HELEN BIANCHIN

Mistress Arrangements

HELEN
BIANCHIN

COLLECTION

February 2016

March 2016

April 2016

May 2016

June 2016

July 2016

HELEN BIANCHIN

Mistress Arrangements

First Published in Great Britain 2016
By Mills & Boon, an imprint of HarperCollins*Publishers*
1 London Bridge Street, London, SE1 9GF

MISTRESS ARRANGEMENTS © 2016 Harlequin Books S.A.

Passion's Mistress © 1994 Helen Bianchin
Desert Mistress © 1996 Helen Bianchin
Mistress by Arrangement © 1999 Helen Bianchin

ISBN: 978-0-263-92148-9

09-0416

Harlequin (UK) Limited's policy is to use papers that are natural, renewable and recyclable products and made from wood grown in sustainable forests. The logging and manufacturing processes conform to the legal environmental regulations of the country of origin.

Printed and bound in Spain
by CPI, Barcelona

PASSION'S MISTRESS
HELEN BIANCHIN

Helen Bianchin was born in New Zealand and travelled to Australia before marrying her Italian-born husband. After three years they moved, returned to New Zealand with their daughter, had two sons and then resettled in Australia.

Encouraged by friends to recount anecdotes of her years as a tobacco sharefarmer's wife living in an Italian community, Helen began setting words on paper and her first novel was published in 1975.

Currently Helen resides in Queensland, the three children now married with children of their own. An animal lover, Helen says her two beautiful Birman cats regard her study as much theirs as hers, choosing to leap onto her desk every afternoon to sit upright between the computer monitor and keyboard as a reminder they need to be fed...like right now!

CHAPTER ONE

IT WAS ONE of those beautiful southern hemispheric summer evenings with a soft balmy breeze drifting in from the sea.

An evening more suited to casual entertainment outdoors than a formal gathering, Carly mused as she stepped into a classically designed black gown and slid the zip in place. Beautifully cut, the style emphasised her slim curves and provided a perfect foil for her fine-textured skin.

A quick glance in the mirror revealed an attractive young woman of average height, whose natural attributes were enhanced by a glorious riot of auburn-streaked dark brown curls cascading halfway down her back.

The contrast was dramatic and far removed from the elegant chignon and classically tailored clothes she chose to wear to the office.

Indecision momentarily clouded her expression as she viewed her pale, delicately boned features. *Too* pale, she decided, and in a moment of utter recklessness she applied more blusher, then added another touch of eyeshadow to give extra emphasis to her eyes.

There, that would have to do, she decided as she

viewed her image with critical appraisal, reflecting a trifle wryly that it was ages since she'd attended a social function—although tonight's soirée was entirely business, arranged for the express purpose of affording a valuable new client introduction to key personnel, and only her employer's insistence had been instrumental in persuading her to join other staff members at his house.

'All done,' she said lightly as she turned towards the small pyjama-clad girl sitting cross-legged on the bed: a beautiful child whose fragility tore at Carly's maternal heartstrings and caused her to curse silently the implicit necessity to attend tonight's party.

'You look pretty.' The voice held wistful admiration, and a wealth of unreserved love shone from wide, expressive dark eyes.

'Thank you,' Carly accepted gently as she leant forward and trailed slightly shaky fingers down the length of her daughter's dark, silky curls.

Tomorrow the waiting would be over. In a way, it would be a relief to know the medical reason why Ann-Marie's health had become so precarious in the past few months. The round of referrals from general practitioner to paediatrician, to one specialist and then another, the seemingly endless number of tests and X-rays had proven emotionally and financially draining.

If Ann-Marie required the skills of a surgeon and private hospital care...

Silent anguish gnawed at her stomach, then with a concentrated effort Carly dampened her anxiety and forced her wide, mobile mouth into a warm smile as she clasped Ann-Marie's hand in her own.

'Sarah has the telephone number if she needs to contact me,' she relayed gently as she led the way towards the lounge.

Leaving Ann-Marie, even with someone as competent as Sarah, was a tremendous wrench. Especially tonight, when apprehension heightened her sense of guilt and warred violently with any need for divided loyalty. Yet her work was important, the money earned essential. Critical, she added silently.

Besides, Ann-Marie couldn't be in better hands than with Sarah, who, as a nursing sister at the Royal Children's Hospital, was well qualified to cope with any untoward eventuality.

'The dress is perfect.'

Carly smiled in silent acknowledgement of the warmly voiced compliment. 'It's kind of you to lend it to me.'

The attractive blonde rose from the sofa with unselfconscious grace. 'Your hair looks great. You should wear it like that more often.'

'Yes,' Ann-Marie agreed, and, tilting her head to one side, she viewed her mother with the solemn simplicity of the very young. 'It makes you look different.'

'Sophisticated,' Sarah added with a teasing laugh as she collected a book from the coffee-table. It was a popular children's story, with beautiful illustrations. 'Ann-Marie and I have some serious reading to do.'

Carly blessed Sarah's intuitive ability to distract Ann-Marie's attention—and her own, if only momentarily.

Their friendship went back seven years to the day they'd moved into neighbouring apartments—each fleeing her own home town for differing reasons, and each desperate for a new beginning.

'I won't be away any longer than I have to,' she assured quietly, then she gave Ann-Marie a hug, and quickly left.

In the lobby, Carly crossed to the lift and stabbed the call-button, hearing an answering electronic hum as the lift rose swiftly to the third floor, then just as swiftly transported her down to the basement.

The apartment block comprised three levels, and was one of several lining the northern suburban street, sharing a uniformity of pale brick, tiled roof, and basement car park, the only visual difference being a variation in the grassed verges and gardens, dependent on the generosity of any caring tenant who possessed both the time and inclination to beautify his or her immediate environment.

Carly unlocked her sedan, slid in behind the wheel and urged the aged Ford on to street level, taking the main arterial route leading into the city. It was almost seven-thirty, and unless there were any delays with traffic she should arrive at the requested time.

Clive Mathorpe owned an exclusive harbourside residence in Rose Bay, and a slight frown creased her forehead as she attempted to recall a previous occasion when her employer had organised a social event in his home for the benefit of a client—even the directorial scion of a vast entrepreneurial empire.

Acquiring Consolidated Enterprises had been quite a *coup*, for Mathorpe and Partners bore neither the size nor standing of any one of the three instantly recognisable internationally affiliated accounting firms.

Carly's speculation faded as she caught a glimpse

of towering multi-level concrete and glass spires vying
for supremacy in a city skyline, followed within minutes by an uninterrupted view of the unique architectural masterpiece of the Opera House.

It was a familiar scene she'd come to appreciate,
for it was here in this city that she had developed
a sense of self-achievement, together with an inner
satisfaction at having strived hard against difficult
odds and won. Not handsomely, she admitted a trifle
wryly, aware of the leasing fee on her apartment and
the loan on her car.

Negotiating inner-city evening traffic demanded
total concentration, and Carly gave a silent sigh of
relief when she reached Rose Bay.

Locating her employer's address presented no problem, and she slid the car to a halt outside an imposing
set of wrought-iron gates.

Minutes later she took a curving path towards the
main entrance, and within seconds of pressing the
doorbell she was greeted by name and ushered indoors.

It was crazy suddenly to be stricken with an attack of nerves; mad to consider herself a social alien
among people she knew and worked with.

Soft muted music vied with the chatter of variously
toned voices, and Carly cast the large lounge and its
occupants an idle sweeping glance. Without exception the men all wore black dinner-suits, white silk
shirts and black bow-ties, while the women had each
chosen stylish gowns in a concerted effort to impress.

Within minutes she was offered a drink, and she
managed a slight smile as Bradley Williamson moved
to her side. He was a pleasant man in his early thirties

and considered to be one of Mathorpe and Partners' rising young executives.

His roving appraisal was brief, and his eyes assumed an appreciative sparkle as he met her steady gaze. 'Carly, you look sensational.'

'Bradley,' she acknowledged, then queried idly, 'Has Clive's honoured guest arrived yet?'

His voice took on an unaccustomed dryness. 'You're hoping he'll appear soon and let you off the figurative hook.'

It was a statement she didn't refute. 'Maybe he won't come,' she proffered absently, and caught Bradley's negative shake of the head.

'Doubtful. Mathorpe revealed that the director favours a personal touch in all his business dealings. "Involvement on every level" were his exact words.'

'Which explains why the company has achieved such success.'

Bradley spared her a quizzical smile that broadened his pleasant features into moderate attractiveness. 'Been doing your homework?'

Her answering response was without guile. 'Of course.' Figures, projections, past successes had been readily available. Yet mystery surrounded Consolidated Enterprises' top man, inviting intense speculation with regard to his identity.

'Such dedication,' he teased. 'The way you're heading, you'll be the first woman partner in the firm.'

'I very much doubt it.'

His interest quickened. 'You can't possibly be considering resigning in favour of working elsewhere.'

'No,' Carly disclaimed. 'I merely expressed the observation that Clive Mathorpe has tunnel vision, and, while an accountant of the feminine gender is quite acceptable in the workforce, taking one on as a partner is beyond his personal inclination.' A faint smile tugged the corners of her generously moulded mouth. 'Besides, I'm comfortable with things as they are.'

He absorbed her words and effected a philosophical shrug. 'Can I get you another drink?'

'Thank you. Something long, cool and mildly alcoholic.' She smiled at his expression, then added teasingly, 'Surprise me.'

Carly watched Bradley's departing back with an odd feeling of restlessness, aware of a time when her slightest need had been anticipated with unerring accuracy, almost as if the man in her life possessed an ability to see beyond the windows of her mind right to the very depths of her soul. Those were the days of love and laughter, when life itself had seemed as exotic and ebullient as the bubbles set free in a flute of the finest champagne.

Entrapped by introspection, Carly fought against the emergence of a vision so vivid, so shockingly compelling, that it was almost as if the image had manifested itself into reality.

Seven years hadn't dimmed her memory by the slightest degree. If anything the passage of those years had only served to magnify the qualities of a man she doubted she would ever be able to forget.

Their attraction had been instantaneous, a combustible force fired by electric fusion, and everything, everyone, from that moment on, had faded into insignificance. At twenty, she hadn't stood a chance against his devastating sexual alchemy, and within weeks he'd slipped a brilliant diamond on to her finger, charmed her widowed mother into planning an early wedding, and succeeded in sweeping Carly into the depths of passionate oblivion.

For the first three months of her marriage she had been blissfully, heavenly happy. Then the demands of her husband's business interests had begun to intrude into their personal life. Initially she hadn't queried the few occasions he rang to cancel dinner; nor had she thought to doubt that his overnight business trips were anything other than legitimate. Their reunions had always been filled with such a degree of sexual urgency that it never occurred to her that there could be anyone else.

Yet the rumours had begun, persistently connecting her husband with Angelica Agnelli. The two families had been linked together in various business interests for more than a generation, and Angelica, with qualifications in business management to her credit, held a seat on the board of directors of numerous companies.

Tall, slim, *soignée*, Angelica was the visual image of an assertive, high-powered businesswoman with her eye firmly set on the main chance. And that had included the man at the top of the directorial board. The fact that he had been legally and morally unavailable was considered of little or no consequence, his wife merely a minor obstacle that could easily be dismissed.

Carly's husband was possessed of an entrepreneurial flair that was the envy of his contemporaries, and his generosity to numerous charities was well known, thus ensuring his presence at prominent social events in and around Perth.

Carly reflected bitterly that it hadn't taken long for

the gossip to take seed and germinate. Nor for the arguments to begin, and to continue unresolved until ultimately a devastating confrontation had finally supplied the will for her to escape.

Throughout her flight east she had been besieged by the machinations of her own imagination as it provided a litany of possible scenarios, and during those first few weeks in Sydney she'd lived on a knife-edge of nervous tension, fearful that her whereabouts might be discovered.

The bitter irony of having figuratively burned her bridges soon had become apparent with the knowledge she was pregnant.

The solution was something she'd chosen to face alone, and even in the depths of her own dilemma it had never occurred to her to consider abortion as the easy way out. Nor in those first few months of her pregnancy had she enlightened her widowed mother, and afterwards it was too late when emergency surgery resulted in her mother's death.

That initial year after Ann-Marie's birth had been difficult, caring for a child while juggling study and attempting a career. However, she'd managed...thanks to a private day-care centre and Sarah's help.

It was a source of pride that not only had she achieved success in her chosen field of accountancy, she'd also added a string of qualifications to her name that had earned respect from her peers.

'Sorry I took so long.'

Carly was brought sharply back to the present at the sound of Bradley's voice, and her lashes swept down to form a protective veil as she struggled to shut out the past.

'Your drink. I hope you like it.'

She accepted the glass with a slight smile, and mur-mured her thanks.

It was relief when several minutes later one of the firm's partners joined them and the conversation shifted entirely to business. A recent change in tax legislation had come into effect, and Carly entered into a lengthy debate with both men over the far-reaching implications on various of their clients' affairs.

Carly became so involved that at first she didn't notice a change in the background noise until a slight touch on her arm alerted her to examine the source of everyone's attention.

Clive Mathorpe's bulky frame was instantly recognisable. The man at his side stood at ease, his height and breadth a commanding entity. Even from this distance there was sufficient familiarity evident to send her heart thudding into an accelerated beat.

A dozen times over the past seven years she'd been shocked into immobility by the sight of a tall, broad-framed, dark-haired man, only to collapse with relief on discovering that the likeness was merely super-ficial.

Now, Carly stood perfectly still as logic vied with the possibility of coincidental chance, and even as she dismissed the latter there was a subtle shift in his stance so that his profile was revealed, eliminating any doubt as to his identity.

For one horrifying second Carly sensed the dark void of oblivion welling up and threatening to en-gulf her.

She couldn't, *dared not* faint. The humiliation

would be too incredible and totally beyond conceivable explanation.

With conscious effort she willed herself to breathe slowly, deeply, in an attempt to retain some measure of composure as every single nerve-end went into a state of wild panic.

Stefano Alessi. Australian-born of Italian parents, he was a proven successor to his father's financial empire and a noted entrepreneur, having gained accolades and enjoyed essential prestige among his peers. In his late thirties, he was known to head vast multinational corporations, and owned residences in several European cities.

It was seven years since she'd last seen him. Seven years in which she'd endeavoured to forget the cataclysmic effect he'd had on her life.

Even now he had the power to liquefy her bones, and she watched with a sense of dreaded fascination as he glanced with seeming casualness round the room, almost as if an acutely developed sixth sense had somehow alerted him to her presence.

Carly mentally steeled herself for the moment of recognition, mesmerised by the sheer physical force of the man who had nurtured her innocent emotions and stoked them into a raging fire.

His facial features were just as dynamically arresting as she remembered, distinctive by their assemblage of broad-sculpted bone-structure, his wide-spaced, piercing grey eyes able to assess, dissect and categorise with definitive accuracy.

Dark brown, almost black hair moulded his head with well-groomed perfection, and he looked older—*harder*, she perceived, aware of the indomitable air of power evident that set him aside from every other man in the room.

She shivered, hating the way her body reacted to his presence, and there was nothing she could do to prevent the blood coursing through her veins as it brought all her senses tingling into vibrant life. Even her skin betrayed her, the soft surface hairs rising in silent recognition, attuned to a memory so intense, so incredibly acute, that she felt it must be clearly apparent to anyone who happened to look at her.

In seeming slow motion he captured her gaze, and the breath caught in her throat as his eyes clashed with hers for an infinitesimal second, searing with laser precision through every protective barrier to her soul, only to withdraw and continue an encompassing appraisal of the room's occupants.

'Our guest of honour is an attractive man, don't you think?'

Carly heard Bradley's voice as if from an immense distance, and she attempted a non-committal rejoinder that choked in her throat.

'I doubt there's a woman present who isn't wondering if he performs as well in the bedroom as he does in the boardroom,' he assessed with wry amusement.

All Carly wanted to do was escape the room, the house. Yet even as she gathered her scattered wits together she experienced a distinct feeling of dread with the knowledge that any form of retreat was impossible.

It became immediately apparent that Clive Mathorpe intended to effect an introduction to key personnel, and every passing second assumed the magnitude of several minutes as the two men moved slowly round the room.

Consequently, she was almost at screaming point when Clive Mathorpe eventually reached her side.

'Bradley Williamson, one of my junior partners.'

The lines fanning out from Clive Mathorpe's astute blue eyes deepened in silent appreciation of Carly's fashion departure from studious employee. 'Carly Taylor, an extremely efficient young woman who gives one hundred per cent to anything she undertakes.' He paused, then added with a degree of reverent emphasis, 'Stefano Alessi.'

It was a name which had gained much notice in the business section of a variety of newspapers over the past few months. Twice his photograph had been emblazoned in the tabloid Press accompanied by a journalistic report lauding the cementing of yet another lucrative deal. Even in the starkness of black and white newsprint, his portrayed persona had emanated an electrifying magnetism that Carly found difficult to dispel.

She held little doubt that the passage of seven years had seen a marked escalation of his investment portfolio. On a personal level, she couldn't help wondering whether Angelica Agnelli was still sharing his bed.

An ache started up in the region of her heart with a physicality so intense it became a tangible pain. Even now she could still hurt, and she drew on all her reserves of strength to present a cool, unaffected façade.

Cool grey eyes deliberately raked her slender frame, pausing imperceptibly on the slight fullness of her breasts before lifting to linger briefly on the generous curve of her mouth.

It was worse, much worse, than if he'd actually touched her. Equally mortifying was her body's instant recognition of the effect he had on all its sensual pleasure spots, and there was nothing she could do to still the betraying pulse at the edge of her throat as it quickened into a palpably visible beat.

Rage flared deep within, licking every nerve-fibre until it threatened to engulf her in overwhelming flame. How *dared* he subject her to such a sexist scrutiny? Almost as if she was an available conquest he was affording due contemplation.

Then his eyes met hers, and she almost died at the ruthlessness apparent, aware that his slight smile was a mere facsimile as he inclined his head in greeting.

'Miss Taylor.' His voice was a barely inflected drawl, each word given an imperceptible mocking emphasis.

'Mr Alessi,' Carly managed in polite response, although there was nothing she could do about the erratic beat of her heart in reaction to his proximity.

Something flared deep within her, a stirring that was entirely sexual—unwarranted and totally unwanted, yet there none the less—and it said much for her acquired measure of control that she managed to return his gaze with apparent equanimity.

His eyes darkened measurably, then without a further word he moved the necessary few steps to greet the next employee awaiting introduction.

Carly's mind reeled as several conflicting emotions warred in silent turmoil. Was his presence here tonight sheer coincidence, or did he have an ulterior motive?

She'd covered her tracks so well. She had even consulted a solicitor within days of arrival in Sydney, instructing that a letter be dispatched requesting any formalities to be handled by their individual legal representatives.

In seven years there had been no contact whatsoever.

It seemed incredibly ironic that Stefano should reappear at a time when she'd been forced to accept that he was the last ace in her pack should she have to raise more money for Ann-Marie's medical expenses.

Where her daughter's well-being was concerned there was no contest. Even it if meant sublimating her own personal reservations, and effecting a confrontation. His power and accumulated wealth could move figurative mountains, and if it was necessary she wouldn't hesitate to beg.

Carly caught the lower edge of her lip between two sharp teeth, then winced in silent pain as she unconsciously drew blood.

The desire to make some excuse and leave was strong. Yet only cowards cut and ran. This time she had to stay, even if the effort almost killed her.

Carly found each minute dragged interminably, and more than once her eyes strayed across the room to where Stefano Alessi stood conversing with Clive Mathorpe and two senior partners.

In his presence, all other men faded into insignificance. There was an exigent force apparent, which, combined with power and sexual magnetism, drew the attention of women like bees to a honeypot.

It was doubtful there was one female present whose pulse hadn't quickened at the sight of him, or whose imagination wasn't stirred by the thought of being able to captivate his interest.

Carly waited ten minutes after Stefano left before

she crossed the room to exchange a few polite pleasantries with Clive Mathorpe and his wife, then she
slipped quietly from the house and walked quickly
down the driveway to her car.

Safely behind the wheel, she activated the ignition
and eased the car forward. A quick glance at the illuminated dashboard revealed it was nine-thirty. One
hour, she reflected with disbelief. For some reason it
had seemed half a lifetime.

Stefano Alessi's disturbing image rose up to taunt
her, and she shivered despite the evening's warmth.
He represented everything she had come to loathe
in a man.

For one brief milli-second she closed her eyes, then
opened them to issue a silent prayer that fate wouldn't
be so unkind as to throw her beneath his path again.

It was a relief to reach the sanctuary of her apartment building, and after garaging the car she rode the
lift to the third floor.

'Hi,' Sarah greeted quietly as Carly entered the
lounge. 'Ann-Marie's fine. How was the evening?'

I met Ann-Marie's father, she longed to confide.

Yet the words stayed locked in her throat, and she
managed to relay an informative account as they
shared coffee together, then when Sarah left she
checked Ann-Marie before entering her own bedroom, where she mechanically removed her make-
up and undressed ready for bed.

Sleep had never seemed more distant, and she
tossed restlessly from one side to the other in a bid to
dispel a flood of returning memories.

Haunting, invasive, they refused to be denied as

one by one she began to recall the angry words she'd exchanged in bitter argument with a man she'd chosen to condemn.

CHAPTER TWO

CARLY SLEPT BADLY, haunted by numerous dream sequences that tore at her subconscious mind with such vivid clarity that she woke shaking, shattered by their stark reality.

A warning, perhaps? Or simply the manifestation of a fear so real that it threatened to consume her?

Tossing aside the covers, she resolutely went through the motions entailed in her early morning weekday routine, listening to Ann-Marie's excited chatter over breakfast as she recounted events from the previous evening.

When pressed to reveal just how *her* evening had turned out, Carly brushed it off lightly with a smile and a brief but satisfactory description.

It was eight-thirty when Carly deposited Ann-Marie outside the school gates, and almost nine when she entered the reception area of Mathorpe and Partners.

There were several files on her desk demanding attention, and she worked steadily, methodically checking figures with determined dedication until mid-morning when she reached for the phone and punched out a series of digits.

The specialist's receptionist was extremely polite, but firm. Ann-Marie's results could not be given over the phone. An appointment had been set aside this afternoon for four o'clock.

It sounded ominous, and Carly's voice shook as she confirmed the time.

The remainder of the day was a blur as anxiety played havoc with her nervous system, and in the specialist's consulting-rooms it was all she could do to contain it.

Consequently, it was almost an anticlimax when she was shown into his office, and as soon as she was comfortably seated he leaned back in his chair, his expression mirroring a degree of sympathetic understanding.

'Ann-Marie has a tumour derived from the supporting tissue of the nerve-cells,' he informed her quietly. 'The astrocytoma varies widely in malignancy and rate of growth. Surgery is essential, and I recommend it be carried out as soon as possible.'

Carly's features froze with shock at the professionally spoken words, and her mind immediately went into overdrive with a host of implications, the foremost of which was *money*.

'I can refer you to a neuro-surgeon, someone I consider to be the best in his field.' His practised pause held a silent query. 'I'll have my nurse arrange an appointment, shall I?'

The public hospital system was excellent, but the waiting list for elective surgery was long. Too long to gamble with her daughter's life. Carly didn't hesitate. 'Please.'

It took only minutes for the appointment to be con-

firmed; a few more to exchange pleasantries before
the receptionist ushered Carly from his rooms.

She walked in a daze to her car, then slid in behind
the wheel. A sick feeling of despair welled up inside
as innate fear overruled rational thought, for no matter how hard she tried it was impossible to dispel the
terrible image of Ann-Marie lying still and helpless
in an operating theatre, her life reliant on the skill of
a surgeon's scalpel.

It will be all right, Carly determined as she
switched on the ignition, then eased her car on to
the street. One way or another, she'd make sure of it.

The flow of traffic was swift, and on a few occasions it took two light changes to clear an intersection. Taxis were in demand, their drivers competent
as they manoeuvred their vehicles from one lane to
another, ready to take the first opportunity ahead of
city commuters.

The cars in front began to slow, and Carly eased
her sedan to a halt. Almost absently her gaze shifted
slightly to the right, drawn as if by some elusive mag-
net to a top-of-the-range black Mercedes that had
pulled up beside her in the adjacent lane.

Her eyes grazed towards the driver in idle, almost
speculative curiosity, only to have them widen in
dawning horror as she recognised the sculpted male
features of none other than Stefano Alessi behind the
wheel.

Her initial reaction was to look away, except she
hesitated too long, and in seeming slow motion she
saw him turn towards her.

With a sense of fatalism she saw his strong features harden, and she almost died beneath the intensity of his gaze.

Then a horn blast provided a startling intrusion, and Carly forced her attention to the slow-moving traffic directly ahead. In her hurry she crashed the gears and let the clutch out too quickly for her aged sedan's liking, causing it to stall in retaliatory protest.

Damn. The curse fell silently from her lips, and she twisted the ignition key, offering soothing words in the hope that the engine would fire.

An audible protest sounded from immediately behind, quickly followed by another, then a surge of power shook the small sedan and she eased it forward, picking up speed as she joined the river of cars vacating the city.

It wasn't until she'd cleared the intersection that she realised how tight a grip she retained on the wheel. A light film of moisture beaded her upper lip in visible evidence of her inner tension, and she forced herself to relax, angry that the mere sight of a man she professed to hate could affect her so deeply.

It took almost an hour to reach Manly, yet it felt as if she'd been battling traffic for twice that long by the time she garaged the car.

Upstairs, Sarah opened the door, her eyes softening with concern at the sight of Carly's pale features.

'Sarah helped me draw some pictures.'

Carly leant forward and hugged her daughter close. Her eyes were suspiciously damp as Ann-Marie's small arms fastened round her neck in loving reciprocation.

'I'll make coffee,' Sarah suggested, and Carly shot her friend a regretful smile.

'I can't stay.' Her eyes assumed a haunting vulnerability. 'I'll ring you.' She paused, then attempted a
shaky smile. 'After eight?'

Entering her own apartment, Carly moved through
to the kitchen and prepared their evening meal, then
when the dishes had been dealt with she organised
Ann-Marie's bath, made the little girl a hot milky
drink, then tucked her into bed.

It was early, and she crossed to the phone to dial
directory service, praying they could supply the number she needed.

Minutes later she learned there was no listing for
Stefano Alessi, and the only number available was
ex-directory. *Damn.*

Carly queried Consolidated Enterprises, and was
given two numbers, neither of which responded at this
hour of the night. There was no after-hours number
listed, nor anything connected to a mobile net.

Carly cursed softly beneath her breath. She had no
recourse but to wait until tomorrow. Unless she rang
Clive Mathorpe at home and asked for his coveted
client's private telephone number.

Even as the thought occurred, it was instantly dismissed. What could she offer as the reason for such an
unorthodox request? Her esteemed boss would probably suffer an instant apoplectic attack if she were to
say, 'Oh, by the way, Clive, I forgot to mention that
Stefano Alessi is my estranged husband.'

Tomorrow, she determined with grim purpose.
Even if she had to utilise devious means to obtain
her objective.

A leisurely shower did little to soothe her fractured
nerves, nor did an attempt to view television.

Long after she'd switched off the bedside lamp Stefano's image rose to taunt her, and even in dreams he refused to disappear, her subconscious mind forcing recognition of his existence, so that in consequence she spent another restless night fighting off several demons in numerous guises.

The next morning Carly dropped Ann-Marie at school then drove into the city, and on reaching her office she quietly closed her door so that she could make the necessary phone call in private.

It was crazy, but her nerves felt as if they were shredding to pieces as she waited for the call to connect, and only Ann-Marie's plight provided the courage needed to overcome the instinctive desire to replace the receiver.

Several minutes later, however, she had to concede that Stefano was virtually inaccessible to anyone but a chosen few. The majority were requested to supply verbal credentials and leave a contact telephone number.

The thought of waiting all day for him to return the call, even supposing he chose to, brought her out in a cold sweat. There was only one method left open to her whereby she retained some small measure of power, and she used it mercilessly.

'Stefano Alessi,' she directed coolly as soon as the receptionist answered, and, hardly giving the girl a chance to draw breath, she informed her, 'Tell his secretary his wife is on the line.' That should bring some response.

It did, and Carly derived some satisfaction from the girl's barely audible surprise. Within seconds the call was transferred, and another female voice requested verification.

Stefano's personal staff were hand-picked to handle any eventuality with unruffled calm—and even a call from someone purporting to be the director's wife failed to faze his secretary in the slightest.

'Mr Alessi isn't in the office. Can I have him call you?'

Damn. She could hardly ask for his mobile number, for it would automatically be assumed that she already had it. 'What time do you expect him in?'

'This afternoon. He has an appointment at three, followed by another at four.'

Assertiveness was the key, and Carly didn't hesitate. 'Thank you. I'll be there at four-thirty.' She hung up, then quickly made two further calls—one to Sarah asking if she could collect Ann-Marie from school, and another to Ann-Marie's teacher confirming the change in routine.

The day loomed ahead, once again without benefit of a lunch-hour, and Carly worked diligently in an effort to recoup lost time.

At precisely four-fifteen Carly entered the lobby of a towering glass-faced edifice housing the offices of Consolidated Enterprises, stabbed the call-button to summon one of four lifts, then when it arrived stepped into the cubicle and pressed the designated disk.

The nerves she had striven to keep at bay surfaced with painful intensity, and she mentally steeled herself for the moment she had to walk into Reception and identify herself.

By now Stefano's secretary would have informed him of her call. What if he refused to see her?

Positive, think *positive*, an inner voice urged.

The lift paused, the doors opened, and Carly had little option but to step into the luxuriously appointed foyer.

Reception lay through a set of wide glass doors, and, acting a part, she stepped forward and gave her name. Her eyes were clear and level, and her smile projected just the right degree of assurance.

The receptionist's reaction was polite, her greeting civil, and it was impossible for Carly to tell anything from her expression as she lifted a handset and spoke quietly into the receiver.

'Mr Alessi is still in conference,' the receptionist relayed. 'His secretary will escort you to his private lounge where you can wait in comfort.'

At least she'd passed the first stage, Carly sighed with silent relief as she followed an elegantly attired woman to a room whose interior design employed a mix of soft creams, beige and camel, offset by opulently cushioned sofas in plush chocolate-brown.

There were several current glossy magazines to attract her interest, an excellent view of the inner city if she chose to observe it through the wide expanse of plate-glass window. Even television, if she were so inclined, and a well-stocked drinks cabinet, which Carly found tempting—except that even the mildest measure of alcohol on an empty stomach would probably have the opposite effect on her nerves.

Coffee would be wonderful, and her hand hovered over the telephone console, only to return seconds later to her side. What if the connection went straight through to Stefano's office, instead of to his secretary?

Minutes passed, and she began to wonder if he wasn't playing some diabolical game.

Dear lord, he must know how difficult it was for her to approach him. Surely she'd suffered enough, without this latest insult?

The thought of seeing him again, alone, without benefit of others present to diffuse the devastating effect on her senses, made her feel ill.

Her stomach began to clench in painful spasms, and a cold sweat broke over her skin.

What was taking him so long? A quick glance at her watch determined that ten minutes had passed. How much longer before he deigned to make an appearance?

At that precise moment the door opened, and Carly's eyes flew to the tall masculine frame outlined in the aperture.

Unbidden, she rose to her feet, and her heart gave a sudden jolt, disturbed beyond measure by the lick of flame that swept through her veins. It was mad, utterly crazy that he could still have this effect, and she forced herself to breathe slowly in an attempt to slow the rapid beat of her pulse.

Attired in a dark grey business suit, blue silk shirt and tie, he appeared even more formidable than she'd expected, his height an intimidating factor as he entered the room.

The door closed behind him with a faint decisive snap, and for one electrifying second she felt trapped. Imprisoned, she amended, verging towards silent hysteria as her eyes lifted towards his in a gesture of contrived courage.

His harshly assembled features bore an inscrutability that was disquieting, and she viewed him warily as he crossed to stand within touching distance.

He embodied a dramatic mesh of blatant masculinity and elemental ruthlessness, his stance that of a superior jungle cat about to stalk a vulnerable prey, assessing the moment he would choose to pounce and kill.

Dammit, she derided silently. She was being too fanciful for words! A tiny voice taunted that he had no need for violence when he possessed the ability verbally to reduce even the most worthy opponent to a state of mute insecurity in seconds.

The silence between them was so acute that Carly was almost afraid to breathe, and she became intensely conscious of the measured rise and fall of her breasts, the painful beat of her heart as it seemed to leap through her ribcage. Her eyes widened fractionally as he thrust a hand into his trouser pocket with an indolent gesture, and she tilted her head, forcing herself to retain his gaze.

'Shall we dispense with polite inanities and go straight to the reason why you're here?' Stefano queried hardily.

There was an element of tensile steel beneath the sophisticated veneer, a sense of purpose that was daunting. She was aware of an elevated nervous tension, and it took every ounce of courage to speak calmly. 'I wasn't sure you'd see me.'

The eyes that speared hers were deliberately cool, and an icy chill feathered across the surface of her skin.

'Curiosity, perhaps?' His voice was a hateful drawl,

and her eyes gleamed with latent anger, their depths
flecked with tawny gold.

She wanted to *hit* him, to disturb his tightly held
control. Yet such an action was impossible, for she
couldn't afford to indulge in a display of temper.
She needed him—or, more importantly, Ann-Marie
needed the sort of help his money could bring.

'Coffee?'

She was tempted to refuse, and for a moment she
almost did, then she inclined her head in silent acquiescence. 'Please.'

Dark grey eyes raked her slim form, then returned
to stab her pale features with relentless scrutiny. Without a word he crossed to the telephone console and
lifted the handset, then issued a request for coffee and
sandwiches before turning back to face her.

His expression became chillingly cynical, assuming an inscrutability that reflected inflexible strength
of will. 'How much, Carly?'

Her head lifted of its own volition, her eyes wide
and clear as she fought to utter a civil response.

One eyebrow slanted in a gesture of deliberate
mockery. 'I gather that is why you're here?'

She had already calculated the cost and added a
fraction more in case of emergency. Now she doubled
it. 'Twenty thousand dollars.'

He directed her a swift calculated appraisal, and
when he spoke his voice was dangerously soft. 'That's
expensive elective surgery.'

Carly's eyes widened into huge pools of incredulity
as comprehension dawned, and for one brief second
her eyes filled with incredible pain. Then a surge of

anger rose to the surface, palpable, inimical, and beyond control.

Without conscious thought she reached for the nearest object at hand, uncaring of the injury she could inflict or any damage she might cause.

Stefano shifted slightly, and the rock-crystal ashtray missed its target by inches and crashed into a framed print positioned on the wall directly behind his shoulder.

The sound was explosive, and in seeming slow motion Carly saw the glass shatter, the framed print spring from its fixed hook and fall to the carpet. The ashtray followed its path, intact, to bounce and roll drunkenly to a halt in the centre of the room.

Time became a suspended entity, the silence so intense that she could hear the ragged measure of her breathing and feel the pounding beat of her heart.

She didn't move, *couldn't*, for the muscles activating each limb appeared suspended and beyond any direction from her brain.

It was impossible to gauge his reaction, for the only visible sign of anger apparent was revealed in the hard line of his jaw, the icy chill evident in the storm-grey darkness of his eyes.

The strident ring of the phone made her jump, its shrill sound diffusing the electric tension, and Carly watched in mesmerised fascination as Stefano crossed to the console and picked up the handset.

He listened for a few seconds, then spoke reassuringly to whoever was on the other end of the line.

More than anything, she wanted to storm out of the room, the building, *his life*. Yet she couldn't. Not yet.

Stefano slowly replaced the receiver, then he straightened, his expression an inscrutable mask.

'So,' he intoned silkily. 'Am I to assume from that emotive reaction that you aren't carrying the seed of another man's child, and are therefore not in need of an abortion?'

I carried yours, she longed to cry out. With determined effort she attempted to gather together the threads of her shattered nerves. 'Don't presume to judge me by the numerous women you bed,' she retorted in an oddly taut voice.

His eyes darkened until they resembled shards of obsidian slate. 'You have no foundation on which to base such an accusation.'

Carly closed her eyes, then slowly opened them again. 'It goes beyond my credulity to imagine you've remained celibate for seven years.' *As I have*, she added silently.

'You're here to put me on trial for supposed sexual misdemeanours during the years of our enforced separation?'

His voice was a hatefully musing drawl that made her palms itch with the need to resort to a display of physical anger.

'If you could sleep with Angelica during our marriage, I can't even *begin* to imagine what you might have done after I left!' Carly hurled with the pent-up bitterness of *years*.

There was a curious bleakness apparent, then his features assumed an expressionless mask as he cast his watch a deliberate glance. 'State your case, Carly,' he inclined with chilling disregard. 'In nine minutes I have an appointment with a valued colleague.'

It was hardly propitious to her cause continually to thwart him, and her chin tilted fractionally as she held his gaze. 'I already thought I had.'

'Knowing how much you despise me,' Stefano drawled softly, 'I can only be intrigued by the degree of desperation that forces you to confront me with a request for money.'

Her eyes were remarkably steady, and she did her best to keep the intense emotion from her voice. 'Someone I care for very much needs an operation,' she said quietly. It was true, even if it was truth by partial omission. 'Specialist care, a private hospital.'

One eyebrow lifted with mocking cynicism. 'A man?'

She curled her fingers into a tight ball and thrust her hands behind her back. 'No,' she denied in a curiously flat voice.

'Then who, Carly?' he queried silkily. His eyes raked hers, compelling, inexorable, and inescapable.

'A child.'

'Am I permitted to know *whose* child?'

He wouldn't give in until she presented him with all the details, and she suddenly hated him, with an intensity that was vaguely shocking, for all the pain, the anger and the futility, for having dared, herself, to love him unreservedly, only to have that love thrown back in her face.

Seven years ago she'd hurled one accusation after another at the man who had steadfastly refused to confirm, deny or explain his actions. As a result, she'd frequently given vent to angry recrimination which rarely succeeded in provoking his retaliation.

Except once. Then he'd castigated her as the child

he considered her to be, and when she'd hit him he'd unceremoniously hauled her back into their bed and subjected her to a lesson she was never likely to forget.

The following morning she'd packed a bag, and driven steadily east until hunger and exhaustion had forced her to stop. Then she'd rung her mother, offered the briefest of explanations and assured her she'd be in touch.

That had been the last personal contact she'd had with the man she had married. Until now.

'My daughter,' she enlightened starkly, and watched his features reassemble, the broad facial bones seeming more pronounced, the jaw clearly defined beneath the taut musculature bonding fibre to bone. The composite picture portrayed a harsh ruthlessness she found infinitely frightening.

'I suggest,' he began in a voice pitched so low that it sounded like silk being razed by steel, 'you contact the child's father.'

Carly visibly shivered. His icy anger was almost a tangible entity, cooling the room, and there was a finality in his words, an inexorability she knew she'd never be able to circumvent unless she told the absolute truth—*now*.

'Ann-Marie was born exactly seven months and three weeks after I left Perth.' There were papers in her bag. A birth certificate, blood-group records— hers, Ann-Marie's, a copy of *his*. Photos. Several of them, showing Ann-Marie as a babe in arms, a toddler, then on each consecutive birthday, all showing an acute similarity to the man who had fathered her: the same colouring, dark, thick, silky hair, and grey eyes.

Carly retrieved them, thrusting one after the other

into Stefano's hands as irrefutable proof. 'She's your daughter, Stefano. *Yours.*'

The atmosphere in the lounge was so highly charged that Carly almost expected it to ignite into incendiary flame.

His expression was impossible to read, and as the seconds dragged silently by she felt like screaming—anything to get some reaction.

'Tell me,' Stefano began in a voice that was satin-smooth and dangerous, 'was I to be forever kept in ignorance of her existence?'

Oh, dear lord, how could she answer that? Should she even dare, when she wasn't sure of the answer herself? 'Maybe when she was older I would have offered her the opportunity to get in touch with you,' she admitted with hesitant honesty.

'*Grazie.*' His voice was as chilling as an ice floe in an arctic wasteland. 'And how, precisely, did you intend to achieve that? By having her turn up on my doorstep, ten, fifteen years from now, with a briefly penned note of explanation in her hand?'

He was furiously angry; the whiplash of his words tore at her defences, ripping them to shreds. 'Damn you,' he swore softly. 'Damn you to hell.'

He looked capable of anything, and she took an involuntary step backwards from the sheer forcefield of his rage. 'Right at this moment, it would give me the utmost pleasure to wring your slender neck.' He appeared to rein in his temper with visible effort. 'What surgical procedure?' he demanded grimly. 'What's wrong with her?'

With a voice that shook slightly she relayed the details, watching with detached fascination as he scrawled a series of letters and numbers with firm, swift strokes on to a notepad.

'*Your* address and telephone number.' The underlying threat of anger was almost a palpable force. She could sense it, almost *feel* its intensity, and she felt impossibly afraid.

It took considerable effort to maintain an aura of calm, but she managed it. 'Your assurance that Ann-Marie's medical expenses will be met is all that's necessary.'

His eyes caught hers and held them captive, and she shivered at the ruthlessness apparent in their depths. 'You can't believe I'll hand over a cheque and let you walk out of here?' he said with deadly softness, and a cold hand suddenly clutched at her heart and squeezed hard.

'I'll make every attempt to pay you back,' Carly ventured stiffly, and saw his eyes harden.

'I intend that you shall.' His voice was velvet-encased steel, and caused the blood in her veins to chill.

A knock at the door provided an unexpected intrusion, and Carly cast him a startled glance as his secretary entered the room and placed a laden tray down on to the coffee-table. It said much for the secretary's demeanour that she gave no visible indication of having seen the deposed picture frame or the glass that lay scattered on the carpet.

Carly watched the woman's movements as she poured aromatic coffee from a steaming pot into two cups and removed clear plastic film from a plate of delectable sandwiches.

'Contact Bryan Thorpe, Renate,' Stefano instructed

smoothly. 'Extend my apologies and reschedule our meeting for Monday.'

Renate didn't blink. 'Yes, of course.' She straightened from her task, her smile practised and polite as she turned and left the room.

Carly eyed the sandwiches with longing, aware that the last meal she'd eaten was breakfast. The coffee was tempting, and she lifted the cup to her lips with both hands, took a savouring sip, then shakily replaced it down on to the saucer.

The need to escape this room was almost as imperative as her desire to escape the man who occupied it, for despite her resolve his presence had an alarming effect on her equilibrium, stirring alive an entire gamut of emotions, the foremost of which was fear. The feeling was so intense that all her senses seemed elevated, heightened to a degree where she felt her entire body was a finely tuned instrument awaiting the maestro's touch. Which was crazy—*insane*.

'There's no need to cancel your appointment,' she told him with more courage than she felt, and she collected her bag and slid the strap over one shoulder in a silent indication of her intention to leave.

'Where do you think you're going?' Stefano said in a deadly soft voice, and she looked at him carefully, aware of the aura of strength, the indomitable power apparent, and experienced a stirring of alarm.

'Home.'

'I intend to see her.'

The words threw her off balance, and she went suddenly still. 'No,' she denied, stricken by the image of father and daughter meeting for the first time, the effect it would have on Ann-Marie. 'I don't want the disruption your presence will have on her life,' she offered shakily.

'Or yours,' he declared with uncanny perception. His eyes were hard, his expression inexorable. 'Yet you must have known that once I was aware of the facts there could be no way I'd allow you to escape unscathed?'

A shiver shook her slim frame; she was all too aware that she was dealing with a man whose power was both extensive and far-reaching. Only a fool would underestimate him, and right now he looked as if he'd like to shake her until she begged for mercy.

'There is nothing you can do to prevent me from walking out of here,' she said stiltedly.

'I want my daughter, Carly,' he declared in a voice that was implacable, emotionless, and totally without pity. 'Either we effect a reconciliation and resume our marriage, or I'll seek legal custody through court action. The decision is yours.'

A well of anger rose to the surface at his temerity. 'You have no right,' Carly retaliated fiercely. 'No—'

'You have until tomorrow to make up your mind.' He stroked a series of digits on to paper, tore it from its block, and handed it to her. 'You can reach me on this number.'

'Blackmail is a criminal offence!'

'I have stated my intention and given you a choice,' he said hardly, and her eyes glittered with rage.

'I refuse to consider a mockery of a marriage, with a husband who divides his time between a wife and a mistress!'

His eyes narrowed, and Carly met his gaze with fearless disregard. 'Don't bother attempting to deny it,' she advised with deep-seated bitterness. 'There was a succession of so-called friends and social acquaintances who took delight in ensuring I heard the latest gossip. One, in particular, had access to a Press-clipping service, and never failed to ensure that I received conclusive proof of your infidelity.'

'Your obsession with innuendo and supposition hasn't diminished,' Stefano dismissed with deadly softness.

'Nor has my hatred of you!'

His smile was a mere facsimile, and she was held immobile by the dangerous glitter in his eyes, the peculiar stillness of his stance. 'It says something for your maternal devotion that you managed to overcome it sufficiently to confront me.'

Angry, futile tears diminished her vision, and she blinked furiously to dispel them. 'Only because there was no other option!'

Without a word she turned and walked to the door, uncaring whether he attempted to stop her or not.

He didn't move, and she walked down the carpeted hallway to Reception, her head held high, pride forcing a faint smile as she inclined a slight nod to the girl manning the switchboard before sweeping out to the foyer.

A lift arrived within seconds of being summoned, and it wasn't until she reached ground level that reaction began to set in.

CHAPTER THREE

IT TOOK AN hour for Carly to reach Manly, and she uttered a silent prayer of thanks to whoever watched over her as she traversed the car-choked arterial roads leading north from the city. Concentration was essential, and her own was in such a state of serious disarray that it was a minor miracle her sedan survived the drive intact.

Sarah answered the door at once, and Carly cast her a grateful glance as she entered her friend's apartment.

'Thanks for collecting Ann-Marie. I got held up, and the traffic slowed to a complete halt in places.'

'Sarah read me a story, and we watched television. I've already had my bath,' Ann-Marie informed her as she ran into her mother's outstretched arms.

Carly hugged the small body close, and felt the onset of emotion-packed tears. For more than six years she'd fought tooth and nail to support them both without any outside financial assistance. Soon that would change, and she wasn't sure she'd ever be ready for the upheaval Stefano Alessi would cause in their lives.

'Would you like some coffee?' Sarah queried. 'I'll put the kettle on.'

Carly shot her friend a distracted smile. 'Why not

come over and share our meal?' It was the least she could do, and besides, it would be lovely to have company. Then she would have less time alone in which to think.

Sarah looked suitably regretful. 'I'd love to, but I'm going out tonight.'

Carly glimpsed the indecision apparent, the pensive brooding evident in Sarah's lovely blue eyes.

'I take it this isn't the usual casual meal shared with a female friend?' she queried slowly. 'Who's the lucky man?'

'A doctor who performed emergency surgery several months ago while I was on night duty. He's recently moved south from Cairns. We ran into each other a few days later, in the supermarket of all places, and we chatted. Then I saw him again at the hospital.' She paused, and effected a faint shrugging gesture. 'He's…' She paused, searching for the right words. 'Easy to talk to, I guess. Last week he asked me out to dinner.' Her eyes clouded, then deepened to cerulean blue. 'I said yes at the time, but now I'm not so sure.'

Aware that Sarah's disastrous first marriage and subsequent messy divorce had left her with a strong dislike and distrust of men, almost to the point where she refused to have anything to do with them other than in a professional capacity, Carly could only wonder at the man who had managed to break through her friend's defences.

'I'm delighted for you,' she declared with genuine sincerity.

'I'm terrified for me,' Sarah acknowledged wryly as she filled both mugs with boiling water.

The aroma of instant coffee was no substitute for

the real thing, but the hot, sweet brew had a necessary reviving effect and Carly sipped the contents of her mug with appreciative satisfaction.

'What time is he picking you up?'

'Seven.' An entire gamut of emotions chased fleetingly across Sarah's attractive features. 'I'm going to ring him and cancel.'

If he was at all intuitive, he would have deliberately left his answering machine off with just this possibility in mind, Carly reflected as Sarah crossed to the telephone and punched out the requisite digits, only to listen and replace the receiver.

'Damn. Now what am I going to do?'

Carly viewed her with twinkling solemnity. 'Go out with him.'

'I can't. I'm nuts,' Sarah wailed. '*Nuts.*' Her expression assumed a sudden fierceness. 'If the situation were reversed, would *you* go out with another man?'

Her heart lurched, then settled into an accelerated beat in the knowledge that she would soon be inextricably involved with someone she'd sworn never to have anything to do with again, coerced by a set of circumstances that denied any freedom of choice. Yet her academic mind demanded independent legal verification of Stefano's threat of custody, even as logic reasoned that in a court of law the odds would be heavily stacked against Stefano being denied access to his daughter. Tomorrow was Saturday, but there was a friend she could contact outside office hours who would relay the vital information she needed.

'Carly?'

She proffered a faint smile in silent apology and shook her head. 'Not all men are made from the same mould as our respective first husbands,' she managed, evading Sarah's close scrutiny as she lifted the mug to her lips and sipped from it.

'When he arrives, I'll tell him I've changed my mind,' Sarah declared, and, placing a light hand on Carly's arm, she queried softly, 'Are you OK?'

There was no time for confidences, and Carly wasn't sure she was ready to share Stefano's ultimatum with anyone. 'I'm fine,' she assured quietly as she deliberately forced a slight smile. 'Let me give Ann-Marie dinner, then I'll come and help with your hair.'

Sarah shot her a dark musing glance. 'He's seen me in denim shorts, a T-shirt, trainers, and no make-up.' Her expression became faintly speculative as she took in the paleness of Carly's features, the edge of tension apparent. 'Give me twenty minutes to shower and change.'

Once in her own apartment, it took only a few minutes to heat the casserole she'd prepared the previous evening, and although Ann-Marie ate well Carly mechanically forked small portions from her plate with little real appetite.

Afterwards Ann-Marie proved an interested spectator as Carly used hot rollers to good effect on Sarah's hair.

'Why do I feel as nervous as a teenager about to go on a first date?' Sarah queried with wry disbelief. 'No, don't answer that.'

'All done,' Carly announced minutes later as she stepped back a pace to view the style she'd effected with critical favour. 'You look really great,' she assured her gently, her eyes softening with genuine feeling for her friend's state of panic. 'Are you going to tell me his name?' she prompted with a faintly teasing smile.

'James Hensley,' Sarah revealed. 'Surgeon, late thirties, widower, one son. He's slightly aloof and distinguished, yet warm and easy to talk to, if that makes sense.' Indecision, doubt and anxiety clouded her attractive features. A deprecatory laugh merged with an audible groan of despair. 'Why am I doing this to myself? I don't *need* the emotional aggravation!'

The intercom buzzed, and Carly reached out and caught hold of Ann-Marie's hand. 'Have a really fantastic time,' she bade Sarah gently. 'We'll let ourselves out.'

It was after eight before Ann-Marie fell asleep, and Carly gently closed the storybook, then gazed at her daughter's classic features in repose. She looked so small, so fragile. Far too young to have to undergo extensive surgery. Her beautiful hair—

A lump rose in Carly's throat, a painful constriction she had difficulty in swallowing. It wasn't fair. *Life* wasn't fair. Dammit, she wouldn't cry. Tears were for the weak, and she had to be strong. For both of them. At least her daughter would have the best medical attention money could buy, she consoled herself fiercely.

Carly remained seated in the chair beside Ann-Marie's bed for a long time before she stirred herself sufficiently to leave the room, and after carefully closing the door she crossed the lounge to the phone.

Twenty minutes later she slowly replaced the receiver. With a sinking heart she attempted to come to terms with the fact that any claim for custody by Stefano could succeed. Sole custody was not a consideration unless he could prove indisputably that

Carly was an unfit mother. However, he could insist on joint custody—alternate weekends, half of each school holiday—and be granted any reasonable request for access.

On that premise, Carly was sufficiently intelligent to be aware of what would happen if she contested his claim in a court of law, or what emphasis his lawyer would place on her decision to leave Stefano in ignorance of Ann-Marie's existence.

She closed her eyes, almost able to hear the damning words uttered with appropriate dramatic inflexion. The moral issue would be played out with stunning effect. With the added weight of Stefano's wealth, she wouldn't stand a chance of him being refused custody.

Without conscious thought she sank into a nearby chair in despair. Dear God, she agonised shakily. How could she do that to her daughter? Ann-Marie would be pulled and pushed between two people who no longer had anything in common, torn by divided loyalties, and unsure whether either parent's affection was motivated by genuine love or a desire to hurt the other.

In years to come Ann-Marie would understand and comprehend the truth of her parents' relationship. But what damage would be done between now and then? It didn't bear thinking about.

There was really no choice. None at all.

Impossibly restless, she flung herself into completing a punishing few hours of housework, followed by a stint of ironing. At least it provided an outlet for her nervous tension, and she tumbled wearily into bed to toss and turn far into the early hours of the morning.

'You look—terrible,' Sarah declared with concern

as Carly answered the door shortly after eleven. 'Is Ann-Marie OK?'

'She's fine,' Carly responded with a faint smile, then winced at the increasing pain in her head. 'She's dressing her doll in the bedroom and deciding what she should wear to Susy's party this afternoon. Come on in, we'll have some coffee.'

'I'll make the coffee, *and* get you something for that headache,' Sarah insisted, suiting words to action with such admirable efficiency that Carly found herself seated at the dining-room table nursing a hot cup of delicious brew.

'Now, tell me what's wrong.'

Carly effected a faint shrugging gesture. 'I must be feeling my age,' she qualified with a faint smile. 'One late night through the week, and it takes me the next two to get over it.'

'OK,' Sarah accepted. 'So you don't want to talk. Now take these tablets.'

'Yes, Sister.'

'Don't be sassy with me, young woman. It won't work,' Sarah added with mock-severity.

'How was your date with James?' Carly queried in an attempt to divert the conversation away from herself.

'We had dinner, we talked, then he delivered me home.' Sarah lifted her shoulders in a non-committal gesture. 'It was all right, I guess.'

'That's it?' Carly looked slightly incredulous. '*All right* wraps it up?'

'OK, so he was the perfect gentleman.' Sarah's expression became pensive. 'I was surprised, that's all.'

James was beginning to sound more astute by the minute.

'He's asked me out to dinner next Saturday evening,' Sarah informed her quietly, and Carly applauded his perception in taking things slowly.

'He sounds nice.'

'I get the feeling he's streets ahead of me,' Sarah owned. 'Almost as if he knows what I'm thinking and how I'll react. It's—uncanny.'

Carly sipped her coffee and attempted to ignore her headache. It would take at least ten minutes before the pain began to ease, maybe another ten before it retreated to a dull heaviness that would only be alleviated by rest. After she dropped Ann-Marie at Susy's house, she'd come back and rest for an hour.

Sarah left a short while later, and Carly headed for a long leisurely shower, choosing to slip into tailored cotton trousers and a sleeveless top in eau-de-Nil silk. The pale colour looked cool and refreshing, and accentuated the deep auburn highlights of her hair and the clear honey of her skin.

Lunch was a light meal, for Ann-Marie was too excited to eat much in view of all the prospective fare available at Susy's party.

'Ready, darling?'

Ann-Marie's small features creased into an expression of excited anticipation, and Carly felt a tug on her heartstrings.

'Checklist time,' she bade lightly with a smile. 'Handkerchief? No last-minute need to visit the bathroom?'

'Yes,' Ann-Marie answered, retrieving a white

linen square from the pocket of her dress. 'And I just did. Can we go now?'

'After you,' Carly grinned, sweeping her arm in the direction of the front door.

The drive was a relatively short one, for Susy lived in a neighbouring suburb, and in no time at all Carly brought the car to a halt behind a neat row of several parked cars.

'We're cutting the cake at three,' Susy's mother bade with an expressive smile. 'And I'm planning a reviving afternoon tea for the mothers at three-thirty while Susy opens her presents. I'd love you to be here if you can.'

Carly accepted the invitation, wished Susy 'Happy Birthday', then bent down to kiss Ann-Marie goodbye.

On returning home she garaged the car in its allotted space, sparing its slightly dusty paintwork a faint grimace as she closed and locked the door. Perhaps she could leave early and detour via a carwash.

The apartment seemed strangely empty, and she drifted into the kitchen to retrieve a cool drink from the refrigerator.

The buzz of the doorbell sounded loud in the silence of the apartment, and Carly frowned in momentary perplexity as she crossed the lounge. Sarah?

Instead, a tall, broad-shouldered, disturbingly familiar male frame filled the doorway.

The few seconds between recognition and comprehension seemed uncommonly long as she registered his dominating presence.

'What are you doing here?'

'Whatever happened to *hello*?' Stefano drawled,

and his dry mocking tones sent an icy shiver down the length of her spine.

Her eyes sparked with visible anger, dark depths of sheer mahogany, and it irked her unbearably that she'd discarded her heeled sandals on entering the apartment, for it put her at a distinct disadvantage.

Impossibly tall, he towered head and shoulders above her, his impeccably tailored suit seeming incredibly formal on a day that was usually given to informality and relaxation.

Three nights ago his presence had shocked and dismayed her. Yesterday, she'd been momentarily numbed, grateful for the impartiality of his office. Now, there was no visible shield, no barrier, and she felt inordinately wary.

'Aren't you going to ask me in?'

He projected a dramatic mesh of elemental ruthlessness and primitive power, an intrinsic physical magnetism that teased her senses and rendered them intensely vulnerable.

Her chin lifted fractionally, her eyes locking with his, and she caught the lurking cynicism evident, almost as if he guessed the path her thoughts had taken and was silently amused by their passage.

'What if I refuse?' Brave words, given his sheer strength and indomitable will.

'Would you prefer an amicable discussion, or have me channel everything through my lawyers?'

His voice was deadly quiet, and she felt the cold clutch of fear.

'This isn't a convenient time.' She was mad, *insane* to thwart him continually, yet she was damned if she'd meekly stand aside and allow him entry into the privacy of her apartment.

His expression hardened, the assemblage of muscle and bone tautening into a chilling mask depicting controlled anger. 'You've just returned from delivering our daughter to a birthday party. How long before you need to collect her? An hour? Two?'

Sheer rage rushed to the surface, destroying any semblance of restraint. 'You've had me watched— *followed*?' Words momentarily failed her. 'You *bastard*,' she flung at last, sorely tempted to slam the door in his face, yet even as the thought occurred to her she negated the action as not only foolish but extremely dangerous.

For one infinitesimal second his eyes leapt with icy anger, then sharpened and became infinitely compelling as he raked her slender frame.

A shivery sensation feathered its way down the length of her spine as she fought against the intrinsic pull of his innate sexuality, and of its own volition her body seemed to flare into life as if ignited by some hidden combustible flame.

Seven years ago she'd gone willingly into his arms, his bed, and tasted every sensual delight in a sexual discovery that had set her on fire, enraptured by an ecstasy so acute that it hadn't seemed possible such pleasure existed. A passionate lover, he'd teasingly dispensed with each and every one of her inhibitions, and taught her to become so in tune with her own sensual being that each time they made love it was a total conflagration of the senses.

To deny him access to her apartment would gain absolutely nothing, and, drawing in a deep breath, she gathered her scattered emotions together as she aimed for contrived politeness.

'Please,' Carly indicated as she gestured towards two sofas and a chair in the small lounge. 'Sit down.'

Stefano chose to ignore the directive, and moved slowly across the room to examine a large frame containing a montage of small snapshots showing Ann-Marie in various stages of development from birth to as recently as a month ago.

A palpable silence filled the room until it enveloped everything. A silence so incredibly damning that it was almost tangible.

At long last he turned towards her, his eyes so remarkably dark that it was impossible to discern anything from his expression. 'Why did you choose not to tell me you were pregnant?' he began with deceptive softness.

Her throat felt impossibly dry, and so constricted that she doubted if her larynx could cope with emitting so much as a sound. 'If I had, you would have hauled me back to Perth,' she said at last.

'Indeed,' Stefano agreed. 'And I wouldn't now brand you a thief for stealing from me the first six years of my daughter's life.'

'If you'd had sufficient respect for our marriage, I wouldn't have felt compelled to leave,' she managed carefully. There was an inherent integrity apparent, a strength that came from deep within. 'And rehashing the past has no relevance to Ann-Marie's future.'

She could feel his anger emanating through the pores of his skin, and all her fine body hairs rose in protective self-defence. He could have shaken her to within an inch of her life, and taken extreme pleasure in her pain. It was there in his eyes, the tautly bunched muscles as he held himself rigidly in control. The promise of retribution was thinly veiled, and she felt immeasurably afraid, aware that such punishment would be swift and without warning—an utter devastation. But not yet, she reasoned shakily. A superb tactician, he would derive infinite satisfaction from playing out her fear.

'You've reached a decision?'

Her heart stopped, then clamoured into a thudding beat. 'Yes.' One look at his hard, obdurate features was sufficient to ascertain his inflexibility.

'Must I draw it from you like blood from stone?' he pursued, his voice assuming a deadly softness, and her eyes flared with resentment.

'I won't allow Ann-Marie to be a metaphorical bone we fight over in a lawcourt,' she said hardily. 'Nor will I put her through the emotional trauma of being bandied back and forth between two parents.' Her head lifted slightly and her chin tilted with determination. 'However, I have one condition.'

One eyebrow slanted in silent cynicism. 'And what is that?'

'You give up your women friends.'

He looked at her for what seemed an age, and she was conscious of an elevated nervous tension as the silence between them stretched to an unbearable length.

'Could you be more specific?'

'Lovers,' she said tightly, hating him.

'Does that mean you are prepared to accommodate me in bed?' he pursued with deadly softness.

Her heart stopped, then clamoured into a thudding beat at the memory his words evoked, and the nights when she'd behaved like a mindless wanton in his passionate embrace. With concentrated effort she managed to keep her gaze steady. 'No, it doesn't, damn you!'

Stefano remained silent, his eyes watchful as he witnessed the fleeting change of her emotions, then after a measurable silence he ventured silkily, 'You expect me to remain celibate?'

Of its own volition, her hand lifted to her hair and eased a stray tendril behind on ear, the gesture unconscious and betraying her inner nervousness. 'I'll live in the same house,' she declared quietly. 'I'll play at being your social hostess. For Ann-Marie's sake, I'll pretend everything between us is fine.' Her eyes were wide, clear, and filled with resolution. 'But I refuse to share your bed.'

The edge of his mouth lifted in a gesture of musing mockery. 'I shall insist you share the same room.'

'Why?' Carly demanded baldly.

His eyes speared hers, their depths hard and inflexible. 'Because I choose never to lose.'

'Our marriage meant nothing to you!'

'You think not?' Stefano countered with unmatched cynicism. 'I retain a clear memory of your...' He paused imperceptibly, then added mockingly, 'Contentment.'

'You gave me beautiful things, put me in a beautiful home, took me out to beautiful parties where beautiful people mingled and made out they were friends.' She felt incredibly sad. 'Except nothing was beautiful. Not really. I was a new playmate, someone you could show off when the occasion demanded.' Her

eyes clouded, and her lashes fluttered down to form
a protective veil. 'I was too young, too naïve, and I
didn't know the rules.'

His expression hardened, and only a fool would
choose to disregard the element of tensile steel beneath
his sophisticated veneer, for apparent was a sense of
purpose, a formidability that was infinitely daunting.

'And now you do?' he taunted silkily.

Her eyes were remarkably clear and steady, her resolve derived from an inner strength she would never
allow him to destroy. 'I care for my daughter more
than life itself,' she vowed quietly. 'Her health and
well-being take precedence over anything you can
throw at me.'

His eyes reflected an indomitable strength of will,
and, unless she was mistaken, a chilling degree of silent rage.

Self-preservation was a prime motivation, yet right
at this instant she felt as vulnerable as a cornered
vixen. 'I insist on continuing with my career—even
if it's only on a part-time basis.'

He didn't display any emotion whatsoever, and she
shivered, aware of the force she was dealing with.

'You'll take an extended leave of absence, effective
almost immediately, until Ann-Marie has recovered
fully from surgery and is able to return to school.'

An angry flush crept over her cheeks as she fought
to remain calm beneath his deliberate appraisal. 'It
never entered my head to do otherwise,' she retaliated,
determined to press home every point in her intention to set a personal precedent. 'However, I studied
very hard to achieve my present position, and I have
no intention of giving it up.'

'I'm sure Clive Mathorpe will be amenable to your working a reduced number of hours consistent with the time Ann-Marie spends at school.'

Cool, damning words, but carrying a weight she found impossible to ignore. She felt drained, emotionally and physically, and she needed to be alone.

'Will you please leave?'

'When do you collect Ann-Marie from the party?'

Carly's eyes flew to her watch, confirming with immeasurable relief that it was only minutes past three.

'Soon,' she acknowledged. 'I told Susy's mother I'd join her and the other mothers for afternoon tea.'

'In that case, I'll drive you there.'

A surge of anger rose to the surface, colouring her cheeks and sharpening her features. 'Damn you,' she cursed fiercely. 'I won't introduce you to Ann-Marie in one breath and reveal you're her father in the next!'

'Putting off the inevitable won't achieve anything,' Stefano stated in a voice that was infinitely dangerous. 'Invite me to dinner tonight.'

She closed her eyes, then slowly opened them again. 'Can't it wait a few days?'

'I've spoken to the specialist and arranged an appointment with the neurosurgeon for Tuesday. It's highly possible she'll undergo surgery within a week.' His gaze seemed incredibly dark as his features assumed a harsh, implacable mask. 'It's imperative that you're both established in my home as soon as possible. Emotional stability is crucial to her recuperation.'

'When she's fully recovered is soon enough,' Carly cried, hating the way he was taking charge.

'Tomorrow,' he informed her with diabolical insistence.

'No,' she denied at once. 'It will only cause her anxiety and add to the trauma of hospitalisation and surgery.'

'Use whatever guise you choose,' he insisted softly. 'But do it, Carly. Ann-Marie will soon accept I have a rightful place in her life—as she has in mine.'

A holiday, a brief stay, was the only tenable explanation, she decided, aware that Ann-Marie would probably view the proposal as something of an adventure.

'I'll be back at five,' he declared hardly. 'And I'll bring dinner. All you'll have to do is serve it.' His gaze seared her soul. 'Don't even think about running away, Carly,' he warned softly. 'This time, I'll search until I find you, and afterwards you'll wish you were dead.'

She stood transfixed as he turned and walked to the door, then quietly left the apartment.

It took ten minutes for her to regain some measure of composure, a further five before she took the lift down to the underground car park.

To sit with several other young mothers sipping tea and sharing party fare proved an anticlimax, and Carly felt as if she was operating on automatic pilot while her brain whirled off on a tangent.

She smiled a lot, and she even managed to laugh with apparent spontaneity at an amusingly told anecdote. Inside, she was a mess, conscious with every passing minute, each glance at Ann-Marie, of the impact Stefano would have on their lives. Especially her own.

The most pressing problem was finding the right

words that would prevent Ann-Marie from forming any prejudice, one way or the other, about her mother's actions. Children were incredibly curious, and Ann-Marie was no exception.

For the following half-hour Carly watched Susy unwrap her presents, unable afterwards to remember more than a few, then, when the birthday cake was cut, she helped distribute the pieces.

Soon it was time to leave, and in the car she tussled with her conscience, agonising over how she should explain Stefano and their reconciliation, aware that the little girl was too excited after the party to really absorb much of what her mother had to say.

While driving a car in traffic was hardly the time or place, and as soon as they entered the apartment she plugged in the kettle, made herself a cup of strong tea, then settled down beside Ann-Marie on the sofa.

'Someone very special is going to have dinner with us tonight,' Carly began quietly, aware that she had her daughter's undivided attention by the bright curiosity evident in a pair of grey eyes that were identical to Stefano's.

'Sarah?'

'No, darling.' She hesitated slightly, then offered quietly, 'Your father.'

Ann-Marie's eyes widened measurably and her expression assumed a solemnity beyond her tender years. 'You said my father lived a long, long way away, and you left him before he knew about me.' The eyes grew even larger. 'Why didn't you want to tell him?'

Oh, dear lord. Out of the mouths of babes! 'Because we had an argument,' Carly answered honestly. 'And we said things we didn't mean.' An extension of the

truth, for *she* had said them—Stefano hadn't uttered
a single word in his defence.

'How did he find out about me?' Ann-Marie queried slowly.

'Your father moved to Sydney several months ago,'
Carly said quietly, watching the expressive play of
emotions evident. 'I've been in touch with him.'

'Why?'

If only there were a simple answer! 'I thought it
was time he knew about you.'

Ann-Marie's gaze didn't waver, and it seemed an
age before she spoke. 'And you don't not like him
any more?'

She hid a sad smile at Ann-Marie's phraseology,
and prayed the good lord would forgive her for the
fabrication. 'No.'

'Now he wants to meet me,' Ann-Marie said with
childish intuition, and Carly nodded her head in silent
agreement, then endorsed,

'Yes, he does. Very much.'

'Is he angry with you for not telling him about me?'

'A little,' she admitted gently.

Ann-Marie's expression became comically fierce,
and her chin jutted forward. 'If he's nasty to you, I'll
hit him.'

The mental picture of a delicate, curly-haired six-
year-old lashing out at a six-feet-plus male frame
brought a slight smile to Carly's lips. 'That would
be very rude, don't you think? Especially when he's
a very kind man.' Not to her, never to her. However,
she had no doubt he would be kind to his daughter.

'Does he want us to live together and be a family?'

Her answer had to be direct and without hesitation. 'Yes,' she said simply.

'Do *you* want us to live with him?' Ann-Marie persisted, and Carly felt as if she was caught in a trap with no way out.

'Yes.' Two untruths in the space of two minutes. If she wasn't careful, it could become a habit. 'Let's go and freshen up, shall we? He'll be here soon.'

'What do I call him?' Ann-Marie asked several minutes later as she stood quietly while Carly tidied her hair and redid her ribbons.

Carly had a terrible feeling the questions could only get worse! 'What would you like to call him?'

Ann-Marie appeared to deliberate, her eyes pensive as a slight frown creased her small brow. 'Daddy, I guess.' Her eyes moved to meet those of her mother in the mirror. 'Will I like him?'

She forced her mouth to widen into a warm smile, then she bent down to brush her lips against her daughter's temple. 'I'm sure that once you get to know him you'll like him very much,' she assured her quietly.

Ann-Marie looked at her mother's mirrored reflection and queried with puzzlement, 'Aren't you going to put some lipstick on?'

Carly didn't feel inclined to do anything to enhance her appearance, although she reached automatically for a slim plastic tube and outlined her mouth in clear red.

The sound of the doorbell heralded Stefano's arrival, and, catching hold of Ann-Marie's hand, she summoned a bright smile. 'Shall we answer that?'

I don't want to do this, a voice screamed silently

from within, aware that the moment she opened the door her life would change irrevocably.

Carly schooled her features into an expression of welcome, and although she registered his physical presence she felt akin to a disembodied spectator.

Except that this was no nightmarish dream. Stefano Alessi represented reality, and she issued a greeting, aware that he had exchanged the formal business suit worn a few hours earlier for casual dark trousers and an open-necked shirt.

Carly barely hid a gasp of surprise as he reached out and threaded his fingers through hers, tightening them imperceptibly as she attempted to pull away from his grasp.

She registered a silent protest by digging the tips of her nails into hard bone and sinew. Not that it did any good, for he didn't even blink, and she watched in silence as his mouth curved into a warm smile.

Supremely conscious of Ann-Marie's intent gaze, she managed to return it, and she glimpsed the faint narrowing of his eyes, the silent warning evident an instant before they swept down to encompass his daughter.

'Hello, Ann-Marie.'

He made no attempt to touch her, and Ann-Marie looked at him solemnly for several long seconds, her eyes round and unwavering before they shifted to her mother, then back again to the man at her side.

'Hello,' she answered politely.

Carly felt as if her heart would tear in two, and she held her breath, supremely conscious of the man and the child, one so much a part of the other, both aware of their connection, yet each unsure quite how to proceed.

In a strange way, it allowed her to see a different side of the man, a hint of vulnerability evident that she doubted anyone else had ever witnessed. It surprised her, and made her wonder for one very brief minute how different things might have been if she'd stayed in the marriage, and if he would have given up Angelica Agnelli and assumed the role of devoted father.

A knife twisted deep within her, and the pain became intense at the thought of Stefano taking delight in all the changing facets of her pregnancy, the miracle of the birth itself, and the shared joy of their newborn child.

She'd denied him that, had felt justified in doing so, and if it hadn't been for Ann-Marie's illness she doubted that she'd ever have allowed him to become aware of his daughter's existence.

His fingers tightened around her own, almost as if he could read her thoughts, and she summoned the effort to move into the lounge, indicating one of two chairs.

'Please, take a seat.' Her voice sounded strange, not her own at all, and she extricated her hand from his, aware that it was only because he allowed her to do so.

'I hope you like chicken,' Stefano said, holding out a large carrier bag suitably emblazoned with an exclusive delicatessen logo. 'There's a variety of salads, some fresh bread rolls, cheese. And a bottle of wine.'

'Thank you,' Carly acknowledged with contrived warmth, and preceded him into the kitchen.

They ate at six, and Carly was aware of an inner

tension that almost totally destroyed her appetite. There was no lull in conversation, and although Ann-Marie displayed initial reservation it wasn't long before she was chatting happily about school, her friends, Sarah, and how much she'd love to own a dog.

'I have a dog,' Stefano revealed, and Carly stifled a mental groan in the knowledge that he had just won a massive slice of Ann-Marie's interest, for the 'no animals allowed' rule enforced by the apartment managers ensured that tenants couldn't have pets.

Ann-Marie could barely hide her excitement. 'What sort of dog?'

Carly waited with bated breath, and had her worst fears confirmed with Stefano enlightened her. 'A Dobermann pinscher.'

'Mummy said that one day when we live in a house we can have a poodle.'

Stefano cast Carly a musing glance at her choice before turning his attention back to his daughter. 'In that case, we'll have to see about getting you one.'

It was bribery, pure and simple, and Carly hated him for it.

By the time Ann-Marie was settled happily in bed and asleep, it was clear that Stefano had succeeded in winning a place in his daughter's affections.

'I have to congratulate you,' Carly said quietly as she handed him some freshly made coffee. Then she crossed the small lounge and selected a chair as far distant from his as possible.

His gaze was startlingly level. 'On developing an empathy with my daughter?'

She met his eyes and held their gaze with all the

force of her maternal instincts. 'If you do anything to hurt her—*ever*,' she emphasised softly, 'I'll kill you.'

He didn't speak for several long seconds, and Carly felt close to screaming point. 'You wanted for her to hate me?'

'*No*. No,' she repeated shakily, knowing that it wasn't true.

'Yet you decry the speed with which she has gifted me a measure of her affection,' Stefano pursued.

She refused to admit it, and stirred her coffee instead, wanting only for the evening to end so that she could be free of his disturbing presence.

'Gaining her trust won't be achieved overnight,' he discounted drily, adding, 'And love has to be earned.'

'Why agree to gift her a poodle?'

'I said *we* would have to see about getting her one,' he responded evenly, and she instantly flared,

'A Dobermann and a poodle both on the same property?'

'Prince is a well-trained guard dog who is exceptionally obedient. I doubt there will be a problem.'

'And it matters little to you that I might have a problem moving into your home?'

His eyes were hard, with no hint of any softness. 'I'm sure you'll manage to overcome it.'

Suddenly she'd had enough, and she replaced her cup down on the coffee-table, then rose to her feet. 'I'm tired and I'd like you to leave.'

He followed her movements with a lithe indolence, then covered the distance to the front door. 'Be packed and ready at midday. I'll collect you.'

She wanted to hit him, and she lifted her hand, only to have it caught in a merciless grip.

'Don't even think about it,' Stefano warned silkily. 'This time I won't be so generous.'

There could be little doubt about the veiled threat, and she looked at him in helpless anger, wanting so much to strike out in temper, yet forced to contain it out of consideration to a sleeping child who, should she wake and perchance witness such a scene, would be both puzzled and frightened, and unable to comprehend the cause.

Stefano released her hand, then he opened the door and moved out into the foyer without so much as a backward glance.

CHAPTER FOUR

CARLY EXPERIENCED A sense of acute nervousness as she caught sight of Stefano's imposing double-storeyed French-château-style home. Situated in the exclusive suburb of Clontarf and constructed of grey stone, it sat well back from the road in beautifully kept grounds.

A spreading jacaranda tree in full bloom with its carpet of lilac flowers provided a fitting backdrop to an assortment of precision-clipped shrubs, and symmetrical borders filled with a variety of colourful flowers that were predominantly red, pink, white and yellow.

Dear lord, what had she *done*? The enormity of it all settled like a tremendous weight on her slim shoulders. In the space of fifteen hours she had packed, cleaned the apartment, notified the leasing agent, and confided in Sarah. *And* tossed and turned for the short time she'd permitted herself to sleep. Now she had to face reality.

The car drew to a halt adjacent to the main entrance, and no sooner had Stefano slid out from behind the wheel than a short, well-built man of middle years emerged from the house to retrieve several suitcases from the capacious boot.

'Joe Bardini,' Stefano told them as Carly and Ann-Marie slid from the car. 'Joe and his wife Sylvana look after the house and grounds.'

The man's smile was warm, and his voice when he spoke held the barest trace of an Italian accent. 'Sylvana is in the kitchen preparing lunch. I will tell her you have arrived.'

Some of Carly's tension transmitted itself to her daughter, for Ann-Marie's fingers tightened measurably within her own as Stefano led the way indoors.

The foyer was spacious, with cream-streaked marble tiles and delicate archways either side of a magnificent double staircase leading to the upper floor. The focal point was a beautiful crystal chandelier, spectacular in design by day. Carly could only wonder at its luminescence by night.

'Would you prefer to explore the house before or after lunch?'

'Can we now?' Ann-Marie begged before Carly had a chance to utter so much as a word, and Stefano cast his daughter a musing glance.

'Why not? Shall we begin upstairs?'

'Yes, please.'

They ascended one side of the curving staircase, and on reaching the upper floor he directed them left to two guest rooms and a delightful bedroom suite with a connecting bathroom.

'Is this where I'm going to sleep?' Ann-Marie asked as she looked at the softly toned bedcovers.

'Do you like it?' Stefano asked gently, and she nodded.

'It's very pretty. Can Sarah come visit sometimes?'

'Of course,' he answered solemnly.

'Sarah lives in the apartment next door,' Ann-Marie explained carefully. 'She is our very best friend.'

To the right of the central staircase Stefano opened a door leading into the main suite, and Carly's eyes flew to two queensize beds separated by a double pedestal. A spacious *en suite* was visible, and there was an adjoining sitting-room complete with soft leather chairs, a television console, and escritoire.

'We'll use this suite,' Stefano indicated, and Carly refrained from comment, choosing instead to shoot him a telling glance as she preceded him to the head of the stairs.

If he thought she'd share the same bedroom with him, he had another think coming!

Once downstairs he led them into a formal lounge containing items of delicate antique furniture, deep-seated sofas and single chairs, employing a visually pleasing mix of cream, beige and soft sage-green. Oil-paintings graced the walls, a sparkling crystal chandelier hung suspended from a beautiful filigree-plastered ceiling, and wide floor-to-ceiling sliding glass doors opened out on to a covered terrace.

Even at a glance it was possible to see the blue-tiled swimming-pool beyond the terrace, and catch a glimpse of the magnificent view out over the harbour.

The formal dining-room was equally impressive, and his study held an awesome arsenal of high-tech equipment as well as a large mahogany desk, and wall-to-wall bookshelves.

The southern wing comprised an informal family room, dining-room and an enormous kitchen any chef would kill for.

A pleasantly plump middle-aged woman turned as they entered, and her kindly face creased into a warm welcoming smile as Stefano effected introductions.

'Lunch will be ready in ten minutes,' Sylvana declared.

'Is Prince outside? Can I see him?' Ann-Marie asked, and she made no objection when Stefano reached forward and caught hold of her hand.

'Come and be properly introduced.'

The dog was huge, and looked incredibly fearsome, yet beneath Stefano's guidance he became a docile lamb, his eyes large and soulful, his whimpering enthusiasm as close to canine communication as it was possible to get.

'After lunch we'll take him for a walk round the grounds, and you can watch him go through his paces.'

Lunch was served in the informal dining-room, and Ann-Marie did justice to the tender roast chicken with accompanying vegetables, as well as the delicious crème caramel dessert.

The excellent glass of white wine Carly sipped through lunch helped soothe her fractured nerves, and afterwards she walked quietly with Ann-Marie as Stefano led the Dobermann through a series of commands.

It was very warm outdoors, and Carly glimpsed a few tell-tale signs of her daughter's tiredness. The symptoms of her condition could descend with little warning, and it was essential that her reserves of strength were not overtaxed.

'Shall we go upstairs?' Carly suggested, catching hold of Ann-Marie's hand. 'You can lie down while I unpack your clothes.'

Stefano shot her a quick glance, his expression pensive as Ann-Marie stumbled slightly.

'Can I see Prince again before dinner?'

'Of course. You can watch Joe feed him.'

Carly lifted her into her arms, and Ann-Marie nestled her head into the curve of her mother's shoulder, her small hands lifting to link together around Carly's neck.

'Let me take her,' Stefano bade quietly, and Carly made to demure, barely able to control her surprise as Ann-Marie allowed Stefano to transfer her into his arms without protest.

Ann-Marie fought against encroaching lassitude as they made their way indoors, and by the time Stefano deposited her gently down on to the bed she was asleep.

His eyes were dark and slightly hooded as he watched Carly deftly remove the little girl's shoes then draw up a light cover before crossing to the window to close the curtains.

'She just needs to rest,' she said quietly. 'She'll be all right in an hour or two.'

Carly turned and walked from the room, supremely conscious of a distinct prickling sensation feathering her spine as he followed close behind.

It was damnable to be so aware of him, and in the hallway she quickened her step towards the main suite. 'I'll begin unpacking.' Her voice sounded incredibly stilted and polite, almost dismissing, for he had the power to ruffle her composure more than she was prepared to admit.

Their combined luggage was stacked neatly on the floor, and her eyes swept the room, hating the invidious position in which she'd been placed and the man who deliberately sought to put her there.

'Afraid, Carly?' a deep voice drawled from behind, and she turned slowly to face him, her eyes steady.

'You intend me to be,' she said with hesitation, aware of an inner resentment. 'This is part of a diabolical game, isn't it?' she flared, on a verbal rollercoaster. 'Separate beds, but having to share the same room. An *en suite* with no lock, ensuring you can invade my privacy any time you choose.' A degree of bitterness made itself apparent. 'And you will choose, won't you, Stefano? Just for the hell of it.' Her eyes darkened measurably, the gold flecks appearing like chips of topaz against brown velvet. 'Don't ever mistake your bed for mine,' she warned with deadly softness. 'I'd mark you for life.'

His gaze raked hers, harsh and unrelenting. 'Be grateful I've allowed you a separate bed,' he drawled smoothly. 'It wasn't my original intention.'

Her heart lurched, then missed a beat as sensation unfurled deep within her, the pain so acute that she almost gasped at its intensity. For one horrifying moment she held a clear vision of their bodies locked in lovemaking, aware that if he chose to take her now it would be a violation motivated by revenge.

Her eyes grew large, expressing a mixture of shock and anger, yet she refused to be subjugated to him in any way. 'Rape, even between husband and wife,' she reminded stiltedly, 'is a criminal offence.'

Something flickered in the depths of his eyes, then it was successfully masked. 'You know me well enough to understand that rape would never be a consideration.'

No, she thought shakily. He was too skilled a lover to harm his partner with any form of physical pain. His revenge would be infinitely more subtle.

As it had been on one previous occasion, when she'd driven him to anger with a heated accusation she'd refused to retract or explain, and he had simply hauled her unceremoniously over his shoulder and carried her into the bedroom where he had conducted a deliberate leisurely assault on her senses until she was on fire with a desire so intense that she had possessed no reason, no sanity, only base animal need and a wild driven hunger for the release that only he could give. Except that he had taken pleasure in making her wait until she was reduced to begging unashamedly like a craven wanton caught in the throes of some primeval force, and then, only then, had he taken her with a merciless mastery that knew no bounds in a totally erotic plundering of her senses. With no energy left to move, she'd drifted into sleep, only to waken in the early morning hours, where self-loathing had surfaced, and a degree of shame. It had been the catalyst that had motivated her to leave.

Carly shivered suddenly, hating him more than she thought it was possible to hate anyone, and she watched in silence as he crossed to a concealed wall-safe, activated the mechanism, then removed a small jeweller's box before covering the distance between with calm, leisurely steps.

'Your rings,' Stefano declared, extracting the exquisite square-cut diamond with its baguette-cut diamond mounting, and its matching band.

Surprise momentarily widened her eyes as she recalled tearing both from her finger in a fit of angry rage. 'You kept them?'

His gaze was remarkably steady. 'What did you expect me to do with them?'

She was lost for words, her mobile features hauntingly expressive for a few seconds before she schooled them into restrained reserve, unable in the few ensuing seconds to make any protest as he took hold of her left hand and slid both rings in place.

Of their own volition her fingers sought the large stone, twisting it back and forth in a gesture that betrayed an inner nervousness.

His proximity disturbed her more than she was prepared to admit, and she was aware of a watchful quality in his stance, an intentness so overpowering that she felt almost afraid.

Her whole body stirred, caught up in a web of sensuality so acute that it seemed as if every vein, every nerve cell in her body flamed in electrifying recognition of *his*, which was totally opposite to the dictates of her brain.

To continue standing here like this was madness, and without a further word she turned away from him, crossing to her luggage to begin the chore of unpacking.

Carly's movements were steady and unhurried as she placed clothes on hangers in a capacious walk-in wardrobe, and she was aware of the instant he turned and left the room.

Dinner was a simple meal comprising minestrone followed by pasta, and afterwards Sylvana served coffee in the informal lounge.

Settling Ann-Marie to bed was achieved without

fuss, and Stefano willingly agreed to his daughter's request to listen to a bedtime story.

A novelty, Carly assured herself as she chose the opposite side of Ann-Marie's bed, conscious that she was the focus of two pair of eyes—one pair loving and direct, the other musing and faintly speculative.

Forget he's there, a tiny voice prompted as she picked up the book and began to read. Who do you think you're kidding? another derided.

Somehow Carly managed to inject her voice with its customary warmth and enthusiasm, and she had almost finished when Ann-Marie's eyes fluttered down.

Minutes later Stefano rose quietly to his feet and waited at the door for Carly to precede him from the room.

'Does she usually wake in the night?' he queried as they neared the head of the stairs, and Carly shook her head.

'Very rarely.' She was a nervous wreck, she had a headache, and all she wanted to do was have a long leisurely shower, then slip into bed. She said as much, adding, 'I'll drop Ann-Marie at school in the morning, then go into the office for a few hours.'

'Clive Mathorpe isn't expecting you,' Stefano drawled, and she felt a *frisson* of alarm at his long hard glance. 'I've already enlightened him that his highly regarded Carly Taylor is Carly Taylor *Alessi*.'

Anger surged to the surface at his high-handedness. 'How dare you?' she vented in softly voiced fury. 'I am quite capable of telling him myself!'

'As my wife, there's no necessity for you to work. Your first priority lies with Ann-Marie.' The velvet smoothness in his voice should have been sufficient warning, but she was too stubborn to take any heed.

'I agree,' she conceded, determined to win points against him. 'However, as she'll be at school from eight forty-five until two-thirty, I don't see why I shouldn't spend those hours delegating work to who-ever will take my place over the next few weeks.'

'I'll allow you tomorrow,' Stefano agreed hardly. 'But that's all.'

'Don't begin dictating what I can and can't do!' Carly said fiercely. She felt defensive, and very, very angry. 'And don't you *dare* imply that I'm an irrespon-sible mother! What sort of father will *you* be?' she demanded. 'It isn't nearly enough to provide a child with a beautiful home and numerous possessions. The novelty soon wears off when you can't be present at the school fête, or attend the end-of-year play.' Her eyes flashed with fiery topaz as her anger deepened. 'What happens next week, the week after that, and all the long months ahead?' she queried fiercely. 'You'll be too busy jetting off to God knows where, cement-ing yet another multi-million-dollar deal. When you *are* home, you'll probably leave in the morning before she wakes, and return long after she's given up any hope of catching a glimpse of you. How am I going to explain that your liaison with fatherhood will be conducted by remote control?'

His eyes were dark and unfathomable, and she was aware of a degree of anger apparent. 'Why are you so sure it will be?'

'Because you lead such a high-profile existence,' she flung in cautiously. 'It can't be any other way, damn you!'

He looked at her in silence for what seemed an age, and it was all she could do to hold his gaze. Yet she wouldn't subvert her own beliefs in deference to a man whose credo was different from her own.

'Tell me, are you staging a fight as a matter of principle, or merely as an attempt to vent some of your rage?'

'Both!'

'With any clear thought to the consequences?' Stefano pursued, his eyes never leaving hers for a second.

'Don't you dare threaten me!'

One dark eyebrow rose in cynical query. 'If you imagine I'll take any invective you choose to throw in my direction without retaliation, you're mistaken,' he warned silkily.

Carly felt as if she was on a rollercoaster leading all the way down to hell. 'I'm damned if I'll play happy families at a flick of your fingers!'

'I doubt you'll do or say anything to upset Ann-Marie.'

He was right. She wouldn't. Yet she desperately wanted to hit out at him for invading her life and turning it upside-down.

'Do you enjoy the power it gives you to use my daughter as an excuse to blackmail me?'

'Are you making an allegation?' Stefano countered in a voice that would have quelled an adversary.

For a few fateful seconds they seemed locked in silent battle, and she felt as if she was shattering into a thousand pieces. 'It's the truth!'

He stood regarding her in silence, his eyes darkly inscrutable, yet there was an air of leashed anger apparent, a sense of control that was almost frightening.

'Quit while you're ahead, Carly.'

She felt the need to be free of him, and preferably alone. For a few hours at least. 'I'm going to take a shower and watch television for a while.'

One eyebrow rose fractionally. 'A desire for solitude?'

'I'm off duty,' she declared, uncaring of his reaction.

'Careful with your claws, my little cat,' Stefano warned softly. 'Or I may choose to unsheathe my own.'

There was nothing she could add, so she didn't even try. Instead, she turned and walked towards their suite, and once inside she carefully closed the door.

He didn't follow, and she moved into the *en suite* and shed her clothes, then took a long shower, and, towelled dry, she pulled on a thin cotton shift and emerged into the bedroom, to stand hesitantly, unsure which of the two beds she should occupy.

Dammit, she swore softly. With her luck, she'd choose the wrong one, and then Stefano would be cynically amused by her mistake.

There was only one solution, and she caught up a towelling robe and slid it on, then walked through to the sitting-room, activated the television, and sank into a comfortable chair.

If necessary, she determined vengefully, she'd sleep here, rather than slip into the wrong bed!

Sunday evening television offered the choice of three movies, an intellectual book review, or a play spoken entirely in Hungarian. A karate-kickboxer epic wasn't her preferred viewing, nor was a terminator blockbuster, and she wasn't in the mood for a chilling thriller. After switching channels several times, she simply selected one for the sake of it and allowed her attention to wander.

At some stage she must have dozed, for she was aware of a strange sense of weightlessness, a desire to sink more comfortably into arms that seemed terribly familiar.

A small sigh escaped her lips, and she burrowed her face into the curve of a hard, muscular shoulder, then lifted her hands to encircle a male neck.

It felt so good, so *right*, and she murmured her appreciation. Her lips touched against warm skin, moving involuntarily as they savoured a texture and scent her subconscious recognised—not only recognised, but delighted in the discovery.

Except that she wanted more, and the tip of her tongue ventured out in a tentative exploratory tasting, edging up a deeply pulsing cord in search of a mouth she instinctively knew could bestow pleasure.

Then the barriers between unconsciousness and awareness began to disperse, bringing a horrifying knowledge that, although the arms that held her belonged to the right man, it was the wrong time, the wrong room, and her dream-like state owed nothing to the reality!

For a moment her eyes retained a warm luminescence, a musing witchery, then they clouded with pain before being hidden by two thickly lashed veils as she struggled to be free of him.

'Put me down!'

'I was about to,' Stefano drawled as he placed her between fragrantly clean sheets, and her lashes swept up to reveal intense anger.

His touch was impersonal, yet she felt as if she was on fire, with every separate nerve-end quivering into vibrant life, each individual skin-cell an ambivalent entity craving his touch.

Carly snatched the top sheet and pulled it up to her chin in a defensive gesture. 'Get away from me!'

His eyes speared hers, darkly mesmeric as she forced herself not to look away.

'You're as nervous as a kitten,' he drawled musingly. 'Why, when we've known each other in the most intimate sense?'

Reaching out, he brushed gentle fingers down the length of her cheek to the edge of her mouth, then traced the curving contour with a stray forefinger. 'What are you afraid of, *cara*?'

'Nothing,' Carly responded carefully. 'Absolutely nothing at all.'

Liar, she derided silently. No matter how hard she tried she was unable to still the fast-beating pulse that hummed through her veins, seducing every nerve and fibre until she felt incredibly *alive*.

His smile was wholly cynical, and his eyes held a gleam of mockery as they conducted a deliberately slow appraisal of her expressive features, lingering over-long on the visible pulsebeat at the base of her throat before travelling up to meet her gaze.

'Goodnight, Carly,' he bade her lazily. 'Sleep well.'

She mutinously refused to comment, and she watched as he turned and walked from the room. Damn him, she cursed silently. She *wouldn't* sleep in this bed, this room!

Anger fuelled her resolve, and she flung aside the

covers, grabbed hold of her robe, then retreated quietly to an empty suite near by.

It held a double bed—made up in readiness, she discovered—and she slid beneath the covers, then switched off the bedside lamp.

Quite what Stefano's reaction would be when he found her missing wasn't something she gave much thought to for a while. She was too consumed with numerous vengeful machinations, all designed to cause him harm.

By the time she focused on what he might do, she was drifting off to sleep, too comfortable and too tired to care.

At some stage during the night she came sharply awake as a light snapped on, and she blinked against its brightness, disorientated by her surroundings for one brief second before realisation dawned. Except that by then it was too late to do anything but struggle as hard hands lifted her unceremoniously to her feet.

The face above her own was set in frightening lines, jaw clenched, mouth compressed into a savagely thin line, and eyes as dark as obsidian slate burning with controlled anger.

'You can walk,' Stefano drawled with dangerous softness. 'Or I can carry you.' His eyes hardened with chilling intensity, and Carly felt immensely afraid. 'The choice is yours.'

He resembled a dark brooding force—lethal, she acknowledged shakily, noting a leashed quality in his stance that boded ill should she dare consider rebellion.

'I won't share the same bedroom with you,' she ventured with a brave attempt at defiance, and saw his eyes narrow for an instant before they began a deliberately slow raking appraisal of her slim curves.

It was terrifying, for her skin flamed as if he'd actually trailed his fingers along the same path, and her eyes filled with futile rage. Her fingers curled into her palms, the knuckles showing white as she restrained herself from lashing out at him.

'We agreed to a reconciliation,' he reminded her with icy detachment. 'For Ann-Marie's benefit.' His dark gaze seared hers, then struck at her heart. 'I think we each realise our daughter is sufficiently intelligent to know that happily reconciled parents don't maintain separate bedrooms.' He knew just how to twist the knife, and he did it without hesitation. 'Are you prepared for the questions she'll pose?'

Carly's slim form shook with anger, and her eyes blazed with it as she held his gaze. 'If you so much as touch me,' she warned as she collected her wrap and slipped it on, 'I'll fight you all the way down to hell.'

It took only seconds to reach the master suite, and only a few more to discard her wrap and slip into one of the two beds dominating the large room. With determination she turned on to her side and closed her eyes, uncaring whether he followed her or not.

She heard him enter the room and the soft decisive snap as the door closed, followed by the faint rustle of clothes being discarded, then the room was plunged into darkness, and she lay still, her body tense, until sheer exhaustion triumphed and she fell asleep.

Monday rapidly shaped up to be one of those days where Murphy's Law prevailed, Carly decided grimly, for whatever could go wrong did, from a ladder in her tights to a traffic jam *en route* to the city.

On reaching the office, there appeared to be little improvement. She didn't even manage coffee mid-morning, and lunch was a salad sandwich she sent out for and washed down quickly with apple juice as she checked and double-checked details required urgently for an eminent client.

Given normal circumstances she excelled under pressure, regarding it as a challenge rather than nerve-destroying, and it was with mixed feelings that she tidied her desk, took leave of her colleagues and drove to collect Ann-Marie from school.

They arrived at Stefano's elegant mansion—Carly refused to call it home—shortly after three to find a silver-grey BMW standing in the driveway.

'For you,' Joe Bardini informed Carly as he emerged from the house to greet them. 'Mr Alessi had it delivered this morning.'

Had he, indeed! 'It's very nice, Joe,' she accorded quietly, and she veiled her eyes so that he wouldn't see the anger evident.

'Mr Alessi suggested you might like to take it for a test drive.'

She managed a warm smile, and indicated her briefcase. 'I think I'll get changed first.'

'It's really hot,' Ann-Marie declared as she followed Carly indoors. 'Can we go for a swim?'

Ten minutes later they were laughing and splashing together in the shallow end of the pool, and after half an hour Carly persuaded her daughter to emerge on the pretext of having a cool drink.

'Look,' Ann-Marie alerted her from the pool's

edge. 'Daddy's home.' The name slid so easily, so naturally off the little girl's tongue, with no hesitation or reservation whatsoever, and Carly felt her stomach clench with pain.

She was suddenly supremely conscious of the simply styled maillot, and, although it was perfectly respectable when dry, wet, it clung lovingly to soft curves. Much too lovingly, she saw with dismay, conscious of the way it hugged her breasts.

Slowly she turned to face him, a faint false smile pulling at the edges of her mouth as she wound a towel around Ann-Marie's small frame, then she quickly reached for another, draping it over one shoulder in the hope that it would provide some sort of temporary cover.

Her action amused him, and she met his gaze with equanimity, heighteningly aware of his studied appraisal and her own damning reaction.

It was difficult to keep the smile in place, but she managed—just. If she'd been alone she would have slapped his face.

It was perhaps as well that he turned his attention to his daughter, whose wide, solemn eyes switched from one parent to the other as she assessed his show of affection and her mother's reaction.

Consequently Carly presented a relaxed façade, deliberately injecting some warmth as she enquired as to his day, and commented on his early return.

'I thought we might drive out to one of the beaches for a barbecue,' Stefano suggested, and was immediately rewarded with Ann-Marie's enthusiastic response.

'Can we go in the new car?'

His answering smile was her reward. 'I don't see why not.'

There was no way Carly could demur, and with a few words and a fixed smile she directed her daughter upstairs to shower and change.

It was after five when Stefano drove the BMW out of the driveway and headed towards one of the northern beaches, where he played chef, cooking steak and sausages to perfection while Carly busied herself setting out a variety of salads, sliced a freshly baked French breadstick, and enjoyed a light wine spritzer.

The air was fresh and clean, slightly tangy with the smell of the sea. A faint warm breeze drifted in from the ocean, teasing the length of her hair, and she gazed out to the horizon, seeing deep blue merge with clear azure, aware in that moment of a profound feeling of awe for the magnitude and greatness of nature. There was a sense of timelessness, almost an awareness that life was extremely tenuous, gifted by some powerful deity, and that each day, each hour, should be seized for the enjoyment of its beauty.

Tears welled at the backs of her eyes and threatened to spill. Dear God, what would she do if anything happened to Ann-Marie? How could she cope?

'Mummy, what's wrong?'

Carly caught her scattered thoughts together and summoned a smile. 'I'm admiring the view,' she explained, and, reaching down, she lifted Ann-Marie into her arms and directed her attention out over the ocean. 'Look, isn't that a ship in the distance?'

They ate sausages tasting faintly of smoke, tender steak, and the two adults washed it all down with a light fruity wine, then they packed everything back into the boot of the car and walked along the foreshore.

Ann-Marie chattered happily, pausing every now and then to inspect and collect seashells, which she presented for Carly's inspection, then when she grew tired Stefano lifted her high to sit astride his shoulders, and they made their way slowly back to the car.

A gentle breeze tugged at Carly's long cotton skirt and teased the length of her hair. The sun's warmth was beginning to cool as the giant orb sank lower in the sky, its colour flaring brilliantly as it changed from yellow to gold to orange, then to a deep rose before sinking below the horizon. The keening seagulls quietened, and took their last sweeping flight before seeking shelter for the night.

There was a sense of peace and tranquillity, almost a feeling of harmony with the man walking at her side, and for a moment she wondered if their marriage could have worked... Then she dismissed it in the knowledge that there were too many 'if only's. There was only *now*.

'You take the wheel,' Stefano instructed as they reached the car, and Carly shook her head, unwilling to familiarise herself with a new vehicle while he sat in the passenger seat. 'I insist,' he added quietly, and in Ann-Marie's presence she had little option but to accede.

It was almost nine when they arrived home, and Ann-Marie was so tired that she fell asleep almost as soon as her head touched the pillow.

CHAPTER FIVE

'COFFEE?' STEFANO queried as they descended the staircase, and Carly nodded her head in silent acquiescence.

In the kitchen she filled the percolator with water, selected a fresh filter, spooned in a measure of freshly ground coffee-beans, then activated the machine before reaching for two cups and saucers, sugar.

'From now on, use the BMW.'

Resentment flared in his mocking command. 'There's nothing wrong with my car,' she retaliated at once. 'It's roadworthy and reliable.'

His gaze trapped hers and she felt every single hair on her body prickle with inexplicable foreboding. 'When was it last fully serviced?'

Too long ago, Carly admitted silently, all too aware that over the past few months all her money had gone on expensive medical bills.

'You don't like the BMW?' Stefano queried with deceptive mildness, and she summoned a false smile.

'I presume it's the "in" vehicle that wives of wealthy corporate directors are driving this year.'

His eyes narrowed fractionally, and the edges of

his mouth curved with cynicism. 'That wasn't the reason I chose it.'

'No?' Her faint smile was tinged with mockery. 'It does, however, fit the required image.'

'And what is that, Carly?' Stefano pursued with dangerous softness.

'You're a very successful man,' she returned solemnly, 'who has to be seen to surround himself with the trappings of success.' She lifted an expressive hand and effected an encompassing gesture. 'This house, the cars. Even the women who grace a part of your life.'

His eyes locked with hers, and she suppressed a faint shivery sensation at the dark implacability evident.

'You know nothing of the women in my life.'

It was like a knife twisting deep inside her heart, and she fought visibly to contain the pain. She even managed to dredge up a smile as his eyes seared hers, dark, brooding, and infinitely hard.

Carly felt as if she couldn't breathe, and the beat of her heart seemed to thud right through her chest, fast-paced and deafening in its intensity. She wanted to escape—from the room, the man, the *house*. Except that she had to stay. For a while, at least. Until Ann-Marie was fully recovered. Then...

'The coffee is ready.'

His voice intruded, and she turned blindly towards the coffee-machine. Dear God, she doubted her ability to walk the few paces necessary and calmly pour the brew into cups, let alone drink from one. She'd probably scald her mouth, or drop the cup. Maybe both.

'I no longer feel like any,' she managed in a voice that sounded indistinct and far removed from her own.

'Add a dash of brandy, and cream,' Stefano ordered steadily. 'It will help you sleep.'

She opened her mouth to respond, only to have him pursue with dangerous softness, 'Don't argue.'

'I'm not arguing!'

'Then stop wasting energy on being so stubbornly determined to oppose me.'

'You must know how much I hate being here,' she flung with restrained anger. She was so infuriated that it took every ounce of control not to lash out at him.

'Almost as much as you hate me,' Stefano drawled imperturbably as he moved to pour the coffee, then he added brandy and cream to both cups.

'You have no intention of making things easy for me, do you?' Carly demanded bitterly.

His eyes assumed a chilling bleakness, his features assembling into a hard, inflexible mask. 'You're treading a mental tightrope.' He lifted a hand and caught hold of her chin, his fingers firm and faintly cruel. 'And I'm in no mood to play verbal games.'

'Then stop treating me like a fractious child.' It was a cry from within, heartfelt, and more revealing than she intended.

'Start behaving like a woman and I'll respond accordingly,' he said hardly, and flecks of fiery topaz lightened the darkness of her eyes.

'Close my mind and open my legs?' Rage bubbled to the surface and erupted without thought to the consequence. 'Sorry, Stefano. I'm not that desperate.'

For a moment she thought he meant to strike her,

and she was powerless to escape him as hard hands curled round her arms and pulled her close.

'This time,' he ground out grimly, 'you push me too far.'

He possessed sufficient strength to do her grievous bodily harm, yet she stood defiant, unwilling to retract or apologise for so much as a single word.

With slow deliberation he caught both her hands together, then slid one hand beneath her head, tilting it as he impelled her forward, then his mouth was on hers, hard and possessively demanding.

A silent scream rose and died in her throat, and she began to struggle, hating him with all her heart as he exerted sufficient pressure to force open her mouth, then his tongue became a pillaging destructive force that had her silently begging him to stop.

His stance altered, and one hand splayed down over the gentle swell of her bottom, pressing her close in against him so that the heat of his arousal was a potent virile force that was impossible to ignore.

The invasion of her mouth didn't lessen, and she felt absorbed, overwhelmed, *possessed* by a man who would refuse anything other than her complete capitulation.

Something snapped inside her, swamping her with anger and a need for retribution. She began to struggle more fiercely, managing to free one hand, which she balled into a fist to flail against his back. She clenched her jaw against the considerable force of his, and gained a minor victory when she managed to capture his tongue with her teeth.

Not enough to inflict any damage, but sufficient to cause him to still fractionally, then he was free, but only momentarily, for he lifted her effortlessly over one shoulder and strode from the room.

'You bastard,' Carly hissed vehemently as she pummelled her fists against the hard muscles of his back. 'Put me down, damn you!'

She fought so hard that she lost all sense of direction, and it wasn't until he began to ascend the central staircase that she began to feel afraid. Her struggles intensified, without success, and several seconds later she heard the solid clunking sound of the bedroom door as it closed behind them, then without ceremony she was lowered down to her feet.

Defiance blazed from her expressive features as she met his hardened gaze, and despite their compelling intensity she refused to bow down to fear. Her mouth felt violated, her tongue sore, the delicate tissues grazed and swollen. Even her throat ached, and her jaw.

'If it weren't for Ann-Marie...' She trailed to a halt, too incensed to continue.

'Precisely,' Stefano agreed succinctly. His implication was intentional, and she burst into voluble speech.

'You're so damned *ruthless*,' Carly accused vengefully. 'You dominate everything, *everyone*. I can't wait to be free of you.'

He went completely still, and she was vividly reminded of a superb jungle animal she'd viewed on a television documentary; of the encapsulated moment when every muscle in his body had tensed prior to the fatal spring that captured and annihilated his prey. Stefano looked just as dangerous, portraying the same degree of leashed violence.

'You believe our reconciliation to be temporary?'

he queried in a voice that sounded like the finest silk being torn asunder.

She drew in a deep breath, then slowly released it. 'When Ann-Marie is completely recovered, I intend to file for divorce.'

His eyes lanced hers, killing in their intensity. 'You honestly believe I'd allow you to attempt to take her away from me?'

'Dear lord in heaven,' Carly breathed shakily. 'Who do you think you are? *God*?'

He was silent for so long that she thought he didn't mean to answer, then he drawled with deliberate softness, 'I have the power to hound you through every lawcourt in the country for whatever reason I choose to nominate.'

She felt sickened, and *raw* with immeasurable pain. 'Are you so bent on revenge that you'd punish yourself as well as me?'

His eyes raked her slim frame. 'Punish? Aren't you being overly fanciful?'

'Angelica Agnelli. I imagine she still—' She paused fractionally, then continued with deliberate emphasis, '*Liaises* with you?'

His voice was tensile steel, and just as dangerous. 'In a professional capacity—yes.'

'And is she still based in Perth?' Carly pursued unrepentantly. 'Or has she also moved to Sydney?'

'Sydney.'

'I see,' she said dully, and wondered at her own stupidity in querying if the relationship between Stefano and Angelica still existed. It hadn't ceased and probably never would.

'Do you?' Stefano queried, and she smiled with infinite sadness, all the fight in her suddenly gone.

'Oh, yes,' she assented wearily. 'I was way out of my league right from the beginning.'

'You should have stayed and fought the battle.' He sounded impossibly cynical, and it rankled unbearably.

'I tried.' Dear lord, how she'd tried. But one battle didn't win the war, as she had discovered to her cost. Carly tilted her head at a proud angle. 'Being figuratively savaged by a female predator held no appeal. I much preferred to retreat with dignity.' Her eyes were remarkably clear. 'Besides, it's impossible to lose what you never had.'

'I willingly slid a ring on your finger, and pledged my devotion.' His voice held a soft drawling quality that sent shivers scudding down the length of her spine. 'Was your faith in me so lacking that there was no room for trust?'

The entire conversation had undergone a remarkable change, and she wasn't comfortable with its passage. 'That was a long time ago,' she responded slowly, aware of the tug at her heartstrings, the ecstasy as much as the agony of having loved him. 'Your concept of marriage was different from mine.'

'You're so sure of that?'

A lump rose unbidden in her throat—she doubted her voice could surmount it—and a great weariness settled down on to her young shoulders, making her feel suddenly tired.

'If you don't mind, I'd like to shower and go to bed.'

'Enjoy your solitude, *cara*,' Stefano told her with soft mockery. 'I have a few international calls to make.' His expression was veiled, making it impossible to detect his mood, and she watched as he walked to the door, then he turned towards her.

'Incidentally, I've located a reputable breeder who will deliver Ann-Marie's poodle late tomorrow afternoon.' He paused, a faint smile tugging his lips at her surprise. 'A house-trained young female, black, with impeccable manners, who answers to Françoise. I'll see that I'm home to ensure she has a proper introduction to Prince.'

He opened the door, then closed it quietly behind him before Carly had a chance to say so much as a word.

He was an enigma, she decided as she became caught up in a maelstrom of contrary emotions. There was a sense of unresolved hostility, an inner need that bordered on obsession, to get beneath his skin and test the strength of his anger.

Or his passion, her subconscious mind taunted mercilessly. Wasn't that what she really wanted?

No. The silent scream rose in her throat, threatening, agonising in its intensity, and she gazed sightlessly around the room for several seconds as she attempted to focus on something—anything—that would rationalise her feelings.

All she could see were the two pieces of furniture that totally dominated the large room. Two queensize beds, each expensively quilted in delicately muted matching colours that complemented the suite's elegant furnishings.

A leisurely shower would surely ease some of her emotional tension, she rationalised as she stripped off her outer clothes, wound the length of her hair into a knot atop her head, and stepped beneath the therapeutic warm spray.

Ten minutes later she stood before the mirror clad in a towelling robe, her hair brushed and confined into a single braid. Her features were too pale, she decided, and with a slight shrug she transferred her gaze to the opulence of her surroundings.

It provided an all too vivid reminder of another house, in another city, and another time. Then, she'd followed her heart, so totally enthralled with the man she had married that every hour apart from him was an agonising torment.

In those days she'd behaved like a love-crazed fool, she reflected a trifle grimly. So young, so incredibly naïve, *aching* all day for the evening hours she could spend in his arms.

Beautiful, soul-shaking hours filled with a lovemaking so incredibly passionate that she would often wake trembling at the thought that she might lose him and have it end.

Carly studied her reflection, seeing the subtle changes seven years had wrought. Her èyes lacked the luminescent lustre of love, and held an elusive quality that bore evidence of a maturity gained from the responsibility of caring emotionally and financially for herself and her child. Any hint of naïveté had long since departed, and there was an inherent strength apparent, an inner determination to succeed. There was also pain, buried so deep within her that she rarely allowed it to emerge.

Now she had to fight against the memories that rose hauntingly to the surface, each one a separate entity jealously guarded like a rare and precious jewel.

If she closed her eyes she could almost imagine that seven years had never passed, that any moment Stefano would step behind her and slowly, erotically tease her tender nape with a trail of lingering kisses, then gently slide the robe from her shoulders, and extend the physical sense of touching that had begun hours before over dinner with the veiled promise of passion in the depths of those dark eyes. The shared flute of wine; a morsel of food proffered from his plate; the deliberate lingering over coffee and liqueurs, almost as if they were delaying the moment when they'd rise leisurely to their feet and go upstairs to bed.

Even then, they'd rarely hurried, and only once could she recall him being so swept away that he'd lost control, kissing her with such savage hunger that she'd responded in kind, evincing no protest as he'd swiftly slaked his desire. Afterwards he'd enfolded her close in his arms, then he'd made love to her with such exquisite gentleness that she'd been unable to still the soft flow of silent tears.

Carly blinked, then shook her head faintly in an effort to clear away any further treacherous recollection from the past. Yet it wouldn't quite submerge, and she gazed sightlessly into the mirror as she pondered what Stefano's reaction had been when he'd discovered she'd left him.

Good grief! What are you? she demanded of her reflected image. A masochist? He didn't choose to instigate a search to discover your whereabouts, and in all probability he was pleased to be relieved of a neurotic young wife who warred with him over his indiscretions.

Damn. The silent curse whispered past her lips,

and with a gesture of disgust she turned off the light and moved into the bedroom.

There was no purpose to damaging introspection, she resolved as she slid into bed. She was an adult, and, if he could handle spending the night hours lying in another bed in the same room, then so could she.

The challenge was to fall asleep *before* he entered the bedroom, rather than afterwards, and despite feeling tired it proved impossible to slip into a state of somnolent oblivion.

How long she lay awake she had no idea, but it seemed *hours* before she heard the faint click of the bedroom door as it unlatched, followed by another as it was quietly closed.

Every nerve-end tautened to its furthest limit as she heard the indistinct sound of clothing being discarded, and she unconsciously held her breath as she visualised each and every one of his movements, her memory of his tightly muscled naked frame intensely vivid from the breadth of shoulder to his slim waist, the whorls of dark hair on his chest that arrowed down to his navel before feathering in a delicate line to a flaring montage at the junction of his loins. Firm-muscled buttocks, lean hips, and an enviable length of strong muscled legs. Beautiful smooth skin, a warm shield for the blood that pulsed through his veins and entwined with honed muscle and sinew.

It was a body she had come to know as intimately as her own as he had tutored her where to touch, when to brush feather-light strokes that had made him catch his breath, and how the touch of her lips, her tongue, could drive him almost beyond the edge of sensual sanity.

But it had been little in comparison to the response he was able to evoke in her, for all her senses had leapt with fire at his slightest touch, and she had become a willing wanton in his arms, encouraging everything he chose to give, like a wild untamed being in the throes of unbelievable ecstasy. Abandoned, exultant—passion's mistress.

Carly closed her eyes, tight, then slowly opened them again. Dear lord, she must have been insane to imagine she could share this room with him and remain unaffected by his presence.

Was this some form of diabolical revenge he'd deliberately chosen? Did he really intend to *sleep*?

The acute awareness was still there, a haunting pleasurable ache that fired all her senses and ate into her soul. In the past seven years there hadn't been a night when she didn't think of him, and many a time she'd woken shaking at the intensity of her dreaming, almost afraid in those few seconds of regained consciousness that she had somehow regressed into the past. Then she would look at the empty pillow beside her and realise it had all been a relayed figment of her overstimulated imagination.

Several feet separated each bed, yet the distance could have been a yawning chasm ten times that magnitude. Carly heard the almost undetectable sound of the mattress depressing with Stefano's weight as he slid in between the sheets, followed by the slowly decreasing rhythm of his breathing as it steadied into a deep, regular beat denoting total relaxation.

It seemed unbelievable that he could summon sleep so easily, and a seed of anger took root and began to germinate deep within her, feeding on frustration, pain and a gamut of emotions too numerous to delineate.

Rational thought disappeared as her febrile brain pondered the quality of his lovemaking, and whether it would be any different now from what it had been seven years ago.

In that moment she realised how much she was at his mercy, and that the essence of Stefano Alessi the man *now* was inevitably different from the lover she had once known.

At some stage she must have fallen into a blissful state of oblivion, for she gradually drifted into wakefulness through various layers of consciousness, aware initially in those few seconds before comprehension dawned that something was different. Then her lashes slowly flickered open, and she saw why.

In sleep she had turned to lie facing the bed opposite her own, and her eyes widened as she encountered Stefano's steady gaze. Reclining on his side, head propped in one hand, he regarded her with unsmiling appraisal.

Carly's first instinct was to leap out from the bed, and perhaps something in her expression gave her intention away, for one of his eyebrows arched in silent musing cynicism.

The gesture acted as a challenge, and she forced herself to remain where she was. 'What's the time?' she asked with deliberate sleepiness, as if this were just another morning in a series of mornings she woke to find herself sharing a room.

'Early. Not long after six.' His eyes slid lazily down to her mouth, then slipped lower to pause deliberately on the soft swell of her breast. 'No need to rush into starting the day.'

Carly's fingers reached automatically for the edge of the sheet and pulled it higher, aware of a tell-tale warmth tingeing her cheeks, and her eyes instantly sparked with fire. 'If you think I'm going to indulge in an exchange of pleasantries, you're mistaken!'

'Define *pleasantries*,' Stefano drawled, and she froze, her eyes widening into huge pools of uncertainty in features that had suddenly become pale. There wasn't a shred of softness in his voice, and she was frighteningly aware of her own vulnerability in the face of his superior strength.

'Afraid, Carly?'

'Of a display of raging male hormones?' she managed with a calmness she was far from feeling. He looked dangerous, like a sleek panther contemplating a helpless prey, and it was impossible not to feel apprehensive.

Her lashes flicked wide as his gaze travelled to the base of her throat, then his eyes captured hers with an indolent intensity, and she dredged up all her resources in an attempt to portray some measure of ease.

'Is that all you imagine it will be?' he queried silkily.

'Sex simply to satisfy a base animal need?'

'Cynicism doesn't suit you,' he said in a voice that was deadly soft.

'I've learnt to survive,' she returned with innate dignity. 'Without benefit of anyone other than myself.'

Stefano looked at her for what seemed an age, his gaze dark and inscrutable. 'Until now.'

'Payback time, Stefano?' She forced herself to

study him, noting the almost indecently broad shoulders, the firm, sculptured features that embodied an inherent strength of will. 'Are you implying I should slip into your bed and allow you to score the first instalment?'

'With you playing the role of reluctant martyr?' He paused, and his voice hardened slightly. 'I think not, my little cat. I don't feel inclined to give you that satisfaction.'

Her stomach lurched, then appeared to settle. It was only a game, a by-play of words designed to attack her composure. Well, she would prove she was a worthy opponent.

'What a relief to know I don't have to fake it,' she told him sweetly. 'Is there anything else you'd like to discuss before I hit the shower?'

There was lurking humour evident in those dark eyes, and a measure of respect. 'Last week I extended an invitation to Charles and his wife to dine here this evening. They flew in from the States yesterday.'

The thought of having to act the part of gracious hostess in his home, while appearing capable and serene, was a hurdle she wasn't sure she was ready to surmount—yet. However, Charles Winslow the Third was a valued colleague, who, the last time she'd dined in his presence, had been in the throes of divorcing one wife in favour of wedding another.

'What time had you planned for them to arrive?' she queried cautiously, unwilling to commit herself.

'Eight. Sylvana will prepare and serve the meal.'

She had to ask. 'Are they the only guests?'

'Charles's daughter, Georgeanne.'

Seven years ago Georgeanne had been a precocious teenager. Time could only have turned her into a stunning beauty. 'Another conquest, Stefano?' she queried with musing mockery.

'I don't consciously set out to charm every female I come into contact with,' he drawled, and she gave a soundless laugh.

'You don't have to. Your potent brand of sexual chemistry does it for you.'

'An admission, Carly?'

'A statement from one who has sampled a dose and escaped unscathed,' she corrected gravely, and glimpsed the faint edge of humour curve his generous mouth.

'And tonight?'

She looked at him carefully. 'What if I refuse?'

'Out of sheer perversity, or a disinclination to mix and mingle socially?'

'Oh, *both*,' she disclaimed drily. 'I just love the idea of being a subject of conjecture and gossip.'

'Charles is a very good friend of long standing,' Stefano reminded her.

'In that case, I'll endeavour to shine as your hostess,' Carly conceded. 'What of *my* friends?' she pursued.

'Sarah?'

'Yes.' And James. She would mention it when she phoned Sarah this afternoon.

'Feel free to issue an invitation whenever you please.'

Stefano watched with indolent amusement as she slid from the bed, slipped her arms into a towelling wrap, then escaped to the adjoining *en suite*.

Breakfast was a shared meal eaten out on the terrace, after which Stefano withdrew upstairs only to re-emerge ten minutes later, immaculately attired in a dark business suit.

He looked every inch the directorial business-man that he was, and arrestingly physical in a way that set Carly's pulse racing in an accelerated beat. She watched with detached interest as he crossed to the table and brushed gentle fingers to Ann-Marie's cheek.

Somehow she managed to force her features into a stunning smile when his gaze assumed musing in-dolence as it rested on her mobile mouth.

'Bye. Don't work too hard.' The words sounded light and faintly teasing, but there was nothing light in the glance she spared him beneath dark-fringed lashes.

Minutes later there was the muted sound of a car engine as the Mercedes traversed the long curving driveway.

Ann-Marie's appointment with the neuro-surgeon was at ten, and afterwards Carly drove home in a state of suspended shock as she attempted to absorb Ann-Marie's proposed admission into hospital the follow-ing day, with surgery scheduled for late Wednesday afternoon.

So *soon*, she agonised, in no doubt that Stefano's influence had added sufficient weight to the surgeon's decision to operate without delay.

It was impossible not to suffer through an entire gamut of emotions, not the least of which was very real fear. Even the neuro-surgeon's assurance that the success-rate for such operations was high did little to alleviate her anxiety.

Stefano arrived home shortly after four, and half an

hour later the breeder delivered Françoise—a small, intelligent bundle of black curls who proved to be love on four legs.

The delightful pup took an instant liking to the hulking Prince, who in turn was initially tolerant, then displayed an amusing mixture of bewitchment and bewilderment as Françoise divided her attention equally between him and her new mistress.

There was a new kennel, an inside sleeping-box, leads, a collar, a few soft toys, and feeding bowls.

Ann-Marie looked as if she'd been given the world, and Carly experienced reluctant gratitude for Stefano's timing.

'Thank you,' she said quietly as they emerged from their daughter's bedroom, having settled an ecstatically happy little girl to sleep. Françoise was equally settled in her sleeping-box beside Ann-Marie's bed.

His smile was warm, genuine, she perceived with a slight start of surprise, for there was no evidence of his usual mockery.

'She has waited long enough to enjoy the company of a much wanted pet.'

Carly felt a pang of remorse for the years spent living in rented accommodation which had excluded the ownership of animals. It seemed another peg in the victory stakes for Stefano—a silent comparison of provision. His against hers.

'We have fifteen minutcs before Charles is due to arrive,' Stefano intimated as they reached their suite. 'Can you be ready in time?'

She was, with a few seconds to spare, looking attractive in a slim-fitting dress in vivid tones of peacock-green and -blue. Her hair was confined in

a simple knot, her make-up understated with practised emphasis on her eyes... Eyes which met his
and held them unflinchingly as she preceded him
from the room.

CHAPTER SIX

CHARLES WINSLOW THE THIRD was a friendly, gregarious gentleman whose daughter was of a similar age to his second wife.

If appearances were anything to go by, each young woman had worked hard to outdo the other in the fashion stakes, for each wore a designer label that resembled creations by Dior and Ungaro.

Carly felt her own dress paled by comparison, for although the classic style was elegant it was hardly new.

Within seconds of entering the lounge Charles took hold of Carly's hand and raised it, Southern-style, to his lips.

'I'm delighted the two of you are together again,' he intoned solemnly. 'You're too beautiful to remain unattached, and Stefano was a fool to let you escape.'

Carly caught Stefano's faintly lifted eyebrow and was unable to prevent the slight quiver at the edge of her mouth. Without blinking an eyelid, she sent Charles her most dazzling smile. 'Charles,' she greeted with equal solemnity. 'You haven't changed.'

His faintly wolfish smile was no mean complement to his sparkling brown eyes. 'My wife tells me I become more irascible with every year, and Georgeanne only tags along because I pay her bills.'

'Ignore him,' Kathy-Lee advised with a light smile.

'Stefano...' Georgeanne purred, offering Carly a sharp assessing glance before focusing her attention on her father's business associate. 'It's wonderful to see you again.'

'Wonderful' was a pretty fine superlative to describe Charles's daughter, Carly mused, for the young woman was all grown up and pure feline.

Kathy-Lee, at least, opted to observe the conventions and set out to charm superficially while choosing to ignore the machinations of her stepdaughter. Which, Carly noted circumspectly, grew more bold with every passing hour. Perhaps it was merely a game, she perceived as they leisurely dispensed with one delectable course after another.

Whatever the reason, Carly refused to rise to the bait, and instead drew Charles into a lengthy and highly technical discourse on the intricacies of computer programming. As he owed much of his fortune to creating specialised programs, his knowledge was unequalled.

Stefano, to give him his due, did nothing to encourage Georgeanne's attention, but Carly detected an implied intimacy that hurt unbearably. It clouded her beautiful eyes, leaving them faintly pensive, and, although her smile flashed with necessary brilliance throughout the evening, her hands betrayed their nervousness on one occasion, incurring Stefano's narrowed glance as she swiftly averted spilling the contents of her wine glass.

Carly told herself she couldn't care less about her

husband's past indiscretions, but deep within her resentment flared, and mingled with a certain degree of pain.

Outwardly, Stefano was the perfect host, his attention faultless, and only she knew that the implied intimacy of his smile merely depicted a contrived image for the benefit of their guests.

It was almost eleven when Charles indicated that they must leave.

'It's so early,' Georgeanne protested with a pretty pout. 'I thought we might go on to a nightclub.'

'Honey,' Charles chided with a slow sloping smile before directing Carly a wicked wink, 'I have no doubt Stefano and Carly have a different kind of socialising in mind.'

His daughter effected a faint moue, then sent Stefano a luscious smile. 'Don't be crude, Daddy. I'm sure Stefano has the stamina for both.'

Charles gave Kathy-Lee the sort of look that made Carly's toes curl before switching his attention to his daughter. 'It's no contest, darlin',' he drawled.

Georgeanne evinced her disappointment, then effected a light shrugging gesture. 'If you say so.' She moved a step closer to Stefano and placed scarlet-tipped nails against his jacket-encased arm. '*Ciao, caro.*' She reached up and brushed her lips against his cheek—only because he turned his head and she missed his mouth. Her smile was pure celluloid, and there was a faint malicious gleam as she turned towards Carly. 'You look—tired, sweetie.'

Without blinking, Carly met the other girl's sultry stare, and issued softly, 'Stefano doesn't allow me much time to sleep.'

Charles's eyes danced with ill-concealed humour. 'Give it up, Georgeanne.' With old-fashioned charm he took hold of Carly's hand and squeezed it gently. 'You must be our guests for dinner before we fly back to the States.'

Carly simply smiled, and walked at Stefano's side to the foyer. Minutes later Charles, Kathy-Lee and Georgeanne were seated in their hired car, and almost as soon as the rear lights disappeared through the gates Carly moved upstairs to check on Ann-Marie and Françoise.

A tiny black head lifted from the sleeping-box to regard her solemnly, then nestled back against the blanket.

'I'll take her outside for a few minutes, then she should be all right until morning.'

Carly turned slowly at the sound of Stefano's voice, and she nodded in silent acquiescence. Ann-Marie was lost in sleep, her features relaxed and cherubic in the dull reflected glow of her night-light, the covers in place, and her favourite doll and teddy bear vying for affection on either side of her small frame.

Carly felt the sudden prick of tears, and blinked rapidly to dispel them. Her daughter was so small, so dependent—so damned vulnerable.

She was hardly aware of Stefano's return, and it took only seconds to settle the poodle comfortably among its blankets.

Once inside their own suite, Carly stepped directly through to the bathroom and removed her make-up with slightly shaking fingers. Her nerves felt as if they were shredding into a thousand pieces, and she needed a second attempt at replacing the lid on the jar of cleanser.

When she re-entered the bedroom Stefano was propped up in bed, stroking notes into a leatherbound book, and her stomach executed a series of flips at his breadth of shoulder, the hard-muscled chest with its liberal whorls of dark hair tapering down to a firm waist.

The pale-coloured sheet merely highlighted the natural olive colour of his skin, and as if sensing her appraisal he looked up and pinned her gaze, only to chuckle softly as she quickly averted her eyes.

'Shy, Carly?' he drawled, and she hated the faint flood of pink that warmed her cheeks as she moved towards her bed.

He possessed all the attributes of a superb jungle animal, resplendent, resting, yet totally focused on his prey.

An arrow of pain arched up from the centre of her being in the knowledge that seven years ago she would have laughed with him, tantalisingly slid the nightgown from her shoulders—if she'd even opted to wear one—and walked towards him, sure of his waiting arms, the rapture that would take them far into the night.

Now, she fingered the decorative frill on the pillowslip, and made a play of plumping the pillow, feeling oddly reluctant to skip into bed, yet longing for the relaxing effect of several hours' sleep.

'How delightful, *cara*,' Stefano teased mercilessly. 'You can still blush.'

Carly lifted her head and her eyes sparked with latent fire. 'If you wanted a playmate for the evening, you should have gone nightclubbing with Georgeanne.'

One eyebrow slanted in silent mockery. 'Why—when I have my very own playmate at home?'

Anger mingled with the fire, and produced a golden-flecked flame within the brilliant darkness of her gaze. 'Because I don't like playing games, and I particularly don't want to play them with *you*!'

'Georgeanne is—'

'I know perfectly well what Georgeanne is!' she vented quietly, hating his level gaze. She was angry, without any clear reason *why*.

'—the daughter of a very good friend of mine,' he continued as if she hadn't spoken, 'who delights in practising her feminine witchery.' His eyes hardened fractionally. 'Charles should have disciplined her precociousness at a young age.'

'Oh—*fiddlesticks*,' Carly responded, unwilling to agree with him. 'Georgeanne suffers from acute boredom, and views any attractive man as a contest. If he's married, that presents even more of a challenge.'

Stefano's eyes speared hers, and his expression assumed a lazy indolence. 'Jealous, *cara*?'

'Stop calling me that!'

'You're expending so much nervous energy,' he drawled imperturbably. 'You'll never be able to relax sufficiently to sleep.'

Without thinking she picked up the pillow and threw it at him, then gasped as he fielded it with one hand and moved with lightning speed to trap her before she had the chance to move. She wrenched her arm in an effort to be free of him, then she cried out as he tightened his grip and pulled her down on to the bed.

There wasn't a chance she could escape, yet to lie quiescent was impossible, and she flailed at him with her free arm, then groaned with despair as he caught it and held her immobile.

His mouth was inches above her own, and she just looked at him, unable to focus her gaze on anything except his strong, chiselled features and the darkness of his eyes.

Time became suspended as she lay still, mesmerised by the look of him, imprisoned in a spellbinding thrall of all her senses. This close, the warmth of his breath skimmed her mouth, and she could smell the faint musky tones of his aftershave, the clean body smell emanating from his skin, and the essential maleness that was his alone. An answering awareness unfurled deep within her, flaring into vibrant life as it coursed through her body with the intensity of flame.

She could see the knowledge of it reflected in his eyes, the waiting expectancy evident as every cell, every nerve-end flowered into a sexual bloom so vivid, so hauntingly warm that she caught his faint intake of breath an instant before his head slowly lowered to claim her mouth in a teasingly gentle kiss that was so incredibly evocative that she was powerless to still the faint prick of tears.

His lips trailed to the sensitive cord at the edge of her neck, nuzzling the sweet hollows, before continuing a slow descent to a highly sensitised nub peaking at her breast.

The anticipation was almost more than she could bear, and she murmured indistinctly, craving the exquisite pleasure of his touch, exulting when he took the tender peak into his mouth and began teasing it with the edge of his teeth.

A deep shooting pain arrowed through her body, and she slid her hands up over his shoulders in a tactile voyage of discovery until her fingers reached the dark curling hair at his nape.

An ache began at the junction of her thighs, and she arched her body against his in unbidden invitation, then she gave a pleasurable sigh as his fingers slid to caress the aroused orifice to a peak of exquisite pleasure, his movements deftly skilled, until nothing less than total possession was enough.

She became mindless, caught in the thrall of a passion so intense that she began to beg, pleading with him in wanton abandon, until with sure movements he plunged deep inside, stilling as she gasped at his level of penetration.

Then slowly he began to withdraw, only to repeat the initial thrust again and again, increasing in rapidity until her body caught hold of his rhythm and then paced it in unison until the momentum tipped them both over the edge into an explosion of ecstasy so tumultuous that she began to shake uncontrollably as the tremors radiated through her body, incandescent, shattering, primitive, the most primal of all the emotions, subsiding gradually to assume a piercing sweetness that stayed with her long after he curled her close in against him and his breathing steadied with her own into the slow, measured pattern of sleep.

Carly retained very little memory of the ensuing few days, for one seemed to run into the other as she spent all her waking hours at the hospital.

'I want to stay with her,' she said quietly to the sister on duty shortly after Ann-Marie was admitted.

'My dear, I understand your concern, but we've found a young child tends to become distraught if the mother rooms in with the child. It really is much more practical if you visit frequently for short periods. Quality time is much better than quantity. Besides,' she continued briskly, 'it allows the medical staff to do their job more efficiently.'

It made sense, but it didn't aid Carly's natural anxiety, for she had hardly slept the night prior to Ann-Marie's surgery, and was a nervous wreck all through the following day, choosing to sit in silent vigil well into the evening, despite being advised to go home and rest.

Stefano came and fetched her, his voice quietly insistent, and she was too mentally and emotionally exhausted to give more than a token protest as he led her out to the car. At home he heated milk, added a strong measure of brandy, and made sure she drank it all.

One day seemed to run into another without Carly having any clear recollection of each, for Ann-Marie was her entire focus from the time of waking until she fell wearily into bed at night.

From Intensive Care, Ann-Marie was released into a suite of her own, and designated a model patient as she began the slow path towards recuperation.

Carly, however, became increasingly tense, for there were still tests to be run, and by the fifth evening she was powerless to prevent the silent flow of tears long after she'd crept into bed.

Reaction, she decided wearily, to all the tension, the anxiety, and insufficient sleep. Yet she couldn't stop, and after a while she slid soundlessly to her feet, gathered up a wrap and walked silently down the hall.

Ann-Marie's bedroom door was closed, and she opened it, her breath catching as she saw the nightlight burning and two bright button eyes as Françoise lifted her head to examine the intruder.

A lump rose in her throat as she crossed to the sleeping-box and scooped the curly-haired black bundle into her arms.

The poodle's nose was cool and damp, and Carly hugged her close. A small, wet pink tongue emerged to lick her cheek, then began to lap in earnest at the taste of salty tears. After several long minutes she restored the poodle into its sleeping-box, then slowly crossed to the window.

The curtains were closed, and she opened them fractionally, looking out at the moonlit grounds in detached contemplation.

The small shrubs appeared large with their looming shadows, and everything seemed so still, almost lifeless. Pin-pricks of electric light glittered across the harbour, merging with splashes of flashing neon advertisements gracing several city buildings. By night it resembled a tracery of fairy-lights, remote, yet symbolising activity and pulsing life.

She had no idea how long she remained motionless, for there was no awareness of the passage of time, just a slide into introspection that took her back over six years to the day her daughter was born, and the joy, the tears and the laughter that had followed through a few childhood illnesses, the guilt of having to leave her in child care while she worked, Ann-Marie's first day at kindergarten, her first visit to the zoo, and the day she had started school. She was a quiet, obedient child, but with a mind of her own.

'Unable to sleep?' The query was quietly voiced, and Carly turned slowly to face the man standing in the aperture.

For an age she just looked at him, her eyes large and unblinking in a face that was pale and shadowed, then she turned back to the scene beyond the window. 'I wish it was all over and she was home,' she managed in an emotion-charged voice, and felt rather than heard him move to stand behind her.

'Likewise,' Stefano muttered in agreement.

No power on earth could speed up time, and she closed her eyes in an effort to gain some measure of inner strength. She had to be strong, she *had* to be, she resolved silently.

Hard, muscular arms slid around her waist from behind and pulled her gently back against a solid male frame.

For a moment she resisted, stiffening slightly, then she became prey to the protective shelter he offered, and she relaxed, allowing his strength to flow through her body.

It was like coming home, and the sadness of what they'd once shared, then lost, overwhelmed her. She closed her eyes tightly against the threat of tears, feeling them burn as she fought for control.

For all of a minute she managed to keep them at bay, then they squeezed through to spill in warm rivulets down each cheek to fall one after the other from her chin.

Firm hands slid up to her shoulders and turned her into his embrace, one hand slipping through the thickness of her hair while the other slid to anchor the base of her spine.

It felt so good, so right, so *safe*, and after a long time she slid her hands round his waist, linking them together behind his back.

The strong, measured beat of his heart sounded loud against her ear, and she rested against him for a long time, drawing comfort from his large frame, until at last she stirred and began to pull free of him.

Without a word he loosened his hold, and, slipping one arm about her waist, he led her back to their suite. Both beds bore evidence of their occupation, and she viewed each, feeling strangely loath to leave the sanctuary of his embrace, yet to go tacitly to his bed would reveal an unspoken willingness for something she was as yet unprepared to give.

For what seemed an age he stood in silence, watching the expressive play of emotions chase across her features, then he leant forward and brushed his lips against her cheek, trailing gently up to her temple before tracing slowly down to the edge of her mouth.

It was an evocative caress, his lips gently tracing her own with such a heightened degree of sensitivity, it was almost more than she could bear.

It would be so easy to allow him to continue, to follow a conflagrating path to total possession and its resultant euphoria. Except that it would only be a merging born out of sexual desire, not the meeting of two minds, two souls, the sharing of something so beautiful, so exquisite, that the senses coalesced and became one.

She went still, lowering her hands slowly down to her side, and Stefano lifted his head slightly, viewing the soft mouth, the faint smudges beneath her shimmering eyes, and his expression became watchful, intent, as she sought to swallow the sudden lump that had risen in her throat.

Carly wanted to cry out, yet no sound emerged, and she willed herself to breathe slowly, evenly, as he drew her down on to his bed and pulled her gently into the circle of his arms.

His quietly voiced, 'Sleep easy, *cara*,' sent goosebumps scudding in numerous directions to places they had no right to invade. She lay there, unable to make so much as a sound, and within minutes she became aware of the steady pattern of his breathing. Then slowly she began to relax, and gradually sheer emotional exhaustion provided a welcome escape into somnolence.

CHAPTER SEVEN

ANN-MARIE CONTINUED to improve with each passing day, and there was immense relief at the week's end to receive the neuro-surgeon's voiced confidence of a complete recovery. It balanced the shock of seeing the bandages removed for the first time, and evidence of a vivid surgical scar.

Carly was so elated on leaving the hospital that she decided against phoning Stefano, and opted to tell him the news in person. Consequently it was almost four when she entered the towering modern city block and rode the lift to Reception.

There was a sense of *déjà vu* on stepping into the luxuriously furnished foyer, although this time there was the advantage of needing no introduction. Carly entertained little doubt that an expurgated version of her previous visit had filtered through the office grapevine, and she kept her eyes steady with a friendly smile pinned in place as the receptionist rang through to Stefano's personal secretary.

Renate appeared almost immediately, her features schooled to express warmth and a degree of apologetic charm. 'Stefano is in conference with a colleague,' she enlightened Carly as she ushered her into his private lounge. 'I've let him know you're here, and he said he'll be with you in a matter of minutes.' The smile deepened. 'Can I get you a drink? Coffee? Tea? Something cool?'

'I'd like to use the rest-room first, if I may?' Carly returned the woman's smile with one of her own. 'And something cool would be great.'

As she was about to re-enter the lounge several minutes later a door opened several feet in front of her to reveal a tall, attractive brunette whose stunning features were permanently etched in Carly's mind.

Recognition was instantaneous, and Carly's whole body went cold as she watched Angelica Agnelli turn back to the man immediately behind her and bestow on him a lingering kiss.

Carly felt as if the scene was momentarily frozen in her brain, like the delayed shutter of a camera, then the figures began to move, and she watched as Stefano stood back a pace and let his hands fall from Angelica's shoulders.

His expression held warm affection, and stabbed at Carly's heart. At the same moment he lifted his head, and Carly watched with a sort of detached fascination as they each became aware of her presence.

It was rather like viewing a play, she decided as she glimpsed the darkness in Stefano's eyes an instant before he masked it, and she was prepared to go on record that the dismay evident in Angelica's expression was deliberate, for the faint smile of contrition failed to reach her eyes.

'Carly,' Angelica greeted her with apparent warmth. 'Stefano told me you were back.' Her expression pooled into one of apparent concern. 'How is your daughter?'

The faint emphasis on 'your' wasn't missed, and Carly marshalled innate dignity as a weapon in her mythical arsenal. 'Ann-Marie is fine, thank you,' she responded steadily. Her eyes lifted to meet Stefano's slightly narrowed gaze, and she summoned a deliberately sweet smile. 'Renate is fetching me a cool drink. I'll wait in the lounge while you see Angelica out.' She placed imperceptible stress on the last word, then softened it with a studied smile as she turned towards the beautifully attired young woman whose *haute-couture* clothes hugged a perfect figure. 'Goodbye, Angelica. I'm sure we'll run into each other again.' Not if I see you first, she added silently as she turned into the private lounge.

With extreme care Carly closed the door behind her, then crossed towards the bar where an iced pitcher of orange juice stood beside a tall frosted glass.

Pouring herself a generous measure, she sipped at it abstractly and told herself she felt no pain. Dammit, she swore softly. There had to be subversive psychic elements at play somewhere in the vicinity, for each time she entered Stefano's private lounge she was moved to blinding rage.

However, *this* time she'd be calm. Another voluble, visible display of temper would have the staff labelling her a shrew. Yet she defied even the most placid woman not to be driven to anger when she was faced with evidence of her husband's *affaire de coeur*.

It was five minutes before Stefano joined her, and she turned quietly to face him as he entered the room. His expression was inscrutable, his eyes faintly hooded, and he made no attempt at any explanation.

He looked the epitome of a successful businessman, his three-piece suit dark and impeccably tailored, the pale blue shirt made of the finest silk, and his shoes hand-stitched imported leather.

She was reminded of the saying that 'clothes made the man'. Yet her indomitable husband could have worn torn cut-off jeans and a sweatshirt, and he'd still manage to project a devastating raw virility that had little to do with the physical look of him.

If his relationship with Angelica Agnelli continued to extend beyond that of friends, then anything Carly said would only fuel her own anger and lead inevitably to another confrontation.

Besides, she was twenty-seven, and no longer the naïve, trusting young girl who had believed in one true love. Reality was the knowledge that love didn't conquer all, nor did it always last forever.

'How was Ann-Marie this afternoon?'

Carly met his dark gaze with equanimity. 'Improving,' she informed him steadily. 'The specialist is confident she'll make a full recovery.'

His features relaxed into an expression of immense relief. '*Grazie a Dio*,' he breathed with immense gratitude.

'Obviously it would have been better if I'd phoned with the news.'

One eyebrow slanted above a pair of eyes that had become strangely watchful. 'Why *obviously*?'

'Business, pleasure and personal affairs are an incompatible mix,' she hinted with unaccustomed cynicism, and saw his eyes narrow.

'Angelica—'

'Don't even consider proffering the rather hackneyed explanation that she's merely an associate.' She lifted her chin, and her eyes were remarkably clear as they held his. 'I've heard it all before.'

'Angelica is a valued family friend,' he continued with hard inflexibility, and the gold flecks in her eyes flared with brilliant topaz as she refused to be intimidated in any way.

'*Valued* is a very tame description, Stefano,' Carly responded, wondering what devilish imp was pushing her in a direction she'd sworn not to tread.

'Perhaps you'd care to offer a more lucid alternative,' he drawled with dangerous silkiness, and she was powerless to prevent the surge of anger coursing through her body.

'She wants *you*,' she declared with quiet conviction. 'She always has. For a while I stood in her way. Now that I'm back…' She trailed off deliberately, then effected a slight shrug. 'If she can hurt me emotionally, she will.' The need to be free of him was paramount, and she turned to leave, only to have a detaining hand catch hold of her arm and pull her back to face him.

Any escape could only be temporary. It was there in his eyes, the latent anger a silent threat should she continue to thwart him.

'Let me go.' The words left her throat as his head lowered, and she turned slightly so that his lips grazed her cheek. Then she cried out as he slid his fingers through the thickness of her hair, and his mouth captured hers in a kiss that was nothing less than a total possession of her senses.

A muffled groan of entreaty choked in her throat

as he brought her even closer against his hard, muscular frame, and when he finally lifted his head she stood quite still, bearing his silent scrutiny until every nerve stretched to its furthest limit.

His hands slid with seductive slowness to her waist, then cradled her ribcage, the pads of each thumb beginning an evocative circle over the hardening peaks of her breasts in a movement that was intensely erotic.

She had to stop him *now*, before she lost the will to move away. 'Sex in the office, Stefano? Whatever will Renate think?' she taunted softly. 'Or maybe she's accustomed to her boss's...discreet diversions?'

His eyes narrowed, and a muscle hardened at the edge of his jaw. 'Watch your foolish tongue.'

Carly laughed, a soft mocking sound that was the antithesis of anything related to humour. Gathering courage, she added with unaccustomed cynicism, 'I imagine many women shared your table as well as your bed in the last seven years.'

His eyes stilled for a second, then assumed a brooding mockery. 'You want me to supply a list, *cara*?'

For one heart-stopping moment she looked stricken. The thought of that long, superbly muscled body giving even one other woman the sort of sexual pleasure he gave her was sickening. To consider there had probably been *several* made her feel positively ill. Suddenly she'd had enough, and was in dire need of some breathing space—preferably as far away from her inimical husband as possible.

If she didn't leave soon, the ache behind her eyes would result in silent futile tears, and without a further word she turned and left the room.

Within minutes of reaching home she crossed to

the phone and dialled Sarah's number. At the sound
of her friend's voice she clutched hold of the receiver
and sank down into a nearby chair for a long conversation that encompassed an exchange of news as well
as providing a link to normality.

'You must bring James to dinner,' Carly insisted as
Sarah exclaimed at the time. 'I'll check with Stefano
and give you a call.'

'Lovely,' the other girl declared with enthusiasm.
'Give Ann-Marie a big hug from me, and tell her I'll
visit tomorrow.'

Dinner was a strained meal, for Carly found it difficult to contribute much by way of conversation that
didn't come out sounding horribly banal. In the end,
she simply gave up, and pushed her food around the
plate before discarding her cutlery to sip iced water
from her glass.

Stefano, damn him, didn't appear a whit disturbed,
and he did justice to the dishes Sylvana provided before finishing with fresh grapes, biscuits and cheese.

Carly sat in silence during the drive to hospital,
unwilling to offer so much as a word in case it ended
in a slanging match—or worse.

There was such a wealth of resentment at having
witnessed the touching little departure scene between
Angelica and Stefano that afternoon—and unabating
anger. It almost eclipsed the joy of witnessing Ann-
Marie's pleasure in their visit, and the expressive smile
when Stefano presented her with yet another gift.

'I'm getting spoilt,' Ann-Marie concluded, hugging
the beautifully dressed doll close to her small chest,
and her eyes gleamed when her father leaned down to
brush his lips against her cheek. 'Thank you, Daddy.'

The words held such poignancy that Carly had to blink fast against the threat of tears.

'My pleasure, *piccina*.'

'What's a *piccina*?'

'A special endearment for a special little girl,' he responded gently.

It was almost eight when the Mercedes pulled into the driveway leading to Stefano's elegant home, and once indoors Carly made her way through to the kitchen.

'Coffee?' It was a perfunctory query that incurred his narrowed gaze.

'Please.'

Her movements were automatic as she filled the percolator, selected a fresh filter, then spooned in a blend of ground coffee-beans.

'Would you prefer yours here, or in the lounge?'

'The lounge.'

Damn, that meant she'd have to share it with him, yet if she opted out he'd only be amused, and she refused to give him the satisfaction.

Five minutes later she placed cups and saucers, sugar and milk on to a tray and carried it through to the informal lounge. Placing his within easy reach, she selected a chair several feet distant from where he was seated.

'We've been invited out to dinner tomorrow evening,' Stefano informed her with indolent ease as he spooned in sugar and stirred the thick black liquid in his cup. 'Charles Winslow will be there with Kathy-Lee.' His eyes seared hers, darkly analytical in a manner that raised all her fine body hairs in a gesture of self-defence.

'And Georgeanne?' She arched a brow in deliberate query. 'I'm not sure I want to go.' The thought of standing at his side for several hours playing a part didn't figure very high in her order of preferred entertainment.

'Most of the men present will have their wives or partners in attendance,' he drawled, and she said sweetly,

'Why not invite Angelica? I'm sure she'd delight in the opportunity. Then you could have two women vying for your attention.'

One eyebrow slanted in quizzical mockery, although anything approaching humour was sadly lacking in his expression. 'I'll ignore that remark.'

A crazy imp prompted her to query, 'Good heavens, *why*? It's nothing less than the truth.'

His expression didn't alter. 'Watch your unwary tongue, *mi moglie*,' he cautioned in a deadly soft voice.

'Don't threaten me,' she responded swiftly, feeling the deep-rooted anger begin to surge to the surface.

'Warn,' he amended with quiet emphasis.

'There's a difference?'

His eyes lanced hers, silent and deadly in their intent. 'Give it up, Carly.'

'And concede defeat?'

'If you want to fight,' Stefano drawled with dangerous silkiness, 'I'm willing to oblige.' He paused deliberately, then continued, 'I doubt you'll enjoy the consequences.'

A shaft of exquisite pain arrowed through her body, although defiance was responsible for the angry tilt of her chin as she berated, 'I seem to remember you preferred your women warm and willing.'

'What makes you think you won't be, *cara*?' Stefano drawled, his expression veiled as pain clouded her beautiful eyes, rendering her features hauntingly vulnerable for a few heart-stopping seconds before the mask slipped into place.

She was treading dangerous waters, yet she was too incensed to desist. 'Did it never occur to you that my taste in men may have changed?'

'Have there been that many?' His voice sounded like finely tempered steel grazing satin, and she had the incredible desire to shock.

'Oh—*several*.'

Something leapt in the depth of his eyes, and she wanted to cry out a denial, yet the words remained locked in her throat.

What on earth was the matter with her in taunting him? Playing any kind of game with a man of Stefano's calibre was akin to prodding a sleeping jungle animal.

'I had a life during the past seven years, Stefano,' she flung, more angry than she'd care to admit. 'Didn't you?'

'Do you really want to pursue this topic?'

'Why?'

'Because it will have only one ending,' he warned with incredible silkiness, although his eyes were hard and obdurate, and there could be no doubt as to his meaning.

'Go to hell,' she whispered, hating him more at that precise moment than she'd thought it possible to hate anyone.

The need to get away from him was paramount, and, uncaring of his reaction, she turned and walked out of the room, out of the house, moving with a quick measured pace along the driveway to the electronically locked steel gates.

For the first time she damned Stefano's security measures as logic and sanity temporarily vanished in the face of a fierce, unbating anger.

The house, the grounds, were like an impenetrable fortress, necessary in today's age among the exceedingly wealthy in a bid to protect themselves, their family and their possessions.

She could return indoors, collect her keys and the necessary remote module to release the main gates, but even in anger sufficient common sense exerted itself to warn silently against walking the suburban streets alone after dark. And if she took her car, where would she go? It was too late for visiting, and Sarah, if she wasn't working, would probably be out with James.

Carly turned back towards the house and slowly retraced her steps. The air was warm, with the faintest breeze teasing a few stray tendrils of her hair, and she lifted her face slightly, looking deep into the indigo sky with its nebulous moon and sprinkling of stars.

Drawing in a deep breath, she released it slowly. A strange restlessness besieged her, and she felt the need for some form of exercise to help expel her pent-up emotions.

There was a pool in the rear of the grounds, and she instinctively took the path that skirted the southern side of the house.

Reflected light from several electric lamps strategically placed in the adjacent rockery garden lent the pool a shimmering translucence, and, without giving too much thought to her actions, Carly stripped off her outer clothes and executed a neat dive into the pool's clear depths. Within seconds she was cleaving clean strokes through the cool water, silently counting as she completed each length. After twenty-five she rested for a few minutes, clearing the excess water from her face, her hair.

'Had enough?'

Carly lifted her head and looked at the tall figure standing close to the pool's edge. In the subdued light he loomed large, his height and breadth magnified by reflected shadows.

'Is there some reason why I shouldn't take advantage of the pool?'

'None whatsoever,' Stefano declared mockingly. 'Shall I help you out?' At his drawled query she raised a hand, then when he grasped it she tugged *hard*, experiencing a thrill of exultation as he lost his balance and was unable to prevent a headlong fall into the water.

Fear of retaliation lent wings to her limbs as she levered herself up on to the pool's edge, then, scooping up her clothes, she sped quickly into the house.

A faint bubble of laughter emerged from her throat as she entered the bedroom. She'd have given almost anything to glimpse the expression on his face!

Moving straight through to the adjoining bathroom, she turned on the shower, discarded her briefs and bra, then stepped beneath the warm, pulsing water.

Selecting shampoo, she massaged it through the length of her hair, then rinsed it off before reaching for the soap—and encountered a strong male hand.

'Is this what you're looking for?'

She went still with shock as fear unfurled in the region of her stomach. Slowly she pushed back the wet length of her hair, and a silent gasp parted her lips at the sight of him standing within touching distance, every last vestige of clothing removed from his powerful frame.

'Ready to cry wolf, Carly?'

No sooner had the soft taunt left his lips than she felt the soap sweep in a tantalisingly slow arc from the tip of her shoulder to the curve at her waist. She had to get out *now*. She tried, except that one hand closed over her arm, holding her still, while the other curved round her shoulder, and she was powerless to resist as he turned her round to face him.

'I'm sorry.' It was a half-hearted apology, and his answering smile was wholly cynical as his fingers trailed an evocative path over the surface of her skin, tracing the delicate line of her collarbone, then brushing lower to the dark aureole surrounding the tight bud of her left breast.

'Don't.' The single plea went unheeded, and her stomach quivered as his hand slid to caress her hip, the narrow indented waist, before traversing to cup the soft roundness of her bottom.

Without her being aware of it, he'd managed to manoeuvre her so that the jet of water streamed against his back, and she stood still, her eyes wide and luminous beneath his hooded gaze.

'Stefano—' she protested as he pulled her close against him. His arousal was a potent virile force, and she arched back, straining against the circle of his arms in an effort to put some distance between them.

'You can't do this,' she whispered in a broken voice.

Yet he could, very easily. He knew it, just as she did. All it would take was one long drugging open-mouthed kiss to destroy any vestige of her self-restraint.

One strong hand slid up to cup her nape, his thumb tilting the uppermost edge of her jaw, holding it fast as she attempted to twist her head away from him. Then his lips brushed hers, lightly at first, teasing, nibbling, tasting in a manner that was deliberately erotic, and left her aching with a terrible hunger, that longing for the satisfaction only he could give.

She resisted for what seemed a lifetime, but playing cool to Stefano's undoubted expertise wreaked havoc with her nervous system, and she gave a hollow groan of despair as he lifted her high up against him, parting her thighs so that she straddled his waist, then she cried out as he lowered his head and took one tender peak into his mouth, suckling with such flagrant eroticism that she clutched hold of his hair in an effort to have him desist.

Just when she thought she could stand it no longer, he transferred his attention and rendered a similar attention to its twin until she begged him to stop.

Then he slowly raised his head, his eyes incredibly dark as they speared hers, and she felt her lips tremble uncontrollably at the sense of purpose evident. Time became a suspended entity, and she couldn't have torn her gaze away if her life depended on it.

With a sense of impending fascination she watched in mesmerised silence as his mouth lowered down over her own, and she gave a silent gasp as he plundered the moist cavern at will, punishing, tantalising, until she gave the response he sought.

When at last he lifted his head she wanted to weep,

and she just looked at him, her soft mouth quivering and faintly bruised as she blinked rapidly against the rush of warm tears.

As soon as his hands curved beneath her bottom she knew what he meant to do, and she swallowed convulsively.

His entry was slow, stretching silken tissues to their furthest limit as they gradually accepted his swollen length, and his eyes trapped hers, witnessing her every expression as he carefully traversed the tight, satiny tunnel leading to the central core of her femininity.

Her beautiful eyes widened measurably as his muscular shaft attained its pinnacle. The feeling of total enclosure was intense, and a slow warmth gradually flooded her being, radiating in a tumultuous tide until her whole body was consumed with it. The blood vessels swelled and became engorged, activating muscle spasms over which she had no control, and she unconsciously clenched her thighs, instinctively arching away from him as a pulsating rhythm took her towards fulfilment.

At the zenith, she threw back her head, gasping as he drew her close and feasted shamelessly at her breast, tossing her so close to the edge between pain and pleasure that the two became intermingled, and she cried out, caught in the sweet torture of sexual ecstasy.

Then his hands shifted to her hips, lifting her slightly as he began a slow, tantalising circular movement that sent her to the brink and beyond before he took his pleasure with deep driving thrusts that drew soft guttural cries of encouragement which she refused to recognise as her own.

Afterwards he held her close for what seemed an age, then he gently withdrew and lowered her carefully to her feet.

She stumbled slightly, and clutched hold of him, then she stood transfixed as he caught up the soap and slowly cleansed every inch of her body.

When he'd finished he held out the bar of soap and when she shook her head he placed it in her palm before covering it with his own and transferring it to his chest. His eyes never left hers as he carefully traversed every ridge, every muscle, until his ablutions were complete.

She ached, everywhere. Inside and out. And she stood quiescent as he gently towelled her dry, then transferred his attention to removing the moisture from his own body.

Carly felt totally enervated, and she was powerless to resist as he placed a thumb and forefinger beneath her chin. She wanted to cry, and there were tears shimmering, welling from the depth of her eyes. There was a deep sense of emotional loss for the passion of mind and spirit they'd once shared. For then it had been a joy, a total merging of all the senses, transcending everything she'd ever dreamed...and more.

Her lashes fluttered down, veiling her expression, and concealing the haunting vulnerability she knew to be evident.

Without a word he slid an arm beneath her knees and carried her through to the bedroom, sweeping back the covers on the bed before slipping with her beneath the sheets.

Carly craved the sweet oblivion of sleep, but it had never seemed more distant, and she provided little resistance as Stefano curved her close in against him. She felt his lips brush the top of her head, and the gentle caress of his hand as it stroked the length of her body before coming to rest on the soft silken curls at the junction between her thighs. His fingers made a light probing foray, and she stiffened as they encountered the slight ridge caused by endless sutures.

'You had a difficult birth with Ann-Marie?'

Carly closed her eyes, then opened them again. 'Yes,' she acknowledged quietly, and felt silent anger emanate through his powerful body as he swore softly, viciously, in his own language. There was no point informing him that her meagre savings hadn't allowed for the luxury of private care.

Nor, in the long silent minutes that slowly ticked by, could she assure him that the wonder of holding Ann-Marie in her arms for the first time swept aside the trauma of a painful birth.

Even now it was a vivid memory, and she stared sightlessly into the darkness as she recalled the joy and the tears associated with those initial few years as she'd struggled to support them both.

Carly became aware of the soft brush of his fingers against her skin, and felt the faint stirring deep within her as her body responded to his touch. She wanted to move away, but she was caught in a mystical mesmeric spell, and she gave a faint despairing moan as his lips sought the soft hollows at the base of her throat in an erotic savouring that sent the blood coursing through her veins like quicksilver.

Not content, he trailed a path to her breasts to begin an evocative tasting that made her arch against him, and she barely registered the faint guttural sounds that whispered into the night air as his mouth travelled lower, teasing, tantalising, until she was driven almost mad with need.

When he reached the most intimate crevice of all she cried out at the degree of pleasure he was able to arouse, until ecstasy transcended mere pleasure, and she begged, pleading with him to ease the ache deep within her. Yet he stilled her limbs, soothing her gently as he brought her to a climax so tumultuous that it was beyond any mortal description, then he took her in his arms and rolled on to his back, carrying her with him so that she straddled his hips, his mouth warm as he pulled her head down to hers in a kiss so sweetly passionate that she almost cried.

His mouth left hers and trailed to nuzzle the sweet hollows at the base of her throat, then he shifted his hands to her ribcage as he gently positioned her, his eyes dark and intently watchful of the play of emotions chasing across her expressive features as she accepted his full length.

Carly felt a heady sense of power, and her eyes widened slightly as she glimpsed the slumberous passion evident in his dark eyes, the gleam of immense satisfaction, and knew the measure of his control. Unconsciously she arched her body, stretching like a playful young kitten, and revelled at his immediate response.

'Careful, *cara*,' he bade teasingly. 'Or you may get more than you bargained for.'

She moved against him with slow deliberation, undulating her hips in a gentle erotic movement that drew a warning growl, then his hands closed over her lower waist, and she lost control as he set the pace, taking her higher and higher until she cried out and clung on to his arms in a bid to gain some balance in an erotic ride that had no equal. At least, not in her experience.

Slowly, gradually, his movements began to ease, and then his hands slid to her hips, holding her still as he gently stroked his length, almost withdrawing before plunging with infinite slowness until she felt a wondrous suffusing of heat that swelled, triggering a miasma of sensation spiralling through her body until every nerve-end seemed to radiate with exquisite sweetness.

He shuddered, his large body racked with emotion, and she looked at him with an incredible sense of wonder as he became caught in the throes of passion: man at his most vulnerable, adrift in a swirling vortex of sexual experience.

Then his breathing began to slow, and the madly beating pulse at his throat settled into a steady beat. His features softened and his eyes became luminescent for a few heart-stopping minutes, and just for a milli-second she glimpsed the heart of his soul.

Then his hands slid up to cup her breasts, caressing with such acute sensitivity that she caught her breath, and she made no demur as he gently drew her down to him, cradling her head against a muscled shoulder. His fingers trailed over her hair, while a hand slid with tactile softness down the length of her spine. She felt his lips brush across her forehead, then settle at her temple, soothing, until the shivery warm sensation gradually diminished and she was filled with a dull, pleasurable ache.

'I hurt you.' The words held a degree of regretful remorse, and she stirred faintly against him.

Tomorrow there would be an unaccustomed tenderness evident, but she didn't care, for it had nothing to do with physical pain, merely satiated pleasure in its most exhilarating extreme. She sought to reassure him, and moved her lips against his throat, then gently nipped a vulnerable hollow.

'You still want to play?' His voice reverberated against her mouth, and she felt rather than heard his soft husky laughter when she shook her head in silent negation.

'Then go to sleep, *cara bella*,' Stefano bade her gently.

And she did, drifting easily into dreamless oblivion, unaware that he carefully disengaged her and curled her into the curve of his body before reaching for the sheet to cover their nakedness.

CHAPTER EIGHT

CARLY PUT THE final touches to her hair, then stood back and surveyed her reflection. The deep jacaranda-blue gown was classically styled, comprising a figure-hugging skirt and a camisole top with twin shoestring straps that emphasised her slim curves and pale honey-gold skin. Make-up was understated, with emphasis on her eyes, and a clear peach lipstick coloured her generous mouth. Her only jewellery was a slim gold chain at her neck and small gold hoops at her ears. With the length of her hair confined in an elaborate knot atop her head, she looked…passable, she decided. Or at least able to feel sufficiently confident among guests at a dinner to be held in one of Stefano's business associate's home in nearby Seaforth.

'Stunning,' a deep voice drawled, and she turned slowly to see Stefano standing a few feet distant, looking the epitome of sophistication in an impeccably tailored dark suit, white silk shirt and dark silk tie.

Carly proffered a slight smile and let her eyes slide to a point just beyond his left shoulder. 'Thank you.' Turning, she collected a black beaded evening bag, slipped in a lipstick and compact, then drew in a deep breath as she preceded him from the room to the head of the staircase.

Several minutes later she was seated in the Mercedes as it purred down the driveway towards the street.

When they reached the hospital Ann-Marie was sitting up in bed, together with the doll Stefano had given her, a favoured book, and a teddy bear slightly the worse for wear from which she refused to be parted because, she assured her mother, he was as old as she was, and watched over her as she slept.

She looked, Carly decided with maternal love, as bright as a proverbial button, although there were still slight smudges beneath the beautiful dark eyes, and her skin was transparently pale—visible effects of the aftermath of extensive surgery, the specialist had assured.

Soon she would be able to come home. By the start of the new school year in February, she would be able to resume her classes. Except for the short curly hair, no one would ever know she'd undergone extensive neuro-surgery.

Stefano was wonderful with her, gently teasing, warm, ensuring that Ann-Marie's initial wariness was a thing of the past.

'You look tired, Mummy. Didn't you sleep well last night?'

The words brought a faint smile to Carly's lips. Out of the mouths of babes! 'I stayed up too late,' she relayed gently. 'And woke early.' Was woken up, she amended silently, and persuaded to share a spa-bath, then put back into bed and brought fresh orange juice, toast and coffee on a tray.

'You should rest, like me,' Ann-Marie advised with the ingenuousness of the very young, and Stefano lifted a hand to ruffle her curls.

'I shall ensure she does.'

It was eight when they left, and Carly turned slightly towards him as he eased the car on to the main road.

'How many people will be there tonight?' Her features assumed a faint pensive expression. 'Perhaps you should fill me in with a few background details of key associates.'

'Relax, Carly. This is mainly a social occasion.'

'Yet the men will inevitably gravitate together and discuss business,' she said a trifle drily, and incurred a long probing look as he paused through an intersection.

'Nervous?'

'Should I be?' she countered with remarkable steadiness, considering the faint fluttering of butterfly wings already apparent in her stomach.

'I have no doubt you'll cope admirably.'

She sat in silence during the drive, and glanced out of the window with interest as he turned the Mercedes into a suburban street bordered on each side by tall, wide-branched trees. Seconds later the car turned into a curved driveway lined with late-model cars.

The butterflies in her stomach set up an increasing beat as she slid out from the passenger seat and moved to his side, unprepared within seconds to have him thread his fingers through hers as they walked towards the main entrance. The pressure of his clasp was light, yet she had the distinct feeling he wouldn't allow her to pull free from him.

They were almost the last to arrive, and after a series of introductions Carly accepted a glass of mineral water and attempted to relax.

It wasn't a large group, sixteen at most, she decided as she cast a circumspect glance around the elegantly furnished lounge.

Stefano possessed a magnetic attraction that wasn't contrived, and Carly couldn't help but be aware of the attention he drew from most of the women present.

Seven years ago she'd lacked essential *savoir-faire* to cope with the socially élite among Stefano's fellow associates. Nervous and unsure of herself, she'd chosen to cling to his side and smile, whereas now she was well able to stand on her own feet. It had to make a difference in her ability to cope with his lifestyle.

Canapés and hors-d'oeuvres were proffered at intervals over the next half-hour, and it was almost nine when Charles and Kathy-Lee Winslow arrived with Georgeanne.

'We were held up,' Charles declared with droll humour as he steered his wife to where Carly stood at Stefano's side.

'By a taxi driver who decided to take advantage of the obvious fact we weren't residents, and drove us via a few scenic routes that lost us twenty minutes and gained him twenty extra dollars,' Georgeanne declared in explanation.

'Stop complaining,' Charles chastised with a broad smile. 'We enjoyed a pleasant ride, we're here, and I doubt anyone has missed us.'

'I need a drink,' his daughter vowed, her eyes settling deliberately on Stefano. 'Would you mind?' The

smile she bestowed was nothing short of total bewitchment. 'I'm thirsty.'

Not just for a drink, Carly surmised wryly, for
Georgeanne's behaviour fell just short of being blatant, and she watched with faint bemusement as Stefano elicited Georgeanne's preference.

'Why, there's Angelica,' Charles's daughter announced, and her eyes flew towards Carly with a
very good imitation of expressed concern. 'Oh, dear,
how—awkward.'

This could, Carly decided, become one of those
evenings where Murphy's Law prevailed, and she
wondered what on earth she could have done to upset
some mythical evil spirit who clearly felt impelled to
provide her with such an emotional minefield.

With detached fascination she watched Angelica
locate Stefano's tall frame at the bar, then cross leisurely to join him. She saw the beautiful brunette lift
a manicured hand and touch his arm, saw him turn,
and caught his smile in greeting. Angelica's expression was revealingly warm. *Loving*, Carly added, feeling as if she'd just been kicked in the stomach.

A confrontation was inevitable, and when they
were seated for dinner Carly cursed the unkind hand
of fate as she saw Georgeanne opposite at the large
dining-table, with Angelica slightly to Georgeanne's
right.

Wonderful, she groaned silently as she sipped a
small quantity of white wine in the hope that it would
provide a measure of necessary courage with which
to get through the evening.

Their hosts provided a sumptuous meal comprising
no fewer than five courses if one counted the fresh

fruit and cheeseboard that followed dessert. The pre-
sentation of the food was impressive, and Carly duti-
fully forked morsels into her mouth without tasting
a thing.

Conversation flowed, and she was aware of an increasing tension as she waited for the moment Angelica would unsheathe her claws.

'How is *your* daughter?'

Again, the faint emphasis didn't go unnoticed, and
Carly turned slightly to meet the brunette's seemingly
innocent gaze as she summoned a polite smile. 'Ann-
Marie is improving steadily.' She aimed for a subtle
emphasis of her own. '*We're* hopeful it won't be long
before she's released from hospital.'

Angelica picked up her wine glass and fingered the
long crystal stem with studied deliberation. 'Stefano
appears to delight in playing the role of devoted *Papà*.'

Carly effected a negligible shrug. 'You, more than
anyone, should appreciate that Italian men are re-
nowned for their love of family.'

Carefully shaped eyebrows rose a fraction in unison with the faint moue of evinced surprise that was
quickly camouflaged with a smile. 'Proud of their
sons, protective of their daughters.'

Carly couldn't resist the dig. 'And their wives.'

'Well, of course.' The voice resembled a husky
purr, infinitely feline. 'And their mistresses.' Her eyes
assumed a warm intimacy that was deliberate. 'What
female of any age could resist Stefano?'

Carly felt like screaming, but she forced her
mouth to curve into a soft smile, and her beautiful
eyes assumed a misty expression that was deliberately contrived as she lifted her shoulders in a help-

less shrugging gesture that she tempered with a light musing laugh. 'None, I imagine.'

Stefano, damn him, was seemingly engrossed in conversation with Charles, and appeared oblivious to the content of her conversation with Angelica.

What on earth did he imagine they had to discuss, for heaven's sake? The weather? The state of the nation?

It seemed forever before their host suggested adjourning to the lounge for coffee, and she felt strangely vulnerable as the men gravitated together on the pretext of sharing an after-dinner port while the women sought comfortable chairs at the opposite end of the large room—with the exception of Angelica, who stood at Stefano's side, a blatant disparity among men, yet totally at ease with their conversation. It was carrying feminism and equality among the sexes a little too far, surely? Carly couldn't help wondering if the men felt entirely comfortable. Yet she knew Angelica didn't give a fig what her male colleagues thought. Her main motivation in joining the men was to clarify the contrast between two women—herself and Stefano's wife.

The difference was quite marked in every way, from physical appearance to business qualifications. Seven years ago it had seemed important, the chasm too wide for Carly to imagine she would ever bridge. Except that in her own way she had, for there was now a diploma, experience and added qualifications in her field, as well as respect from her peers. There wasn't a thing she needed to prove, and if she so chose she could join Stefano's associates and discuss any topic relating to corporate accounting and tax legislation.

The coffee was liquid ambrosia, and Carly sipped it appreciatively, wondering just how long it would be before they left.

'You must visit when Stefano brings you to the states.'

Carly smiled, then thanked Charles's wife for the invitation. 'It's quite a few years since I was last there.'

'The house is large,' Kathy-Lee pursued. 'We'd be delighted if you'd stay. We love having guests.'

Carly could only admire Kathy-Lee for keeping pace with Charles's high-flying existence, *and* playing stepmother—a masterly feat in keeping the peace, for Charles adored his precocious daughter.

'I'll leave the decision to Stefano,' she said gently, indulging in inconsequential conversation for almost thirty minutes before Kathy-Lee had her cup refilled and was drawn by their hostess to join another guest who had professed an interest in Kathy-Lee's preoccupation with interior design.

Carly let her gaze wander round the room, settling on the broad frame of her husband as he stood idolently at ease and deep in conversation with two of his associates—one of whom was Angelica.

Carly forced herself to study them with impartial eyes—difficult when she wanted physically to tear Stefano and Angelica apart.

Angelica was a seductive temptress beneath the designer gown, leaning imperceptibly towards Stefano, her eyes, hands, *body* receptive to the man at her side, whereas Stefano stood totally at ease, his stance relaying relaxed confidence, an assurance that wasn't contrived. And, try as she might, Carly could find no visible sign of any implied intimacy—on his part.

Almost as if he was aware of her scrutiny, he turned slightly and met her gaze. For a moment everything else faded into obscurity, and she watched in bemused fascination as he excused himself and crossed the room to settle his length comfortably on the padded arm of her chair.

His proximity put her at an immediate disadvantage, for she was extremely aware of the clean smell of his clothes, the faint aroma of soap intermingling with his chosen aftershave, an exclusive mixture of spices combined with muted musk that seemed to heighten the essence of the man himself.

Within minutes his associates followed his actions in joining their wives, and Carly wasn't sure which she preferred...being alone with a clutch of curious women, or having to contend with Stefano's calculated attention.

'Almost ready to leave, *cara*?'

His voice was a soft caress, and if anyone was in any doubt as to his affection for his wife he lifted a hand and swept back a swath of curls that had fallen forward, letting his fingers rest far too long at the edge of her throat.

There was a degree of deliberation in his movement, almost as if he was attempting to set a precedent, and it made her unaccountably angry.

She wanted to move away, yet such an action was impossible, and it took all her acting ability to sit still as he brushed gentle fingers across her collarbone then slid them down her arm to thread through her own. The look in his eyes was explicitly seducing, and to any interested observer it was only too apparent that he couldn't wait to get her home and into bed.

Well, two could play at that game, and she gently dug the tips of her nails into the tendons of his hand, then pressed *hard*. 'Whenever you are,' she acquiesced lightly, casting him a soft winsome smile that was deceptively false. She would have liked to *kill* him, or at least render some measure of physical harm, yet in a room full of people she could only smile. As soon as they were alone, she'd verbally *slay* him.

He knew, for his eyes assumed a mocking gleam that hid latent amusement, almost in silent acceptance of an imminent battle.

With an indolent movement he rose to his feet, and Carly followed his actions, adding her appreciation with genuine politeness as they thanked their hosts and bade Charles and Kathy-Lee goodbye.

'So early, Stefano?' Angelica queried, effectively masking her displeasure.

'My wife is tired.'

It was nothing less than the truth, but she resented the implication.

Angelica's eyes narrowed, then assumed speculative amusement as she proffered Carly a commiserating smile. 'Can't stand the pace?'

'Quite the contrary,' Carly demurred sweetly. 'Stefano is merely providing a clichéd excuse.'

The resentment was simmering just beneath the surface of her control, and she contained it until the Mercedes had swept from the driveway.

'You enjoyed setting me among the pigeons, didn't you?' she demanded in a low, furious tone.

'Was it so bad?'

To be honest, it hadn't been. Yet she was loath to agree with him—on anything. 'On a scale of one to

ten in the curiosity stakes, our reconciliation has to
rate at least a nine,' she declared drily as he sent the
opulent vehicle speeding smoothly through the darkened streets.

'You more than held your own, *cara*,' he said with
drawled humour.

Inside she felt like screaming, aware that it would
take several weeks before the speculative looks, the
gossip abated and eventually died. In the meantime
she had to run the gauntlet, and she felt uncommonly
resentful.

'Nothing has changed,' Carly voiced with a trace
of bitterness, and incurred his swift scrutiny.

'In what respect?'

'You have to be *kidding*,' she declared vengefully.
'Angelica would have liked to eat you alive.' She was
so incensed that she wasn't aware of the passion evident in her voice, or the pain.

Turning her attention to the darkened city streets,
she watched the numerous vehicles traversing the
well-defined lanes with a detached fascination. The
bright neon signs provided a brilliant splash of colour
that vied with the red amber and green of traffic-lights
controlling each intersection.

Transferring her attention beyond the windscreen,
she looked sightlessly into the night, aware that Stefano handled the car with the skilled ease of long
practice.

The same ease with which he handled a woman:
knowledgeable, experienced, and always one step
ahead. Just once she'd like to be able to best him,
catch him off guard.

Yet even as the resentment festered she knew in-

stinctively that he'd never allow her to win. A solitary battle, possibly, in their ongoing private war, as a
musing concession to her feminine beliefs. But never
the war itself.

It was twenty minutes before the Mercedes drew
to a halt inside the garage, and Carly made her way
upstairs to the main suite.

She was in the process of removing her make-up
when Stefano entered the room, and her eyes assumed
a faint wariness as she completed the task.

It required only a few steps to move into the bedroom, a few more to reach the bed. Yet she was loath
to take them, knowing what awaited her once she
slipped between the cool percale sheets.

Fool she derided silently. It's not as if you lack enjoyment in the marital bed.

The knowledge of her exultant abandon in Stefano's arms merely strengthened her resolve to provide delaying tactics, and she plucked the pins from
the elaborate knot restraining her hair, only to catch
hold of her brush and stroke it vigorously through the
length of tumbled auburn-streaked curls.

It was mad to want more, insane to build an emotional wall between them. A tiny logical voice rationalised that she should be content. She had a beautiful
home, and a husband whose business interests ensured they were among the denizens of the upper social echelon.

Many women were confined in marriages of mutual convenience, happy to bury themselves in active
social existences as their husbands' hostesses, in return for the trappings of success: the jewellery, exotic
luxury cars, trips abroad.

Carly knew she'd trade it all willingly to erase the past seven years, to go back magically in time to the days when *love* was an irrepressible joy.

Now it was an empty shell, their sexual coupling merely an expression of physical lust untouched by any emotion from the heart.

Perhaps she was too honest, with too much personal integrity to survive within the constraints of such a marriage. Yet she was trapped, impossibly bound to Stefano by Ann-Marie. To remove her daughter from her father and return to their former existence would cause emotional scarring of such magnitude that the end result would be worthless.

'If you continue much longer, you'll end up with a headache.'

Carly's hand stilled at the sound of that deep drawling voice, and she stood motionless as Stefano moved to stand behind her.

'I have nothing to say to you,' she managed in stilted tones, watching him warily.

He was close, much too close for her peace of mind, and all her fine body hairs quivered in anticipation of his touch.

'We seem to manage very well without words,' he said with a degree of irony, and she lashed out verbally at his implication.

'Sex isn't the answer to everything, damn you!'

Her eyes unconsciously met his in the mirror, large and impossibly dark as she took in the image her body projected against the backdrop of his own.

Without the benefit of shoes, the tip of her head was level with his throat, and his breadth of shoulder had a dwarfing effect, making her appear small and incredibly vulnerable.

'No?' he queried softly, and she was damningly aware of the subtle pull of her senses as she fought his irresistible magnetism.

Her gaze remained locked with his, their darkness magnifying as he slowly lifted a hand and swept a heavy swath of her hair aside, baring the edge of her neck. His head slowly lowered as his mouth sought the pulsing cord in that sensitive curve, and she was powerless to prevent the sweet spiralling sensation that coursed through her body at his touch.

Carly was conscious of his hands as they shifted to her shoulders, then slid slowly down her arms to rest at her waist, before slipping up to cup the swollen fullness of her breasts.

She wanted to close her eyes and pretend the seduction was real, and for a few minutes she succumbed to temptation.

His fingers created a tactile magic, sensitising the engorged peaks until she moved restlessly against him, craving more than this subtle pleasuring. A hollow groan whispered from her throat as his hands slid to her shoulders, slipping the thin straps of her nightgown down over her arms, so that the thin silk slithered in a heap at her feet.

He didn't move, and she slowly opened her eyes to focus reluctantly on their mirrored image, watching in mesmerised fascination as his hands slid round her waist and pressed her back against him.

Her eyes widened as she watched the effect he had on the texture of her skin, the tightening of her breasts, each tumescent peak aroused in anticipation of his possession.

It was almost as if he was forcing her to recognise something her conscious mind refused to acknowledge, and she gazed in mesmeric wonder as her body reacted to the light brush of his fingers as he trailed them across the curve of her waist, then slid to trace the soft mound of her stomach before allowing his fingers to splay into the soft curls protecting the central core of her femininity.

Of their own volition, her lower limbs swayed into the curve of his hand as they sought closer contact, and she was totally unprepared for the soft dreaminess evident in her eyes, the faint sheen on her parted lips.

She looked…incandescently bewitched, held in thrall by passionate desire, and in that moment she felt she hated him for making her see a side of herself she preferred to keep well-hidden. Especially from him.

Yet it was too late, and even as she arched away he turned her fully into his arms, his mouth successfully covering hers in a manner that left her no hope of uttering so much as a word.

Her initial struggle was merely a token gesture, as was her determination to prevent his open-mouthed kiss. Seconds later she cried out as one long arm curved down the length of her back in a seeking quest for the tell-tale dewing at the aroused nub of her femininity.

Every nerve in her body seemed acutely sensitised, the internal tissues still faintly bruised from the previous night's loving, so much so that she tensed involuntarily against his touch.

Without a word he placed an arm beneath her knees

and lifted her high against his chest to carry her to his bed, sinking down on to the mattress in one fluid movement as he cradled her gently into the curve of his body.

His lips trailed a path to her mouth, soothing her slight protest, before tracing a path down her neck. Slowly, with infinite care, he traversed each pleasure pulse, anointing the tender peak of each breast with delicate eroticism.

Her stomach quivered in betrayal beneath the seductive passage of his mouth, and when he reached the junction between her thighs she gave a beseeching moan, an entreaty to end the consuming madness that flared through her body, igniting it with flame.

Carly consoled herself that nothing mattered except this wonderful slaking of sensual pleasure in a slow, gentle loving that touched her soul. But in her subconscious mind she knew she lied, and she drifted into sleep wondering if there could ever be a resolution between the dictates of her brain and the wayward path of her emotions.

CHAPTER NINE

'I HAVE TO attend a meeting on the Central Coast,' Stefano declared as he rose from the breakfast table. 'I doubt I'll be home before seven.'

'Angelica is naturally one of the associates accompanying you.' It wasn't a question, and he shot her a dark encompassing glance.

'She is on the board of a number of family companies,' he informed coolly. 'And a dedicated businesswoman.'

'Very dedicated,' Carly mocked, and was unable to resist adding, 'Have fun.'

After he left she finished her coffee, then moved quickly upstairs to change into a white cotton button-through dress, slipped her feet into flat sandals, then collected the keys to the BMW, informed Sylvana she'd be home in the late afternoon, and drove into the city.

There were a few things she wanted to pick up for Ann-Marie, and she'd fill in time between hospital visits by browsing the shops in the hope of gaining some inspiration for Christmas gifts.

Carly returned home at five, and after a leisurely shower she changed into a cool sage-green silk shift, wound her hair up into a casually contrived knot, then went downstairs to check on dinner with Sylvana.

The portable television was on in the kitchen, and highlighted on the screen was an area of dense bush-covered gorge and a hovering rescue helicopter. The presenter's modulated voice was relaying information regarding a light plane crash just south of the Central Coast. There were no survivors, and names had not yet been released of the pilot and two passengers.

Carly went cold. It was as if her limbs were frozen, for she couldn't move, and she gazed sightlessly at the flashing screen without comprehending a single thing.

Then she began to shake, and she clutched her arms together in an effort to contain her trembling limbs.

It couldn't be the plane carrying Stefano and Angelica—*could it*? A silent agonised scream rose in her throat. Dear God—*no*.

The thought of his strong body lying broken and burned in dense undergrowth almost destroyed her. His image was a vivid entity, and she saw his strongly etched features, the dark gleaming eyes, almost as if he were in the same room.

The phone rang, but the sound barely registered, nor did Sylvana's voice as she answered the call, until it seemed to change in tone and Carly realised that Sylvana was attempting to gain her attention.

'Stefano rang to say he'll be home in twenty minutes.'

The words penetrated her brain, barely registering in those initial few seconds, then she turned slowly, her eyes impossibly large. 'What did you say?'

Sylvana repeated the message, then added in puzzlement, 'Are you all right?'

Carly inclined her head, then murmured something indistinguishable as her stomach began to churn, and she only just made it upstairs to the main suite before she was violently ill.

Afterwards she clenched her teeth, then she sluiced warm water over her face in an effort to dispel the chilled feeling that seemed to invade her bones.

Attempting to repair the ravages with make-up moved her to despair, for she looked incredibly vulnerable—*haunted*, she amended silently as she examined her mirrored image with critical deliberation.

How could you *love* someone you professed to hate? Yet an inner voice taunted that love and hate were intense emotions and closely entwined. Legend had it that they were inseparable.

Stefano's arrival home was afforded a restrained greeting. If she'd listened to her heart she would have flown into his arms and expressed a profound relief that he was alive. Yet then he couldn't fail to be aware of her true feelings, and that would never do.

Consequently dinner was strained, and Carly failed to do any justice to Sylvana's beautifully prepared food, and throughout the meal she was conscious of his veiled scrutiny, so much so that she felt close to screaming with angry vexation.

'Did it bother you that it might have been my body lying lifeless in some rocky gorge?'

The blood drained from her face at his drawled query, and she got to her feet, wanting only to get away from his ill-disguised mockery.

She hadn't moved more than two paces when hard hands closed over her shoulders, and she struggled in

vain, hot, angry tears clouding her eyes as she fought
to be free of him.

One hand slid to hold her nape fast, tilting her head,
and her lashes swept down to form a protective veil,
only to fly open as his mouth closed over hers in a
hard open-mouthed kiss that was impossibly, erotically demanding.

It seemed to go on forever, and when it was over
she lifted shaking fingers to her lips.

His eyes were dark with brooding savagery, their
depths filled with latent passion and an emotion she
didn't even attempt to define. Carly glanced past him
and fixed her eyes on a distant wall in an attempt to
regain her composure. If she looked at him she knew
she'd disgrace herself with stupid ignominious tears.

'I rang through the instant we touched base,' he
enlightened quietly. 'Our helicopter pilot sighted the
crash, radioed for help, then circled the area until a
rescue unit arrived.' He raised a hand and trailed gentle fingers along the edge of her cheek.

She lifted her shoulders in a faint shrugging gesture. Somehow she had to inject an element of normality, otherwise she was doomed. 'Would you like
some coffee?'

A forefinger probed the softness of her swollen
lower lip, then conducted a leisurely tracery of its
outline. 'I'd like *you*,' Stefano drawled in mocking
tones, and watched the expressive play of emotions
chase each other across her mobile features.

'It's early,' she stalled, hating the way her body was
reacting to the proximity of his.

'Since when did time have anything to do with
making love?' His head lowered and he touched his

mouth to the thudding pulse at the edge of her neck, then traced a path to her temple. His lips pressed closed one eyelid, then the other, and his hands shifted as he caught her up in his arms.

'What are you doing?' The cry was torn from her lips as he calmly strode from the room, and headed for the stairs.

'Taking you to bed,' Stefano declared in a husky undertone, 'in an attempt to remove the look of shadowed anguish lurking in your beautiful eyes.'

She struggled in helplessness against him, aware of an elemental quality that was infinitely awesome. No one man deserved so much power, or quite such a degree of latent sensuality.

'Must you be so—physical?' she protested as he entered their suite and closed the door.

He lowered her down to stand within the circle of his arms, and her limbs seemed weightless as he caught her close. Then he kissed her, slowly and with such evocative mastery that she didn't have the energy to voice any further protest as he carefully removed her clothes, then released the pins holding her hair before beginning on his own.

'Tell me to stop,' he murmured seconds before his mouth closed over hers, and the flame that burned deep within them flared into vibrant life, consuming them both in a passionate storm that lasted far into the night.

The following days settled into a relatively normal routine. The nights were something else as Carly fought a silent battle with herself and invariably lost.

Their lovemaking scaled hitherto unreached

heights, transcending mere pleasure, and it was almost as if some inner song were demanding to be heard, yet the music was indistinct, the words just beyond her reach.

Introspection became an increasing trap in which she found herself caught, in the insidious recognition that *love* was inextricably interwoven with physical desire—which inevitably led to the agonising question of Angelica, and the degree of Stefano's personal involvement. Were they still on intimate terms? *Had they ever been*? Dear God, could she have been wrong all these years?

One day in particular she couldn't bear the tension any more, and she moved restlessly through the house, unsure how to fill the few hours until it was time to visit Ann-Marie.

Making a split-second decision, she changed clothes, stroked a clear gloss over her lips, then caught up her sunglasses and bag, and made her way down to the car, intent on spending a few more hours in the city looking for suitable Christmas gifts. She might even do lunch.

Two hours later Carly wasn't sure shopping was such a good idea. It was hot, there were crowds of people all intent on doing the same thing, and it took ages to be served. All she'd achieved was a bottle of Sarah's favourite French perfume, a book and an educational game for Ann-Marie, and nothing for Stefano. What did you buy a man who had everything? she queried with scepticism. Another silk tie? A silk shirt? Something as mundane as *aftershave*, when she didn't even recognise what brand he preferred?

A glance at her watch revealed that it was after one.

Something to eat and a cool drink would provide a welcome break, and ten minutes later she was seated in a pleasant air-conditioned restaurant eating a succulent chicken salad.

'Mind if I join you?'

Carly glanced up and endeavoured to contain her surprise. Coincidence was a fine thing, and the chance of choosing the same restaurant as Angelica Agnelli had to run at a thousand to one. 'If you must,' she responded with bare civility. The restaurant *was* crowded, after all, and short of being rude there wasn't much she could do except accept the situation with as much grace as possible.

'Shopping?' Angelica queried, arching an elegantly shaped eyebrow as she caught sight of the brightly designed bags.

'Yes.' As if an explanation was needed, she added, 'Christmas.'

'Stefano is caught up in a conference, so I came on ahead.' She allowed the information to sink in, then added with deadly timing, 'This is a charmingly secluded place, don't you agree?' For furtive assignations. The implication was there for anyone but the most obtuse, but just in case there was any doubt she added smoothly, 'You don't normally lunch here, do you?'

'No. I preferred to eat a packed lunch at my desk,' Carly explained with considerable calm, and tempered the words with a seemingly sweet smile.

Angelica deliberately allowed her eyes to widen. 'Rather clever of you to present Stefano with a child conveniently the right age to be his own.' Her mouth curled fractionally. 'I almost advised him to insist on a DNA test.' She lifted a hand and appeared to study her immaculately manicured nails. 'But of course, I wouldn't presume to interfere in his...' She trailed off deliberately, then added with barbed innuendo, 'Private affairs.'

'You've obviously changed your strategy,' Carly returned with considerable fortitude, when inside she felt like screaming.

'Whatever do you mean?'

Carly had quite suddenly had enough. 'You had no such compunction about interfering in his private life seven years ago. You deliberately set out to destroy me. Like a fool, I ran.' Her eyes sparked gold-flecked fire that caused the other woman's expression to narrow. 'I realise your association with Stefano goes back a long time, but perhaps you should understand it was *he* who did the chasing in our relationship, and he who insisted on a reconciliation.' She drew in a deep breath, then released it slowly. 'Stefano has had seven years to instigate divorce proceedings.' Her voice assumed a quietly fierce intensity. 'I would suggest you ask yourself why he never did.'

'*Brava*,' a deep voice drawled quietly from behind, and Carly closed her eyes in vexation, only to open them again.

Stefano stood indolently at ease, his expression strangely watchful as he took in Carly's pale features. All of her pent-up emotion was visible in the expressive brilliance of her eyes, their gold-flecked depths ringed in black.

'Stefano.' Angelica's tone held a conciliatory purr, yet his eyes never moved from Carly's features.

'If you'll excuse me?' She had to get out of here before she erupted with volatile rage—with Angelica for being a bitch, and Stefano simply because he was *here*.

Rising to her feet, she collected her bag and assorted carriers. 'Enjoy your lunch.'

His hand closed on her arm, bringing her to a halt, and she just looked at him, then her lashes swept down in a bid to hide the pain that gnawed deep inside.

'Please. Let me go.' Her voice was softly pitched, yet filled with aching intensity, and there was nothing she could do to prevent the descent of his mouth or the brief, hard open-mouthed kiss he bestowed.

Then he released her, and it took all her reserve of strength to walk calmly from the restaurant.

By the time she reached the street her lips were quivering with pent-up emotion, and she fumbled for her sunglasses, glad of their protective lenses as they hid the well of tears that blurred her vision.

Tonight there would be no respite, for Sarah and James were coming to dinner. To present anything approaching a normal façade would take every ounce of acting ability, and Carly wished fervently for the day to be done, and the night.

Only a matter of weeks ago everything had seemed so uncomplicated. Ann-Marie and work had been the total focus of her life. Now she was in turmoil, her emotions as wild and uncontrollable as a storm-tossed sea.

At the hospital, Ann-Marie's exuberant greeting, the loving hug and beautiful smile acted to diffuse Carly's inner tension, and she listened to her daughter's excited chatter about a new patient who had been admitted that morning.

As Carly left the hospital and drove home she

couldn't help wishing her life were clear-cut, and there were no tensions, no subtle game-playing that ate at the heartstrings and destroyed one's self-esteem.

Perhaps she should stop fighting this conflict within herself and just accept the status quo, be content with her existence as Stefano's wife, and condone the pleasure they shared each night. To hunger for anything more was madness.

After garaging the car, Carly consulted with Sylvana, made suitably appreciative comments, then opted to cool off with a leisurely swim in the pool.

Stefano arrived home as Carly was putting the finishing touches to her make-up, and she turned as he entered their suite, her expression deliberately bland as she registered his tall, dark-suited frame before lifting her head to meet his gaze.

His eyes were dark, probing hers, and after a fleeting glance her own skittered towards the vicinity of his left shoulder. The last thing she needed was a confrontation. Not with Sarah and James due within minutes.

'I'll go down and check with Sylvana,' Carly said evenly. 'I'll wait for you in the lounge.'

It was a relief to escape his presence, and she was grateful for Sarah's punctuality, immensely glad of her friend's warm personality.

The meal was a gourmet's delight, and although conversation flowed with ease Carly merely operated on automatic pilot as she forked food intermittently into her mouth, then toyed with the remainder on her plate.

She laughed, genuinely enjoying Sarah's anecdotes

intermingled with those of James, but all the while she felt like a disembodied spectator.

It was almost ten when they rose from the table.

'I'll make the coffee,' Carly declared, and smiled when Sarah rose to her feet.

'I'll help you.'

Sylvana had set everything ready in the kitchen, so that all Carly had to do was percolate the coffee.

'How are things going—?' Carly broke off with a laugh in the realisation that Sarah was asking the same question simultaneously with her own. 'You go first,' she bade her, shooting her friend a smiling glance.

'Where shall I start?' Sarah returned with a grin as she crossed to the servery, and cast the stylish kitchen an appreciative glance. 'Lucky you,' she smiled without a trace of envy. 'All this, and Stefano, too.'

'Sarah…' Carly warned with a low growl, and Sarah grinned unrepentantly.

'James and Stefano seem to have a lot in common,' Sarah offered innocuously, her eyes sparkling as Carly shot her a speaking glance. 'James is nice,' she admitted quietly. 'I like him.'

'*And*?' Carly prompted.

'Sometimes I think I could get used to the idea of a relationship with him, then I'm not sure I want to make that sort of change to my life.' Her eyes sought Carly's, and her voice softened. 'How about you?'

'Ann-Marie is improving daily.'

'That wasn't what I asked,' Sarah admonished teasingly, and Carly's expression became faintly pensive.

'I seem to swing like a pendulum between resentment and acceptance.'

'You look...' Sarah paused, her eyes narrowing with thoughtful speculation. 'Pregnant. Are you?'

Carly opened her mouth to deny it, then closed it again as her mind rapidly calculated dates. Her eyes became an expressive host to a number of varying fleeting emotions.

'You have that certain look a woman possesses in the initial few weeks,' Sarah observed gently. 'A subtle tiredness as the body refocuses its energy. You had the same look the day we met moving into neighbouring apartments,' she added softly.

'It could be stress from juggling twice-daily hospital visits, marriage,' Carly offered in strangled tones as the implications of a possible pregnancy began to sink in. She *couldn't* be, surely? Yet the symptoms were all there, added to facts she'd been too busy to notice.

She lifted a shaking hand, then let it fall again, and for one heartfelt second her eyes filled with naked pain before she successfully masked their expression.

'The coffee is perking,' Sarah reminded gently, and Carly crossed to turn down the heat, then when it was ready she placed it on the tray.

The men were deep in conversation when Carly and Sarah re-entered the lounge, and if either detected that the girls' smiles were a little too bright they gave no sign.

It was almost eleven when Sarah indicated the need to leave, explaining, 'I'm due to go on duty tomorrow morning at seven.' She rose to her feet, thanked both Stefano and Carly for a delightful evening, and at the door she gave Carly a quick hug in farewell. 'Ring me when you can.'

Carly turned back towards the lobby the instant the car headlights disappeared down the drive, moving into the lounge to collect coffee-cups together prior to carrying them through to the kitchen.

'Leave them,' Stefano instructed as he saw what she was doing. 'Sylvana can take care of it in the morning.'

'It will only take a minute.' In the kitchen, she rinsed and stacked them in the dishwasher, then turned to find him leaning against the edge of the table, watching her with narrowed scrutiny.

She stood perfectly still, despite every nerve-end screaming at fever pitch, and her chin lifted fraction-ally as he took the necessary steps towards her.

'What now, Stefano?' Carly queried with a touch of defiance. 'A post-mortem on lunch?'

One eyebrow slanted in mocking query. 'What part of lunch would you particularly like to refer to?'

'I disliked being publicly labelled as your posses-sion,' she insisted, stung by his cynicism.

'Yet you are,' he declared silkily. 'My feelings where you're concerned verge on the primitive.'

A tiny pulse quickened at the base of her throat, then began to hammer in palpable confusion as she absorbed the essence of his words. 'Is that meant to frighten me?'

Tension filled the air, lending a highly volatile quality that was impossible to ignore. 'Only if you choose to allow it,' he mocked, and she stood per-fectly still as he conducted a slow, all-encompassing appraisal, lingering on the deepness of her eyes, and her soft, trembling mouth.

He lifted a hand to brush gentle fingers across her cheek, and she reared back as if from a lick of flame.

'Don't touch me.'

'Whyever not, *cara*?'

'Because that's where it starts and ends,' she asserted with a mixture of despair and wretchedness.

'You find my lovemaking so distasteful?'

His musing indulgence was the living end, and she lashed out at him with expressive anger. '*Lust*, damn you!' she corrected heatedly, so incensed that she balled both hands into fists and punched him, uncaring that she connected with the hard, muscular wall of his chest.

'Lust is a bartered commodity. What would you like me to give you?' His voice was a low-pitched drawl that cut right through to the heart. 'An item of jewellery, perhaps?'

For several long seconds she just looked at him, filled with an aching pain so acute that it took all her effort to breathe evenly. What was the use, she agonised silently, of aiming for something that didn't exist?

'In return for which I reward you in bed?' The words were out before she had time to give them much thought, and afterwards it was too late to retract them.

His dark brooding glance narrowed fractionally, then his mouth curved in mocking amusement. 'Ah, *cara*,' he taunted softly. 'You reward me so well.'

The need to get away from him, even temporarily, was paramount, and she turned towards the door, only to be brought to a halt as hard hands caught hold of each shoulder and spun her round.

Her eyes blazed with anger through a mist of tears

as she tilted her head in silent apathy, hating him more at that precise moment than she thought it possible to hate anyone.

'Stop making fun of me! I won't have it, do you hear?' Angry, frustrated tears filled her eyes as he restrained her with galling ease, and she shook her head helplessly as he drew her inextricably close.

'*Don't*—' Carly begged, feeling the familiar pull of her senses. It would be so easy to succumb, simply to close her eyes and become transported by the special magic of their shared sexual alchemy.

'When have I ever made fun of you?' he teased gently, and she shivered slightly as one hand slid down over the soft roundness of her bottom, pressing her close against the unmistakable force of his arousal, while the other slid up to cup her nape.

'Every time I oppose you,' she began shakily, then, gathering the scattered threads of her courage, she continued with strengthened resolve. 'You resolve it by sweeeping me off to bed.' Lifting her hands, she attempted to put some distance between them, only to fail miserably.

'Am I to be damned forever for finding you desirable?'

The thread of amusement in his voice hurt unbearably. 'I'm not a sex object you can use merely to satisfy a need for revenge.'

His eyes searched hers, dark and unfathomable as he held her immobile.

'Let me go, damn you!'

He looked at her in silence for what seemed an age, his eyes darkening until they resembled the deepest slate—hard and equally obdurate.

'Does it feel like revenge every time I take you in my arms?' he queried with dangerous silkiness.

It was heaven and the entire universe rolled into one, ecstasy at its zenith. She looked at him for what seemed an age, unable to utter so much as a word.

Dared she take the chance? All the pent-up anger, her so-called resentment, dissipated as if it had never existed.

'No,' Carly voiced quietly, and he shook her gently, sliding his hands from her shoulders up to cup her face.

'From the moment I first met you I wanted to lock you in a gilded prison and throw away the key. Except such a primitive action wouldn't have been condoned in this day and age.' His eyes were level, and she was unable to drag her own away from the darkness or the pain evident. 'You were a prime target...young, and incredibly susceptible,' he enlightened her softly.

'If I had been able to get my hands on you during those first few weeks after you left Perth I think I would have strangled you,' he continued slowly. 'Your mother disavowed any knowledge of your whereabouts, and I soon realised you had no intention of contacting me.' His voice hardened measurably, and assumed a degree of cynicism. 'The letter dispatched from your solicitor merely confirmed it.'

He was silent for so long that she wondered if he intended to continue.

'A marriage has no foundation without trust, and as you professed to have lost your trust in me I let you go. Fully expecting,' he added with a trace of mockery, 'to be officially notified of an impending divorce.'

He hadn't been able to instigate such proceedings any more than she had. Her heart set up a quickened beat.

'Not long after shifting base to Sydney I attended an accounting seminar with a fellow associate at which Clive Mathorpe was a guest speaker. I was impressed. Sufficiently so to utilise his services.' He proffered a faint smile. 'Coincidence, *fate* perhaps, that Carly Taylor *Alessi* should be a respected member of his firm. The night I met you at Clive's home I was intrigued by your maturity and self-determination. And very much aware that the intense sexual magic we once shared was still in evidence.' His eyes held hers, and his voice was deliberate as he continued, 'For both of us.'

Carly looked at him carefully, seeing his innate strength, the power in evidence, and knew that she would never willingly want to be apart from him. It was always easy, with hindsight, to rationalise—to indulge in a series of 'what if's, and 'if only's. Maturity had taught her there could only be *now*.

'Angelica's ammunition was pretty powerful,' she offered quietly. 'I found it emotionally damaging at the time.'

There was a mesmeric silence, intensifying until she became conscious of every breath she took.

'I have known Angelica from birth,' Stefano revealed with deceptive mildness, and a muscle tensed along the edge of his jaw. 'Our affiliation owes itself to two sets of parents who immigrated to Australia more than forty years ago. They prospered in one business venture after another, achieving phenomenal success. So much so that hope was fostered that the only Alessi son might marry an Agnelli daughter and thus form a dynasty.' He paused fractionally, and searched her pale features, seeing the faint shadows evident beneath her eyes. 'It was a game I chose not to play,' he added gently.

Carly swallowed the lump that had suddenly risen in her throat. 'The way Angelica told it,' she informed him shakily, 'you were unofficially betrothed when you met me. If our engagement surprised her, our wedding threw her into a rage,' she continued, unwilling to expound too graphically on just how much she'd been hurt by a woman who refused to face reality. 'It appeared I was merely a temporary diversion, and there was little doubt she intended to be there to pick up the pieces.' She effected a deprecatory shrug that hid a measure of pain.

'Angelica,' Stefano declared hardly, 'possesses a vivid imagination. After today,' he grained out with chilling inflexibility, 'she has no doubt whom I love, or why.' His expression softened as he watched the expressive play of emotions chasing each other across her features. '*You*, Carly,' he elaborated gently. 'Always. Only you.'

Stefano shifted his hold, catching both her hands together in one of his, feeling her body quiver slightly as he traced a gentle pattern over the slim curve of her stomach before resting possessively at her trim waist. When his gaze met hers, she nearly died at the lambent warmth revealed in those dark depths.

'There is nothing else you want to tell me?'

Carly stood hesitantly unsure, and at the last moment courage failed her. Slowly she shook her head.

Tomorrow, she'd visit the doctor and undergo a pregnancy test. Then she'd tell him.

CHAPTER TEN

THE MORNING BEGAN the same as any other week day. Stefano rose early, swam several lengths of the pool, ate breakfast with his wife, then showered, dressed and left for the city.

At nine Carly checked with Sylvana, then changed into a smart lemon-yellow button-through linen dress, applied make-up with care, slid her feet into elegant shoes, and went downstairs to the car.

The pregnancy test was performed with ease, and pronounced positive. Carly drove on to the hospital in a state of suspended euphoria.

Ann-Marie looked really *well*, her eyes bright and shining as Carly walked into her room, and her beautiful hair was beginning to show signs of growth. A consultation with the specialist revealed that Ann-Marie could be discharged the following day.

Carly almost floated down the carpeted corridor, and on impulse she crossed to the pay-phone, checked the directory, slotted in coins and keyed in the appropriate series of digits, then relayed specific instructions to the voice on the other end of the phone.

A small secretive smile tugged the edges of her mouth as she drove into the city, and twenty minutes later she stood completing formalities in Reception at one of the inner city's most elegant hotels.

The lift whisked her with swift precision to the eleventh floor, and inside the luxurious suite she swiftly crossed the room, lifted the handset and dialled a memorised number.

She was mad, absolutely crazy, she derided as the line engaged after a number of electronic beeps. What if Stefano wasn't in the office? Worse, what if he was in an important meeting, and couldn't leave? she agonised as the number connected with his personal mobile net.

'Alessi.' His voice sounded brisk and impersonal, and her stomach flipped, then executed a number of painful somersaults.

'Stefano.'

'Carly. Is something wrong?'

'No—' *Hell*, she was faltering, stammering like a schoolgirl. Taking a deep breath, she clenched the receiver and forced herself to speak calmly. 'I'm fine.' Dammit, this was proving more difficult than she'd envisaged.

'Ann-Marie?'

'She's coming home tomorrow.' The joy in her voice was a palpable entity that was reciprocated in his.

Do it, *tell* him, a tiny voice prompted. 'I wanted to ring and say…' She hesitated slightly, then uttered the words with slow emphasis. '*I love you.*'

A few seconds of silence followed, then his voice sounded incredibly husky close to her ear. 'Where are you?'

'In a hotel room, in the city.'

His soft laughter sent spirals of sensation shooting through her body. 'Which hotel, *cara*?'

She named it. 'It's Sylvana's day to vacuum,' she explained a trifle breathlessly.

'Ensuring that total privacy is out of the question,' he drawled with a tinge of humour.

'Totally,' she agreed, and a tiny smile teased the edges of her mouth. 'Is this a terribly inconvenient time for you?'

'It wouldn't make any difference.'

Her heart leapt, then began thudding to a quickened beat. 'No?'

His husky chuckle did strange things to her equilibrium. 'I'll be with you in twenty minutes.'

Carly relayed the room number, then softly replaced the receiver.

Twenty minutes, she mused as she eased off her shoes. How could she fill them? Make a cup of coffee, perhaps, or select a chilled mineral water from the variety stocked in the bar-fridge.

Her eyes travelled idly round the large room, noting the customary prints, the wall-lights, before settling on the bed.

If she turned down the covers, it would look too blatant, and she didn't quite possess the courage to remove all her clothes. What if she opened the door to find a maid or steward on the other side? she thought wildly.

Damn. Waiting was agony, and she crossed to the sealed window and stood watching the traffic on the busy street below.

Everyone appeared to be hurrying, and when the southbound traffic ground to a halt a clutch of people surged across the road to the opposite side. The lights turned green, and the northbound traffic gathered momentum, moving in a seemingly endless river of vehicles until green changed to amber and then to red, when the process began all over again.

From this height everything seemed lilliputian, and she watched the cars, searching for the sleek lines of Stefano's top-of-the-range Mercedes, although the likelihood of catching sight of it when she wasn't even sure from which direction he'd be travelling seemed remote.

It was a beautiful day, she perceived idly. There was a cloudless sky of azure-blue, the sun filtering in shafts of brilliant light between the tall city buildings.

Time became a suspended entity, and it seemed an age before she heard the quiet double knock at the door.

Her stomach reacted at once, leaping almost into her throat, and she smoothed suddenly damp hands down the seams of her dress as she crossed the suite to open the door.

Stefano stood at ease, his tall frame filling the aperture, and she simply looked at him in silence. There was a vital, almost electric energy apparent, an inherent vitality that was compelling, and her pulse accelerated into a rapid beat.

A faint smile teased his generous mouth, and his eyes were so incredibly warm that she almost melted beneath their gaze.

'Do you intend to keep me standing here?'

Pale pink tinged her cheeks as she stood to one side. Fool, she berated herself silently, feeling about as composed as a lovestruck teenager as she followed him into the centre of the room.

When he turned she was within touching distance, yet he made no attempt to draw her into his arms.

'I gather there was a degree of urgency in the need to book in to a hotel room?'

There was no mistaking his soft teasing drawl, nor the expression evident in his eyes. It gave her the confidence to resort to humour.

The sparkle in the depths of her eyes flared into brilliant life, and she laughed softly. 'Tonight we're supposed to dine out with Sarah and James to celebrate Sarah's birthday. If it were anyone else, I wouldn't hesitate to cancel.' A devilish gleam emerged, dancing in the light of her smile. 'I did consider a confrontation in your office, but the thought of Renate or any one of the staff catching sight of their exalted boss deep in an erotic clinch might prove too embarrassing to be condoned.'

His lips twitched, then settled into a sensual curve. 'Erotic?'

'There's champagne in the bar-fridge,' Carly announced inconsequentially. 'Would you like some?'

'I'd like you to repeat what you said to me on the phone,' he commanded gently, and her eyes were remarkably clear as they held his.

'I love you. I always have,' she stressed.

'*Grazie amore*.' He reached out and pulled her close in against him. His lips brushed her forehead, then began a slow, tantalising trail down to the edge of her mouth.

'You're my life,' he said huskily. 'My love.'

There was such a wealth of emotion in his voice;

she felt a delicious warmth begin deep within her as a thousand tiny nerve-endings leapt into pulsating life.

'So many wasted years,' she offered with deep regret. 'Nights,' she elaborated huskily. 'Dear heaven, I *missed* you.'

Her eyes widened as she glimpsed the expression in those dark depths mere inches above her own, then she gasped as his mouth moved to cover hers in a kiss that left her feeling shaken with a depth of emotion so intoxicating that it was as if she was soaring high on to a sensual pinnacle of such incredible magnitude that she felt weightless, and totally malleable.

'*Don't*,' Stefano chastised softly. 'We have today, and all the tomorrows. A lifetime.'

Her eyes were wondrously expressive as she lifted her hands and wound them round his neck. 'What time do you have to be back at the office?'

'I told Renate to reschedule the remainder of the day's appointments,' he revealed solemnly.

A delightfully bewitching smile lit her features, and her lips curved to form a teasing smile. 'We have until two, when I visit Ann-Marie in hospital.'

His hands slid down over her hips, and she gloried in the feel of him as he drew her close and brushed his lips close to her ear. 'We'll go together.' The tip of his tongue traced the sensitive whorls, and she shivered as sensation shafted through her body.

A soft laugh bubbled up from her throat to emerge as an exultant sound of delicious anticipation. 'Meantime, I have a few plans for the next few hours.' Leaning away from him, she murmured her pleasure as he loosened his hold so that she could slip the jacket from his shoulders.

His eyes gleamed with humour, and a wealth of latent passion. 'Do you, indeed?'

'Uh-huh.' Her fingers set to work on his tie, then the buttons of his shirt. The belt buckle came next, and she hesitated fractionally as she undid the fastener at his waist and freed the zip. 'Something wildly imaginative with champagne and strawberries.' A bubble of laughter emerged from her throat. 'It's rather decadent.'

His shoes followed, his socks, until all he wore was a pair of silk briefs.

'My turn, I think.'

With unhurried movements he removed every last vestige of her clothing, then he leaned down and tugged back the covers from the large bed before gently pulling her down to lie beside him.

His kiss melted her bones, and she gasped as his mouth began a treacherous path of discovery that encompassed every inch, every vulnerable hollow of her body.

By the time his lips returned to caress hers, there wasn't one coherent word she was capable of uttering, and she clung to him, eager, wanting, *needing* the sweet savagery of his lovemaking.

A long time afterwards she lay catching her breath as she attempted to control the waywardness of her emotions, then slowly she moved, affording him a similar pleasuring until he groaned and pulled her to lie on top of him.

'Minx,' he growled softly, curving a hand round her nape and urging her mouth down to his. 'Keep doing that, and I won't be answerable for the consequences.'

'Promises, promises,' Carly taunted gently as she

initiated a kiss that he allowed her to control. Then she rose up and arched her back, stretching like a kitten that had just had its fill of cream.

The soft sigh of contentment changed to a faint gasp as he positioned her to accept his length, and now it was he who was in command, watching her fleeting emotions with musing indulgence as he led her towards a climactic orgasmic explosion that had her crying out his name as wave after wave of sensation exploded from deep within her feminine core, radiating to the furthest reaches of her body in an all-consuming pleasurable ache that gradually ebbed to a warm afterglow, lasting long after they'd shared a leisurely shower and slipped into the complimentary towelling robes.

'Hmm,' Carly murmured as Stefano came to stand behind her and drew her back into the circle of his arms. 'I'm hungry.' She felt his lips caress her nape, and she turned slightly towards him. 'For food, you insatiable man!'

'Do you want to dress and go down to the restaurant, or shall I order Room Service?'

She pretended to consider both options, then directed him a teasing smile. 'Room Service.' She was loath to share him with anyone, and although the time was fast approaching when they must dress and leave she wanted to delay it as long as possible. 'Besides,' she teased mercilessly, 'there's still the champagne.'

Choosing from the menu and placing their order took only minutes, and afterwards Stefano pulled her back into his arms and held her close.

She drew in a deep breath, then released it slowly.

'I've been giving some thought to going back to work next year.'

His eyes took on a new depth, then assumed a musing speculative gleam. 'What if I were to make you a better offer?'

'Such as?'

'Working from home, maintaining order with my paperwork, liaising with Renate?'

Carly pretended to consider his proposal, tilting her head to one side in silent contemplation.

'Flexible hours, harmonious working conditions, and intimate terms with the boss?' she teased.

'Very intimate terms,' he conceded with a sloping smile.

'I accept. Conditionally,' she added with attempted solemnity, and was unable to prevent the slight catch in her breath. 'I'm not sure of your stance on employing pregnant women.'

He didn't say anything for a few seconds, then he kissed her, so gently and with such reverence that it was all she could do not to cry.

'Thank you,' Stefano said simply, and she smiled a trifle tremulously.

'If this pregnancy follows the same pattern as it did with Ann-Marie,' she warned with musing reflection, 'I'll begin feeling nauseous within the next few weeks.' She wrinkled her nose at him in silent humour. 'How will you cope with a wife who has to leap out of bed and run to the bathroom every morning?'

'Ensure that you have whatever it is you need until such time as you feel you can face the day.'

Carly blinked rapidly, then offered shakily, 'Did I tell you how much I love you?'

Room Service delivered their lunch, but it was another hour before they ate the food. Afterwards they slowly dressed and made their way down to the car park.

'I'll follow you to the hospital,' Stefano said gently as he saw her seated behind the wheel of her car. 'Travel carefully, *cara*.'

'We really should stop meeting like this,' Carly declared with impish humour, and heard his husky laugh. Her smile widened into something so beautiful that he caught his breath. 'People might get the wrong idea,' she said with mock-solemnity.

'Indeed?'

'Indeed,' she concurred with a bewitching smile. 'I think we should limit it to special occasions.'

'Such as?'

She fastened her seatbelt, then fired the engine. 'Oh, I'm sure I'll think of something.' With a devilish grin, she engaged the gear, then eased the car out of its parking bay. '*Ciao, caro*.'

She felt deliciously wicked as she cleared the exit and slid into the flow of traffic. An exultant laugh emerged from her throat.

Anyone could be forgiven for thinking she was a mistress having an affair with a passionate lover. And she was. Except that the lover was her husband, and there was nothing illicit or furtive about their relationship.

Only mutual love and a shared bond that would last a lifetime.

* * * * *

DESERT MISTRESS

HELEN BIANCHIN

CHAPTER ONE

KRISTI PUT THE finishing touches to her make-up, then stood back from the mirror to scrutinise her reflected image. An image she had deliberately orchestrated to attract one man's attention. That it would undoubtedly gain the interest of many men was immaterial.

The dress she'd chosen was fashioned in indigo raw silk; its deceptively simple cut emphasised her generously moulded breasts and narrow waist, and provided a tantalising glimpse of silk-clad thigh. Elegant high-heeled shoes completed the outfit.

Dark auburn hair fell to her shoulders in a cascade of natural curls, and cosmetic artistry highlighted wide-spaced, topaz-flecked hazel eyes, accented a delicate facial bone structure and defined a sensuously curved mouth. Jewellery was kept to a minimum—a slim-line gold watch, bracelet and earstuds.

Satisfied, Kristi caught up her evening coat, collected her purse and exited the hotel suite.

Downstairs the doorman hailed her a taxi with one imperious sweep of his hand, and once seated she gave the driver a Knightsbridge address, then sank back in contemplative silence as the vehicle eased into the flow of traffic.

The decision to travel to London had been her own, despite advice from government officials in both Australia and England that there was little to be gained in the shift of location. '*Wait*,' she'd been cautioned, 'and allow them to do their job.'

Except she'd become tired of waiting, tired of hearing different voices intoning the same words endlessly day after day. She wanted action. Action that Sheikh Shalef bin Youssef Al-Sayed might be able to generate, given that his assistance with delicate negotiations in a similar situation more than a year ago had resulted in the successful release of a hostage.

The slim hope that she might be able to persuade him to use his influence to set her brother free had been sufficient for her to book the next available flight to London and arrange accommodation.

Yet in the two weeks since her arrival Kristi's telephone calls had been politely fielded, her faxes ignored. Even baldly turning up at his suite of offices had met with failure. The man was virtually inaccessible, his privacy guarded from unwanted intrusion.

Kristi's long-standing friendship with Georgina Harrington, the daughter of a foreign diplomat, with whom she'd attended boarding-school, provided the opportunity to meet the Sheikh on a social level. There could be no doubt that without Sir Alexander Harrington's help she would never have gained an invitation to tonight's soirée.

The decision to replace Georgina with Kristi as Sir

Alexander's partner had been instigated by a telephone call to the Sheikh's secretary, and had been closely followed by a fax notifying him that Georgina had fallen prey to a virulent virus and would not be able to attend. It had gone on to ask if there would be any objection to Kristi Dalton, aged twenty-seven, a friend of long-standing, taking Georgina's place. Details for security purposes were supplied. Acknowledgement together with an acceptance had been faxed through the following day.

The taxi cruised through the streets, the glisten of recent rain sparkling beneath the headlights. London in winter was vastly different from the Southern hemispheric temperatures of Australia, and for a moment she thought longingly of bright sunshine, blue skies and the sandy beaches gracing Queensland's tropical coast.

It didn't take long to reach Sir Alexander's elegant, three-storeyed apartment, and within minutes of paying off the taxi she was drawn into the lounge and handed a glass containing an innocuous mix of lime, lemonade and bitters.

'Ravishing, darling,' Georgina accorded with genuine admiration for Kristi's appearance—a compliment which was endorsed by Sir Alexander.

'Thank you,' Kristi acknowledged with a slightly abstracted smile.

So much rested on the next few hours. In her mind she had rehearsed precisely how she would act, what she would say, until the imagery almost assumed reality. There could be no room for failure.

'I've instructed Ralph to have the car out front at

five-thirty,' Sir Alexander informed her. 'When you have finished your drink, my dear, we will leave.'

Kristi felt the knot of tension tighten in her stomach, and she attempted to disguise her apprehension as Georgina gave her a swift hug.

'Good luck. I'll ring you tomorrow and we'll get together for lunch.'

Sir Alexander's car was an aged Rolls, the man behind the wheel a valued servant who had been with the Harrington family for so many years that employer and employee had given up trying to remember the number.

'The traffic is light, sir,' Ralph intoned as he eased the large vehicle forward. 'I estimate we will reach the Sheikh's Berkshire manor in an hour.'

It took precisely three minutes less, Kristi noted as they slowed to a halt before a massive set of wrought-iron gates flanked by two security guards.

Ralph supplied their invitation and sufficient proof of identity, then, as the gates swung open, he eased the Rolls towards the main entrance where they were greeted by yet another guard.

'Miss Dalton. Sir Harrington. Good evening.'

To the inexperienced eye he appeared to be one of the hired help. Given the evening's occasion, there was a valid reason for the mobile phone held in one hand. Yet the compilation of information that Kristi had accumulated about his employer left her in little doubt that there was a regulation shoulder-holster beneath his suit jacket, his expertise in the field of martial arts and marksmanship a foregone conclusion.

A butler stood inside the heavily panelled front door,

and Kristi relinquished her coat to him before being led at Sir Alexander's side by a delegated hostess to join fellow guests in a room that could only have been described as sumptuous.

Gilt-framed mirrors and original works of art graced silk-covered walls, and it would have been sacrilege to suggest that the furniture was other than French antique. Multi-faceted prisms of light were reflected from three exquisite crystal chandeliers.

'I'll have one of the waiters bring you something to drink. If you'll excuse me?'

An elaborate buffet was presented for personal selection, and there were several uniformed waitresses circling the room, carrying trays laden with gourmet hors d'oeuvres.

Muted background music was barely distinguishable beneath the sound of chattering voices, and Kristi's smile was polite as Sir Alexander performed an introduction to the wife of an English earl who had recently presented her husband with a long-awaited son.

Kristi scanned the room idly, observing fellow guests with fleeting interest. Black dinner suit, crisp white cotton shirt and black bow-tie were *de rigueur* for the men, and her experienced eye detected a number of women wearing designer gowns whose hair and make-up bore evidence of professional artistry.

Her gaze slid to a halt, arrested by a man whose imposing height and stature set him apart from everyone else in the room.

Sheikh Shalef bin Youssef Al-Sayed.

Newspaper photographs and coloured prints in the

pages of glossy magazines didn't do him justice, for in the flesh he exuded an animal sense of power—a physical magnetism that was riveting.

An assemblage of finely honed muscle accented a broad bone structure, and his facial features bore the sculpted prominence of inherited genes. Dark, well-groomed hair and olive skin proclaimed the stamp of his paternal lineage.

Information regarding his background gleaned from press releases depicted him as the son of an Arabian prince and an English mother—a woman who, it was said, had agreed to an Islamic wedding ceremony which had never been formalised outside Saudi Arabia, and after a brief sojourn in her husband's palace had fled back to England where she'd steadfastly refused, despite giving birth to a much coveted son, to return to a country where women were subservient to men and took second place to an existing wife.

Yet the love affair between the Prince and his English wife had continued to flourish during his many visits to London, until her untimely death, whereupon the ten-year-old Shalef had been removed from England by his father and introduced to his Arabian heritage.

Now in his late thirties, Shalef bin Youssef Al-Sayed had won himself international respect among his peers for his entrepreneurial skills, and in the years since his father's demise his name had become synonymous with immense wealth.

A man no sensible person would want as an enemy, Kristi perceived wryly. Attired in a a superbly cut evening suit, there was an elemental ruthlessness beneath his sophisticated façade.

As if some acute sense alerted him to her scrutiny, he lifted his head, and for a few timeless seconds his eyes locked with hers.

The room and its occupants seemed to fade to the periphery of her vision as she suffered his raking appraisal, and she was unable to control the slow heat coursing through her veins. Intense awareness vibrated from every nerve cell, lifting the fine body hairs on the surface of her skin.

No man of her acquaintance had made her feel so acutely vulnerable, and she found the sensation disconcerting. Had it been any other man, she would have displayed no interest and openly challenged his veiled evaluation. With Shalef bin Youssef Al-Sayed she couldn't allow herself the luxury of doing so.

For one split second she glimpsed lurking cynicism in his expression, then his attention was diverted by a man who greeted him with the earnest deference of the emotionally insecure.

The study of body language had been an integral part of her training as a photographer, inasmuch as she'd consciously chosen to emphasise the positive rather than the negative in the posed, still shots that had provided her bread and butter in the early days of her career in her parents' Double Bay photographic studio.

Kristi's gaze lingered, her interest entirely professional. Or so she told herself as she observed the slant of Shalef bin Youssef Al-Sayed's head, the movement of his sensually moulded mouth as he engaged in po-

lite conversation, the piercing directness of his gaze.
To the unwary he appeared totally relaxed, yet there
was tensile steel apparent in his stance, a silent strength
that was entirely primitive. And infinitely dangerous.

A feather of fear pricked the base of her neck and
slithered slowly down the length of her spine. As an
enemy he would be lethal.

'Kristi.'

She turned at the sound of her name and gave Sir
Alexander a warm smile.

'Allow me to introduce Annabel and Lance Shrews-
bury.' His voice was so incredibly polite that Kristi's
eyes held momentary mischief before it was quickly
masked. 'Kristi Dalton, a valued friend from Australia.'

'*Australia*!' Annabel exclaimed in a voice that diminished the country to a position of geographical obscurity. 'I'm fascinated. Do you live on a farm out there?'

'Sydney,' Kristi enlightened her politely. 'A city with
a population in excess of five million.' She shouldn't
have resorted to wry humour, she knew, but she couldn't
help adding, 'The large farms are called stations, each
comprising millions of acres.'

The woman's eyes widened slightly. 'Good heavens. *Millions*?'

'Indeed,' Kristi responded solemnly. 'A plane or
helicopter is used to check boundary fences and monitor stock.'

Annabel suppressed a faint shudder. 'All that red
dirt, the heat, and the snakes. My dear, I couldn't live
there.' Red-tipped fingers fluttered in an aimless gesture, matching in colour the red-glossed mouth, and

in perfection the expensive orthodontic work, and the considerable skill of cosmetic surgery.

Thirty, going on forty-five, married to a wealthy member of the aristocracy, and born to shop, Kristi summarised, endeavouring not to be uncharitable.

'Sir Alexander.'

Awareness arrowed through her body at the sound of that smooth, well-educated drawl, and she turned slowly to greet their host.

His shirt was of the finest cotton, his dinner suit immaculately tailored to fit his broad frame, and this close she could sense the clean smell of soap mingling with the exclusive tones of his cologne.

Unbidden, her eyes were drawn to his mouth, and she briefly examined its curve and texture, stifling the involuntary query as to what it would be like to have that mouth possess her own. Heaven and hell, a silent voice taunted, dependent on his mood. There was a hint of cruelty apparent, a ruthlessness that both threatened and enticed. A man who held an undeniable attraction for women, she perceived, yet willing to be tamed by very few.

It was almost as if he was able to read her thoughts, for she glimpsed musing mockery in those slate-grey eyes—a colour that was in direct defiance of nature's genetics, and the only visible feature that gave evidence of his maternal ancestry.

'Miss Dalton.'

'Sheikh bin Al-Sayed,' Kristi acknowledged formally, aware that his gaze rested fractionally long on her hair before lowering to conduct a leisurely appraisal of her features.

It was crazy to feel intensely conscious of every single breath, every beat of her pulse. Silent anger lent her eyes a fiery sparkle, and it took considerable effort to mask it. An effort made all the more difficult as she glimpsed his amusement before he turned his attention to Sir Alexander.

'Georgina is unwell, I understand?'

'She asks me to convey her apologies,' Sir Alexander offered. 'She is most disappointed not to be able to attend this evening.'

Shalef bin Youssef Al-Sayed inclined his head. 'It is to be hoped she recovers soon.' He moved forward to speak to a woman who showed no reticence in greeting him with obvious affection.

'Would you care for another drink?'

Kristi felt as if she'd been running a marathon, and she forced herself to breathe evenly as everything in the room slid into focus. The unobtrusive presence of the waiter was a welcome distraction, and she placed her empty glass on the tray. 'Mineral water, no ice.' She didn't need the complication of a mind dulled by the effects of alcohol.

'Would you like me to get you something to eat, my dear?' Sir Alexander queried. 'Several of the guests seem to be converging on the buffet.'

Kristi summoned a warm smile as she linked her hand through his arm. 'Shall we join them? I'm feeling quite hungry.' It was a downright lie, but Sir Alexander wasn't to know that.

There was so much to choose from, she decided minutes later: hot and cold dishes, salads, hot vegetables, delicate slices of smoked salmon, seafood, chicken, turkey, roast lamb, slender cuts of beef. The selection of desserts would have put any of the finest London restaurants to shame, and the delicate ice sculptures were a visual confirmation of the chef's artistic skill.

Kristi took two slices of smoked salmon, added a small serving of three different salads, a scoop of caviare, then drifted to one side of the room.

How many guests were present tonight? she pondered idly. Fifty, possibly more? It was impossible to attempt a counting of heads, so she didn't even try.

Sir Alexander appeared to have been trapped by a society matron who seemed intent on discussing something of great importance, given the intensity of her expression.

'All alone, *chérie*? Such a crime.'

The accent was unmistakably French, and she moved slightly to allow her view to encompass the tall frame of a man whose smiling features bore a tinge of practised mockery.

'You will permit me to share a few minutes with you as we eat?'

She effected a faint shrug. 'Why not? We're fellow guests.'

'You are someone I would like to get to know—very well.' The pause was calculated, the delicate emphasis unmistakable.

Kristi's French was flawless, thanks to a degree in Italian and French, her knowledge and accent honed by a year spent in each country. 'I am selective when it comes to choosing a friend—or a lover, *monsieur*.' Her smile was singularly sweet. 'It is, perhaps, unfortunate that I do not intend to remain in London long enough to devote time to acquiring one or the other.'

'I travel extensively. We could easily meet.'

His persistence amused her. 'I think not.'

'You do not know who I am?'

'That is impossible, as we have yet to be introduced,' she managed lightly. Perhaps she presented a challenge.

'*Enchanté, chérie.*' His eyes gleamed darkly as he reached for her hand and raised it to his lips. 'Jean-Claude Longchamp d'Elseve.' He paused, head tilted slightly as he waited for an expected reaction. When she failed to comply, his mouth assumed a quizzical slant. 'I cannot believe you lack the knowledge or the intelligence to be aware of the importance my family hold in France.'

'Really?'

He was an amusing diversion, and he was sufficiently astute to appreciate it. 'I am quite serious.'

'So am I, Jean-Claude,' she declared solemnly.

'You make no attempt to acquaint me with your name. Does this mean I am to be rejected?' The musing gleam in his eyes belied the wounded tone.

'Do you not handle rejection well?'

His mouth parted in subdued laughter. 'I am so rarely in such a position, it is something of a novelty.'

'I'm relieved. I would hate to provide you with an emotional scar.'

He still held her hand, and his thumb traced a light

pattern over the veins of her wrist. 'Perhaps we could begin again. Will you have dinner with me?'

'The answer is still the same.'

'It will be relatively easy for me to discover where you are staying.'

'Please don't,' Kristi advised seriously.

'Why not?' His shrug was eloquent. 'Am I such objectionable company?'

She pulled her hand free. 'Not at all.' She cast him a slight smile. 'I simply have a tight business schedule and a full social calendar.'

The edge of his mouth curved in pensive humour. 'You mean to leave me to another woman's mercy?'

In different circumstances he might have proved to be an amusing companion. 'I'm sure you can cope.'

His eyes gleamed with hidden warmth. 'Perhaps. Although I may choose not to.'

'Your prerogative,' she accorded lightly. 'If you'll excuse me? I should rejoin Sir Alexander.'

Jean-Claude inclined his head and offered a teasing smile. *'Au revoir, chérie.'*

Her food had remained almost untouched, and she handed the plate to a passing waitress, her appetite gone.

Sir Alexander wasn't difficult to find, although he appeared deep in conversation with a distinguished-looking guest and she was loath to interrupt them.

'Champagne?'

Kristi cast the waitress and the tray she carried a fleeting glance. Perhaps she *should* have a glass to diffuse her nervous tension. Even as the thought occurred, she dismissed it. Coffee, strong black and sweet was

what she needed, and she voiced the request, then made
her way to the end of the buffet table where a uniformed
maid was offering a variety of hot beverages.

Declining milk, she moved to one side and sipped
the potent brew. The blend was probably excellent, but
she hardly noticed as she steeled herself to instigate a
planned action.

Seconds later her cup lay on the carpet, and the
scalding liquid seared her midriff. The pain was intense—far more so than she'd anticipated.

'Oh, my dear, how unfortunate. Are you all right?'
The voiced concern brought attention, and within minutes she was being led from the room by the hostess
who had greeted them on arrival.

'We keep the first-aid equipment in a bathroom next
to the kitchen.' The hostess's voice was calm as she
drew Kristi down a wide hallway and into a room that
was clinically functional. 'If you'll remove your dress
I'll apply a cold compress to cool the skin.'

Kristi complied, adding a sodden half-slip to the
heap of ruined silk, then stood silently as the hostess
efficiently dealt with the burn, applied salve, then covered the area with a sterile dressing.

'I'll organise a robe and have someone take care of
your dress.'

Minutes later Kristi willed the hostess a speedy return, for despite central heating the room was cool, and
a lacy bra and matching wispy bikini briefs were hardly
adequate covering.

A frown creased her forehead, and she unconsciously
gnawed at her lower lip, uneasy now that she had im-

plemented her plan. There was a very slim chance that Sheikh bin Al-Sayed would check on her himself. Yet she was a guest in his home, and courtesy alone should ensure that he enquired as to her welfare—surely?

Her scalded flesh stung abominably, despite the hostess's ministrations. A wide, raised welt of red skin encompassed much of her midriff and tapered off in the region of her stomach. Even she had been surprised that one cup of hot liquid was capable of covering such an area.

A sound alerted Kristi's attention an instant before the door swung inwards. Her eyes widened measurably as Shalef bin Youssef Al-Sayed stood momentarily in its aperture.

He held a white towelling robe, his features schooled into a fathomless mask, and she shivered, unable to control the slither of apprehension as he moved into the room and closed the door.

Its soft clunking sound was somehow significant, and her hands moved instinctively to cover her breasts.

'I suggest you put this on. It would be unfortunate to compound your accident with a chill.'

The room suddenly seemed much smaller, his height and breadth narrowing its confines to a degree where she felt stifled and painfully aware of the scarcity of her attire.

Reaching forward, she took the robe and quickly pushed her arms into the sleeves, then firmly belted the ties, only to wince and ease the knot. 'Thank you.'

'Rochelle assures me the burn, while undoubtedly painful, is not serious enough to warrant professional medical attention. Your gown is silk and may not fare well when cleaned. Replace it and send me the bill.'

'That won't be necessary,' Kristi said stiffly.

'I insist.' His gaze was startlingly direct, and difficult for her to hold.

'It was a simple accident, and the responsibility is entirely mine,' she declared, hating her body's reaction to his presence. It had been bad enough in a room full of people. Alone with him, it was much worse.

His eyes narrowed. 'You decline the replacement of an expensive dress?'

'I don't seek an argument with you.'

With easy economy of movement he slid one hand into a trouser pocket—an action which parted the superbly tailored dinner jacket and displayed an expanse of snowy white cotton shirt, beneath which it was all too easy to imagine a taut midriff and steel-muscled chest liberally sprinkled with dark, springy hair.

'What precisely is it that you do seek, Miss Dalton?' The words were a quizzical drawl laced with cynicism.

There was an implication, thinly veiled, that succeeded in tightening the muscles supporting her spine. It also lifted her chin and brought a brightness to her eyes.

His smile was totally lacking in humour. 'All evening I have been intrigued by the method you would choose to attract my attention.' His mouth assumed a mocking slant. 'No scenario I envisaged included a self-infliction of injury.'

CHAPTER TWO

KRISTI FELT THE color drain from her face. 'How dare you suggest—?'

'Save your breath, Miss Dalton. An investigation fell into place immediately after your second phone call to my office,' Shalef bin Youssef Al-Sayed informed her with deadly softness. His gaze never left her features as he listed the schools she'd attended, her educational achievements, her parents' names and the cause of their accidental death, her address, occupation, and a concise compilation of her inherited assets. 'Your visit to London was precipitated by a desire to accelerate the release of your brother, Shane, who is currently being held hostage in a remote mountain area,' he concluded in the same silky tones.

Anger surged through her veins, firing a helpless fury. 'You *knew* why I was trying to contact you, yet you denied me the courtesy of accepting one of my calls?'

'There seemed little point. I cannot help you, Miss Dalton.'

The words held a finality that Kristi refused to accept. 'Shane was unfortunate to be in the wrong place at the wrong time—'

'Your brother is a professional news photographer who ignored advice and flouted legal sanction in order to enter a forbidden area,' Shalef bin Youssef Al-Sayed declared hardly. 'He was kidnapped by an opposing faction and taken beyond reach of local authorities, who would surely have instigated his arrest and incarcerated him in prison.'

'You consider his fate is better with a band of political dissidents?'

His mouth curved into a mere facsimile of a smile. 'That is debatable, Miss Dalton.'

Concern widened her eyes and robbed her features of their colour. The image of her brother being held captive kept her awake nights; then, when she did manage to sleep, her mind was invaded by nightmares. 'I implore you—'

'You beg very prettily,' Shalef bin Youssef Al-Sayed taunted mercilessly, and in that moment she truly hated him. 'However, I suggest you direct all your enquiries through the appropriate channels. Such negotiations take time and require the utmost delicacy. And patience,' he added with slight emphasis. 'On the part of the hostage's family.'

'You could help get him out,' she declared in impassioned entreaty.

His gaze speared through her body and lanced her very soul, freezing her into speechlessness. There was scarcely a sound in the room, only the whisper of her breathing and she couldn't have looked away from him if she'd tried.

'We are close to the twenty-first century, Miss Dalton,' he drawled. 'You did not imagine I would don a *thobe* and *gutra*, mount an Arab steed and ride into the desert on a rescue mission with men following on horseback, taking water and food from conveniently placed oases along the way?'

Kristi ignored his sardonic cynicism, although it cost her considerable effort not to launch a verbal attack. 'I have a sizeable trust fund which is easily accessed,' she assured him with determined resolve, grateful in this instance for inherited wealth. 'Sufficient to cover the cost of hiring Jeeps, men, a helicopter if necessary.'

'No.'

The single negation sparked a feeling of desperation. She held one ace up her sleeve, but this wasn't the moment to play it. 'You refuse to help me?'

'Go home, Miss Dalton.' His expression was harsh, and his voice sounded as cold as if it had come direct from the North Pole. 'Go back to Australia and let the governments sort out the unfortunate incident.'

She wanted to hit him, to lash out physically and berate him for acting like an unfeeling monster.

He knew, and for one fraction of a second his eyes flared, almost as if in anticipation of her action—and the certain knowledge of how he would deal with it. Then the moment was gone, and it had been so swift, so fleeting that she wondered if it hadn't been a figment of her imagination.

'You will have to excuse me. I have a party to host,'

he imparted with smooth detachment. 'Rochelle will bring you something suitable to wear. Should you wish to return to your hotel, it will be arranged for a driver to transport you there. Otherwise, I can only suggest that you attempt to enjoy the rest of the evening.'

'Please.' Her voice broke with emotional intensity.

His eyes flayed every layer of protective clothing, burning skin, tissue, seeming to spear through to her very soul. With deliberate slowness he appraised her slender figure, resting over-long on the curve of her breasts, the apex between her thighs, before sweeping up to settle on the soft fullness of her mouth. 'There is nothing you can offer me as a suitable enticement.'

Anger brightened her eyes, and pride kept her head high. 'You insult my intelligence, Shalef bin Youssef Al-Sayed. I was appealing for your compassion. Sex was never a consideration.'

'You are a woman, Miss Dalton. Sex is always a consideration.'

A soft tinge of pink coloured her cheeks as she strove to keep a rein on her temper. She drew a deep, ragged breath, then released it slowly. 'Not even for my brother would I use my body as a bartering tool.'

His eyes narrowed with cynical amusement. 'No?'

She was sorely tempted to yell at him, but that would only have fuelled his amusement. 'No.' The word was quietly voiced and carried far more impact than if she'd resorted to angry vehemence.

He turned towards the door, and the blood seemed to roar in her ears, then she felt it slowly drain, leaving her disoriented and dangerously light-headed for an instant before she managed to gather some measure of control.

'What would it take for you to make a personal appeal to Mehmet Hassan on my behalf?' The words were singularly distinct, each spoken quietly, but they caused Shalef bin Youssef Al-Sayed to pause, then turn slowly to face her.

His features were assembled into an inscrutable mask, and his eyes held a wariness that was chilling.

'Who precisely is Mehmet Hassan?' The voice was dangerously quiet, the silky tones deceptive, for she sensed a finely honed anger beneath their surface.

She felt trapped by the intentness of those incredible eyes, much like a rabbit caught in the headlights of a car, and she took a deep, shuddering breath, then released it slowly. 'You attended the same school and established a friendship which exists to this day, despite Mehmet Hassan's little-known link with political dissident leaders.'

Dark lashes lowered, successfully hooding his gaze. 'I know a great many people, Miss Dalton,' he drawled, 'some of whom I number as friends.'

She had his attention. She dared not lose it.

'You travel to Riyadh several times a year on business, occasionally extending your stay to venture into the desert with a hunting party to escape from the rigours of the international corporate world. You never go alone, and it has been whispered that Mehmet Hassan has been your guest on a number of occasions.'

He was silent for what seemed to be several minutes but could only have been seconds. 'Whispers, like grains of sand, are swept far by the desert winds and retain no substance.'

'You deny your friendship with Mehmet Hassan?'

His expression hardened, his eyes resembling obsidian. 'What is the purpose of this question?'

Steady, an inner voice cautioned. 'I want you to take me with you to Riyadh.'

'Entry into Saudi Arabia requires a sponsor.'

'Something you could arrange without any effort.'

'If I was so inclined.'

'I suggest you *are* inclined,' Kristi said carefully.

Shalef bin Youssef Al-Sayed's appraisal was all-encompassing as it slowly raked her slim frame. 'You would dare to threaten me?' he queried with dangerous softness, and she shivered inwardly at the ominous, almost lethal quality apparent in his stance.

'I imagine the media would be intensely interested to learn of the link between Sheikh Shalef bin Youssef Al-Sayed and Mehmet Hassan,' she opined quietly. 'Questions would undoubtedly be raised, public opinion swayed, and at the very least it would cause you embarrassment.'

'There is a very high price to pay for attempted blackmail, Miss Dalton.'

She pulled the figurative ace and played it. 'I am applying the rudiments of successful business practice. A favour in exchange for information withheld. My terms, Sheikh bin Al-Sayed, are unrestricted entry into Riyadh under your sponsorship. For my own protection, it is necessary for me to be a guest in your home. By whichever means you choose you will make contact with Mehmet Hassan and request his help in negotiating for my brother's release. In return, I will meet whatever expenses are incurred.' Her eyes never wavered from his. 'And pledge my silence.'

'I could disavow any knowledge of this man you call Mehmet Hassan.'

'I would know you lie.'

If he could have killed her, he would have done so. It was there in his eyes, the flexing of a taut muscle at the edge of his cheek. 'What you ask is impossible.'

A faint smile lifted the corner of her mouth. 'Difficult, but not impossible.'

The sound of a discreet knock at the door, and seconds later Rochelle entered the room with a swathe of black draped over her arm.

'Perhaps we can arrange to further this discussion at a more opportune time?' Kristi offered with contrived politeness. 'It would be impolite to neglect your guests for much longer.'

Shalef bin Youssef Al-Sayed inclined his head. 'Indeed. Shall we say dinner tomorrow evening? I will send a car to your hotel at six.'

A tiny thrill of exhilaration spiralled through her body. 'Thank you.'

His eyes were hooded and his smile was barely evident. 'I shall leave you with Rochelle,' he declared formally, then, with a dismissing gesture, he moved into the passageway and closed the door behind him.

'I think these should be adequate,' Rochelle indicated as she held out the evening trousers and an elegant beaded top.

They were superb, the style emphasising Kristi's slender frame and highlighting the delicate fragility of her features.

'Do you feel ready to rejoin the party? Sir Alexander Harrington has expressed anxiety as to your welfare.'

'Thank you.'

It really was a splendid gathering, Kristi acknowledged silently some time later as she sipped an innocuous fruit punch. She had attended many social events in the past ten years in numerous capital cities around the world, with guests almost as impressive as these, in prestigious homes that were equally opulent as this one. Yet none had proved to be quite as nerve-racking.

Shalef bin Youssef Al-Sayed was not a man to suffer fools gladly. And deep inside she couldn't discount the fact that she was indeed being foolish in attempting to best him. Twice in the past hour she had allowed her gaze to scan the room casually, unconsciously seeking the autocratic features of her host among the many guests.

Even when relaxed he had an inherent ruthlessness that she found vaguely disturbing. Yet familial loyalty overrode the need for rational thought, and she dampened down a feeling of apprehension at the prospect of sharing dinner with him the following evening.

A strange prickling sensation began at the back of her neck, and some inner force made her seek its source, her gaze seeming to home in on the man who silently commanded her attention.

Dark eyes seared her own, and the breath caught in her throat for a few long seconds as she suffered his silent annihilation, then she raised one eyebrow and slanted him a polite smile before deliberately turning towards Sir Alexander.

'Would you like to leave, my dear?'

Kristi offered him a bemused look, and glimpsed his concern. 'It *is* getting late,' she agreed, moving to his side as they began circling the room to where their host stood listening to an earnest-looking couple conducting what appeared to be an in-depth conversation.

'Sir Alexander, Miss Dalton.' The voice was pleasant, the tone polite.

'It has been a most enjoyable evening,' Sir Alexander said cordially, while Kristi opted to remain silent.

'It is to be hoped the effects of your accident will be minimal, Miss Dalton,' Shalef drawled, and she responded with marked civility,

'Thank you, Sheikh bin Al-Sayed, for the borrowed clothes. I shall have them cleaned and returned to you.'

He merely inclined his head in acknowledgement, and Kristi found herself mentally counting each step that led from the lounge.

As they reached the foyer, instruction was given for the Rolls to be brought around. Within minutes they were both seated in the rear and Ralph began easing the vehicle down the long, curving driveway.

'I trust you were successful, my dear?'

Kristi turned towards Sir Alexander with a faint smile. 'To a degree, although he was aware of the deliberate orchestration. We're to dine together tomorrow evening.'

'Be careful,' he bade her seriously. 'Shalef bin

Youssef Al-Sayed is not someone with whom I would choose to cross words.'

A chill finger feathered its way down her spine. A warning? 'Shane's welfare is too important for me to back down now.'

A hand covered hers briefly in conciliation. 'I understand. However, as a precaution, I would suggest you keep me abreast of any developments. I feel a certain degree of responsibility.'

'Of course.'

It was after midnight when Ralph slid the Rolls to a halt outside the main entrance to her hotel, and an hour later she lay gazing sightlessly at the darkened ceiling, unable to sleep. There was still a slight rush of adrenalin firing her brain, a feeling of victory mixed with anxiety that prevented the ability to relax. Would Shalef bin Youssef Al-Sayed present a very clever argument in opposition to her bid to have him take her to Riyadh? Call her bluff regarding her threat to inform the media of his friendship with Mehmet Hassan? She had seventeen hours to wait before she found out.

Kristi stepped out of the lift at precisely five minutes to six and made her way to the foyer. It was raining heavily outside, the sky almost black, and the wind howled along the space between tall buildings and up narrow alleyways with a ferocity of sound that found its way inside each time the main entrance doors swung open.

An omen? It wasn't a night one would have chosen to venture out in, not if a modicum of common sense was involved. The occasional blast of cold air penetrated the warmth of the central heating like icy fingers reaching in to pluck out the unwary.

Kristi drew the edges of her coat together, adjusted the long woollen scarf, then plunged her hands into her capacious pockets.

Where would they dine? There was an excellent restaurant in the hotel. She would feel infinitely safer if they remained in familiar surroundings.

She watched as a black Bentley swept in beneath the portico. The driver emerged, spoke briefly to the attendant, then strode indoors to receive the concierge's attention, who, after listening intently, gave an indicative nod in Kristi's direction.

Intrigued, she waited for him to reach her.

'Miss Dalton?' He produced ID and waited patiently while she scrutinised it. 'Sheikh bin Al-Sayed has instructed me to drive you to his home in Berkshire.'

Her stomach performed a backward flip, then settled with an uneasy fluttering of nerves. *His* territory, when she'd hoped for the relative safety of a restaurant in which to conduct negotiations.

The success of her ploy rested on one single fact: information that was known to only a privileged few. Her source had extracted a vow of secrecy—a promise she intended to honour despite any threat Shalef bin Youssef Al-Sayed could throw at her.

The large vehicle escaped the city's outskirts, gathered speed, its passage becoming much too swift for Kristi's peace of mind.

It was stupid to feel so nervous, she rationalised as the Bentley slid between the heavy wrought-iron gates and progressed up the curved drive. Insane to feel afraid when the house was staffed with a complement of servants. Yet she was consumed with a measure of both when the door opened and Rochelle ushered her inside.

'May I take your coat?' With it folded across one arm, she indicated a door to her right. 'Come through to the lounge.'

The room was measurably smaller than the large, formal lounge used for last night's party, Kristi observed as she followed Rochelle's gesture and sank down into one of the several deep-seated sofas.

'Can I get you something to drink? Wine? Orange juice? Tea or coffee?'

Hot, fragrant tea sounded wonderful, and she said as much, accepting the steaming cup minutes later.

'If you'll excuse me?' Rochelle queried. 'Sheikh bin Al-Sayed will join you shortly.'

Was it a deliberate tactic on his part to keep her waiting? In all probability, Kristi conceded as she sipped the excellent brew.

He had a reputation as a powerful strategist, a man who hired and fired without hesitation in his quest for dedication and commitment from his employees. The pursuit of excellence in all things, at any cost. Wasn't that the consensus of everything she'd managed to learn about him? Admires enterprise, respects equals and dismisses fools.

But what of the man behind the image? Had the contrast between two vastly different cultures caused a conflict of interest and generated a resentment that he didn't totally belong to either? Little was known of his personal life as a child, whether his mother favoured a strict British upbringing or willingly allowed him knowledge of his father's religion and customs.

If there had been any problems, it would appear that he'd dealt with and conquered them, Kristi reflected as she replaced the cup down on its saucer.

'Miss Dalton.'

She gave a start of surprise at the sound of his voice. His entry into the room had been as silent as that of a cat.

'Sheikh bin Al-Sayed,' she acknowledged with a calmness that she was far from feeling. If she'd still been holding the cup it would have rattled as it touched the saucer.

'My apologies for keeping you waiting.'

He didn't offer a reason, and she didn't feel impelled to ask for one. Her eyes were cool and distant as they met his, her features assembled into a mask of deliberate politeness.

'You've finished your tea. Would you care for some more?'

The tailored black trousers and white chambray shirt highlighted his powerful frame—attire that verged on the informal, and a direct contrast to the evening suit of last night.

It made her feel overdressed, her suit too blatant a statement with its dramatic red figure-hugging skirt and fitted jacket. Sheer black hose and black stilettos merely added emphasis.

'No. Thank you,' she added as she sank back against the cushions in a determined bid to match his detachment.

'I trust the burn no longer causes you discomfort?'

The skin was still inflamed and slightly tender, but there was no sign of blistering. 'It's fine.'

He accepted her assurance without comment. 'Dinner will be served in half an hour.'

'You do intend to feed me.' The words emerged with a tinge of mockery, and she saw one of his eyebrows slant in a gesture of cynicism.

'I clearly specified dinner.'

Kristi forced herself to conduct a silent study of his features, observing the broad, powerfully defined cheekbones and the sensual shaping of his mouth. Dark slate-grey eyes possessed an almost predatory alertness, and she couldn't help wondering if they could display any real tenderness.

A woman would have to be very special to penetrate his self-imposed armour. Did he ever let down his guard, or derive enjoyment from the simple pleasures in life? In the boardroom he was regarded as an icon. And in the bedroom? There could be little doubt that he would possess the technique to drive a woman wild, but did he ever care enough to become emotionally involved? Was he, in turn, driven mad with passion? Or did he choose to distance himself?

It was something she would never know, Kristi decided with innate honesty. Something she never *wanted* to know.

'Shall we define what arrangements need to be made?' It was a bold beginning, especially when she felt anything but bold.

One eyebrow rose in a dark curve. 'We have the evening, Miss Dalton. An initial exchange of pleasantries would not be untoward, surely?' It was a statement, politely voiced, but there was steel beneath the silk. A fact she chose to heed—in part.

'Do you usually advocate wasting time during a business meeting?' Kristi proffered civilly.

'I conduct business in my office.'

'And entertain in your home?'

'Our discussion contains a politically delicate element which would be best not overheard by fellow diners, don't you agree?' he drawled, noting the tight clasp of her fingers as she laced her hands together.

She drew a deep breath and deliberately tempered its release. 'We are alone now.'

His smile held no pretension to humour. 'I suggest you contain your impatience until after dinner.'

It took a tremendous effort to contain her anger. 'If you insist.'

He registered the set of her shoulders as she unconsciously squared them, the almost prim placing of one silk-encased ankle over the other. 'Why not enjoy a light wine? Diluted, if you choose, with soda water.'

It might help her relax. She needed to, desperately. 'Thank you. Three-quarters soda.'

Why couldn't he be older, and less masculine? Less forceful, with little evidence of a raw virility that played havoc with her nervous system? Last night he had dominated a room filled with guests and succeeded in diminishing her defences. A fact she'd put down to circumstance and acute anxiety. Yet tonight she was aware that nothing had changed.

His very presence was unnerving, and she consciously fought against his physical magnetism as she accepted the glass from his hand.

'You are a photographer,' Shalef bin Youssef Al-Sayed stated as he took a comfortable chair opposite. His movements were fluid, lithe, akin to those of a large cat. 'Did you chose to follow in your brother's footsteps?'

Conversation. That's all it is, she reminded herself as she took an appreciative sip of the spritzer. It was cool and crisp to the palate, pleasant.

'Not deliberately. Shane was the older brother I adored as a child,' Kristi explained, prey to a host of images, all of them fond. 'Consequently I was intensely interested in everything he did. Photography became his obsession. Soon it was mine,' she concluded simply.

'Initially within Australia, then to various capitals throughout the world.'

'Facts you were able to access from my dossier.'

He lifted his tumbler and took a long draught of his own drink. 'A concise journalistic account.' His eyes speared hers, dark and relentless beneath the slightly hooded lids. 'Words which can't begin to convey several of the offbeat assignments you were contracted to undertake.'

'Photographs, even video coverage, don't adequately express the horror of poverty, illness and famine in some Third World countries. The hopelessness that transcends anger, the acceptance of hunger. The utter helplessness one feels at being able to do so little. The impossibility of distancing yourself from the harsh reality of it all, aware that you're only there for as long as it takes to do your job, before driving a Jeep out to the nearest airstrip and boarding a cargo shuttle that transports you back to civilisation, where you pick up your life again and attempt to pretend that what you saw, what you experienced, was just a bad dream.'

'Until the next time.'

'Until the next time,' Kristi echoed.

He surveyed her thoughtfully for several long seconds. 'You're very good at what you do.'

She inclined her head and ventured, with a touch of mockery, 'But you can't understand why I failed to settle for freelancing and filling the society pages, in a photographic studio, as my parents did.'

'The lack of challenge?'

Oh, yes. But it had been more than that—a great deal more. The photographic studio still operated, as a mark of respect for their parents, run by a competent photographer called Annie who doubled as secretary. It was an arrangement which worked very well, for it allowed Kristi freedom to pursue international assignments.

'And a desire to become your brother's equal.'

She digested his words, momentarily intrigued by a possibility that had never occurred to her until this man had voiced it. 'You make it sound as if I wanted to compete against him,' she said slowly, 'when that was never the case.'

'Yet you have chosen dangerous locations,' he pursued, watching the play of emotions on her expressive features.

Her eyes assumed a depth and dimension that mirrored her inner feelings. 'I don't board a plane and flit off to the other side of the world every second week. Sometimes there are months in between assignments, and I spend that time working out of the studio, attending social events, taking the society shots, sharing the family-portrait circuit with Annie.' She paused momentarily. 'When I undertake an assignment I want my work to matter, to encapsulate on film precisely what is needed to bring the desired result.' The passion was clearly evident in her voice, and there was a soft tinge of pink colouring her cheeks. 'Whether that be preserving a threatened environmental area or revealing the horrors of deprivation.'

'There are restrictions imposed on women photographers?'

It was a fact which irked her unbearably.

'Unfortunately feminism and equality in the workforce haven't acquired universal recognition.'

'Have you not once considered what your fate might have been if it had been you, and not your brother, who had taken a miscalculated risk and landed in the hands of political dissidents?' Shalef bin Youssef Al-Sayed queried with dangerous softness as he finished his drink and placed the glass down on a nearby side-table.

Topaz-gold chips glowed deep in her eyes as she subjected him to the full force of a hateful glare. A hand lifted and smoothed a drifting tendril of hair behind one ear. 'Shane refused to allow me to accompany him.'

'Something for which you should be eternally grateful,' he stated hardly.

Kristi caught the slight tightening of facial muscles that transformed his features into a hard mask. Impenetrable, she observed, together with a hint of autocratic arrogance that was undoubtedly attributable to his paternal forebears, and which added an element of ruthlessness to his demeanour.

'It would appear that, although a fool, your brother is not totally stupid.'

'Don't you dare—'

She halted mid-sentence as Rochelle entered the room unannounced. 'Hilary is ready to serve dinner.'

Shalcf bin Youssef Al-Sayed nodded briefly, and Rochelle exited as soundlessly as she had appeared.

'You were saying?'

'You have no reason to insult my brother,' she asserted fiercely.

He smiled, although it didn't reach his eyes. 'Familial loyalty can sometimes appear blind.' He stood and moved towards her. 'Shall we go in to dinner?'

Kristi tried to bank down her resentment as she vacated the chair. 'I seem to have lost my appetite.'

'Perhaps you can attempt to find it.'

CHAPTER THREE

THE DINING ROOM was smaller than she'd imagined, although scarcely *small*, with its beautiful antique table and seating for eight, and a long chiffonier. Glassed cabinets housed an enviable collection of china and crystal. Expensive paintings and gilt-framed mirrors adorned the walls, and light from electric candles was reflected in an exquisite crystal chandelier. Several silver-domed covers dominated the table, with its centrepiece of exotic orchids.

Kristi slid into the chair that Shalef bin Youssef Al-Sayed held out for her, then he moved round to take a seat opposite.

A middle-aged woman with pleasant features busied herself removing covers from the heated platters, then indicated a choice of desserts and the cheeseboard, laid out atop the chiffonier.

With a cheerful smile, Hilary—it had to be Hilary, Kristi surmised—turned toward her employer. 'Shall I serve the soup?'

'Thank you, Hilary. We'll manage.'

'Ring when you require coffee.'

He removed the lid from a china tureen. 'I trust you enjoy leek and potato soup, Miss Dalton?'

'Yes.'

He took her plate and ladled out a medium portion before tending to his own. *'Bon appetit,'* he said with a tinge of mockery, and she inclined her head in silent acknowledgement.

The soup was delicious, and followed by superb beef Wellington with an assortment of vegetables.

'Wine?'

'Just a little,' Kristi agreed, motioning for him to stop when the glass was half-filled.

He ate with an economy of movement, his hands broad, with a sprinkling of dark hair, the fingers long, well formed and obviously strong. She could imagine them reining in a horse and manoeuvring the wheel of a rugged four-wheel drive. Gently drifting over the skin of a responsive woman. *Hell,* where did that come from? Her hand paused midway to her mouth, then she carefully returned the fork to rest on her plate. The pressure of the past few weeks, culminating over the last two days, had finally taken its toll. She was going insane. There seemed no other logical explanation for the passage of her thoughts.

'Can I help you to some more vegetables?'

Her vision cleared, and she swallowed in an endeavour to ease the constriction in her throat. 'No. Thank you,' she added in a voice that sounded slightly husky.

He had eaten more quickly than she, consuming twice the amount of food.

'Dessert?'

She settled for some fresh fruit, and followed it with a sliver of brie, observing his choice of apple crumble with cream. The man had a sweet tooth. Somehow it made him seem more human.

'Shall we return to the lounge for coffee?'

'Thank you,' she returned politely, watching as he dispensed with his napkin. Kristi did likewise and then stood.

He moved to the door and opened it, ushering her into the hallway.

A host of butterfly wings began to flutter inside her stomach. The past two hours had been devoted to observing the conventions. Now it was down to business. And somehow she had to convince him that she'd use the information she held against him in order to ensure that he would enlist Mehmet Hassan's help in freeing her brother.

'Make yourself comfortable,' Shalef bin Youssef Al-Sayed bade her as they entered the lounge, and she watched as he pressed an electronic button beside the wall-switch. 'Hilary will bring coffee.'

Kristi sank into the same chair she'd occupied on her arrival. 'Sheikh bin Al-Sayed.' Now that the moment had come, it was costing her more effort than she'd envisaged. 'Dinner was very pleasant,' she began. 'But now—'

'You want to discuss business,' he concluded with a touch of mockery as he took the chair opposite.

'Yes.'

He placed an elbow on each arm of the chair and steepled his fingers, assuming an enigmatic expression that she couldn't begin to fathom. 'The ball is in your court, Miss Dalton. I suggest you play it.'

Her eyes were steady, the tip of her chin tilting at a firm angle as she carefully put the metaphorical ball in motion. 'When do you plan leaving for Riyadh?'

'Next week.'

The butterfly wings increased their tempo inside her stomach. 'With your influence I imagine that allows sufficient time to have the necessary sponsorship papers processed.'

'Indeed.'

So far, so good. 'Perhaps you could let me have flight details, and any relevant information I need.'

He was silent for several seconds, and the silence seemed to grow louder with each one that passed.

'The flight details are simple, Miss Dalton. We board a commercial airline to Bahrain, then take my private jet to Riyadh.' He regarded her with an intensity that had the butterfly wings beating a frantic tattoo. 'Not so simple is the reason for your accompanying me.'

It seemed such a small detail. 'Why?'

'My father's third wife and her two daughters live in the palace, each of whom will be wildly curious as to why I have chosen to bring a woman with me.'

Surprise widened her eyes. 'You're joking. Aren't you?' she queried doubtfully.

'Since I can avail myself of any woman I choose,' he drawled hatefully, 'the fact that I have brought one with me will be viewed as having considerable significance—not only by my late father's family, but by several of my friends.' He smiled—a mere facsimile which held an element of pitiless disregard. 'Tell me, Miss Dalton, would you prefer to be accepted as the woman in my life, or a—' he paused imperceptibly '—transitory attraction?'

Hilary chose that moment to enter the room, wheeling a trolley bearing a silver coffee-pot, two cups and saucers, milk, cream and sugar, together with a plate of petit fours.

'Thank you, Hilary. The meal was superb, as usual,' Shalef bin Youssef Al-Sayed complimented her while Kristi inwardly seethed with anger. Somehow she managed to dredge up a smile and add to her host's praise. However, the instant that Hilary disappeared out the door she launched into immediate attack.

'What is wrong with presenting me to your family as a guest?' she demanded heatedly.

His eyes hardened measurably, and she felt the beginnings of unease. 'I accord Nashwa and her two daughters the respect they deserve. Whenever I visit Riyadh I observe the customs of my father's country for the duration of my stay. As sponsor, I must vouch for your good behaviour while you are in Saudi Arabia, take responsibility for your welfare, and ensure your departure when it is time for you to leave.'

Kristi lifted a hand, then let it fall in a gesture of helpless anger. Her main consideration was Shane, and the influence that Shalef bin Youssef Al-Sayed could wield with Mehmet Hassan in negotiating her brother's release.

'OK,' she agreed. 'I don't particularly like the idea of pretending to be your woman but I'll go along with it.'

He made no comment. Instead, he rose to his feet and proceeded to pour dark, aromatic coffee into the two cups. 'Milk, cream, or a liqueur?'

'Black.' She helped herself to sugar, then sipped the strong brew, watching as he did likewise. When she finished she placed her cup and saucer down on a nearby table and stood up. 'If you could arrange a taxi for me, Sheikh bin Al-Sayed, I'd like to return to my hotel.'

'Shalef,' he corrected silkily. 'As we're to be linked together, it will be thought strange if you continue to address me with such formality.' He unfolded his lengthy frame with lithe ease. 'I'll drive you into the city.'

Why did that cause an immediate knot to form in her stomach? 'A taxi would be less inconvenient.'

'To whom?'

She looked at him carefully. 'To you, of course. An hour's drive each way seems unnecessary at this time of night.'

'There are several spare bedrooms, any one of which you would be welcome to use.'

The hint of mockery brought a fiery sparkle to her eyes. 'As long as you're aware it wouldn't be yours.'

One eyebrow slanted. 'I wasn't aware I implied it might be.'

She drew in a deep breath. 'I don't find verbal games in the least amusing.'

It was impossible to detect anything from his expression. 'I'll get your coat.'

Polite civility edged her voice. 'Thank you.'

In the car she sat in silence, grateful when he activated the stereo system and Mozart provided a soothing background that successfully eliminated the need for conversation.

He drove well, with considerably more speed than his chauffeur. Or had it been his bodyguard? The miles between Berkshire and London diminished quickly, although once they reached the inner city any attempt at swift passage was hampered by computer-controlled intersections and traffic.

Kristi sighted the entrance to her hotel and prepared to alight the instant that Shalef bin Youssef Al-Sayed brought the car to a halt.

'Thank you.' Her hand paused on the door-clasp as she turned towards him. It was difficult to fathom his expression. 'I imagine you'll be in touch with the flight time?'

'I have been invited to a formal dinner on Saturday evening. I'd like you to accompany me.'

'Why?' The single query slipped out unbidden, and his eyes hardened slightly.

'In less than a week you will meet members of my late father's family. It would be preferable if we are seen to share a rapport.'

'Does it matter?'

'I consider it does. Be ready at seven.'

She felt the stirrings of resentment. 'I don't like being given an order.'

'Are you usually so argumentative?'

'Only with people who refuse to respect my right to decline an invitation,' she responded coolly.

'Are you dismissing my request?' His voice was dangerously soft, and despite the car's heating system she felt suddenly cold.

'No,' she said quietly, 'merely stating that I prefer to be asked rather than told.' She activated the door clasp and stepped from the car, hearing the refined clunk as she carefully closed the door behind her; then she turned towards the main entrance and made her way into the foyer without a backward glance.

It wasn't until she was inside her suite that she allowed herself the luxury of releasing an angry exclamation.

Sheikh Shalef bin Youssef Al-Sayed was beginning to threaten her equilibrium in more ways than one. She didn't like it, any more than she liked him. Nor did she particularly like the idea of partnering him to a formal dinner party. Except she couldn't afford to anger him.

Not yet, a tiny imp inside her taunted with mischievous intent. Not yet.

'Formal' was particularly apt, Kristi reflected with idle interest as she scanned the room's occupants. Twenty-four people sat at the table, and were served cordon bleu courses by uniformed maids and offered finest vintage wines by impeccably suited waiters. Gold-rimmed bone china vied with gleaming silver and sparkling crystal, and the floral centrepieces were a work of art.

Expensive jewellery adorned the fingers of the female guests, and there was little doubt that their gowns were designer originals.

'Dessert, Miss Dalton? There is a choice of tiramisu, strawberry shortcake, or fresh fruit.'

Although each single course had comprised a small portion, she'd lost count of the courses served and was reluctant to accept yet another. She offered the waitress a faint smile. 'No, thank you.'

'You have no need to watch your figure.'

Kristi turned towards the man seated on her left and felt the distinct pressure of his knee against her own. Without any compunction she carefully angled the tip of her slender-heeled shoe to connect with his ankle. 'I doubt Shalef would appreciate your interest,' she ventured sweetly.

'Point taken,' he acknowledged with sardonic cynicism. 'Literally.'

Her smile held no sincerity. How much longer before they could leave the table and adjourn to the lounge?

'Try some of this cheese,' Shalef suggested smoothly as he speared a small segment onto a wafer then offered it to her. His eyes were dark, their expression enigmatic, and her own widened marginally at the studied intimacy of his action.

Kristi's mouth curved slightly in response as she sampled the wafer. 'Superb,' she acknowledged. She had never doubted that he was dangerous. When he set out to charm, he was positively lethal.

'Would you like some more?'

'No. Thanks,' she added.

'So polite.'

'Don't amuse yourself at my expense,' she warned in a silky undertone.

He considered her thoughtfully. 'Is that what you think I'm doing?'

'You're playing a game for the benefit of fellow guests who are intent on displaying a discreet interest in Sheikh Shalef bin Youssef Al-Sayed's latest companion.'

'What is it you particularly object to?' he queried musingly. 'Being a subject of interest, or labelled as my latest conquest?'

Her gaze was level. 'I have little control over the former, but as the latter doesn't apply I'd prefer it if you would decline from indicating an intimacy which doesn't exist.'

'You have a vivid and distorted imagination.'

'While you, Sheikh bin Al-Sayed,' she re-sponded evenly, 'parry words with the skill of a master chess-player.'

A soft chuckle started at the back of his throat and emerged with a genuine humour that was reflected in the gleaming warmth of his eyes. 'Shalef,' he insisted quietly.

Kristi looked at him carefully. 'I imagine it is much too early to request that you take me back to the hotel?'

His mouth curved with slow indolence. 'Much too early.'

'In which case I shall attempt dazzling conversation with a fellow guest.'

'Alternatively, you could attempt to dazzle me.'

She picked up her glass and sipped the chilled water, then set it down carefully. 'Don't you tire of women who strive to capture your attention?'

'It depends on the woman,' he said mockingly. 'And

whether it's more than my attention she attempts to capture.'

The request for guests to adjourn to the lounge was timely, and Kristi rose to her feet with relief, glad of the opportunity to escape the close proximity of Shalef bin Youssef Al-Sayed.

But her freedom was short-lived as he moved to her side, and she didn't pull away when he caught her elbow in a light clasp as they made their way from the dining room.

Her senses seemed more acute, and she was conscious of his clean male smell mingling with the subtle tang of his cologne. His touch brought an awareness of sexual alchemy together with a heightened degree of sensuality that quickened her pulse and had the strangest effect on her breathing.

Such feelings were a complication she couldn't afford, and she deliberately sought to impose a measure of control.

'Shalef, how wonderful to see you again.'

Kristi heard the distinct purr in the light, feminine voice and glimpsed the perfection of scarlet-tipped fingers an instant before a model-slim, dark-haired young woman slid an arm through his.

Beauty enhanced by the skilful application of cosmetics and the clothes of a noted European couturier lent and exclusivity that was unmatched by any of the other female guests, and Kristi couldn't help the uncharitable thought that such a stunning result had probably taken the entire afternoon to achieve.

'Fayza.'

Was it her imagination or did she sense a barrier of reserve fall into place?

'Allow me to introduce Kristi Dalton. Fayza Al-Khaledi.'

The features were exquisitely composed, and her mouth curved into a smile that revealed perfectly even white teeth. But the brilliant dark eyes were as cold as an Arctic floe.

'If you'll excuse me, I'll fetch some coffee.' Kristi took longer than necessary in adding sugar and a touch of cream to the aromatic brew.

She started to show an interest in the mingling guests, assured her hostess that the coffee was fine and indulged in polite small talk. Not once did she glance towards Shalef bin Youssef Al-Sayed or the glamorous woman who had commandeered his attention.

'There was no need for you to desert me.'

She turned slightly as he rejoined her, and met his solemn gaze. 'Just as there was no need for me to compete.'

Shalef chose not to comment, and Kristi finished her coffee, refused a second cup and managed to contain her relief when he indicated that they would leave.

'You found the evening boring?'

The illuminated clock on the dashboard revealed that it was after midnight, and she sank back against the deep-cushioned seat as the large car gained the motorway and gathered speed.

'Not at all,' Kristi assured him with polite civility.

'The food was superb, and one would have to grant that the company was equally so.'

'Including the guest who indulged in a surreptitious play for your attention during the main course?'

'You noticed.'

'He has a certain reputation,' Shalef informed her drily.

'I don't need a protector.'

'In London you can rely on Sir Alexander Harrington for friendship and support. In Riyadh it will be different.'

She turned to look at him in the semi-darkness of the car, noting the harsh angles and planes of his profile. 'Are you issuing a subtle warning?'

'A suggestion that you accept the political and religious dictates of my father's country,' he corrected.

'I won't attempt to wield any Western influence or encourage the younger members of your family to challenge your will, Sheikh bin Al-Sayed,' Kristi said with a touch of mockery.

'Shalef.' His voice was silky soft, and her stomach began to knot with nerves as she focused her attention on the scene beyond the windscreen.

It had begun to snow—light flakes that settled with an eerie whiteness on tree branches and hedges.

City lights appeared in the distance, and soon they were traversing inner suburbia at a reduced speed. Streetlights gave out a regimented glow, and most of the houses were shrouded in darkness, their occupants tucked up warmly in bed.

Kristi shivered despite the car's heating. In a few

days she would board a plane in the company of a man she hardly knew, forced to place not only herself but the fate of her brother in his hands.

How long would the rescue mission take? It *had* to be successful. She couldn't, *wouldn't* contemplate failure.

The car eased to a halt outside the hotel's main entrance, and she turned towards the man behind the wheel.

'What time shall I meet you at the airport?'

He shifted in his seat and leaned an arm against the wheel. 'My chauffeur will collect you from the hotel. I will have you notified of the time.'

'Thank you.' She reached for the door-clasp and stepped out of the car. 'Goodnight.'

'Goodnight, Kristi.' His voice was a deep drawl that seemed to mock her long after she'd gained her suite and undressed for bed.

It kept her awake, then haunted her dreams as she slept.

CHAPTER FOUR

RIYADH ROSE FROM the desert like a high-tech oasis of glass, steel and concrete, with office towers, freeways, hotels, hospitals and, Shalef informed Kristi as his private jet landed and taxied down the runway, the largest airport in the world.

The subdued whine of the engines wound down to an electronic hum as the pilot wheeled the jet round towards an allotted bay. With almost simultaneous precision they slid to a halt as the hostess released the door and activated the steps for disembarkation.

Ten minutes later Kristi followed Shalef into the rear seat of a black stretch Mercedes. A man already occupied the opposite seat and Shalef effected an introduction.

'Fouad is the son of the daughter of my father's first wife,' he informed her quietly. 'He holds a managerial position with one of the family companies here.'

Kristi turned towards the man and inclined her head in silent acknowledgement. 'How many daughters are there?'

'Four. Two from my father's first wife, both of whom

are older than me, and two younger, the daughters of my father's third wife.'

'Happy families,' she quipped lightly. 'I imagine there is a variety of distant aunts and cousins?'

'Several. My father's first wife developed cancer and died five years ago.'

The two men lapsed into Arabic as the large vehicle slipped free of the terminal traffic, and Kristi transferred her attention beyond the tinted windows.

This was a land where the muezzin called the faithful to prayer five times a day, where the male was revered while the female remained subservient.

She was intrigued by a culture that viewed women as less important than their male counterparts, their role so defined and protected that it amounted to almost total discrimination.

Did the women silently crave for more freedom, both in speech and action? To dispense with the *abaaya* and the veil, and adopt westernised apparel? And, if they did, would they dare speak of it to a stranger, albeit a stranger presented to them as Shalef bin Youssef Al-Sayed's current companion?

The Mercedes began to slow, and Kristi felt the nerves in her stomach awaken as it paused beside massive gates, cleared security, then swept through to a large courtyard.

The architecture was interesting—solid walls plastered in stark white, surprisingly small windows, given the hot climate, and an impressive set of carved wooden doors overlaid with ornate, metal-pressed panels.

One of the doors swung inwards as the Mercedes

slid to a halt, and a middle-aged couple emerged to extend a greeting.

'Amani and Abdullah manage the house and staff,' Shalef informed her when he'd completed an introduction.

Indoors there was an assemblage of neatly attired staff waiting to greet their sheikh, and, although Shalef made no attempt at individual introductions, he presented her as a close friend from England.

The reception hall was the largest that Kristi had seen, with imposing marble columns and Carrara marble floors covered in part by a matched selection of exquisitely woven rugs. Tapestries adorned the walls, and expensive works of art vied with gilt-edged mirrors.

'At your request I have made ready the east suite for Miss Dalton,' Amani revealed. 'Refreshments are ready to be served in the sitting room.'

'Thank you. Shall we say half an hour?'

'I will take Miss Dalton to her room.'

Shalef inclined his head, then turned towards Kristi. 'I am sure you'll find everything to your satisfaction.'

Dismissal, she determined wryly. Yet she had expected no more. With a faint smile she turned and followed Amani towards a wide, curving staircase leading to an upper floor.

The palace was sufficiently substantial to house several families and still ensure individual privacy, she realised as she traversed a long, marble-tiled hallway.

Ornate side-tables and velvet-upholstered, gilt-framed chairs lined the walls and expensive silk rugs covered the marble floor.

'I'm sure you'll be very comfortable here, Miss Dalton. If there is anything you need, please don't hesitate to ask.'

Kristi preceded the manageress into a magnificent suite comprising sitting room, bedroom and *en suite* bathroom. The furnishings were an exotic blend of deep emerald, gold and white.

'Thank you.'

With twenty-five minutes in which to shower and change, Kristi managed it in less, choosing to use minimum make-up and leave her hair loose. Aware of a preference for women to wear clothes that covered their legs and arms, she'd packed smartly tailored, loose-fitting trousers, a variety of blouses and a few tunic-style tops.

As she added a spray of perfume to her wrists she couldn't help a wry smile, for the trousers and tunic top were a deep emerald…a perfect match for the suite's furnishings.

Would members of his family join them for refreshments? She had an intense curiosity to meet the woman who had been content to take second place to an existing wife. Had a sense of rivalry existed between the two women? And what of Shalef's mother? One could only wonder at her situation—an English rose, unversed in Islamic customs, set among the desert jewels. Yet if the Prince had displayed his son's obvious attraction for the opposite sex it was probable that Shalef's mother had been caught up in a dream that had soon dissipated in the light of reality.

Kristi emerged from her suite to find a Filipino servant waiting to escort her down to the sitting room.

It was a courtesy for which she was grateful, as the palace was vast, the rooms many, and she'd begun to wonder if she would need to embark on an adventure of seek and find.

They arrived downstairs and walked along a main corridor from which led three long hallways, linking, the servant informed her, further wings of the palace. No wonder there was such a large complement of staff!

The room Kristi was shown into was large and airy and filled with exquisite gilt-framed furniture, priceless items of gold-painted porcelain and original works of art.

Her eyes flew to the tall man who stood to one side of the window, his breadth of shoulder and stature emphasised by the silk-edged white *thobe* with Western-style collar and French cuffs. A white headscarf secured with an *agal* provided an electrifying effect, and made her all the more aware of the extent of his wealth, and his mantle of power.

'Kristi. Allow me to introduce you to Nashwa.'

She wrenched her eyes away from him and turned towards a slim, attractive woman attired in a royal blue traditional robe, whose dark hair was almost hidden by an exotic royal blue scarf beautifully embroidered in gold thread.

Kristi extended her hand in formal greeting, then followed Nashwa's action by touching her heart with the palm of her right hand.

The gesture brought forth a warm smile. 'I'm very pleased to meet you, Miss Dalton. May I call you Kristi?'

'Please.'

Nashwa's smile widened as she indicated a comfortable chair. 'Do sit down. Would you prefer coffee or something cool to drink? I can have tea served, if you wish.'

Kristi opted for coffee, then took a seat, all too aware that Shalef followed her action by choosing a chair close to her own.

'I understand you are a photographer. It must be an interesting profession.'

Kristi accepted a delicate cup and saucer from the maid, added sugar, then selected a pastry from an offered plate. 'My father founded a photographic studio, which my brother and I still operate. Shane's speciality is freelance photojournalism.' She smiled, unaware that her eyes held a tinge of warm humour which lent their hazel depths a velvety texture. 'He enjoys the challenge of venturing into far-flung territory in search of the unusual.'

'You have brought your camera with you?' Shalef enquired, his dark gaze steady, daring her to resort to any fabrication.

'It forms part of my luggage wherever I travel,' she managed evenly.

'I suggest you exercise caution whenever you use it, and request permission before you do.'

'Including the palace?'

'I would prefer it if you did not photograph any of the rooms within the palace. I have no objection to external shots, or those of the gardens.'

Security? She had no desire to flout his wishes.

She turned towards Nashwa. 'You have two daughters. I'm looking forward to meeting them.'

Nashwa's expression softened. 'Aisha and Hanan.
They are aged twenty-one and nineteen respectively.
Aisha is en-joying a sabbatical after lengthy university
studies. Soon she will leave for Switzerland to spend a
year in finishing school. Hanan is not quite so academi-
cally inclined, and after emerging from boarding-school
in England at the end of last year she too has opted to
join Aisha in Switzerland.' She proffered a warm smile.
'You will meet them both at dinner.'

Kristi sipped the coffee, finding it very pleasant if a
little too strong, and declined anything further to eat.

Shalef, she noted, drank Arabic coffee flavoured
with cardamom from a tiny handleless cup that was
so small it looked ludicrous held between his fingers.

Nashwa was an impeccable hostess, adept at maintaining a flow of conversation, and Kristi found herself
agreeing to a conducted tour of the palace itself, while
Shalef retired to the study for a few hours in order to
apprise himself of business affairs.

The palace was even larger than Kristi had imagined, with innumerable rooms set aside for the sole
purpose of formal and informal entertaining. Opulent, she decided silently as she admired the elaborate
draping. Each room was large, the colours employed
lending a cool, spacious effect that was enhanced by
ducted air-conditioning. An indoor swimming pool was
Olympian in proportion, the tiled surrounding area sufficiently wide to harbour a variety of casual cushioned
loungers and chairs. Beyond that were the Turkish baths

and beautiful paved walkways meandering through an exotic garden.

There were three wings attached to the central building, Nashwa explained—one which she and her daughters used, one designated for Shalef's occupation whenever he was in Riyadh, and the remaining one kept for visiting family and guests. Staff were housed separately.

Encompassing two levels, the internal walls enclosed a central courtyard with lush gardens, palm trees and exotic plants. Numerous columns supported wide, covered verandas which could be reached from every room on the upper floor through arched doorways.

Kristi's tour was restricted to the guest wing and the entire ground level. Not offered were Shalef's quarters or those of Nashwa and her daughters. A dual purpose, perhaps...privacy as well as security?

'You have endured a long flight. Perhaps you would like to rest for a while?'

A flight that had been fraught with a degree of apprehension about the destination and its implications. Added to which, she'd been painfully aware of Shalef's presence and the vibrant energy he'd exuded as he'd relayed information about the history of his father's country, its rulers, and the positive effects of an oil-rich nation.

The thought of solitude for an hour or two sounded ideal. She could write a promised postcard to Annie, and Sir Alexander and Georgina would also value word of her safe arrival.

'Thank you.'

Nashwa inclined her head in polite acceptance. 'Dinner will be served at eight. I will send a servant to your room at seven-thirty, just in case you fall asleep. She will escort you down to the dining room.'

They were back in the reception hall and, with a warm smile, Kristi inclined her head before turning towards the staircase.

Her suite was delightfully cool, and she quickly discarded her outer clothes, then donned a silk wrap. An antique escritoire held paper, a variety of postcards, envelopes and pens.

Twenty minutes later Kristi placed the completed cards to one side, then crossed to the bed and lay down. Half an hour, she told herself as she closed her eyes.

But she must have dozed longer than she'd meant to, for she came awake at the sound of a light double tap against the outer door.

It couldn't be seventy-thirty already! But it was, and she flew to the door, opening it to discover a servant waiting outside.

'Could you come back in twenty minutes?'

'As you wish.'

Kristi closed the door and moved quickly into the bathroom, shedding her wrap and her underclothes, as she went. The shower succeeded in removing the last vestiges of tiredness, and she let the water run cold for ten seconds before turning off the taps.

She was ready with one minute to spare, dressed in long black silk evening trousers and matching top, her make-up understated except for her eyes. Jewellery was confined to a gold pendant and matching earrings, and she'd sprayed perfume to several pulse spots. There wasn't time to do anything other than stroke a brush through her hair.

The servant was patiently waiting when she opened the door, and Kristi attempted to dispel a faint fluttering of nerves as they descended the staircase.

'Dining room' was a slight misnomer, she discovered on being directed to a semi-formal lounge with an adjoining dining room.

Shalef was an impressive figure in a royal blue *thobe* edged with silver, and the butterfly wings inside her stomach beat a faint tattoo as he crossed the room to greet her.

'I hope I haven't kept you waiting.' Her voice sounded faintly husky even to her own ears, and her eyes widened fractionally at his indulgent smile.

'Not at all.' He caught hold of her hand and lifted it to his lips, his eyes silently challenging hers as he glimpsed her inner battle to retain a measure of composure.

He was initiating a deliberate strategy, alluding to a relationship which didn't exist merely to qualify her presence here. Yet Kristi had the distinct feeling that he intended to derive a certain degree of diabolical pleasure from the exercise, and it rankled unbearably that the only time she'd be able to castigate him verbally for his actions would be when they were alone.

Her eyes flashed a silent warning as she offered him a brilliant smile: Don't play games with me.

She saw one eyebrow lift in mocking amusement,

and she had to marshal her features not to reflect the burning anger that simmered deep within her.

'Come and meet Nashwa's daughters,' Shalef bade her smoothly as he turned and led her into the centre of the room. 'Aisha.' He indicated a slim girl of average height whose dark gaze was openly friendly, then the younger girl at her side. 'Hanan.'

Both girls were beautiful, with flawless complexions and dark, liquid brown eyes. Each wore traditional dress, Aisha in gold-embroidered aqua silk, while Hanan had opted for a soft blue. Their mother looked resplendent in deep emerald.

At least she provided a contrast in black, Kristi decided as she smiled and offered the girls a greeting. 'I've been looking forward to meeting you both.' She turned slightly and included the young man standing unobtrusively a short distance from Nashwa. 'Nashwa. Fouad.'

'Mother says you're a photographer,' Aisha said politely. 'It must be a fascinating occupation.'

'Most of the time it's routine,' Kristi acknowledged with a touch of wry humour.

'I am to study fashion design when I return from Switzerland,' Hanan declared. 'Shalef has given permission for me to begin in London. If I do well, he will allow me to study in Paris.'

Nashwa stood up. 'Shall we all go in to dinner?'

Shalef took a seat at the head of the table, and indicated that Kristi should occupy a chair close to him. An honour, she assumed, that merely endorsed her place as his latest 'companion'.

The food was excellent—hot, spicy lamb served with

rice and beans, followed by a variety of sweets laden with dates and honey. There was a platter of succulent fresh fruit, and Kristi opted for some sliced melon and a few dates.

They were waited on by a number of Filipino servants, who stood inconspicuously in the background as each dish was served, then moved forward to remove plates and replace them with each subsequent course, and no sooner was a water glass empty than it was unobtrusively refilled.

'Is your photographic work confined to studio portraits?' Fouad queried politely.

Kristi set down her glass. 'Frequently, in between assignments.'

'Tell us something about these assignments. Are any of them dangerous?'

'Not really,' she answered lightly, deliberately meeting Shalef's hard gaze. 'The risk is minimal.'

Shalef's fingers toyed with the stem of his crystal goblet. 'Indeed?'

Kristi held his gaze without any difficulty at all. 'You hunt in the desert and attempt to master the falcon. Is that without risk?'

'Attempt' was perhaps not the wisest choice of word. There could be no doubt that Shalef bin Youssef Al-Sayed achieved success in everything he did, and to hint at anything less was almost an insult.

'Your concern for my safety warms my heart.'

'As does yours for me,' she responded, offering him a sweet smile.

His eyes gleamed darkly and one eyebrow slanted

in silent amusement. 'When we've had coffee I'll show you the garden.'

She forced her smile to widen slightly, while silently threatening to do mild injury to certain of his male body parts if he dared anything more than a light clasp of her hand.

At the mention of coffee the servants moved forward to clear the dessert plates from the table, and Shalef rose to his feet, indicating the conclusion of the meal.

The partaking of coffee was leisurely, the conversation pleasant, and throughout the ensuing hour Kristi was supremely conscious of the tall man who chose to sit in a chair close to her own.

For a brief moment she almost considered declining when he suggested that they stroll through the illuminated gardens, and she glimpsed the hint of steel in those dark eyes and was aware that he knew the passage of her thoughts. Then she gave him a slow smile and stood up, offering no protest when he clasped her elbow as they left the room.

The warmth of the early evening was evident without the benefit of the palace's air-conditioning, and she surreptitiously lengthened her step in an effort to move further from his side—an action that was immediately thwarted as he captured her hand in a firm clasp that threatened to tighten should she attempt to wrench it from his grasp.

'What in the name of heaven do you think you're doing?' She kept her voice quiet, but he could hardly have failed to detect her anger.

'If we act as polite strangers it will raise questions about our relationship,' Shalef said smoothly.

'We don't have a relationship!'

'For the purposes of this visit we do,' he reminded her.

She turned slightly in the pale evening light and was unable to discern much from his features. 'I'm not in awe of your wealth or of you as a man,' Kristi declared in an undertone. The first was the truth, the latter an outright fabrication.

'No?'

Her eyes acquired a fiery sparkle at the faint mockery evident in his voice. 'If I didn't need your help, I'd leave and be grateful that I never had to see you again.'

'But you do need me,' Shalef pointed out silkily. 'So we shall walk and admire the garden, and appear to be as engrossed in each other as the situation demands.'

A slight breeze riffled the palm fronds and teased the length of her hair. 'Perhaps you'd care to introduce a subject of conversation that we can both pursue?' she said.

'One that won't digress into an argument?'

'You could tell me how you coped when your father first brought you here.'

'Fill in the blanks that have not been written up in the tabloid press?'

'Alternatively, there's Riyadh itself. Islam.'

'Religion and politics are a dangerous mix,' Shalef dismissed.

'They form an important part of life. Especially in the land of the Prophet Mohammed.'

'And if I were to present you with my views what guarantee would I have that they wouldn't be written up and sold to the media?' he said drily.

She looked at him carefully, aware of the caution he felt constrained to exercise with everyone he met. A man in his position would have many social acquaintances, numerous business associates, but few friends in whose company he could totally relax. 'Is that why you retreat here several times a year?'

The gardens were extensive, with carefully tended lawns, shrubs, and an ornamental fountain strategically placed to provide a central focus. Water cascaded over three levels, and at night, beneath illumination, it was nothing less than spectacular.

No doubt for him the palace represented a welcome and familiar sanctuary, whereas she found that it contained an air of Eastern mystery that she wanted to explore. The people, the culture, their beliefs, the vast, definitive division between men and women. To read and be aware of factual reporting was not the same as experiencing it for oneself.

'This is the land of my father,' Shalef began slowly. 'A land where the power of nature can move tonnes of sand for no apparent reason other than to reassemble a shifting terrain. Man has plumbed its depths and channelled the riches, reaping enormous rewards.'

'Yet you choose not to live here.'

He smiled faintly. 'I have homes in many capital cities around the world, and reside for a short time in several.'

'When do you plan on going to the hunting lodge?'

He paused and turned to face her. 'In a few days, when the first of my guests arrive. Meantime, I will ensure that you see some of the sights Riyadh has to offer, such as the museum, Dir'aiyah, the Souk Al-Bathaa. Fouad will continue to see that you are entertained in my absence.'

His features hardened fractionally. 'I must impress on you the fact that as a woman you cannot venture anywhere beyond the palace unless accompanied by Fouad or myself. Is that understood? Women are not permitted anywhere on their own, and cannot use public transport. To do so will result in arrest. Nashwa will provide you with an *abaaya* to wear whenever you leave the palace.'

Kristi made no protest. Despite her personal views on such issues there was nothing to be gained by flouting Saudi Arabian religious dictates. 'Have we been out here sufficiently long, do you think?'

'You have grown tired of my company?'

What could she say? That he unsettled her more than any man she'd ever met? 'I think you're enjoying the pursuit of this particular game,' she ventured, meeting his gaze.

'There are advantages,' Shalef drawled.

'Such as?'

'This.' His hands caught her close as his head lowered and his mouth closed over hers, his tongue a provocative instrument as he explored the delicate interior and wrought havoc with her senses. At her soft intake of breath his mouth hardened, staking a possession with such mastery that it took considerable will-power not to give in to sensation and kiss him back.

When he released her she stood, momentarily bemused, then reality returned, and with it a measure of anger.

'That was unnecessary!'

'But enjoyable, don't you agree?'

She wanted to hit him, and her fist clenched as she summoned a measure of restraint. 'You're despicable.'

'Come,' he bade her easily. 'We'll explore the garden further then return indoors. By that time your anger will have cooled.'

'Don't bet on it,' she returned inelegantly, unsure just how much control she could exert during her sojourn in the desert. Shalef bin Youssef Al-Sayed was a law unto himself, but when it came to a clash of wills she intended to do battle.

Shalef was as good as his word, and during the ensuing few days he assumed the role of perfect host. In the company of Nashwa, with a Filipino chauffeur at the wheel of the Mercedes, he ensured that Kristi saw many of the sights Riyadh had to offer. They visited the museum, the Masmak Fortress and the Murabba Palace, followed by the King Faisal Centre for Research and Islamic Studies. There was also the King Saud University Museum, and Kristi displayed a genuine interest as their assigned guide explained the history attached to each of the finds from the university's archaeological digs at Al-Fao and Rabdhah. The Souk Al-Bathaa, Shalef explained as they explored what remained of it,

had become a victim of Riyadh's rush into the twen-
tieth century.

Being in Shalef's company almost constantly had a
disturbing effect on Kristi's composure, as he meant it
to have. His behaviour was impeccable, although she
was acutely aware of the intensity of his gaze as it lingered on her a trifle longer than was necessary, the
touch of his hand when he directed her attention to
something of interest, the moment he caught hold of
her arm when she almost tripped over the hem of her
borrowed *abaaya*.

Frequently she found her gaze straying to the firm
lines of his mouth…and remembered what it felt like
to have it move over her own.

Kristi didn't know whether to feel relieved or dismayed when one evening he suggested that they dine
together in town.

'The night-life here is notoriously thin,' Shalef revealed, watching the fleeting play of emotions on her
expressive features. 'However, the hotels have excellent restaurants, and the Al-Khozama has one I can
recommend.'

With Nashwa and Fouad present, there wasn't much
she could do but agree.

The *abaaya* was a necessary addition, but beneath
it she wore silk evening trousers and a camisole top,
and kept her make-up to a minimum. In some ways it
had been amusing to discover that Nashwa, Aisha and
Hanan each wore modern Western clothes beneath their

abaayas. Saudi Arabian women, they assured her, spent a fortune on European couture.

Shalef was accorded due deference at the hotel as the *maître d'* escorted them to a table reserved, Kristi surmised, for the privileged few.

Choosing mineral water, she deliberated over the choice of starter and main course, conferred with Shalef and was guided by his selection.

'When do you leave for the hunting lodge?'

'Tomorrow.'

At last, she breathed silently with a sense of relief. There were questions she wanted to ask, but refrained from putting them into words, choosing to wonder in silence when Mehmet Hassan would arrive, and how soon it would be before negotiations for Shane's release could be initiated.

'How long will you be away?'

Their drinks arrived and it was a few minutes before he answered.

'A week.'

'I can only wish you an enjoyable and successful sojourn with your guests.'

He inclined his head in mocking acknowledgement. 'While you will be glad to be free of my presence.'

'Of course,' she agreed sweetly. 'It will be a relief not to have to pretend to be enamoured of you.'

The starter was served and Kristi found it delectable. The main course, when it arrived, was a visual work of art.

'It seems a shame to disturb such artistic symmetry.' She picked up her fork and carefully speared a segment of lamb, then paused in the action of transferring it to her mouth as a waiter approached the table and spoke to Shalef in a respectful undertone, listened to the response, then bowed his head and moved away.

'Fayza is visiting her family in Riyadh,' Shalef revealed. 'She is here with her brother and suggests we join them for coffee. Do you mind?'

Oh, *joy*. 'Why not?' Her smile was bright, her tone vivacious.

'You're in danger of creating a case of overkill,' he drawled.

'Why, *Shalef*,' she reproved with deliberate mockery, 'would I do such a thing?'

His eyes gleamed with dark humour. 'I suspect you might.'

'We could,' Kristi mused thoughtfully, 'consider it pay-back time for your unwarranted kiss in the garden.'

One eyebrow rose. 'Unwarranted?'

'Finish your dinner,' she bade him solemnly. 'We mustn't keep the lovely Fayza waiting.'

'Remind me to exact due punishment.'

'A threat?'

'More in the nature of a promise.'

She pretended deliberation. 'Is she merely one of many women in your life or is she special?'

'I have known Fayza for a number of years.'

'Ah,' Kristi responded with comprehension, 'the "we're just good friends" spiel. Does she know that?' She looked at him, then shook her head. 'No, don't answer. She lusts after you, and your wealth is a magnificent bonus. Or should it be the other way round?'

She savoured another mouthful of food. 'Mmm, this is good.' She summoned a winsome smile. 'Should I play the jealous "companion", do you think? Take your hands off him, he's mine? Or the bored socialite who knows she has you by the… Well, let's just say I'm very sure I have your attention.'

Shalef finished the course and replaced his cutlery. 'One day some man is going to take you severely in hand.'

'Rest assured it won't be you,' Kristi responded, pushing her empty plate to one side. 'Shall we enter the battlefield?'

Fayza greeted Kristi with polite civility, proffered Shalef a stunning smile, and allowed her brother to perform his own introduction.

You just had to admire Fayza's style, Kristi commended her silently almost an hour later. Demure, with a touch of the exotic, the hint of seething passion beneath a chaste exterior. Was Shalef fooled? Somehow she thought not.

'You are a professional photographer?' Fayza made it sound the lowest of lowly occupations, and Kristi had a difficult time remaining calm.

'It's a job,' she dismissed, and glimpsed the young woman's deliberate raising of one eyebrow.

'I have a degree in business management. But, of course, it's unnecessary for me to work.'

'What a shame,' Kristi sympathised. 'All that study and no need to apply it.'

Fayza's eyes darkened. 'Surely a woman's focus

should be looking after a man? Ensuring his home is a tranquil haven?'

Oh, dear, what had she begun? Kristi wondered. She was in the wrong country, and probably in the wrong company, to converse on feminist issues. 'One has to allow that it's possible not all men desire tranquillity,' she opined with due cautiousness.

'Shalef,' Fayza appealed with just the right degree of helpless virtue, 'Miss Dalton has little understanding of a woman's role in Saudi Arabia.' She honed her weapons and aimed for the kill. 'However, I imagine such knowledge is of no importance to her.'

It was obvious that she was unsure of the precise depth of Kristi's relationship with Shalef bin Youssef Al-Sayed, despite the inevitable gossip which would have circulated among the cream of Riyadh society. It allowed Kristi the advantage of responding with an enigmatic smile.

'You're wrong,' she submitted quietly. 'On both counts.'

Fayza managed a creditable attempt at disbelief. 'Really?'

'If you'll excuse us?' Shalef asked Fayza and her brother. 'It's quite late.' He signalled to the *maître d'*, signed the proffered credit slip, then rose to his feet.

The fact that he took hold of Kristi's hand and enfolded it in his didn't escape Fayza's notice.

'One imagines you will fly out to the hunting lodge during your stay in Riyadh?'

Shalef's expression mirrored polite civility. 'It is something I allow time for whenever I am here.'

'Falconry sounds such a fascinating sport,' Kristi offered, and she gave him an adoring glance. 'Perhaps you could take me out to the lodge some time, darling? It would be a fascinating experience to witness your skill with the falcon.'

Shalef's fingers tightened measurably on her own, and there was little she could do to wrench them from his grasp as Fayza and her brother accompanied them to the hotel foyer, then stood briefly while the doorman summoned both cars to the main entrance.

Immediately Shalef and Kristi were seated the chauffeur eased the Mercedes onto the road and headed towards the palace.

'You excelled yourself tonight,' Shalef commented with dangerous smoothness, and she turned to look at him. The dim light inside the car accentuated the strong angles and planes of his facial bone structure.

'I wasn't the only one acting a part.'

'No,' he agreed as the car sped through the quiet city streets.

All too soon they reached the palace gates, and Kristi followed Shalef from the vehicle when it drew to a halt outside the main entrance.

'Thank you for a pleasant evening,' she said politely once they were indoors. 'Will I see you before you leave tomorrow?'

'The helicopter pilot has been instructed to be ready at seven.'

'In that case I'll wish you a pleasant stay and ask that you be in touch with any news.' She turned away only to come to a halt as a detaining hand clasped her shoulder and brought her back to face him.

'Don't,' he warned with threatening intent, 'concoct a scheme to visit the hunting lodge.'

Her eyes were wide and remarkably clear. 'Why would I do that?'

'You've dared many things in your career.' His hands crept up to cradle her head. 'The hunting lodge and the identities of my guests are *my* business. Do you understand?'

'Yes.' She *did* understand. Yet that didn't change her intention to put a carefully devised plan into action. For days she'd surreptitiously observed the servants' routine, and she knew where the keys to the vehicles were kept. She also knew how to disengage the palace alarm system, as well as the system connected to the garages. She had a map, and over the next few days she would encourage Fouad to enlighten her about the art of falconry and to disclose the precise whereabouts of the hunting lodge.

However, Shalef wasn't to know that.

'Make sure that you do,' he said hardly. His head descended and he took possession of her mouth, plundering it in a manner that bordered on the primitive, and when he released her she lifted a shaking hand to her bruised lips.

'I think I hate you.'

His eyes were so dark that they were almost black, and he offered no apology.

Without another word she turned and made her way to the wide, curved stairway that led to the upper floor, and in her room she slowly removed the borrowed *abaaya* and the silken evening clothes beneath it before entering the *en suite* bathroom. Minutes later she slid into bed and systematically went over every aspect of the palace security system, then mentally calculated when she would initiate her plan.

CHAPTER FIVE

KRISTI DRESSED QUICKLY in blue cotton trousers and a matching cotton shirt, dispensed with make-up except for moisturising cream, twisted her hair on top of her head and secured it with pins, pulled on a cap, pushed her feet into trainers, then scrutinised her appearance, satisfied that she could easily pass for a reed-slim young man.

With a swift glance round the elegant suite, she caught up the backpack into which she'd pushed a change of clothes and minimum necessities then moved silently into the hallway.

The palace was quiet. In another hour Amani and Abdullah would begin organising the staff with daily chores.

Part of her deplored the subterfuge of removing the remote control and spare set of keys to the four-wheel drive from Abdullah's desk. It made her feel like a thief.

Kristi gained the ground floor and made her way to a rear side-door, disengaged the security alarm, then slipped outside and moved quickly to the garages.

For the first time she sent a prayer heavenward for

expensive equipment as she depressed the remote control and saw one set of double doors lift upwards with scarcely more than an electronic whisper.

The four-wheel drive was large, with wide tyres and attached spotlights, spare petrol and water cans. There was no time for second thoughts, and she deactivated the alarm, then unlocked and opened the door.

She had driven a Jeep and a smaller four-wheel drive, but this was a monster by comparison. CB radio, car phone...the interior was crammed with every conceivable extra imaginable.

Kristi checked the low reduction, ran through the gears, then started up the engine. All she had to do now was deactivate the security alarm at the gates, release them, and she was on her way.

There wasn't a hitch, and she gave thanks to heaven as she gained the road and moved the heavy vehicle swiftly through its numerous gears.

During the past few days she'd spent considerable time memorising streets, time and distance. At this early hour of the morning there was no other traffic to speak of, and her passage through the city was uneventful.

In another hour it would be light, and by then she'd be on the long road snaking into the desert.

She calculated that she had two hours, perhaps three, before her absence would be noticed. What she couldn't surmise was how Nashwa would react to her carefully penned note. Doubtless Abdullah would be consulted, and Fouad. There was always the possibility that she would reach the hunting lodge before anyone could notify Shalef.

His anger was something she preferred not to envisage, and a faint shiver feathered her skin at the prospect of weathering his wrath.

The buildings began to dwindle, the houses became fewer and far between, then there was nothing except the sparse expanse of desert, stretching out beneath the vehicle's powerful headlights.

Kristi seemed to have driven for ages before the sky began to lighten, dimming the shadows and bathing the land with a soft, ethereal glow. As the sun rose the colours deepened and the sky changed to the palest blue.

There was a sense of isolation—the grandeur of the sand and the gentle undulation of the land, the stark beauty of the contrasting colour between earth and sky.

The desert seemed so vast, so…inhibiting, Kristi mused. Frightening, she added, aware that a sudden sandstorm could cover the road, obliterating it entirely from view.

Don't even think about it, she chastised herself silently. It won't happen. And even if it did she would only be briefly stranded, for she could notify the palace— *anyone*—of her whereabouts via the car phone or CB.

As the sun rose higher in the sky its warmth began to penetrate the vehicle and Kristi switched on the air-conditioning and donned her sunglasses.

With careful manoeuvring she extracted a water bottle and a packet of sandwiches from her backpack, then ate as she drove, not wanting to stop and waste time.

As the sun rose further the bitumen began to shimmer with a reflective heat haze. It played havoc with her vision and brought the onset of a headache.

There was almost a sense of relief when she glimpsed a vehicle in her rear-view mirror. It gained on her steadily, then pulled out to pass.

There were two men in the front seat and the passenger gave her an intent look then turned to the driver. Instead of passing, they maintained an even pace with her vehicle, then gestured for her to pull over.

It didn't make sense, so she ignored the directive, accelerating to gain speed. Within seconds they were abreast of her once again, and this time there could be no mistaking their intention to have her pull over and stop.

When she didn't comply, the driver positioned the side of his vehicle against hers, and she felt the sickening thud of metal against metal.

She sped ahead, reached for the CB speaker, depressed the switch and spoke into it rapidly, giving her identity, approximate location and indicating the problem.

The men drew level again, and this time the four-wheel drive took a pounding. Kristi held onto the wheel for grim death and managed to get ahead of them.

Risking a quick glance in the rear-view mirror, she felt fear clutch hold of her stomach as she saw their vehicle in hot pursuit.

She was an experienced driver. With luck, skill and divine assistance, she thought she might manage to outdistance them.

Within a matter of seconds the vehicle was right behind her, then it pulled out and inched forward until it was abreast. The passenger gestured with a rifle for her to pull over.

There was no point in arguing with someone wielding a loaded firearm so she began to brake.

There was the sound of a shot, followed almost simultaneously by the soft thud of a blown-out tyre, then the vehicle slewed horribly to one side.

For what seemed like half a lifetime she battled to maintain some sort of control and bring the four-wheel drive to a halt, then she hit the door-locking mechanism, grabbed the car phone, hit a coded button, and when a heavily accented male voice answered she relayed an identical message, hoping, praying that whoever was on the other end of the line understood English. In desperation she repeated it in French before replacing the receiver.

She watched with mounting apprehension as one man crossed to the passenger side while the other attempted to wrench open the door closest to her.

They yelled instructions in Arabic, and shook their fists at her when she indicated a refusal to comply.

The man with the rifle crossed round to the passenger side, carefully took aim, then shot the lock.

There wasn't a flicker of emotion evident in their expressions as they gestured for her to move outside, the command enforced as the driver reached in and hauled her unceremoniously across the passenger seat and threw her down onto the ground.

Two hands grabbed her shoulders and dragged her to her feet. She stood still, returning their heated looks with angry intensity.

The driver reached out and pulled the cap from her head, then gaped in amazement and broke into a heated conversation with his fellow assailant.

Kristi lifted a shaky hand and tucked some of her hair behind one ear. The gesture was involuntary, and both men immediately stopped speaking.

Kristi fixed each of them with a scathing look, then pointed at her four-wheel drive. 'Sheikh Shalef bin Youssef Al-Sayed.' Then she touched a hand to her heart. 'Shalef bin Youssef Al-Sayed,' she repeated with soft vehemence.

The men conversed in rapid Arabic, arguing volubly for what seemed an age, then they turned towards her, subjecting her to a long look that encompassed her slim figure from head to toe before settling with stony-faced anger on her expressive features.

One word was uttered with such force that its explicitness couldn't fail to be universally understood.

It took considerable effort to hold their gazes, but she managed it, unwilling to respond in English, knowing that any verbal exchange would be totally useless.

The car phone rang, its insistent summons sounding loud in the surrounding stillness, and she lifted one eyebrow in silent query.

For several long seconds they seemed undecided as to whether she should answer, then the driver gave a brief nod and she scrambled into the front seat and snatched up the receiver. When she turned round the men were climbing into their vehicle, and, gunning the engine, tyres spinning, they roared at great speed down the road.

'Kristi? Fouad. Shalef is on his way. Are you all right?'

'I'm OK. The four-wheel drive hasn't fared so well.'

'And the two men?'

'They've just left.'

'Did you get the vehicle plate number?'

'It wasn't high on my list of priorities,' Kristi informed him drily. She thought that she detected a faint noise and quickly checked the rear-view mirror, then swung her attention to the road ahead. Nothing. The noise grew louder and her eyes caught a movement to her right. A helicopter. 'I think the cavalry is about to arrive.'

'The CB and car phone automatically access the palace,' Fouad revealed. 'The instant you rang in I notified Shalef on his mobile net.'

'I imagine all hell is about to break loose.'

'For me it already has.'

'None of this is your fault.'

'I am responsible in Shalef's absence. Therefore some of the blame falls on my head.'

The noise was incredibly loud, the rotor-blades whirling up the dust as the machine settled down a short distance away.

'I can't hear a thing. I'll have to hang up,' Kristi shouted into the receiver, then replaced it slowly as the helicopter door swung open and Shalef jumped down to the ground.

With a sense of detached fascination she watched as he strode towards the four-wheel drive. In a black *thobe* and red and white checked *gutra* he presented a formidable figure.

Suppressed rage emanated from his taut frame. She saw it reflected in his harshly set features as she wound down the window and sat waiting for him to say something—anything.

He opened the door and his eyes pierced hers, penetrating their mirrored depths. 'You are unharmed?'

Kristi wanted to laugh. Except that if she did, she'd never stop. Hysterical reaction, she recognised, and banked it down. This wasn't the first tight situation she'd been in, and it probably wouldn't be the last.

'I'm in one piece, as you can see,' she dismissed lightly.

'Then I suggest you get out of the vehicle.'

The four-wheel drive wasn't going anywhere in a hurry until some worthy soul jacked it up and changed the tyre.

With brief economy of movement she slid from the seat and stepped down. He was much too close, his height and breadth much too...intimidating, she decided.

'I'm sorry about this,' Kristi began, indicating the vehicle with a sweep of her hand.

'Shut up,' Shalef directed quietly, and her eyes widened fractionally.

'You're angry,' she said unnecessarily.

'Did you expect me not to be?' Hard words that had the power to flay the skin from her body. His eyes seemed to sear her soul. 'I issued express instructions that you were to stay at the palace.'

'I had a map,' she said.

'And resorted to subterfuge.'

'Fouad had nothing to do—'

'Fouad will answer to me. As you will.' His gaze raked her slim form, noting the graze on one wrist, the light scratch above her temple. 'The helicopter is waiting.'

'I have a backpack in the four-wheel drive.'

He gave her a searching look, then reached in and retrieved it from the floor. 'Let's go.'

Kristi walked at his side, protesting as he placed his hands at her waist and lifted her into the cabin.

'The rear seat. I'll take the front.'

It would have been difficult to do anything but comply, and, once seated, she secured the belt as Shalef swung up behind her.

The pilot set the helicopter in the air, then wheeled it away in a north-westerly direction. The noise precluded conversation, and since she wasn't offered a set of headphones she sat in silence and focused her attention on the swiftly passing ground below.

She saw the road, and three vehicles blocking another. Her assailants, surrounded by a party of men wielding rifles. Were they the police, or guards in Shalef's employ?

Kristi heard Shalef issue instructions in Arabic and the acknowledgement of the pilot as he swung away from the scene.

Were they heading back to the palace? She wanted to ask but dared not, aware that she would see soon enough.

Within minutes she caught sight of a building, and her breathing quickened as the helicopter cruised down to settle on a helipad inside the compound.

The hunting lodge.

The engine cut out and the rotors slowed as Shalef swung out onto the ground. Kristi followed, catching her breath as he lifted her from the cabin.

His eyes clashed with hers for an interminable few seconds, and she almost died when she saw the ruthlessness in their depths.

Retaining hold of her arm, he led her across a large grassed area to the house, and once indoors he traversed a hallway and drew her into a room near its end.

The door closed with a refined clunk, and the sound had an unsettling effect on her nerves.

'Now,' he intoned silkily, 'tell me everything that happened. Not,' he qualified, 'how you evaded the palace security system and commandeered one of my vehicles.' His eyes became faintly hooded, and she had the feeling that he was keeping a tight rein on his temper. 'From the moment you were threatened by those two thugs.'

Her chin lifted and her eyes were faintly clouded. 'What will happen to them?'

A muscle tensed at the edge of his jaw and his expression hardened with controlled anger. 'They will be dealt with, and charges laid against them. Most certainly they face jail.'

She shivered slightly, aware that the scenario could have had a very different ending if she had not been privileged with Shalef's protection.

'They probably wanted to alleviate their boredom by having a bit of fun.'

His hand slid up to cup her chin, lifting it so that she had to look at him. 'Saudi Arabian women are *not* permitted to drive,' he relayed with soft emphasis.

Kristi digested his implication in silence, unwilling to put a connotation she wasn't sure of on the two men's actions.

Her eyes widened as they searched his, and her stomach executed an emotional somersault that sent warning flares to various pulse spots throughout her body, activating a rapid beat that was clearly visible at the base of her throat.

'I'm sorry.'

'At this precise moment I find it difficult not to make you sorry for the day you were born,' he threatened softly.

Apprehension feathered a trail down the length of her spine as she willed herself to hold his gaze. 'Punishing me to appease your own anger will achieve nothing.'

He released her chin and thrust both hands into the pockets of his *thobe*. 'Your story, Kristi,' he reiterated hardly. 'All of it.'

With deliberate detachment she relayed what had happened from the moment the men's four-wheel drive had drawn alongside her.

Shalef listened intently, his eyes never leaving her face, and when she finished he turned and crossed to the window.

It probably wasn't the time to ask, but she had to know. 'Is Mehmet Hassan at the lodge?'

'No.'

Utter dejection dulled her eyes. Her trip to Riyadh had been in vain. 'So he didn't arrive,' she said in a flat voice.

'He flew out yesterday.'

'So he was here,' she breathed in sheer relief. 'Did you speak to him about Shane?'

Shalef turned towards her. 'There can be no guarantees,' he warned. 'None, you understand?'

Elation radiated through her body, turning her expressive features into something quite beautiful. 'It's the best chance Shane has.' Without thinking she crossed to his side and placed her lips against his cheek. 'Thank you.'

Something flickered in the depths of his eyes, then one hand slid to her nape, his fingers spreading beneath her hair to capture her head, while the other settled at the base of her spine.

Vibrant energy emanated from every pore, exuding an erotic power that she consciously fought against in an effort to retain a gram of sanity.

Kristi saw his head descend as if in slow motion, and her lips parted to voice an involuntary protest as his mouth closed over hers.

No man had ever kissed her with quite such a degree of restrained passion, and she shivered at the thought of what force might be unleashed if ever he allowed himself to lose control.

He plundered at will, ignoring the faint protesting groan that rose and died in her throat, and the ineffectual punches she aimed at his shoulders.

Kristi wasn't aware of precisely when the pressure changed, only that it did, and there was a wealth of mastery evident as his tongue explored the softness inside her mouth, then tangled with hers in a swirling dance that took hold of her conflicting emotions and tossed them high.

Almost of its own volition her body swayed into his, and her hands reached for his shoulders, then linked together behind his head.

His hand spread against her lower spine, lifting her in against him, and his mouth hardened in demanding possession.

The kiss frightened her, awakening sensations that tore at her control and ripped it to shreds. She wanted him, badly. So badly that when his hand moved to cup her breast she gave an indistinct groan of despair and closed her eyes, exulting in the moment and the heady emotions that he was able to arouse.

When his mouth left hers she made a slight murmur of protest, then cried out as he teased a trail of evocative kisses down the sensitised cord at the side of her neck. His lips circled the rapidly beating pulse as he savoured it with his tongue, and she went up in flames, uncaring at that precise moment as his fingers loosened the buttons on her blouse.

He dealt with the front fastening of her bra with adept ease, and she arched her throat as his lips sought one taut peak, tasting it gently, then teasing the engorged nipple with the edge of his teeth until she hovered between pleasure and pain.

Just as she thought that she could bear no more, he

drew it in with his tongue and began to suckle shamelessly. Extreme ecstasy arrowed through her body, centring at the junction between her thighs, and she gave a low, gratified groan when his hand slid to ease the ache there.

It wasn't enough. It would never be enough. Yet when his fingers sought the zip-fastener of her jeans she stilled, caught between the heaven of discovering what it would be like to share with him the ultimate intimacy and the hell of knowing that if she did she'd never be the same again.

He sensed her indecision and moved his hand back to the base of her spine, trailing it gently up and down the vertebral column in a soothing motion that heightened her emotions even further.

With considerable care he closed the edges of her blouse and re-did the buttons, then he gently pushed her to arm's length.

'I'll instruct the servants to prepare something for you to eat.'

Kristi wanted to close her eyes and dismiss the previous ten minutes. Yet such a feat wasn't possible. Somehow she had to reassemble her emotions into some sort of order and act as if everything was normal. If *he* could, then so could she.

'I'm not hungry.' She had to look at him, and she managed it bravely.

'If you should change your mind, just go into the kitchen and help yourself.'

She didn't want to ask but the words tumbled out before she could halt them. 'When will you be back?'

'Before dark.'

He turned and left the room, and she could hear his footsteps retreating down the hallway.

Kristi stood where she was for a long time, then she stirred and looked round the room, noting the masculine appointments, the king-size bed. She walked to the *en suite* bathroom and examined the spa, deciding on a whim to fill it and take a leisurely bath.

Half an hour later she switched off the jets and climbed out, then towelled herself dry. She crossed into the bedroom and extracted fresh underwear from her bag, donned clean trousers and blouse, then went in search of the kitchen.

The lodge was reasonably large, comfortably furnished, and entirely male. Kristi wondered idly if Shalef ever brought any women here, then dismissed the idea. He had homes in capital cities all over the world. Why bring a woman here, when he could woo her in luxurious surroundings in an exotic location?

She found the kitchen and discovered it occupied by a middle-aged woman and a young girl. From the aroma permeating the air it was apparent that they were preparing a meal. Simultaneously they turned to look at her as she entered their domain.

The older woman beckoned as she crossed to a bank of cupboards, took out a plate and cutlery, then crossed to the stove and ladled a generous portion from each pot onto the plate.

It was more than Kristi could possibly eat, and she used sign language to indicate that she required less than half. Seconds later she was shown into an informal dining room and seated at the table.

The food was good, the meat tender and succulent, the vegetables cooked with herbs, lending a delicate flavour.

The afternoon seemed to drag, and she wished that she had something to read…anything to pass the time. There was a television somewhere, for she'd seen a satellite dish when they'd flown in. Perhaps if she went on a tour of the lodge she'd eventually find it. There might even be stereo equipment and compact discs.

Kristi discovered both in an informal lounge adjoining the games room, and after checking the electronic remote control she switched on the television and went through numerous channel changes before settling on one.

It was after five when she heard the sound of vehicles returning, and she crossed to the window to watch as four men exited one Jeep and three stepped down from the other.

Shalef was easily identifiable, and she wondered which of the men were friends and which were staff. More importantly, did they speak English? If not, conversation over dinner was going to prove difficult.

From the sound of their voices it seemed that they'd had a successful day. There was deep laughter, followed shortly by the closing of doors as the men retired to their rooms to wash and change for the evening meal.

'I thought I might find you here.'

Kristi turned in surprise, for she hadn't heard Shalef enter the room. His black *thobe* had been exchanged for one of dark brown, and he presented an indomitable figure. A man who held sufficient power to shape his own life and change the lives of many of his fellow men. His effect on women didn't need qualification.

'You have a comprehensive audio-visual system,' she complimented lightly as she rose to her feet. His height was intimidating from a seated position, and she felt the need of any advantage she could gain.

He inclined his head in silent acknowledgement. 'Dinner will be served in half an hour.'

She looked at him carefully, noting the fine lines fanning out from the corners of his eyes, the vertical cleft slashing each cheek, and the strong jawline curving down to a determined chin.

Although she felt at ease in the company of men, she was aware of the segregation of the sexes in this country.

'It won't bother me if you'd prefer to dine alone with your guests.'

His eyes darkened fractionally and he made an impatient gesture. 'They know you are here, and I have no inclination to hide you away in a separate room.'

Kristi effected a slight shrug and cast her clothes a rueful glance. 'I'm not exactly dressed to impress.'

'You are not required to impress,' Shalef returned with mocking amusement. 'Shall we join our guests?'

The four men varied in age from early thirties to mid-fifties, and their status was evident in their distinguished bearing and demeanour. A Western woman in their midst was viewed with polite circumspection, and if they thought Shalef bin Youssef Al-Sayed had tem-

porarily lost a measure of his sanity they were careful
by word and action not to give a hint of this.

English was spoken throughout the evening, but although the conversation flowed easily Kristi gained the
impression that her presence was an intrusion.

After coffee had been served she excused herself
and bade the men goodnight.

In her room she shed her clothes, removed her bra
and briefs, handwashed both and draped them over a
towel stand in the *en suite* bathroom to dry, then she
slid between the crisp, clean sheets of the king-size bed
and switched off the lamp.

The darkness was like an enveloping blanket, and
she lay staring sightlessly ahead, her mind active as
she weighed Mehmet Hassan's influence in negotiating Shane's release.

How long would it take? Days—*weeks*? What if he
wasn't successful at all?

Kristi plumped the pillow and turned on her side.
She'd been up since an hour before dawn and she was
tired.

Overtired, she cursed silently an age later. She should
never have had coffee after her meal.

A shaft of light lanced through the darkness then
disappeared, and she detected the almost silent click
of the bedroom door.

Who—? She reached out and switched on the lamp,
then gave a surprised gasp at the sight of Shalef in the
process of removing his *thobe*.

CHAPTER SIX

'WHAT THE HELL are you doing here?' Kristi's voice was filled with outrage.

Shalef directed her a faintly mocking look. 'This happens to be my personal suite.'

She sat up, carrying the sheet with her. 'Either you go to another room or I will,' she vented with thinly veiled fury.

'The lodge has four guest suites,' he enlightened her. 'I have four guests.'

'Couldn't two of your guests share?'

'Each suite is identical to this one,' he revealed. 'To suggest sharing would constitute a grave insult.' His mouth curved into an amused smile. 'You are my...' he paused deliberately '...woman. Where else would you sleep, except with me?'

'Like hell,' Kristi said inelegantly.

'I don't perceive there is a problem. The bed is large.'

It might not be a problem for him, but there was no way she would calmly accept sharing the same room with him, let alone the same bed.

'I'll get dressed and go sleep on the sofa in the entertainment room,' she declared purposefully.

'And risk the possibility of being discovered by any one of my guests who might find it difficult to sleep and seeks the solace of music or television for an hour or two?' One eyebrow slanted. 'At least here you are beneath my protection.'

Anger lent her eyes a fiery sparkle. 'I don't want to be beneath you for *any* reason.'

He began to laugh softly. 'I'm pleased to hear you enjoy variety.'

Colour flooded her cheeks, and, without thinking, she caught up a nearby pillow and threw it at him, uncaring at that precise moment if he should choose some form of retribution.

He fielded it neatly and tossed it back onto the bed, then he continued undressing, and she was unable to look away from the superb musculature of his near-naked body. Sinews stretched and flexed, their fluid movement beneath silk-sheened skin a visual attestation to a man who took care to maintain a physical fitness regime.

When he reached his briefs she averted her gaze. She wasn't sufficiently bold to watch as he stripped off the last vestige of clothing.

Damn him. Didn't he possess a skerrick of modesty?

Determination set her features into an angry mask. 'I'll opt for the chair.'

Shalef walked calmly to the opposite side of the bed and slid in beneath the covers. 'As you please.'

'It doesn't please me at all,' she vented in a furious

undertone as she scrambled to her feet. She wrenched the sheet from the bed and wrapped it round her slim form, holding it firmly above her breasts with taut fingers as she scooped up the excess length.

'Be careful you don't trip,' came a lazy drawl, and she turned to shoot him a fulminating glare.

The chair was large and looked reasonably comfortable, and she curled into its cushioned depths, adjusting the sheet so that it covered every visible inch of her, then positioned her head on the armrest and closed her eyes.

The early-morning start coupled with the events of the day gradually overcame her resentment, and she drifted into a light doze, only to stir some hours later as the air temperature dropped several points. The sheet was no longer adequate against the coolness of the air-conditioning, and she carefully attempted to reassemble its folds so that it provided another layer of cover.

Half an hour later any thought of sleep was impossible. There had to be a store of blankets somewhere, but as she had no knowledge of where they might be there was no point in trying to search for them in the dark. That only left the clothes she'd discarded earlier.

With considerable care she sat up and attempted to orientate herself to her surroundings. The *en suite* bathroom had to be directly ahead, the bed to her left, and the door to her right. Therefore all she had to do was creep into the bathroom, reach for her clothes, don them, and creep back to the chair.

She dared not risk putting on a light, even had she been able to remember precisely where any one of several switches were located. And the room was dark. Not inky black, but sufficiently shrouded to make any movement in unfamiliar territory a bit of a hazard.

Kristi knew that she could handle the situation in one of two ways: carefully, so that she didn't make any noise and disturb the man sleeping in the nearby bed, or brazenly, by searching for the light switch and waking Shalef. Somehow *carefully* presented itself as the better option.

The sheet had to go. It would rustle with every move. Seconds later she eased out from the chair and trod slowly across the room. Four, six, eight, ten steps. The *en suite* bathroom's door should be a few more steps ahead to her left.

Except that when she reached for the knob she discovered the wall. It had to be further along. Inch by inch she moved to the left, then clenched her teeth as her toe made contact with a solid piece of furniture.

'Kristi?'

She spun towards the sound of that deep male voice and cried out in anguished despair, 'Don't turn on the light!' Dear God, this had to rank high on her list of embarrassing moments. 'The sheet is on the chair!'

'And you're afraid I might catch a glimpse of you *au naturel*?'

He was amused. Oh, how she'd like to wipe the smile from his face and delete the mockery from his voice! 'I was looking for my clothes.'

'I doubt you'll find them in my wardrobe.'

She drew in a deep breath. 'I left them in the *en suite* bathroom.'

'Your sense of direction leaves something to be desired,' Shalef informed her drily. 'The *en suite* is several feet to your left.'

Kristi wanted to throw something at him and, preferably, have it connect with a vulnerable part of his anatomy. 'Thank you,' she acknowledged with as much civility as she could muster, then gave an anguished cry as the room was illuminated. 'I asked you not to do that!' The fact that he had a view of her back didn't make it any less mortifying.

'I doubt I could forgive himself if you were to add to your list of existing injuries.' She detected the soft sound of bedclothes, sensed rather than heard him move.

She began to shake, partly with anger, partly from sheer reaction. 'At least have the decency to get me a shirt—*anything.*'

He hadn't touched her, but she felt the loss of his immediate presence as much as if she'd been in his embrace.

Seconds later he was back. 'Lift your arms.'

She obeyed, feeling the coolness of fine cotton on her skin as he slid the sleeves in place, then smoothed the shirt over her shoulders. Her fingers clutched the front edges and drew them together.

'You look like a child playing with grown-up clothes,' Shalef commented with a soft laugh. The shirt-tail brushed the backs of her calves and the sleeves were far too long. 'Now,' he ordered quietly, 'get into bed before I put you there.'

She turned round to face him, increasingly aware of his essential maleness, and her heart leapt, then thudded into a quickened beat.

One eyebrow lifted in a gesture of silent mockery. 'Do you really want to suffer a loss of dignity?'

What price defeat? Yet she refused to concede easily. 'Don't close your eyes, Shalef,' she warned. 'I might seek vengeance in the night.'

He reached out and caught hold of her chin between thumb and forefinger. 'Be aware that such an action will have only one ending.'

Something clawed at her innermost being, tightening into a deep, shooting pain that radiated from her feminine core. Sex with this man, simply as an assuagement of anger, would tear her emotions to shreds.

'I don't like being manipulated.' Yet she was helpless in this present situation, and she hated the thought of capitulation.

'You placed your fate in my hands when you left the sanctuary of the palace for the desert,' he reminded her, tilting her chin as he studied the conflict visible in her expressive features.

She opened her mouth to voice a protest, only to have it stilled by the placing of his finger over her lips.

Her eyes mirrored her inner anguish, and the pressure on her mouth eased. 'You could have sent me back. Why didn't you?'

The curve of his mouth deepened as it relaxed into a faint smile. 'Perhaps it pleases me to have you here.' His forefinger brushed over the contour of her lower lip, then travelled a similar path along the upper curve.

A deep shiver feathered its way down her spine at his action, and she consciously stilled the flood of warmth that invaded her veins.

'To share with you the stark beauty and the cruelty of a land that holds such an attraction for the men born to it.' His hand moved to cup her chin, while the other lifted and held fast her nape.

Kristi hated the sudden breathlessness that seemed to have taken control of her lungs. She had to stop this *now*. 'It's late, I'm tired, and I'd like to get some sleep.'

His faint smile was tinged with wry humour. 'So too would I.' He released her, and walked round to the opposite side of the bed. 'Get in, Kristi,' he ordered with dangerous softness as he slid in beneath the covers.

Something leapt inside her—anger, fear, *resentment* at his high-handedness. Yet instinct warned her not to voice it. The consequences of doing so hung like a palpable threat, and she had no intention of providing further provocation.

With extreme care she took the few steps to the bed, then lifted the covers and lay down as close to the edge of the mattress as possible.

Seconds later she felt the slight movement as he reached for the lamp switch, then the room was plunged into darkness.

Her body was the antithesis of relaxed, with every cell, every nerve acutely tuned to the presence of the man lying within touching distance. It was almost as if every part of her was silently reaching out to him, *aware* to such a degree that she ached with need.

Imagining what it would be like to have him caress each pleasure pulse, touch his lips to every part of her body was an unbearable torture. And that would be only the prelude to a concerto that she instinctively knew would be wildly passionate, its crescendo bringing such tumultuous joy that a woman might feel as if she'd died and gone to heaven.

Or was it simply a fallacy, a fantasy created by emotions so strong, so impossibly vivid that the reality could only be a disappointment by comparison?

Kristi assured herself that she didn't want to find out. You lie, a tiny voice taunted.

Dammit, *sleep*, she commanded herself silently with irritated frustration. In desperation she forced herself to breathe evenly in an attempt to slow the emotional pendulum.

She wasn't successful, and it seemed an age that she lay staring sightlessly at the ceiling, hating, *hating* the ease with which the man slept beside her.

Eventually she must have dozed, for when she woke the darkness of night had been replaced by an early-dawn light that filtered into the room, dispensing with shadows and providing colour where previously there had been none.

Slowly, carefully, she turned her head, only to find the bed empty, and a long, shuddering breath left her body as she stretched each limb in turn before rolling over onto her stomach. One more blissful hour, then she'd rise from the bed, shower and dress, before seeking some food and strong black coffee.

The next thing she knew was a hand on her shoulder and a deep male voice intoning, 'If you want to accompany me into the desert, you have fifteen minutes to dress and eat.'

Kristi lifted her head from the pillow and felt her

pulse leap at the sight of Shalef standing at the side of the bed.

'I thought you had already left.' With deft movements she secured the top few buttons of her shirt, tugged its length into respectability, then slid to her feet.

'My guests have. I'll join them later in the day.' He reached out and smoothed back the tousled length of her hair.

The breath caught in her throat, momentarily robbing her of the ability to speak. 'Please don't do that.'

His smile was infinitely lazy. 'You sound almost afraid.'

Because I am, she longed to cry out. 'You said fifteen minutes,' she reminded him, neatly sidestepping him as she moved towards the *en suite* bathroom.

'I'll have one of the servants pour your coffee.'

She would have been willing to swear that she detected a tinge of humour in his voice, and she quickly showered, then pulled on her clothes.

When she entered the dining room there was a dish of fresh fruit salad, toast, and the tantalising aroma of freshly brewed coffee, steaming from a small pot.

When she had finished the meal she joined Shalef in the foyer.

'You'll need to wear a *shayla* and apply sunscreen.'

She stood perfectly still as he fixed the long scarf in position. 'Shall we leave?'

The four-wheel drive was the same model as the one she'd driven from the palace, and she wondered if he'd ordered them by the half-dozen.

An hour later Shalef eased the vehicle off the road

and drove along a well-worn track for several kilometres before slowing to a halt close to a large black tent.

He indicated a tall elderly man moving forward to greet them. 'My father sprang from the seed of the Bedouin. I thought it might interest you to meet some of them. We'll be offered coffee, which if we refuse will cause offence. Remember to accept the cup with your right hand. Follow my example.'

He offered her a faintly quizzical smile. 'This man and his family have no command of English. They will accept your dutiful silence as a mark of respect for me.' He leaned forward and caught the edge of her *shayla*, adjusting it to form a partial veil. 'Let the edge fall when we are inside the tent and refreshments are about to be served.'

Kristi was enthralled by their hosts, and she was careful to follow Shalef's brief instructions, all the time aware of their circumspect appraisal.

Her jeans were well washed, their cut generous, and her chambray shirt was buttoned almost to the neck, the sleeves long and cuffed. The *shayla* felt a little strange, but it covered her head and shoulders.

Out here, she could almost sense Shalef's empathy with these people, the link by birth, the inheritance of definitive genes. He was at one with them, yet different.

His education, she knew, had been extensive, and gained in one of the best boarding-schools in England. He was fluent in several languages and held a doctorate. His business acumen and standing in the financial sector were legendary. Yet he spoke Arabic as if it were his first language, mingled with the Bedu, and chose the simplicity and the relative isolation of this desert land for his home for weeks on end at least twice a year.

Was the call of his Bedouin blood so strong? Or was it contrived out of duty to his late father, to Nashwa and her daughters?

The woman in his life would have to understand that, while she could be his hostess in London, New York, Paris, Lucerne or Rome, there would be times when she would need not only to accompany him to Riyadh, but to accept the severe restrictions that extended to women in this land. She would also have to don the *abaaya*, *shayla* and veil—light, gauzy colours in the palace, and black in public. She would have to forgo her independence temporarily, and never in the presence of others would she be able to question his opinions, his direction or his wishes.

Yet there was a dignity, a sense of timelessness, an acceptance that was encapsulated in *inshallah*…if God wills it.

Kristi watched as the coffee was served first to Shalef, then their host. Kristi was careful to accept her cup as Shalef had instructed, then she waited until he drank from his cup before attempting to touch the contents of her own.

She would have liked to know the topic of their conversation, but she sat quietly, instinctively aware that she should not intrude. When she was offered another coffee she didn't refuse.

The encampment was small, and there were a few camels that contrasted sharply with a Japanese-assembled pick-up truck. Even the equipment and utensils were at variance with each other. Water reposed in plastic containers instead of bags made from animal skins, and there was a modern transistor radio close to where their host's wife had prepared the coffee.

At last Shalef rose to his feet, his actions repeated by their host, and Kristi followed suit as it became apparent that they were preparing to leave.

Outside the tent, Shalef was drawn by his host towards the camels, and each was solemnly inspected and commented upon. Then came the formal farewell before Shalef made his way to the four-wheel drive.

As soon as they were on their way he asked, 'You found the encounter interesting?'

The four-wheel drive gathered speed, billowing dust behind it as Shalef headed for the bitumen road.

'Intriguing,' Kristi amended.

'Perhaps you'd care to elaborate?'

'You fit in so well, yet your Arabian persona is totally at variance with the Western image.'

'You find that strange?'

'No,' she said slowly. 'Somehow it suits you. Yet I can't help wondering if you suffer a conflict of interests. Having enjoyed the best of what the West has to offer, doesn't it even bother you that Aisha and Hanan are not free to experience the freedom of their Western sisters?'

He directed her a sharp glance. 'One does not choose the country of one's birth,' Shalef pointed out. 'One simply accepts the dictates of one's heritage until education and personal choice instil the will to change. Aisha and Hanan are fortunate in that their education will be completed abroad, they are free to work in their chosen careers, and they are free to marry—wisely, one hopes—a suitable man of their choosing.'

'Yet, as head of the palace, your opinion is sacrosanct.' It was a statement, not a query.

'Their welfare is very important to me. If they displayed bad judgement, and Nashwa requested me to intervene, I would hope to be able to persuade them to rethink the situation.'

'And if you failed?'

'I would take measures to ensure no mistakes were made.'

'Such as?'

'Refuse to hand over their passports, the restriction of their allowance.'

'Confine them to the palace?'

'The palace is hardly a jail,' Shalef reminded her.

She ventured soberly, 'It could be, if you didn't want to be there.'

'Since this is a purely hypothetical conversation, without any basis of fact, I suggest we change the subject.'

'That's a cop-out,' Kristi protested.

'A tactical sidestep,' Shalef amended.

'Because it's an issue you don't want to discuss?'

'An issue that cannot be addressed without understanding of the Koran in a country which has no constitution. Much of the legal system is based on a straight application of Islamic *sharia* law as interpreted by the Hanbali school of Islamic jurisprudence, the most conservative of Sunni Islam's four main legal schools.'

'I see.' It was a contemplative comment that brought a faint smile to his lips.

'I doubt that you do.'

She studied his features, wanting to dig beneath the surface and determine his personal views, rather than political observations. 'And you, Shalef? Do you consider yourself fortunate to enjoy the best of both worlds? The Western and Islamic? Or are you frequently caught between the two?'

'I accept my Arabian heritage, for that was my father's wish.'

'And when you marry, will you follow the Islamic tradition by taking more than one wife?'

'I would hope to choose a wife whose love for me would be such that there was no need to seek another.'

'But what of your love for her?'

'You doubt I could please a wife?'

He was amused, and it rankled. 'Sex is only one aspect of a marriage. There has to be mutual respect, emotional support,' she ventured. 'And love.'

'Many women would forgo the last three in exchange for wealth and social position.'

'You're a cynic,' Kristi reproved him, and caught the mockery evident in his expression.

'I have reason to be.'

She didn't doubt it. Women flocked to his side like moths dazzled by flame. Yet very few would be interested in the man himself, only what his wealth could provide in terms of jewellery and cash, magnificent homes and social prestige, in exchange for sexual favours.

The hunting lodge was clearly visible, and Kristi evinced surprise.

'Time flies when you're having fun,' Shalef commented, tongue-in-cheek, and she pulled a face at him.

'Lunch,' he announced in response. 'After which you can witness the taming of the falcons.'

'Birds held in captivity, manacled and chained,' she said with veiled mockery.

'Yet when set free they merely circle and eventually return to their master.' He swung the vehicle into the compound. 'They are well housed, well fed, and lead an infinitely better life than they would in the wild.'

'What a shame they can't communicate; they might tell a different story.'

He cut the engine and turned towards her. 'Then again, they may not.'

'You're a superb strategist,' Kristi commended him with intended irony. 'In the business arena you'd be a diabolical adversary.'

'In *any* arena,' Shalef corrected silkily, and she suppressed a faint shiver at the knowledge that there were few men, or women, who could best him.

CHAPTER SEVEN

LUNCH COMPRISED GRILLED chicken, rice and a fava bean dish. The simple fare was filling, and Kristi accepted a small portion, preferring to complete the meal with fresh fruit.

'You wish to rest for an hour?'

She glanced across the table and met Shalef's steady gaze. 'You suggested showing me the falcons. I don't want to delay your joining your guests.'

'In that case we shall leave.' He rose from the table and Kristi did likewise, following him through the hallway to a rear door.

'The falcons are housed opposite the stables,' he indicated as they moved away from the house.

'You have horses?'

'Is that so surprising?'

Nothing about this man would surprise her. 'I didn't expect to find them here.'

'Do you ride?'

'Yes.' Her eyes glowed with remembered pleasure. 'I was taught as a child.' There was something magical about sharing the power rather than controlling it, the wonderful feeling of speed and the empathy one achieved between man and beast. 'They're beautiful animals.'

'Then you shall ride with me at sunrise tomorrow.'

A singularly sweet smile curved her generous mouth. It was months since she'd last ridden, and there could be little doubt that Shalef owned the finest Arabian stock. 'Thank you.'

'Is it the prospect of the ride or the sharing of it with me that affords you such pleasure?'

'The ride,' Kristi returned without hesitation, and heard his soft laughter.

The compound was large, much larger than it had appeared from the air, and she followed Shalef to the end of a long building some distance from the house.

'Stay there,' he bade her as they drew close to a large enclosure. 'You are a stranger, and the falcons will be wary.'

She watched as he unlocked an outer door and disappeared inside, only to emerge some minutes later wearing a heavy leather glove on one arm upon which rested a blue-grey falcon whose lower body was white with blackish-brown bars; it was leg-bound—attached to a short lead whose ring was firmly secured.

'This is one of my most prized falcons,' Shalef explained. 'It is extremely rare, and the most powerful of all the breeds. Its speed when it swoops on its prey is estimated at two hundred and ninety kilometres per hour.'

It looked fearsome, exuding a tremendous sense of predatory strength, and the claws, the beak were undeniably vicious.

'You enjoy the sport?'

'Falconry is a method of hunting game which was begun about four thousand years ago by the Persians. The challenge is in the training of the falcon, for it is an art that takes skill, a lot of time, and endless patience. First they must become used to having men around them. Then they are broken to the hood, which is placed over their head while they are carried in the field. The hood is removed only when the game is seen and the falcon is turned loose to pursue it. Finally, the birds must be trained to lure, so that they will not fly off with the game after they have struck it down or pounced on it.'

She looked at him carefully. 'One assumes you own some of the finest falcons in the country. Is that why Mehmet Hassan retreats here as your guest?'

'He is one of a chosen few.' The falcon rose up on its feet and arched its wings. Shalef said something briefly in Arabic and it immediately quietened. 'He's getting restless. I'll return him.'

Minutes later he rejoined her, and they walked slowly back to the house.

'You like being here.' It was a statement, and one he didn't refute.

'It's a place where I can relax and enjoy the company of valued friends without the intrusion of society.'

Kristi gestured towards the house, then widened the gesture to encompass the desert beyond. 'I can understand why. There is a harshness that challenges the survival of man.'

'Very profound, Kristi Dalton,' he lightly mocked as they entered the house.

Without thinking, she placed a hand on his arm. 'Thank you,' she said quietly.

'For what, precisely? Giving you a few hours of my time?'

'Yes. My being here must be a source of irritation.'

'Are you suggesting I deny it?'

She felt stung, the hurt incredibly strong for one brief second before she was able to mask it. She turned away, wanting only to be free of his disturbing presence, but a hand closed over her shoulder and forced her back to face him.

Kristi met his gaze and held it, hating him at that precise moment for being able to render her vulnerable.

When his head began to descend she averted her own, then she cried out as he cradled her nape so that she couldn't escape the pressure of his mouth.

She had no defence against a kiss that was hard and possessively demanding. He seemed to fill her mouth, exploring, coaxing a capitulation that she was loath to give.

Just as she thought she'd won, the pressure eased, and in its place was a soft, open-mouthed kiss that swamped her emotions and left her weak-willed and malleable.

The desire to kiss him back was impossible to deny, and her body swayed into his as she lifted her arms and linked her hands behind his head.

He permitted her to initiate a kiss, then he subjected her mouth to the explorative sweep of his tongue, teasing, tantalising in a manner that sent an electrifying awareness tingling through her veins, heightening her senses to a frightening degree as she began to melt beneath the magnetic thrill of his sensual onslaught.

Slowly, with infinite care, he eased the flare of passion, tempering it with one lingering kiss after the other on the soft fullness of her lower lip, the edge of her mouth, before trailing his lips up to rest against her temple. Then he gently pushed her to arm's length.

'I must leave.'

Kristi didn't feel capable of uttering so much as a word, yet she managed a sigh before turning away from him to seek the sanctuary and solitude of his bedroom.

A shower would rinse off the desert sand, and she'd shampoo her hair. Then she'd find pen and paper and compose a letter to Georgina Harrington. She'd also write a short note to Annie.

Thoughts of the studio brought forth an image of home. For a moment she almost wished that she were back in Australia. If it hadn't been for Shane, she wouldn't be in a desert a few hundred kilometres from Riyadh. Nor, she vowed silently as she stepped beneath the pulsing jet of warm water, would she be in a constant state of emotional turmoil over a man who could never be a part of her life. Or she a part of his.

It was late when the men returned, and after eight before dinner was served. Conversation was convivial, and it was clear that the falcons had performed well, the kill excellent. Kristi's vivid imagination conjured up their prey, the deadly power of the falcon, and she endeavoured to mask her distaste for a sport that centred on the death of the victim.

The last of the meal was cleared from the table and the men began to move into the lounge for coffee. Two of the guests displayed a penchant for strong cigars, and after an hour Kristi was conscious of a persistent headache as a result of passive smoking.

'If you don't mind, I'll retire for the night.' She stood, smiled at each of the men in turn, then moved towards the door.

Once clear of the room she contemplated taking a walk, but the evening air would not have cooled sufficiently for it to be more pleasant outdoors than in the air-conditioned interior of the house.

The bedroom was blissfully cool, and after brushing her teeth she undressed, donned the shirt that Shalef had provided the night before, then slipped beneath the covers of the large bed.

An hour later she was still awake and the pain in her head had intensified into a full, throbbing ache that showed no sign of dissipating.

Maybe there was some medication in the *en suite* bathroom that might alleviate the pain, she thought, and got up to see.

Switching on the light, she opened a drawer, and was in the process of searching the second when she heard Shalef's unmistakable drawl from the doorway.

'What are you looking for?'

'Paracetamol,' Kristi responded without preamble.

'Try the last cupboard above the vanity to your right.'

She moved towards the designated cupboard, extracted a slim packet, removed two tablets from the blister pack, found a glass and half filled it with water, then swallowed both tablets.

'You are unwell?'

She turned towards him. 'The cigar smoke gave me a headache.' Her fingers shook slightly as she closed the pack, and as she reached for the cupboard the pack slipped from her grasp.

She bent quickly to pick it up, then winced as the downward movement magnified the pain. In her hurry she neglected to foresee that the loosely buttoned shirt would gape, given its voluminous size, and she clutched the edges and held them tightly against her midriff. Her defensive action came too late, and there was little she could do to avoid the firm fingers which extricated her own from the cotton shirt.

'You are bruised.' He undid one button, then the one beneath it, drawing the edge down over her shoulder.

There were more bruises on various parts of her body, and he seemed intent on inspecting them all.

'You assured me you were uninjured,' Shalef said grimly, ignoring her efforts to remove his hands.

'I don't class a few bruises as *injuries*.' Her voice rose as his fingers probed a large, purpling patch close to her hip. *'Don't.'*

'You didn't suffer these from being held at bay, locked in the four-wheel drive,' he observed with deadly softness. 'Did the men undo the door and drag you out?'

His voice was like the finest silk being abraded by steel, and for some inexplicable reason her nerves felt as if they were stretched close to breaking-point.

'They didn't appear to understand English or French,'

she related starkly, and the muscles of his jaw tensed with chilling hardness.

'Did they beat you? Touch you in any way?'

'They stopped when I said your name.' The words sounded stilted even to her own ears, and his eyes narrowed at the fleeting changes in her expression.

She watched in mesmerised fascination as he lifted a hand and brushed his fingers across her cheek then trailed them down to the corner of her mouth. Gently he outlined the contour of her lower lip, then slid down the column of her throat to trace a path over the stitched edge of the shirt to the valley between her breasts.

Then his head lowered to hers, and his lips followed an identical route as he pushed the shirt aside and brushed his mouth back and forth against each bruise in turn.

Something wild and untamed unfurled deep within her, flooding her being with a slow, sweet heat as his lips closed over hers in a kiss that was so erotically evocative that she never wanted it to end.

No man had ever wreaked such havoc with her emotions, nor made her feel so wickedly wanton as she returned his kiss and silently begged for more.

She needed to feel the touch of his skin, the silky external layer sheathing the finely honed muscles and sinews that bound his broad bone structure into a frame that was solely, uniquely *his*.

His clothes followed the path of her shirt, and she gave a silent gasp as he swept an arm beneath her knees and lifted her high against his chest to carry her into the bedroom.

The sheets felt deliciously cool as he laid her down on the bed; then he lowered his body beside her, bracing his weight with his hands as he began an erotic tasting path that slowly traversed every hollow, every intimate crevice until each separate nerve-end screamed for the release she craved.

Not content, he rolled onto his back and carried her with him so that she sat nestled in the cradle of his thighs.

Kristi stilled as he extracted prophylactic protection, broke the seal, then extended it in silent query. She accepted it with fingers that trembled slightly, unsure whether to feel relieved or dismayed. A bubble of silent hysteria threatened to escape her lips as she contemplated whether she could complete the task with any degree of finesse. Perhaps she could opt out and hand it back to him...

His fingers closed over hers, guiding them, and her discomfiture was no longer an issue as his hands slid to her shoulders and captured her head, forcing her mouth down to his as he initiated a long, slow kiss that heated her veins and heightened her emotions to fever-pitch.

The juncture of her thighs ached, and she almost cried out as he gently exposed the aperture then lowered her against the length of his shaft.

She gained some relief, but not enough, not nearly enough, and a low, guttural moan rose in her throat as he drew her forward and brushed his lips against the soft, aching curve of her breast.

His tongue sought one hardened, highly sensitised peak and outlined the dusky aureole, drawing it carefully into his mouth as he gently traced the delicate ridges, before teasing the peak with the edge of his teeth.

'Please... Shalef.' She wasn't aware of uttering the plea, or that she said his name, and she gave a low groan of encouragement as he began to suckle. The pleasure was so intense that it became almost pain, and just as she thought that she could stand no more he diverted his attention to its twin.

His hands spanned her hips, encouraging a delicate sliding movement that almost drove her crazy, and she began to plead with him to ease the torturous ache deep within her.

He did, with such exquisite slowness that the alien invasion merely stretched silken tissues rather than tore them, and, when she gave a slight gasp and momentarily stilled, he stopped, sliding one hand up to cup her jaw as he forced her to look at him.

For long, timeless seconds his gaze raked her flushed features, searing through the moisture shimmering in those heavily dilated hazel eyes, disbelieving, yet having to believe, infinitely curious and filled with a white-hot rage that tightened the fingers at her jaw and sent his hand raking through the tousled length of her hair.

'You would set yourself up to experience the pain of vertical penetration,' he condemned in a dangerously silky voice moving fractionally so that she felt an edge of it, 'unsure whether or not you could accommodate me?'

She wanted to cry, but she was damned if she'd give in to a loss of control. A mixture of anger and despair began to replace passion, and with it came shame and a degree of embarrassment.

It was unnecessary to demand cessation, for he simply removed her, and she was unable to prevent an involuntary gasp at the acute sense of loss.

With an economy of movement he replaced the discarded covers, then settled back against the pillows.

She was incapable of saying so much as a word, although many chased incoherently through her brain. How could she tell him that no other man had made her feel the way he did? Or that there had been no one else because she'd never met a man with whom she'd wanted to share her body? Until now.

She lay quite still, consciously marshalling her breathing into a slow, measured pattern as she silently willed the tears to remain at bay.

They didn't, slowly welling and overflowing from the outer corners of her eyes, rolling down to disappear in her hair.

She wanted to slip out from the bed and dress, then leave the house and drive one of the vehicles through the night to the palace, where at first light she'd pack and have a taxi take her to the airport so that she could catch the first plane back to London. Except that she had no idea where the keys were, or how to neutralise the hunting lodge's security system.

'Why didn't you warn me?'

Kristi wasn't sure if her voice would emerge intact through the constriction in her throat, so she didn't even put it to the test.

The light from the bathroom cast a wide shaft of illumination across the bedroom, highlighting a strip of carpet, a large rosewood cabinet and a valet frame.

He shifted slightly, turning towards her, and even in the shadows he could determine a measure of her distress.

'If I had declared I'd never been this intimate with a man, you probably wouldn't have believed me,' she managed huskily. She'd led an active life, enjoyed numerous sporting pursuits. How could she have known her hymen was still intact?

'No,' Shalef admitted drily. 'Women usually choose to play the coquette, or pretend an innocence which doesn't exist.'

She didn't want to look at him, for she couldn't bear to see the mockery that she was sure must be evident, or glimpse the frustrated anger of a man who had pulled himself back from the brink of achieving sexual satisfaction.

She felt rather than saw his hand move, and she was unable to prevent the faint flinching of her facial muscles as he touched light fingers to her temple and discovered the damp trail of her drying tears.

She closed her eyes tightly as he followed their path, then slowly roamed her cheek with tactile gentleness, pausing at the edge of her mouth as he felt the trembling of her lips.

An arm curved over her waist and slipped beneath her shoulders as he drew her close, ignoring the stiffness of her body as he tucked her head beneath his chin.

Kristi felt his lips against her hair, and the light

caress of his hand as he soothed the taut muscles in her back.

A rawness crawled deep inside her, an aching loss so intense that it was all she could do not to weep silently. She had come so close to an emotional catharsis that not attaining it generated a feeling of deprivation. And deep inside she experienced a measure of anger—with herself for being so blind in believing that her innocence didn't matter, and with him for calling a halt when, at that finite moment, she would have welcomed the pain in order to experience the pleasure she'd believed must surely follow.

She lay very still, lulled by the solid beat of his heart beneath her breast, and she closed her eyes, wishing desperately for sleep to descend and blank out the events of the past hour.

Part of her wanted a separate space, wanted to turn away from him and move to the side of the bed, yet the delicate tentacles of need were too strong, the comfort he offered too pleasurable, so she remained where she was, gradually relaxing until the shadows deepened and she descended into a dreamless state.

CHAPTER EIGHT

NOT QUITE DREAMLESS, Kristi acknowledged from the depths of her subconscious as she ascended through the mists of sleep. She felt deliciously warm, and all her senses seemed to be finely tuned to the faint, musky smell of male skin beneath her lips. She could feel the soft brush of a hand as it trailed along her lower spine, while the other teased the softness of her breast.

Sensation unfurled as her body slowly wakened in response to his feather-light touch, and she murmured indistinctly as her breast burgeoned, its peak hardening in anticipation of the havoc his mouth could create.

She stirred, unable to remain still as the hand at the lower edge of her spine began to explore the contours of her hip, slipping down over her thigh to seek the core of her femininity. Her hastily indrawn breath was followed by a purr of pleasure, and her body arched against his as he began to tantalise her with leisurely expertise.

Every nerve-end began to pulsate until her whole body was consumed with a slow-burning fire that heated her veins and sent the blood pumping at an accelerated rate.

Slowly, with infinite care, he continued an evocative exploration of her body, heightening each sensual pleasure-spot to its ultimate pitch until she became suffused with an aching warmth. Not content with that, he repeated the exploration with the touch of his lips, creating such unbearable sensations that she clung to him unashamedly, silently begging for release from the tumultuous tide of emotion threatening to consume her.

Gently he eased himself between her legs, adjusting her hips as he coaxed her aroused flesh to accept his masculinity.

Kristi felt a sense of total enclosure as silken tissues expanded and stretched, and her faint gasp was caught as his mouth closed in possession over her own, the kiss so erotic that she didn't notice the sting of pain.

He began a gentle pacing, so that she felt every movement, every inch of the journey as the music of passion built deep within her, its tempo increasing as she urged him further and faster in a crashing crescendo that culminated in shock waves shuddering through her body as she reached breathtaking ecstasy.

A total loss of control, she mused as she began the slow descent back to reality. Although reality would never be quite the same again.

Instinct relayed to her the fact that his response had been too controlled, almost as if he had kept a tight rein in order to ensure that she experienced the ultimate pleasure without threat of it being overshadowed by his own.

Awareness defined new dimensions, and she savoured the musky scent secreted by their skin, the warm heat generated by their bodies, their still rapidly beating hearts, his, her own, and felt them slow as languor replaced passion in the sweet aftermath of satisfactory sex.

Lovemaking, Kristi corrected silently. What they'd shared was more than just *sex*.

Slowly she turned her head, marvelling as the first light of the new day's dawn slowly crept up over the horizon, shifting shadows and bathing all before it in a soft, hazy glow.

'Do you want to ride out into the desert?'

The promise of a new day enthralled her, and she couldn't suppress the delight in her voice as she answered him. 'Yes.'

He buried his fingers deep in her hair, then bent his head and bestowed a brief, hard kiss on her mouth before moving to the side of the bed. 'How quickly can you dress?'

Kristi slid out to stand beside him. 'As quickly as you.'

Ten minutes later they were cantering out of the compound, the horses whickering slightly in anticipation of the exercise.

Her mount was a beautiful thoroughbred, with an arrogant head and a fine, pacing step that promised speed once she gave him the rein.

Shalef moved beside her, looking magnificent in traditional *thobe* and *gutra*.

The steed he'd chosen was large and powerful, and as soon as they cleared the compound he urged it into a steady canter.

It felt wonderful to ride again, to enjoy the exhilaration and the power. The terrain of the desert was stark, the sense of isolation intense, yet she could understand the fascination it held, for there was a sense of timelessness apparent, almost a feeling of awe for early civilisation. With a little imagination, one could almost picture the camel train of an ancient era traversing the distant sand-dunes highlighted against the early-morning sky, a caravan of wandering Bedouin seeking food and a temporary camp. And the marauding plunder of tribal bands who sought to gain and mark territory in a land which had known violence since the beginning of time.

A faint shiver ran down Kristi's spine, and in an attempt to dispel such introspection she leaned forward in the saddle and urged her mount to increase his speed. Faster, until every muscle in her body strained and the air rushed through her clothes, tearing at her headscarf and loosening her hair.

Shalef drew abreast and maintained an identical pace as they raced together across the wide plain without any sense of competition, until Kristi eased back slightly, allowing her mount to slow to a canter.

A hand reached out and caught hold of her reins, and she straightened in the saddle, her features alive as she turned towards the man whose thigh was almost brushing her own.

He wasn't even breathing heavily, while she needed precious seconds to gain control of her voice.

'That was incredible!' Her eyes were deep brown velvet specked with glowing topaz, and her cheeks held a blush-pink glow from exertion. The scarf had come adrift, and her hair was in a state of tousled disarray.

'So are you,' Shalef offered softly, and her eyes widened as he leaned close and took her mouth in a long, hard kiss.

It was after seven when they entered the compound, and as they drew close to the stables two Filipino servants emerged to take care of the horses.

'Would you prefer a cold drink or coffee?' Shalef enquired as they entered the house.

'Cold,' Kristi responded without hesitation, following him through to the kitchen.

'Water or orange juice?'

'Juice.' She ran a hand over the taut muscles of one arm. 'Then I'm going to have a long, hot shower.'

The cook looked up as they entered, moving quickly to the refrigerator to extract a carafe of orange juice and chilled water before she tended to the coffee.

Kristi was supremely conscious of the man at her side, and all her fine body hairs seemed to extend like tiny antennae in recognition of his proximity. All her senses appeared to be in a state of heightened anticipation, for she was conscious of every breath she took, every beat of her heart, and it bothered her more than she cared to admit.

The hand that held her glass felt slightly unsteady, and she drank quickly in the need to escape his disturbing presence.

In the bedroom she gathered her spare set of clothes, which seemed to disappear and reappear freshly laundered in a short space of time each morning, and went through to the bathroom.

It took only seconds to discard her jeans and blouse, briefs and bra, and for a moment she looked wistfully at the spa-bath, then decided on the shower.

Kristi moved the dial to 'WARM', stepped beneath the flow of water and picked up the bar of soap. 'Bliss,' she breathed minutes later as she applied shampoo to her hair, only to freeze at the sound of the shower door sliding open.

Shalef stood framed in the aperture, and her eyes flew to his in consternation.

'You can't,' she protested as he stepped in beside her and closed the door.

'I can.' Irrefutable, the words merely confirmed his action, and she gave a startled gasp when he removed the shampoo bottle from her hand and completed her task, massaging her scalp with tactile expertise as the water rinsed the suds from her hair.

The soap came next, and she swept his hand aside as it glided over one breast then moved towards the other. 'Don't.'

The remonstration brought forth a husky laugh. 'You are embarrassed? After what we shared together in the early hours of this morning?'

His hand moved to her abdomen, then traced across to her hip and slid to the base of her spine, soothing in a manner which tugged alive a fierce ache in the pit of her stomach.

'Shalef—'

Whatever else she might have uttered was lost as his

mouth covered hers in a kiss that became flagrantly seductive as it gently coaxed, seeking a response that she was afraid to give. Her hands reached out, touching hard muscle and sinew as her fingers conducted a slow tracing of his ribcage, the indentation of his hard waist, and down over the flat musculature of his stomach.

A deep groan sounded low in his throat as he caught hold of her hands and held them, then his mouth eased away from hers and he rested his chin on the top of her head.

'Enough,' he said heavily. 'Otherwise we'll never get beyond the bedroom and there are guests who expect to sit down to breakfast with me in fifteen minutes.' He moved fractionally, letting his hand slide to cover her breast. 'Go.'

Kristi went, pausing only long enough to collect a towel, basic toiletries and her clothes.

By the time he entered the bedroom she was dressed and doing the best she could to persuade her damp hair into a semblance of order.

She was aware of his every move as he extracted briefs, trousers, shirt, and donned each of them before reaching for a clean *thobe*.

'Ready?'

Physically, although her emotions were in a questionable state!

The meal seemed to last for ever, the men inclined to linger over several cups of coffee, and it was almost ten when Shalef accompanied them out to the waiting helicopter.

The sound of the rotor-blades intensified, then the craft lifted off, paused, then wheeled away to the east.

Kristi listened till the sound disappeared, and she turned as Shalef re-entered the house. Her eyes locked with his as she tried to disguise her uncertainty. 'When do we leave for the palace?'

His expression was impossible to read. 'There is no immediate need to return for a few days.'

Kristi couldn't think of a thing to say.

'Unless, of course, you object,' Shalef added quietly.

She knew she should. Knew that to remain here with him was akin to divine madness. Yet the rational part of her brain was motivated by the dictates of her heart, urging her to embark on an emotional experience that would almost certainly end in heartbreak...although the journey itself would be unforgettable.

'I'll stay.'

Without a word he closed the distance between them and swept her into his arms.

'What do you think you're doing?' she asked in a faintly scandalised voice.

'Taking you to bed.' He carried her down the wide hallway to the room at its very end, then, once inside, he closed the door and allowed her to slide down to her feet.

Her eyes widened slightly at the vital vibrancy evident in those strong facial features, and she was unable to hide her own haunting vulnerability as his head began a slow descent.

The touch of his lips tantalised as they traced the outline of her mouth with evocative persuasion, then slid to the sensitive cord at the edge of her neck, grazing the sweet hollows before trailing up to take possession of her mouth.

Firm fingers dispensed with her clothes, then his own, and before she had time for coherent thought he urged her towards the bed and drew her onto its wide expanse.

Kristi lay still, mesmerised by her heightened senses and enraptured by the dark passion evident in his eyes. This close, she could sense the clean body smell emanating from his skin, and awareness coursed through her body like an igniting flame.

Her lips parted as he sought an erotic exploration of the sweet depths of her mouth, teasing the delicate ridges of her tongue with the tip of his own in an oral dance that matched the rhapsody created by his hands as they drifted with sensual sensitivity over her aroused skin.

She lost track of time, of place, as he submitted her to an erotic tasting of such exquisite proportion that her entire body began to ache with the need for fulfilment, and she began to move, silently enticing his possession.

His lips settled in the vulnerable hollow at the base of her throat, then trailed slowly down to the gentle swell of her breast, and she cried out as he took the engorged peak into his mouth and began a tender suckling that slowly intensified until it became a physical torment.

Kristi was unaware of the soft groan emerging from her throat as she reached for him, instinctively begging him in a voice she didn't recognise as her own.

Wild, pagan need consumed her as he began an intimate exploration, his touch attacking the fragile tenure of her control until she began to sob in helpless despair.

Then with one slow movement he entered her, his hard length enclosed by a tight sweetness that took his breath away.

She clung to him, unashamedly caught in the deep, undulating rhythm as she instinctively matched him stroke for stroke, exulting in the sensation that radiated through her body with such exquisite exhilaration.

Pagan, she acknowledged seconds later as he tipped her over the edge, then joined her there in a shuddering climax of his own.

Kristi was supremely conscious of every nerve-end, every cell in her body as she became filled with a languorous warmth, and she cradled his large frame close, loving the feel of his weight, the heat of his skin, slick with the sweat of his passion.

His heart beat strong and fast close to her own, and she sought his mouth, initiating a kiss which soon became *his* as he deepened her soft foray, changing it to something that staked his possession and branded her his own.

Afterwards he rolled onto his back, carrying her with him, and she arched her body, laughing softly as she felt his immediate response.

His hands slid up her ribcage and cradled her breasts, testing their weight as he began to caress each peak with the pad of his thumb, delighting in her reaction as she threw back her head.

Erotic abandon, she admitted a long time later, unsure whether to be pleased or dismayed that she'd become a begging wanton in his arms as he'd led her down a path to sensual conflagration.

'Should we get up, do you think?' Kristi queried as she lay in his embrace.

'I can't think of one good reason why right at this moment,' Shalef drawled, moving his head to brush his lips against her shoulder.

'Lunch?' she offered hopefully.

He bit her gently, then inched his way to the edge of her neck, nuzzling in a manner that sent a renewed surge of sensation arrowing through her body. 'We could have an early dinner.'

'Alternatively, I could go into the kitchen and bring us back a snack.'

'You're hungry for food?' he asked, and she responded teasingly,

'I need to keep up my strength.'

He levered himself easily off the bed and reached for his clothes. 'Stay here,' he commanded gently.

A slow, witching smile curved her lips, and her eyes sparkled with amusement. 'I wasn't planning on going anywhere.'

Shalef returned with a tray of chicken, salad and fresh fruit. After they'd eaten they talked, discussing anything and everything from early childhood memories to world politics, books, movies, art. Then they made leisurely love, and she became an avid pupil beneath his tutorage, taking pleasure from the depth of passion that she was able to arouse.

When the sun began to descend in the sky they rose from the bed, shared the spa-bath, then dressed and went to the dining room for dinner. And later, when the stars shone bright in an inky night sky, they made passionate love until sleep overcame desire.

It became the pattern for the next three days. Days that were filled with lovemaking and laughter, and with the passing of each night Kristi became more aware that to walk away from this man would bring unimaginable heartache.

Seize each moment, a tiny voice bade her. Treasure it and hold it close.

Yet such time-honoured axioms did nothing to help her sense of approaching despair. They couldn't stay here for ever. Sooner or later a phone call or a fax would summon Shalef back to the palace.

It happened on the morning of the fourth day. They arrived back from their early-morning ride to find a servant waiting for them with a cryptic fax which had come through in their absence. Shalef scanned it, then folded the sheet in three and thrust it into the side-pocket of his *thobe*.

'We have to return to Riyadh. Negotiations for your brother's release have been successful.'

Kristi couldn't believe it. 'Shane is to be freed?' Her face mirrored the immense surge of joy that tore through her body. 'How? When? *Where*?'

'Later today. He'll be transported out of the country and receive debriefing before being put on a plane to London.'

'When will I be able to see him?'

'The media circus will begin within hours of his arrival in England, I imagine,' Shalef declared as they crossed the compound. He cast her a dark, probing look. 'It would be advisable for you to be there before he arrives.'

Kristi felt her heart sink. Within a very short time the helicopter would deposit them at the palace. In less than twenty-four hours she would be on a plane to London.

Mission accomplished.

'I agreed to pay any expenses.'

His eyes darkened with anger. 'You insult me.'

'*Why*?' she demanded.

'I requested a favour from a friend,' he said silkily, 'without any pressure that it be granted.' He looked as if he wanted to shake her. 'There was no cost that you have not repaid me.'

Kristi absorbed his words, and felt part of her slowly die. It took tremendous effort to summon a smile, but she managed a passable facsimile. 'Thank you.'

Shalef inclined his head in silent acknowledgement, his eyes hooded, his features assuming a harsh mask.

It was over. The words echoed inside her brain like a death-knell. Without a word she turned and followed him indoors, showered, collected her spare set of clothes, and was ready to board the helicopter when it arrived less than an hour later.

CHAPTER NINE

THE WHEELS OF the large Boeing hit the tarmac, accompanied by the shrill scream of brakes as the passenger jet decelerated down the runway, then cruised into its designated bay at Heathrow airport.

Kristi moved through the terminal, showed her passport, then made her way to the revolving carousel, waited for her luggage to come through, collected it and completed Customs.

Securing a taxi was achieved without delay, and Kristi sank into the rear seat as the driver stowed her bags in the boot. Minutes later the vehicle eased forward into the queue of traffic seeking exit from the busy terminal.

The weather was dull and overcast, cool after the heat of Riyadh, and she fixed her attention beyond the windscreen as the taxi moved smoothly along the bitumen.

A complexity of emotions racked her body, not the least of which was relief that Shane was safe.

Saying goodbye to Shalef as she'd transferred from his Lear jet onto a commercial flight in Bahrain had been the most difficult part of all. Despite her resolve to keep their parting low-key, his brief, hard kiss had stung her lips, and his words of farewell had held the courteous tones of a business associate rather than the emotional intensity of a lover.

What did you expect? she demanded silently. You were attracted to the man, succumbed to his magnetic sex appeal, and shared a few days and nights of passion. Don't fool yourself it was anything other than that.

A week from now you'll be back in Australia, and a romantic interlude in the desert with a Saudi Arabian sheikh of English birth will gradually fade into obscurity.

But she knew that she'd never be able to forget him, and that no man could take his place.

Love, desire, passion. Were the three interdependent, or could they be separated and judged alone? The cold, hard fact was that women were far more prey to emotions than men.

Kristi viewed the streets of London, the traffic, and watched dispassionately as the taxi slid into the wide parking bay adjacent to her centrally placed hotel.

Within a matter of minutes a porter had taken charge of her bag and she was traversing the wide carpeted foyer to Reception.

On being shown to her room she unpacked only what was necessary, discarded her clothes, took a long, hot shower, then opted for a few hours' sleep, for despite it being mid-morning her body-clock was attuned to a different time-zone and she hadn't closed her eyes during the long flight.

When she woke it was early evening, and she donned a robe, made herself a cup of tea, then perused the room-service menu. After dinner she'd ring Sir Alexander Harrington and apprise him of Shane's release.

At nine she switched on the television and alternated channels until way past midnight, slept briefly, then rose and showered ready for an early breakfast.

Loath to venture far from the hotel in case a message came in regarding Shane's expected arrival, she met Georgina in one of the hotel's restaurants for an extended lunch.

'*Tell* me,' Georgina cajoled when they had eaten the entrée, done justice to the main course, and were partway through a delicious concoction of fresh fruit and ice cream.

Kristi lifted her head and met her friend's teasing smile. 'Tell you what?'

'Shane's release is wonderful. It made the initial subterfuge worthwhile.' Georgina's eyes sparkled with intense interest as she leaned forward. 'But give me the details on Shalef bin Youssef Al-Sayed.'

'What details?'

'I refuse to believe you weren't attracted to the man.'

It would have been so easy to confide in a trusted friend, but to do so would only have caused Kristi pain and, perhaps, a feeling of regret. 'He was a very gracious host,' she said carefully.

'Kristi,' Georgina admonished her, 'you're being evasive.'

'OK, what do you want me to say? That he's a wildly sensual man who has women falling at his feet with practically every step he takes?' As you did, a silent voice taunted. She'd been gone two days. Had he contacted any one of his many women friends in Riyadh—*Fayza*?—dined with her, perhaps sated his sexual appetite in her bed? Dear God, even the thought made her feel physically ill.

'Aren't you going to finish dessert?'

Kristi collected herself together. 'No. Shall we order coffee?'

That evening she dined with Sir Alexander and Georgina, and when she returned to the hotel there was a coded message indicating that Shane was due to arrive the following morning.

Sleep was almost impossible and caught in intermittent snatches. With no knowledge of what flight he'd be on, or where it was coming from, she could only wait.

The telephone call came through shortly before midday, and at the sound of her brother's voice all the pent-up emotion culminated in a rush of tears.

'You're in the same hotel?' She couldn't believe it, wouldn't believe it until she saw him. 'What floor, what room number?'

'Order a meal from Room Service, a magnum of champagne, and give me twenty minutes to shower and shave,' Shane instructed, adding gently, 'Then I'll join you.'

He made it in fifteen, and once inside her room he swooped her up in a bear hug and swung her round in a circle before depositing her on her feet. 'Hi there.' His smile was the same, his laughter as bright as ever, but he looked tired and he'd lost weight. He was tall, his hair darker than hers—a deep brown with a hint auburn—and he had strong features and a skin texture that bore exposure to the sun.

'Hi, yourself,' Kristi said softly, leading him to the table set at one end of the room. The food had arrived only minutes before, and she watched as he took a seat, uncorked the champagne, then filled two flutes.

'Here's to being back in one piece.'

'Unharmed?'

'As you see.'

'I think,' Kristi ventured unsteadily, 'you'd better consider assignments in less politically volatile countries. I don't want to go through this again in a hurry.'

His eyes—deep brown flecked with topaz like her own—speared hers. 'Point taken. Off the record, whose influence did you employ to gain my release?'

'Shalef bin Youssef Al-Sayed's.'

An expressive, soft whistle escaped his lips. 'Should I ask how you made contact with him?'

'Initially through Sir Alexander Harrington.'

'And?'

She effected a faint shrug. 'I gave my word.' There was no need to say why, or to whom. Shane possessed the same degree of integrity with *his* sources.

'Do I get to meet Al-Sayed?'

'Possibly. Maybe.' She lifted a hand and smoothed back her hair. 'I'm not sure.'

He noted the nervous gesture, the faint tenseness at the edge of her mouth, and clenched his teeth. If she'd been hurt, by *anyone*, there would be hell to pay.

'So, tell me what happened,' Kristi encouraged, and Shane took up the story from the time of his capture. She recognised the holes he failed to fill, and accepted them.

'This afternoon a statement will be issued to the media,' he concluded with weary resignation. 'I'll be caught up with interviews, television. Then I fly back to Sydney tomorrow afternoon.'

'So soon?'

'The Australian media will want their piece of the action,' he said wryly. 'Then I'm going to lie low for a while.'

'Maybe I can get the same flight,' she said pensively. It seemed an age since she'd left home, and she wanted to resume her life from where she'd left off...how long ago? Five weeks? It felt like half a lifetime.

'No. That wouldn't be advisable. Give it a few days, then follow me.'

She looked at him carefully, seeing the visible signs of strain and tiredness, and expressed her concern. 'You should get some sleep.'

'I will. I'll ring through when I can, but it may not be until tomorrow morning,' he warned as he stood up.

Kristi saw him out, then closed the door behind him.

Within hours of Shane's departure Kristi secured a flight for Sydney for a few days ahead. Once the booking had been made and she had her ticket, her leaving seemed more of a reality.

Filling those days required little effort as Georgina took charge, first of all dragging her into Harrods, then following it with dinner and a show. The following morning was devoted to attending a beauty parlour for a massage, facial, pedicure, manicure, followed by lunch and a movie.

'Tonight is *mine*,' Kristi declared as they emerged from the cinema in the late afternoon. 'I'm going back to the hotel, ordering room service, followed by an early night.' She gave her friend a stern look. 'And no arguments. I have a long flight ahead of me tomorrow afternoon.'

'So what? You sleep on the plane.' Georgina was carried away with enthusiasm. 'We could go to a nightclub.'

'And get home at three in the morning? No, thanks.'

'It's your last night in town,' Georgina protested. 'You can't spend it alone.'

'Watch me.'

'You leave me no choice but to ring Jeremy and have him take me out.'

'Enjoy,' Kristi bade her, offering a wicked grin, and Georgina laughed.

'I will, believe me.' She leaned forward and pecked Kristi's cheek. 'You only have a block to walk to the hotel. I'll catch a taxi. See you at the airport tomorrow.'

It was almost six when Kristi entered the hotel foyer and took the lift to her floor. There were no messages, and she ordered room service, then stripped off her clothes and pulled on a robe.

Her meal arrived, and she picked at it, then pushed the plate aside. Television failed to hold her interest, and at ten she cleansed her face of make-up, brushed her teeth then slid into bed, only to lie awake staring at the ceiling, fervently wishing that she had agreed to go out with Georgina. At least the bright lights and loud music would have done something to alleviate this dreadful sense of despondency.

She must have fallen asleep, and when she woke the next morning it was late. A shower did much to restore her equanimity, and she ordered breakfast, then made a start with her packing.

A double knock at her door heralded the arrival of Room Service, and she moved across the room to unlock it and allow the waiter access.

But no waiter resembled the tall, dark-haired, immaculately suited man standing in the aperture.

CHAPTER TEN

'SHALEF.' KRISTI HADN'T realised that it would hurt so much to say his name.

Cool grey eyes raked her slender form, lingered briefly on the soft curve of her mouth, then slid to meet her own. 'Aren't you going to ask me in?'

She dug deep into her resources and managed to display a measure of ease, all too aware of the rapid pulse beat at the base of her throat. 'Would there be any point if I refused?'

'None at all.'

He moved into the room as she stood to one side, and his expression hardened as he saw the open suitcase on the bed.

'You're leaving?'

She looked at him carefully, seeing the inherent strength, the indomitable power that allowed him to shape life in the manner he chose. 'Yes.'

The silence in the room was such that it almost seemed a palpable entity, and her nerves stretched until they felt as taut as a finely strung bow. The sensation angered her unbearably, and she silently damned him for being able to generate such havoc.

He looked at her for what seemed an age, his eyes dark, their inscrutable depths successfully shielding him from any possibility of her gauging his emotions.

When at last he spoke, he appeared to select his words with care. 'We need to talk.'

There wasn't a thing she could say that wouldn't sound inane, so she remained silent, waiting for him to continue.

'I'll be in London for a month, then I fly to Paris,' he revealed. 'I want you with me.'

The breath caught in her throat and threatened to choke her.

'No comment, Kristi?' he queried with a degree of mocking cynicism.

'As what?' Was that her voice? Even to her own ears it sounded impossibly husky. 'Your mistress?'

He didn't answer for several long seconds. 'There are many advantages.'

The tissues around her heart began to tear. Her eyes met his and held them without any effort at all. 'I won't be content with second best, waiting for a stolen night or two whenever you could slip away.' She was breaking in two, and the pain was so intense that she was sure it must be clearly visible to him. Her throat began to ache with the constriction of severe control. 'I would rather not have you at all.'

'Then marry me.'

For a moment she was robbed of the ability to speak. 'Why?' she demanded at last. Her eyes clung to his, searching for some hint of passion, any intensity of emotion by way of reassurance.

'You're a rarity among women of my acquaintance,' Shalef said with quiet emphasis. 'Intelligent, courageous. Equally at ease among the social glitterati as you are with my Bedu friends in the desert.'

She closed her eyes in an effort to veil the pain. 'That's hardly a reason for marriage,' she managed slowly.

'You refuse?'

She looked at him carefully, wanting, needing so desperately to accept, yet knowing that if she did she could never be content with good sex and affection as a substitute for love.

It would be so easy to say yes. To accept what he offered and make do with it. Yet she wanted it all, and he wasn't ready to give it.

'I'm flying back to Australia on the early-afternoon flight. Shane is already in Sydney, and it is more than time we both attempted to attend to business.'

'You know I will follow you.'

She looked at him with clear eyes, the pain hidden deep beneath those liquid brown depths. 'Please don't.' Not unless you love me, she added silently.

'You are prepared to discard what we have together?'

It will kill me, she thought. 'Without love there is very little to discard.'

She was mad, *insane* to consider turning him down. A faint bubble of hysteria rose in her throat with the knowledge that she had to be the only woman on any

continent in the world who would consider rejecting
Shalef bin Youssef Al-Sayed.

Yet, if she accepted him *now*, it would be akin to accepting a half-measure. Most—dear heaven, *all* women
of her acquaintance would be content with less. To have
him in their bed, access to his immense wealth and the
rewards it would bring would be enough.

'You offer me everything,' Kristi said slowly, and
was unable to prevent the faint, husky catch in her voice.
Deep inside she felt incredibly sad. She'd hoped for so
much, *prayed* that he would say the words she desperately wanted to hear. 'Everything except your love.'
Her eyes searched his, hoping to pierce the inscrutable
barrier and discover a depth of emotion that was based
on more than just desire for her body.

'I want, *need* to be more to you than just a woman
gracing your arm, a hostess in your home.' She paused,
then added quietly, 'A mistress in your bed.'

There wasn't so much as a flicker in his expression
to give any visible indication of his feelings. It angered
her unbearably, making her want to rage, *shout*, hit him
in order to get some kind of reaction.

'I asked you to be my wife.' The words were softly
spoken, yet deadly, and she shivered inwardly as a sliver
of ice slid down the length of her spine.

She lifted her head, tilting her head fractionally in
silent challenge. 'To bear your sons?' Inside she was
slowly dying. 'If you plant only the seeds of daughters
in my womb, will you cast me aside for another wife
who might sire the son you desire—you *need* to uphold
the coveted name of Al-Sayed?'

Icy rage flared briefly in his eyes before it was quickly masked. 'You would lead an envied lifestyle.'

She thought of Nashwa and her daughters, and knew she could never be meekly accepting of such subjugation.

'It isn't enough,' Kristi offered with incredible sadness, aware that life without him would be like dying a very slow and painful death. 'When I marry, I want to believe it will be for ever. That *I* am as important to the man I accept as my husband as he is to me.' Her eyes felt as if they were drowning in unshed tears. 'Above all others. Beyond material possessions.' The ache in her throat was a palpable lump she dared not attempt to swallow. 'I need to know I am everything you need. All you ever want.' She felt boneless, and in danger of falling in an ignominious heap at his feet.

'You ask for guarantees, when with human emotions there can be none? Assurances are only words, given at a time when the head is ruled by the heart.'

'I feel sorry for you, Shalef. True love is a gift. Priceless.'

'I do not require your sympathy,' he declared with an infinite degree of cynicism.

'No,' she agreed bravely. 'You do not even require me.' It almost killed her to voice the words. 'My position in your life, your bed will be easily filled.'

His eyes narrowed fractionally, their depths so darkly unfathomable that it made her feel immeasurably afraid. 'You play for high stakes.'

Her chin lifted, and it took every ounce of strength she possessed to keep her voice level. 'The highest.'

'And if you lose?'

Kristi was aware of her fragile hold on her emotions. Afterwards, she could cry. But not yet. *'Inshallah,'* she said with quiet simplicity.

A tiny flame leapt in his eyes, flaring briefly before being extinguished beneath the measure of his control.

For one infinitesimal second she thought that he might strike her, so intense was his anger, then she silently damned a vivid imagination. He could employ a far more effective method of retribution if he so chose, without resorting to physical violence.

'You try my patience.'

There were words she could have uttered, but they were meaningless phrases, and not worth uttering. 'Please.' She lifted a hand, then let it fall helplessly down to her side. 'I have to finish packing.'

His eyes resembled dark shards of slate as he thrust one hand into his trouser pocket in a tightly controlled gesture.

'You want me to leave?'

'Yes.'

His facial muscles tensed over sculptured bone. 'As you please. But first—'

He reached for her, and she froze, her eyes widening with an apprehension that had little to do with fear as he lowered his head to hers.

The touch of his mouth was soft against her own, and she was unaware of the tiny, inarticulate sound that emerged from her throat as the edge of his tongue made an exploratory sweep over the full curve of her lower lip.

She wanted to cry out, Don't do this to me. A treacherous warmth invaded her veins, firing her body with a passion that she knew she'd never experience with any other man.

It was like drowning, descending with exquisite slowness into a nirvana-like state where reality faded into obscurity. There was only *now*, and the wealth of sensation that he was able to evoke.

Her body shook slightly as she fought against giving a response, and she felt the ache of unshed tears as he alternately teased and cajoled, pressing home with each small advantage gained, until her mouth aligned with his in involuntary capitulation.

A despairing groan rose and died in her throat as he deepened the kiss, possessing, demanding, *invading* in a manner that made her body tremble, and she clutched at his shoulders in a desperate bid to cling onto something tangible as he swept her into an emotional void from which she doubted she could emerge intact.

His passionate intensity was almost a violation, and when he released her she stood perfectly still, afraid that the slightest movement would rend every crack in her crumbling composure.

Part of her wanted to scream, *Go*; get out of my life before I break into a thousand pieces; the other part wanted to beg him to utter the necessary words that would bind her to him for ever.

His eyes were dark and partly hooded, making it impossible to read anything in his expression.

Lifting a hand to her face, he trailed a forefinger

lightly over the swollen curves of her mouth, then traced a path along the edge of her jaw and back again.

For what seemed an age he simply looked at her, imprinting on his mind her delicate features, the flawless skin, waxen-pale from the intensity of her emotions, the wide-spaced, fathomless deep brown and topaz eyes, and the bruised softness of her mouth.

Then his hand dropped to his side, and he turned towards the door, walking to it, through it without so much as a backward glance.

The sound of the lock clicking into place proved the catalyst for the release of her tears, and she stood exactly where he'd left her as their flow trickled to each corner of her mouth, then slowly slid to her chin.

Kristi stayed locked into immobility for a very long time, then something stirred within her, providing her with sufficient strength to turn and walk back into the bedroom, where she methodically completed her packing.

She even managed to bathe her face and apply fresh make-up before crossing to the in-house phone and alerting Reception that her bags were ready to be taken down.

'Thank you, Miss Dalton. A car is waiting.'

One last check round the suite, then she caught up her shoulder bag and moved out into the hallway. The lift transported her down to Reception, where she was informed that her account had already been settled.

Her fingers shook as she put away her credit card then handed over the key. Shalef. Like the sleek Bentley parked by the kerb outside the main entrance, with its boot open ready to receive her luggage, it represented a final gesture. A silent, mocking attestation to what she had given up.

Kristi stepped through the revolving door and out into the cool air, and the chauffeur opened the rear passenger door.

She didn't hesitate as she crossed to his side. 'Please thank Sheikh bin Youssef Al-Sayed for his kindness,' she said firmly, 'and tell him that I chose to hire a taxi.'

The chauffeur paled with concern. 'Miss Dalton, I have strict instructions to drive you to the airport and assist you through Customs.'

She offered a faint smile of dismissal. 'That won't be necessary.'

'The Sheikh will be annoyed.'

'With me,' she clarified. One eyebrow rose in wry amusement. 'I don't imagine his instructions included bundling me into the car against my will?'

'No, Miss Dalton.'

'Then you are exonerated from any blame.' Turning away, she spoke to the porter and had him beckon a hovering taxi.

Within minutes it pulled out into the flow of traffic and Kristi leaned back against the seat and stared blindly out of the window. There were people briskly walking on the pavements, coats caught tightly closed against the cold. And it began to rain, settling into a heavy deluge that diminished visibility and set the wipers swishing vigorously back and forth against the windscreen.

In less than twenty-four hours she would touch down

to warm summer temperatures, soft balmy breezes, and *home*. The prospect of seeing Shane again, and a few very close friends, should have evoked anticipatory pleasure. Instead, she was filled with a desolation so acute that it became a tangible pain, tearing at her insides and leeching the colour from her face.

CHAPTER ELEVEN

'ANYTHING OF INTEREST in next week's bookings?' Kristi queried as she deposited her camera-case on a nearby chair.

'Nothing outstanding,' Shane relayed as he scanned the appointment book spread out on the desk.

It was late, Annie had left for the day, commuters were on their way home, and outside a traffic lull had emptied the streets.

Soon it would be dark, bright neon signs would vie for attention, and the restaurants and theatres would fill with people seeking food, fun and laughter.

Kristi had been back in Sydney for more than a month. Six weeks, three days and counting, she mused idly as she crossed the floor and stood gazing idly out over the city's skyscape.

The inner harbour waters were a brilliant, sparkling blue beneath the sun's rays, their surface dotted with a mix of pleasure craft, two ferries sailing in opposite directions and a huge freighter led by a pilot tug *en route* to a harbour dock.

Two days after her return from London she'd thrown

herself into work, taking every assignment that was logged into her appointment book in an effort to keep busy during the daylight hours so that she wouldn't have time to *think*.

She had even let it be known that she was prepared to cover the social circuit, and as a consequence she'd been out most nights at one function or another, photographing some of the city's glitterati. Two weddings, two christenings…the list was far too lengthy, the pace too frenetic for one person alone.

The sun's warmth had coloured her skin a light honey-gold, but her eyes held shadows of sadness, her seldom offered smile lacked any real warmth, and her soft curves had become redefined into almost waif-like slenderness.

She could cope, she assured herself silently. She *had* to cope. The nights were the worst—hours when she lay awake staring into the darkness, *remembering*, caught up with visions so graphic, so explicit that it became an agony of the mind as well as of the flesh.

'I've had an offer which I'm tempted to accept,' Shane offered slowly, hating the shadows beneath her eyes, the carefully contrived smile, and the hint of sadness apparent whenever she thought no one was looking.

'Hopefully not in the wilds of Africa, or Bosnia?' Despite her lightly voiced query, there was an underlying concern. Neither location was an impossibility.

'New Zealand. A geographic spread for the tourism industry. It'll provide a contrast to my last assignment,' he noted with wry humour. 'As a bonus I get to go skiing and trek the Milford Sound.'

She turned back to face him. 'When do you leave?'

'How well you know me,' came the slightly wry observation. 'Tomorrow. Is that a problem?'

'When will you be back?'

'The end of next week, providing the weather holds and there are no delays.' His expression softened. 'Why don't you cancel a few appointments and take some time off? You look ragged.'

'Thanks.' She managed a smile that didn't fool him in the slightest. 'Just what I needed to hear.'

'Hey,' Shane chided her gently. Lifting a hand, he brushed his knuckles along the edge of her jaw. 'I care.'

A smile trembled at the edge of her lips. 'I know.'

'Shalef bin Youssef Al-Sayed may have been instrumental in saving my hide,' he said quietly, 'but if I could get my hands on him now I'd kill him for whatever it is that he's done to you.'

Her eyes were remarkably steady as she met his. 'He wanted marriage,' she said evenly. 'For all the wrong reasons.'

'You love him.'

It was a statement she didn't bother to deny. For as long as she could remember they'd shared an affinity, an extra perception that transcended the norm. It generated an indestructible bond—two minds so attuned to each other's thoughts that there had rarely been the need to explain an action.

'It isn't enough.' Her eyes felt large and ached with suppressed emotion.

'The man is a fool,' Shane said gently.

There had been no phone call, no fax. But then,

she hadn't expected any. You lie, a tiny voice taunted. Admit you hoped he would initiate some form of contact. Shalef bin Youssef Al-Sayed was a master player, and she hadn't played the game according to his plan. There were a hundred other women who could fill his bed. Ten times that many who would leap at the chance.

Kristi switched on the answering machine and caught up her camera-bag. 'Let's lock up and get out of here.'

'Dinner. Somewhere that serves good food,' Shane suggested as he followed her to the door.

'I'd rather go home.'

He tended the lock, checked that it was firmly in place, then moved ahead of her down the single flight of stairs. 'A restaurant. I'm buying. And don't argue,' he added softly as they reached the pavement.

French cuisine at its best, Kristi mused almost two hours later. Despite her professed lack of appetite, she'd managed to do justice to chicken consommé followed by a delectable portion of steamed fish with a delicate lemon sauce, accompanied by an assortment of vegetables. To finish, she'd selected a compote of fresh fruit doused in brandy, then flambéed and served with cream.

'Coffee?'

'Please,' she said gratefully. 'Black, very strong.' A few months ago she would have requested a decaffeinated variety and added milk. How some things change, she mused idly as she pushed down the plunger of the cafetière and poured the dark, aromatic brew into two cups. Adding a liberal amount of sugar, she sank back in her chair, then lifted the cup to her lips and took an appreciative mouthful.

The glass of Cabernet Shiraz she'd sipped throughout the meal had had a mellowing effect. 'Thanks.'

'For dinner?'

Kristi smiled. 'For insisting on bringing me here.'

'My pleasure.'

It was late, she was tired, and she knew that she really should go home, but she was loath to return to her empty apartment. So she finished her coffee and poured another for herself and for Shane.

'Want to talk about it?' he queried lightly, and she shook her head.

'Then let's do the business thing. What do you think about allowing Annie to buy a small share of the studio?'

'You're serious?'

'You have reservations?'

'It's been Dalton Photographics for years,' she protested. 'Why change?'

'It will still be Dalton Photographics.'

Comprehension dawned as she remembered the faintly wistful expression on a certain young woman's face whenever Shane was in town. *'Annie?'*

'Is it so obvious?'

'Not to anyone else.' A slow, sweet smile lit her features. 'I can't think of anyone I'd rather have as a sister-in-law.'

'I proposed last night. When I get back from New Zealand we'll make it official. More coffee?'

She shook her head, and he beckoned for the account,

then checked off each item, signed, and handed over a tip as he got to his feet.

He took her key as they reached their parked vehicles, unlocked her door, then saw her safely seated behind the wheel with her belt in place.

'Drive carefully.'

She cast him a teasing glance. 'Always,' she assured him. 'Don't fall off the side of a mountain.'

'No chance.' He reached out a hand and brushed his fingers against her cheek. 'I'll phone.'

'Make sure of it.' She turned the key in the ignition and fired the engine, then put the car into gear. *'Ciao.'*

It took fifteen minutes to reach her apartment, another fifteen for her to shower and slip into bed.

Perhaps it was the wine or the numerous sleepless nights but the next thing she heard was the sound of her alarm the following morning.

Annie was on the phone when Kristi walked into the studio shortly after eight, and in comical sign language she indicated that there was hot coffee in the percolator and could Kristi pour one for her too.

Annie should have opted for a career on the stage, Kristi mused as she extracted two mugs, added sugar, filled each with the hot, deliciously aromatic brew and deposited a mug on Annie's desk. The girl was a natural-born satirist who could mimic anyone you cared to name.

'Miss Dalton,' Annie reiterated in a low, devilishly husky voice as soon as she replaced the receiver, her eyes sparkling with impish humour, 'is summoned to undertake a photographic session at one of *the* most fabulous homes Point Piper has to offer. An interior decorator is being flown in from London *after* she's sighted photographs of each room, the existing landscaping, and the exterior shot from every imaginable angle.'

'When?'

'One gets the feeling it should have been yesterday. I said that you couldn't possibly fit him in until this afternoon.'

Kristi took an appreciative sip of coffee. 'And?'

'He negotiated for this morning.'

'What did you say?'

'I almost considered rescheduling. But he sounded...' She paused, then continued with dramatic intonation, 'frightfully autocratic. I decided he deserved to be taught a little humility.'

'You're incorrigible.'

'I know. I need taking in hand,' she declared with humour, and Kristi gave a subdued laugh.

'Shane assures me he is in line to do just that.' Her features softened with genuine affection. 'I'm delighted for both of you.'

Annie's eyes acquired an extra sparkle. 'Thanks. It'll be a small wedding, just immediate family. Shane wants it to happen three days after he returns from New Zealand.' Her smile widened into a mischievous grin. 'I'm plumping for the end of the month.'

'It will be interesting to see who wins.'

'I'll have fun enjoying Shane's method of persuasion.'

Kristi experienced a shaft of pain at Annie's obvious

happiness, and endeavoured to bury it deep beneath the surface. 'I don't imagine he'll find cause for complaint.'

The strident sound of the phone interrupted their conversation and Annie snatched up the receiver, spoke into it at length, scanned the appointment book, made a booking, then concluded the call.

'Now, where were we?'

'Our so-named autocratic client,' Kristi reminded her. 'What if he wants shots of the pool reflecting the early-morning sun?'

'You develop this afternoon's film then shoot tomorrow,' Annie rationalised, raising her hands in an expressive gesture. 'As long as the courier picks up before five they'll be on a flight out of here tomorrow night.'

'You were able to convince him of that?'

'He didn't threaten to use one of the competition.'

'What time am I supposed to be there?'

'One-thirty. He didn't even query the fee.'

Kristi shot her a sharp look. 'Tell me you didn't load it.'

'*Moi*?' Annie queried with mock humour. 'I simply informed him there was an extra charge for a rush job.'

'What would I do without you?'

'Survive,' the vivacious brunette responded with a sunny smile.

Kristi finished the last of her coffee, then rinsed and put away the mug before checking the appointment book. 'Bickersby, studio, eight-thirty, followed by a ten-thirty session at a client's home in Clontarf. Children's photographs.' She would have enough time to finish, return to the studio, grab some lunch, then be at Point Piper by one-thirty.

* * *

Annie was right—the house was fabulous, Kristi decided a few hours later as she parked her car in a street lined with prestigious homes. Some had been there a long time, while there were a few huge modern structures which had obviously replaced the original houses, comprising three and sometimes four levels against the sloping cliff-face. The view out over the harbour was spectacular, and the price-tag for each home would run into several millions of dollars.

She ran a quick check of the house number, then alighted from the car, collected her gear, and approached the security intercom attached to an ornate steel gate.

At the front door a housekeeper greeted her and led the way through a spacious foyer to an informal lounge.

The interior was a little too ascetic for Kristi's taste. There should have been artwork on the walls, bowls filled with freshly cut flowers, and the primrose-painted walls needed be repainted in cool off-white or pale calico to emphasise the light, airy design.

'My employer requested that I convey his apologies. He's been delayed by a business call which may take up to ten minutes. Would you like a cool drink or a cup of coffee or tea while you wait?'

'Tea would be lovely, thanks.' Lunch had been an apple eaten *en route* from her previous booking. Photographing children was a hazardous occupation, for they tended to be unpredictable when faced with a stranger wielding a camera. This morning's session had run badly over time, with a harried young mother professing that it would be *years* before she could contemplate assembling her normally angelic little darlings for another professional sitting. Despite Kristi's efforts to capture their amusement with a hand puppet, the children, aged eighteen months, three and four years, had collectively gone from shy to awkward to uncooperative, resorted to tears, then finally succumbed to blatant bribery.

There was a sense of relief, Kristi mused wryly, in that this afternoon's booking involved an inanimate house. Crossing to the wide glass window, she turned back and checked the light, mentally choosing the best angles.

The housekeeper appeared with a tray which she set down on a low table. 'I'll leave you to pour.' She indicated a plate of delicately prepared sandwiches. 'Just in case you're hungry.'

Kristi gave an appreciative smile. 'Thanks. I missed lunch.'

The tea was Earl Grey, the sandwiches smoked salmon and cream cheese. Divine, she described them silently as she bit into another and replaced her cup on the tray.

She would have liked to wander through the house while she waited, observing and conducting a professional assessment. It would save time.

With ideal contemplation she wondered at the identity of the new owner. The house was only a few years old, and its design held the stamp of one of Sydney's finest architects whose brilliance commanded an exorbitant fee. Despite the colours not being her personal preference, the workmanship was superb. The fact that he was employing an international interior decorator indicated that no expense would be spared in establishing the owner's individual taste.

'Miss Dalton?'

Kristi turned at the sound of the housekeeper's voice.

'I'll take you down to the office now.'

They descended to the next level via a wide, curved staircase which led to a spacious marble-tiled area complete with an ornate fountain centrally positioned beneath a crystal chandelier. The housekeeper indicated a hallway to her left.

'The office is situated at the end, the last door on the right.'

There was no logical reason for the faint unfurling of nerves inside Kristi's stomach or the prickle of apprehension that settled between her shoulderblades as she drew closer.

Crazy, she dismissed as the housekeeper paused beside the closed door and knocked before standing to one side.

'Please go in, Miss Dalton.'

A faint shiver shook her slim frame, yet her hand was steady as she turned the handle and pushed open the door.

It was a large room, she saw at once, complete with an assortment of high-tech electronic business equipment. Bookcases lined one wall, and the desk was an expensive antique.

Behind it the high-backed swivel-chair was empty, and her eyes slid to a tall figure silhouetted against the floor-to-ceiling plate-glass window.

The man's height and breadth looked achingly familiar, and the breath caught in her throat as she willed him to turn and face her.

Almost as if he sensed her apprehension, he shifted, his movements deliberately slow as he swung away from the window.

Shalef.

There was something primitive in his expression, and every instinct she possessed warned of the need for caution. It vied with a slow-burning anger that made her want to demand a reason for his presence in Sydney—more particularly, *why* he had summoned her to this house.

Innate dignity put a temporary rein on her temper as she studied his features, noting the fine lines fanning out from the corners of his eyes, the chiselled perfection of his mouth, the slashes down each cheek that seemed more deeply etched than she remembered.

Superbly tailored black trousers accentuated the muscular length of his legs, while the white silk shirt lent emphasis to his height and breadth of shoulder. He had loosened the top three buttons of his neck and folded back both cuffs, lending a casual, relaxed look that was belied by the most electric energy projected with effortless ease.

It was an energy that both thrilled and frightened, for she'd witnessed it unfurled and at its most dangerous.

Now she was unsure of its measure, and of his precise reason for requesting her presence.

It took considerable effort to inject her voice with polite civility. 'There are any number of competent photographers listed in the telephone directory capable of providing the services you require.' She drew in a deep breath, then released it slowly. 'It would better if you contacted one of them.'

One dark eyebrow lifted slightly and his smile was faintly cynical. 'Better for whom?'

If he was going to play games, she'd turn around and walk out *now*. 'Shalef—'

'I was assured by your secretary that the photographs would be ready early this evening,' he declared with dangerous silkiness. 'Are you now implying that you intend to renege on a verbal business agreement?'

Professionalism and sheer inner strength brought a lift to her chin and lent her eyes an angry sparkle. She'd complete the session and provide him with his wretched photographs, if only to prove that he no longer possessed the power to affect her. 'Perhaps you could tell me precisely what you want, then I can get started.'

He didn't move, but she sensed his body muscles tense with restrained anger.

'I return to London tomorrow. I'd prefer to take the prints with me.'

Her eyes flashed with brilliant fire. 'Why a London interior decorator? What's wrong with employing an Australian firm?'

'I have utilised this firm's services for a number of years.' He paused, then continued quietly, 'I trust their judgement and have no qualms about leaving them to complete everything to my satisfaction in my absence.'

Pain knotted in the region of her stomach, and she

had to consciously stop herself from gasping out loud. After tonight she'd never see him again.

'Very well.'

He shifted away from the desk and walked to the door. 'We'll begin outside while the light is still good.'

Instead of choosing the staircase, he led the way to a cleverly concealed lift, and in the cubicle's close confines she could feel the fast hammering of her heart. A tell-tale pulse beat in unison at the base of her throat, and she had to fight the temptation to cover it with a protective hand.

There were five buttons on the indicator panel, and she almost cried out in relief when the lift slid to a smooth halt on the lowest level.

Focus, concentrate, she commanded herself silently as she walked at his side through a large, informal area to wide, sliding glass doors opening out onto a terracotta-tiled patio and a free-form swimming pool.

For the next ten minutes Kristi reeled off numerous shots of the pool, external frontage from several angles and the view out over the harbour, before moving inside.

Shalef was never far from her side, suggesting, directing, asking her opinion on occasion as she steadily filled one roll of film, then paused to remove it and insert another.

It was a game, she decided in desperation. Deliberately orchestrated by a man who had no concern for the emotional storm that tore at her insides and ripped her nerves to shreds.

Twice his arm brushed against one of hers, and the

faint muskiness of his cologne combined with his masculine scent almost succeeded in driving her insane.

It seemed for ever before the interior shooting was completed, and she welcomed the fresh, cooling breeze as she moved outdoors and shot the house from the street, the gardens, the driveway.

'That's it,' Kristi announced finally, aware that she had far more than she could possibly need. With care she capped the lens and removed the strap from her neck. Her shoulders felt slightly stiff and she had the beginnings of a headache. Tension, from being in Shalef bin Youssef Al-Sayed's company for the past few hours—three, she noted with surprise as she spared her watch a quick glance.

'I'll collect my bag from the foyer then get back to the studio.' The sooner she made a start on the developing process, the sooner she'd be finished.

Several minutes later, bag in hand, she moved towards the front door. The knot of tension inside her stomach tightened into a painful ball, and her smile was a mere facsimile of one as she turned towards him. 'I can't give you a definite time. Somewhere between seven and eight o'clock?'

He inclined his head and accompanied her to her car, waiting as she unlocked it; then, when she was seated, he shut the door.

The engine fired immediately and she paused only long enough to secure her seat belt before sending the BMW down the road.

It wasn't until she had gained the main New South

Head road that she was able to relax, and even then it was strictly temporary.

'Well? What is he like?' Annie demanded the instant Kristi entered the studio. 'Make my day and tell me he's tall, dark and gorgeous.'

'Any messages?' Kristi crossed to the desk and checked the message pad. 'I'll be in the lab for the next hour. Maybe longer.'

Annie wrinkled her nose in silent admonition, and her eyes sharpened fractionally. 'You look tired. Why don't you go home and come in early in the morning?'

'Because, Annie, darling,' she revealed, 'the client requires the prints tonight.'

'Tell him you can't do it.'

'Too late. I already told him I can.'

'Then I'll make some fresh coffee.'

Kristi gave a smile in thanks. 'You're an angel.'

It was after seven when she examined the last print. With professional dedication she collated them according to floor level, noting each room and its aspect, before pushing them into a large envelope.

Moving her shoulders, she eased the crick in her neck, then massaged each temple in an effort to diminish the dull, aching sensation which had settled there more than an hour ago.

She felt tired, hungry, and would have given almost anything to go home, sink into a spa-bath and have the tiny, pulsing jets work their magic on her tense muscles.

Fifteen minutes later she wound down the window of her car and pressed the security intercom outside the set of high iron gates guarding the entrance to Shalef's harbourfront home. Within seconds they slid open and she eased the car towards the front of the house, parking it right outside the main door...for an easy getaway, she told herself as she retrieved the thick envelope from the passenger seat.

The housekeeper answered the door and Kristi wondered why she should be surprised. Shalef lived in a world where one employed staff to maintain residences. However, this was Sydney, not London or Riyadh.

'Would you please give this to Sheikh bin Al-Sayed?' Kristi requested, holding out the package. 'I've enclosed the account.'

'Sheikh bin Al-Sayed wishes to pay you now. If you'd care to wait in the lounge?'

No, I wouldn't care to wait, Kristi felt like screaming, and I don't want to see Shalef bin Youssef Al-Sayed.

'Thank you, Emily. I'll take care of Miss Dalton.'

She should have known that he wouldn't allow her to get away so easily, she decided in despair. 'I've delivered the prints as you requested,' she ventured quietly.

'Emily has prepared dinner,' Shalef declared smoothly. 'We'll eat, then I'll go through the prints.'

'*No.*' The single negation took the place of a silent, primal scream that sprang from the depths of her soul. 'I can't. I'm expecting a phone call.' She was babbling— short, stark sentences that sounded desperate even to her own ears.

His eyes hardened measurably. 'I imagine whoever it is will leave a message on your answer-ing machine.'

'Damn you, Shalef,' she flung at him, shaky with

anger as he took hold of her arm and led her through to an informal dining room where the table was set for two.

Covered dishes had been placed in the centre, and her stomach clenched in hungry anticipation at the delicious aroma permeating the room.

'Sit down.'

It was easier to capitulate, and she made no protest as he uncorked a bottle of Cabernet Shiraz and poured a generous measure into her glass.

'Emily is an exceptional cook,' Shalef informed her as he uncovered a dish and served her a generous portion, adding rice from the second dish. He served himself, then took the seat opposite. 'Eat, Kristi,' he commanded silkily. He filled his own glass, then raised it in a silent toast.

Kristi picked up her fork and speared a delectable piece of chicken. Sautéed in wine and mushrooms, it tasted out of this world.

She thought of a dozen things to say, and discarded every one of them. The wine was superb, and gradually it began to dissipate the knot of tension inside her stomach.

'Why did you buy this house?' Surely the house was a safe subject?

His eyes lingered on her mouth, then slowly traversed the slope of her nose before locking with her own. 'I wanted an Australian base.'

'Extending your global interests?'

'You could say that.'

She was breaking up inside, fragmenting into a hundred pieces. If she didn't gather her shattered nerves together, she'd never be able to get up and walk out of here with any semblance of dignity.

She put down her fork, then carefully replaced her glass. Not carefully enough, for the rim caught the side of her plate and slipped from her fingers. With horrified fascination she watched the wine spill into an ever widening dark pool on the white damask. 'I'm so sorry.' The apology fell from her lips as a whisper. Moisture welled from behind her eyes, distorting her vision as she plucked up her napkin and dabbed it over the spillage. 'The tablecloth should be rinsed or it will stain,' she said shakily.

'Leave it,' he commanded. 'It isn't important.'

'I'll replace it.'

'Don't be ridiculous.'

She closed her eyes, then slowly opened them again. Hell couldn't be any worse than this. 'If you'll excuse me, I'd prefer to leave.' She rose to her feet and side-stepped the chair. 'Thank you for dinner.' It was amazing. Even at a time like this she could still remember good manners.

She turned blindly away from the table, only to be brought to a halt mid-stride by a hand closing over her arm.

His eyes were dark, their expression so deeply inscrutable that it was impossible to discern his mood.

For what seemed an age he just looked at her, his silence unnerving in the stillness of the room.

She was damned if she'd cry. Tears were for the weak and she had to be strong. Her eyes ached as she strove to keep the moisture at bay, and she almost succeeded. Almost—the exception being a solitary tear which overflowed and spilled slowly down one cheek. It came to rest at the corner of her mouth, and after a few long seconds she edged the tip of her tongue out to dispense with it.

A husky, self-deprecating oath fell from his lips, and she stood in mesmerised silence as he caught hold of her hand and carried it to his mouth.

'Dear God,' Shalef groaned. '*Don't.*' His hand moved to capture her shoulders, then slid upwards to stroke her hair. His eyes were dark—so dark that they mirrored her own emotional pain as he held her head.

'For years I have enjoyed feminine company and never had to work at a relationship. *You*,' he enlightened her with gentle emphasis, 'mentally stripped me of all my material possessions and judged me for the man that I am without them. For the first time I had nothing to rely on except myself. It wasn't an enviable situation,' he said with a touch of self-mockery.

Kristi stood perfectly still, almost afraid to move.

'You didn't conform and I was intrigued. I thought I knew every facet of a woman, but you proved me wrong.' He paused, tilting her face slightly so that she had to look at him. 'You opposed me at every turn, and argued without hesitation. Yet you were angelic with Nashwa, sympathetic with Aisha and Hanan. I knew without doubt that I wanted you as my wife.' His expression became faintly wry. 'I imagined all I had to do was ask and you'd agree.'

He smiled, and the first flutter of hope began to stir inside her stomach.

'Instead you refused and walked out on me. My initial instinct was to follow you. Yet if I had then, even if I'd said the words you so wanted to hear, you would have been disinclined to believe them. So I decided to give you time. Not too much, but enough. Enough for me to set up this house and invent a reason to get you here.'

Her lips parted to protest, and he stilled her flow of words very effectively by taking possession of her mouth.

When he finally lifted his head, her own was reeling with the degree of passion he'd managed to evoke.

'This afternoon I wanted to declare my love the instant you walked in the door, but I had to allow for your outrage,' he qualified with genuine regret, 'and crack the protective barrier you'd erected around your heart.' His lips settled against her temple, then trailed a gentle path down to the edge of her mouth.

She felt shaky, and almost afraid to believe his words.

'I have something for you,' Shalef said gently. He withdrew a ring from his trouser pocket and placed it in the palm of her hand. 'It belonged to my mother, gifted to her by my father.'

Kristi looked at the wide gold ring embedded with diamonds.

'She never wore it, preferring a plain gold band, but she accepted it for what it represented…a symbol of my father's love.'

She raised her eyes to meet his, saw the depth of passion evident, and was unable to tear her gaze away.

'It was held in safe-keeping and handed to me on my twenty-fifth birthday, with the relayed request that I gift it to the woman I chose to be my wife.'

'It's beautiful,' Kristi said simply.

He brushed his fingers down her cheek, and warmth radiated through her body, bringing with it the need for the sweet sorcery of his touch.

'Marriage was something I viewed as a convenient necessity with a woman of whom I could become fond...someone who could be my social hostess, the mother of my children, and pleasure me in bed.' He smiled—a slightly wry gesture that was belied by the warm humour evident in the depths of his eyes. 'Then I met you. And every woman of my acquaintance paled in comparison.' He traced the curves of her mouth with a forefinger, and followed its path with his tongue before seeking the soft inner tissues, to create an emotional demand which she didn't hesitate to answer.

When at last he lifted his head she could only look at him in bemusement as she saw the raw need, the hunger and the passion in his eyes.

'I love you. *Love,*' Shalef declared as he slid trembling hands to frame her face.

His eyes were dark, almost black, and Kristi sensed the faint uncertainty in his touch—a vulnerability she'd thought she would never see. It moved her more than she could bear.

'I know the only worthy gift I can bestow on you is

my heart,' he said deeply. 'It's yours. For as long as it beats within me.'

Joy unfurled from deep within her and soared to an unbelievable height. Without hesitation she lifted her hands and wound them round his neck.

'I'll take great care of it,' she promised softly.

His features assumed a gentleness that almost made her want to cry. 'And you'll marry me?'

Kristi smiled—a wonderfully warm smile that was meant to banish any doubts. The desire to tease him a little was irresistible. 'Are you asking?'

His faint laugh was low and husky as he gathered her close in against him. 'You want me to go down on bended knee?'

'I may never see you so humbled again,' she ventured solemnly, and he slowly shook his head.

'You're wrong. Each day I'll give thanks that I have the good fortune to share your life.'

She felt the prick of tears, and was unable to still the twin rivulets that ran slowly down each cheek.

'You haven't answered.'

Her mouth trembled. 'Yes.'

His mouth closed over hers, possessing it with such incredible passion that she felt dizzy when he finally lifted his head.

'Will you mind if the civil ceremony in London is followed by another in Riyadh?'

It was somehow fitting, and something that would have pleased his father. She thought of sharing the arrangements with Nashwa, Aisha and Hanan, and knew the enjoyment it would give them.

'Not at all.'

'We'll spend the first week of our honeymoon in Taif, then cruise the Greek islands for a month.'

'June is a nice month for brides,' Kristi offered wistfully.

'Next week,' Shalef commanded. 'You fly out to London with me tomorrow. Don't object,' he ordered as she opened her mouth.

'I could follow in a few days. No?' Her eyes sparkled mischievously. 'The day after?'

'Tomorrow,' he reaffirmed, giving her a gentle shake.

'In that case I'd better go home and pack.'

'All you need is your passport and a change of clothes, which we'll collect from your apartment *en route* to the airport in the morning.' His mouth fastened over hers in a kiss that left her weak-kneed and malleable. 'I have plans for what remains of the night.' He revealed precisely what those plans were, none of which involved any sleep. 'You can rest on the planc,' he added gently as he placed an arm beneath her knees and swung her into his arms.

In the bedroom he lowered her to her feet, and she reached for the buttons on his shirt, slipping them free before tackling the belt at his waist.

Kristi uttered a small gasp as his fingers brushed against her breast, then she groaned out loud as he began teasing each burgeoning peak, intensifying an awareness that radiated from the centre of her being until it encompassed every vein, every sensitised nerve-ending.

She was *his*, wholly, completely, to do precisely

whatever he wanted with, and she helped him shed what remained of her clothes while he gave assistance in discarding his own before drawing her down onto the bed.

'My darling,' Shalef whispered with due reverence as he studied the silky sheen of her smooth-textured skin, and his gaze lingered on the soft curves of her breasts, the delicately shaped waist, before settling on the deep auburn curls protecting her womanhood.

He lifted a hand and brushed his fingers back and forth over the soft concavity of her stomach before trailing to trace the bones at one hip.

Her whole body ached with the promise of passion too long denied, and she reached for him.

'I want you *now*,' she whispered fiercely. 'All of you, inside me, without any preliminaries.' She cried out as his fingers slipped beneath the soft curls to initiate a sweet sorcery that quickly tipped her over the edge into a secret place where passion flared into an all-consuming fire, sweeping aside inhibition as it imbued her with an abandon that completely took his breath away as he carefully prepared her to accept his swollen length.

Silken tissues stretched to accommodate him, warm and wonderfully sleek as she met that initial thrust, encouraging his total possession by rising up against him in a rhythm that increased in pace until there was no master, no mistress, only two people in perfect accord, intent on gifting the other with the ultimate pleasure.

Afterwards she rested her cheek against the curve of his shoulder, too satiated to move so much as a muscle as he lightly trailed his fingers up and down the length of her spine.

This time their lovemaking was slow and erotic, ascending to new heights of intoxicating sensuality, and it was almost dawn before they drifted into a deep sleep from which they woke in time to shower, dress and depart for the airport via her apartment.

Once aboard the plane, Kristi slept most of the way to Hawaii, waking to meet the indulgent eyes of the man who would soon be her husband.

'Hello,' she greeted him softly, giving him a smile so warm and so incredibly sweet that it almost robbed him of breath.

Careless of the other passengers travelling in the first-class section of the aircraft, he leaned over and bestowed a lingering kiss on her lips.

'I've booked us into a hotel for a fourteen-hour stopover.'

Her eyes filled with wicked humour. 'Only fourteen hours?'

His mouth softened into a sensual curve. 'You require more than fourteen?'

She reached out a hand and traced the strong sweep of his jawline before covering his cheek with her palm. 'I love you.'

'Now you tell me,' Shalef groaned softly. '*Here*, where I can do very little about it.'

She cast him an angelic smile that was totally at variance with the witching sparkle lighting her eyes. 3'Patience, they tell me, is good for the soul.'

His answering gaze was filled with musing self-mockery. 'Patience,' he stressed lightly, 'will doubtless stretch the limit of my control.'

Kristi laughed softly. 'I promise I'll allow you to make up for it.'

One eyebrow rose in a gesture of wry humour. 'That's supposed to get me through dinner, landing, Customs and a three-quarter-hour drive to the hotel?'

Her eyes teased him unmercifully. 'But think of the reward...for each of us.'

His expression darkened with the promise of renewed passion. 'Indeed,' he agreed gently. 'A lifetime.'

* * * * *

MISTRESS BY ARRANGEMENT

HELEN BIANCHIN

For Alex and Angie Kidas,
with gratitude and affection

CHAPTER ONE

MICHELLE SIPPED SUPERB Chardonnay from a crystal wineglass and cast an idle glance at the room's occupants.

The men were resplendent in black dinner suits, white dress shirts and black bow ties, while the women vied with each other in designer gowns.

This evening's occasion was a simple dinner party for ten guests held in the beautiful home of their hosts, Antonia and Emerson Bateson-Burrows, whose reputation for providing fine wine, excellent food, and scintillating company was almost unequalled in Queensland's Gold Coast society.

'Another drink, darling?'

She felt the proprietorial clasp of Jeremy's arm along the back of her waist.

Mine, the action seemed to shriek. The fond glance of his parents, *hers,* merely served to endorse their approval.

Did they think she was unaware of the subtle manipulative matchmaking attempts of late? It was too much of a coincidence that Jeremy had been a fellow guest at several social events she'd attended in the past four weeks.

Marriage wasn't on her agenda, nor was she willing to drift into a meaningless relationship. Thanks to an annuity from her maternal grandmother, her life was good. At twenty-five, she owned her own apartment, ran a successful art gallery in partnership with a friend, and she had no inclination to change the status quo.

She felt the faint pressure of Jeremy's hand at her waist and she summoned a polite smile. 'Thanks, but I'll wait until dinner.'

Which would be when? Were all the guests not accounted for? Speculation rose as she glimpsed Jeremy's mother spare her wristwatch a surreptitious glance.

Who would dare to be late for a Bateson-Burrows soiree?

'Mother is becoming a tad anxious,' Jeremy revealed, sotto voce. 'Nikos warned he might be unavoidably late.'

Curiosity sparked Michelle's interest. 'Nikos?'

Jeremy cast her an amused look. 'Alessandros. Greek origin, relatively new money, respectably earned,' he added. 'Electronics. Bases in Athens, Rome, Paris, London, Vancouver, Sydney.'

'If his Australian base is in Sydney, what's he doing on the Gold Coast?'

'He has a penthouse in Main Beach,' Jeremy enlightened. 'The man is a consummate strategist. Word has it he's about to close an enviable deal.' His mouth formed a cynical twist. 'Instead of flying directly to Sydney, he's chosen to negotiate from the Gold Coast.'

'Impressive,' she acknowledged, summoning a

mental image of a short, paunchy, balding middle-aged Greek with a stylish much younger wife.

'Very,' Jeremy declared succinctly. 'Father covets his patronage and his business account.'

'And his friendship?'

'It's at an adequate level.'

Adequate presumably wasn't good enough, and Emerson Bateson-Burrows' extended invitation to dine was merely part of a larger plan.

Politics, business and social, involved an intricate strategy of a kind that occasionally sickened her altruistic mind.

'Two hours to dine and socialise over coffee,' Jeremy inclined. 'Then we can escape and go on to a nightclub.'

It irked her that he took her acquiescence for granted. She was on the point of telling him so, when some sixth sense alerted her attention.

Curious, she lifted her head and felt the breath catch in her throat.

'Nikos,' Jeremy informed her, although she barely registered the verbal identification as her interest was captured by the tall male figure who had just entered the room.

He possessed broad-boned features, a strong jaw, and his mouth was chiselled perfection.

A man, Michelle perceived with instinctive insight, who wore the fine clothes of a gentleman, possessed the requisite good manners…and had the heart of a predatory warrior.

It was evident in his stance, the cool assessing quality in those dark slate-grey eyes as they roamed the room and its occupants.

They flicked towards her, paused, then settled in a slow appraisal of her dark honey-blond hair, green eyes, and the slender feminine curves encased in a black designer dress.

There was no power on earth that could suppress the faint shivery sensation feathering its way down her spine at the intensity of that look. She felt as if it stripped away the conventional barrier of clothes, lingerie, and stroked her skin.

It took considerable effort to match his appraisal, but she was damned if she'd concede him any sort of victory by glancing away.

Dark hair, well-groomed. Broad shoulders beneath expensive tailoring, and his shoes were hand-tooled leather. In his mid-thirties, he was the antithesis of the middle-aged paunchy balding man Michelle had envisaged.

She watched as he worked the room during an introductory circuit, noting the undoubted charm, the easy smile, an easy grace of movement that implied a high level of physical fitness.

'Michelle Gerard,' Antonia announced by way of introduction, reaching their side. 'Jeremy's girlfriend.'

Nikos Alessandros reached forward, took hold of her hand, and raised it to his lips.

Michelle's eyes flew wide with shock as he placed a brief open-mouthed kiss to her palm, then he curled her fingers as if to seal in the flagrant action. Heat flooded her veins, coursing through her body as each nerve-end sprang into vibrant life.

'Michelle.' His voice held a faint inflection, an accent that was more international than indicative of his own nationality.

Primitive alchemy, potent and incredibly lethal, was a compelling force, and her skin burned where his lips had touched.

'We meet again.'

Again? She'd never met him in this lifetime. If she had, she'd remember. No woman alive could possibly forget someone of Nikos Alessandros' calibre!

Michelle was at once conscious of Antonia's surprised gaze coupled with Jeremy's sharp attention.

'You've already met?'

'While Michelle was studying at the Sorbonne in Paris,' Nikos declared with knowledgeable ease.

A calculated guess? Somehow she doubted it. Which immediately drew the question as to how he came by the information.

'Really?' Antonia queried lightly after a few seconds silence.

Michelle watched in fascination as he directed her a blatantly sensual smile. 'How could I forget?'

She should refute they'd ever set eyes on each other, and accuse him of being a sexist opportunist.

'Your capacity to remember surprises me.' That much was true, yet as soon as the words left her lips she wondered at the wisdom of playing his game.

Midsummer madness? An attempt to alleviate the matchmaking techniques employed by two sets of parents? Or just plain devilry.

Nikos' eyes never left her own, and she experienced the uncanny sensation he could read her mind. Worse, that he could dissect the conventional barriers she'd learnt to erect and divine the path to her soul.

It wasn't a comfortable feeling. But then, she

doubted there was anything *comfortable* about this man.

Dangerous, occasionally merciless, powerful. And rarely predictable. A tiny imp added, incredibly sexual. An earthy, uninhibited lover who would seek every liberty, and encourage a similar response. Demand, she amended with instinctive knowledge.

Just the thought of what he could do to a woman, and how he would do it was enough to raise all her fine body hairs in a gesture of…what? Self-preservation? *Anticipation?*

Her eyes dilated at a highly erotic image, one that was so evocative she was unable to subdue the flare of heat from her innermost core.

'Indeed?' That deep drawl held a wealth of meaning she didn't even want to explore.

Antonia sensed it, and immediately launched into an attempt at damage control. 'Nikos, you must allow Emerson to get you a drink.' She placed a hand on his sleeve, and for a moment Michelle held her breath at the possibility he might detach Antonia's hand and opt to stay where he was.

Something moved in his expression, then he smiled, inclining his head in mocking acquiescence as he allowed his hostess to steer him away.

The electric force-field evident didn't diminish, and it took considerable effort to lift the glass to her lips and take a sip of wine.

'You know him.'

Michelle's lips parted to deny it, only to pause fractionally too long.

'And to think I've been playing the gentleman,' Jeremy drawled silkily, raising his glass in a silent mocking salute as he conducted a slow encompassing survey from the top of her head to the tip of her toes and back again.

Indignation heightened the dark golden sparks in her green eyes, and anyone who knew her well would have heeded the silent warning.

'One has only to look at Nikos to know his *friendship* with women is inevitably of an intimate nature.'

'Really?' Michelle tempered the query with a deceptive smile. She wanted to hit him. 'You'd dare to accuse me on the strength of another man's reputation?'

Antonia Bateson-Burrows' announcement that dinner was ready proved opportune.

'Can you blame me for being jealous?' Jeremy offered as they crossed to the dining room.

Nikos Alessandros had a lot to answer for, she determined wryly.

Unbidden, her gaze shifted to the tall male Greek a few feet distant, and she watched in fascinated surprise as he turned briefly towards her.

Those dark slate-grey eyes held an expression she couldn't fathom, and for one infinitesimal second everything faded to the periphery of her vision. There was only *him*. The subdued chatter, the other guests, were no longer apparent.

A slight smile curved his lips, but his eyes remained steady, almost as if he withheld a knowledge of something she couldn't even begin to presume.

The breath caught in her throat, and she deliberately broke the silent spell by transferring her attention to the proposed seating arrangements.

With any luck, Nikos Alessandros would be at the

opposite end of the table, precluding the necessity to indulge in polite conversation.

An accomplished hostess, Antonia skilfully manoeuvred her guests into chairs, shuffling them so there were six on one side with five on the other, while she and Emerson took their position at the head of the table.

Oh *hell*. Thirteen at the dinner table on Friday the thirteenth. Could it get any worse?

Don't tempt Fate by even *thinking* about it, a tiny voice taunted, only to discover she faced Nikos across a decorative floral centrepiece.

Emerson poured the wine while Antonia organised the serving of the first course.

'*Salute.*' Nikos' accent was flawless as he lifted his glass, and although his smile encompassed everyone seated at the table, his eyes remained fixed on Michelle.

The soup was delicious vichyssoise, although after the first spoonful Michelle's tastebuds seemed to go on strike.

Succulent prawns in a piquant sauce were served on a bed of mesclan lettuce, and she sipped the excellent white wine, then opted for chilled water in the need for a clear head.

The conversation encompassed a broad spectrum as it touched briefly on the state of the country's financial budget, the possibility of tax reform and its effect on the economy.

'What is your view, Michelle?'

The sound of that faintly accented drawl stirred her senses. Her hand paused midway in its passage from the table to her lips, and her fingers tightened fractionally on the goblet's slim stem.

'Inconsequential, I imagine. Given that whatever my opinion, it will have little effect in the scheme of things.'

Jeremy's silent offer to refill Nikos' glass was met with an equally silent refusal.

The fact that Nikos declined didn't halt Jeremy's inclination to fill his own glass.

'Nevertheless, I would be interested to hear it.'

Having set the cat among the pigeons, it's a source of amusement for you to watch the outcome, she surmised silently. But what if one of the pigeons was unafraid of the cat? Two could play this game.

'As I recall, you were never particularly interested in my mind.'

His eyes held hers, mesmeric in their intensity. She watched as his lips parted to reveal even white teeth, and noticed the movement deepened the vertical slash on each cheek.

'Could anyone blame me, *pedhi mou?*'

His drawled endearment curled round her nerve-ends and sent them spiralling out of control.

'I'll serve the main course.'

Michelle heard Antonia's words, and watched absently as the hired help cleared plates and cutlery and replaced them.

'Some more wine, Nikos?'

Emerson, ever the genial host, merely warranted the briefest glance. 'Thank you, no.' He returned his attention to Michelle. 'I haven't the need for further stimulation.'

This was getting out of hand. It was also gaining the interest of everyone seated at the table.

Chicken in a lemon sauce accompanied by a selection of braised vegetables did little to tempt Michelle's flagging appetite, and she sampled a few mouthfuls of chicken, took a delicate bite of each vegetable, then set down her cutlery.

Water, not wine, was something she sipped at infrequent intervals as she wished fervently for the evening to end.

Yet there was dessert and the cheeseboard to complete the meal, followed by coffee. It would be at least another hour before she could make some excuse to leave.

Jeremy leaned towards her and placed an arm along the back of her chair.

'Tell me, darling.' His voice was a conspiratorial murmur. 'Is he incredibly physical in bed?'

She didn't deign to answer, and deliberately avoided glancing in Nikos' direction as she conversed with the guest seated next to her. Afterwards she had little recollection of the topic or her contribution.

Dessert was an exotic creation of baklava, together with fresh fruit and brandied cream.

Michelle passed on both, and selected a few grapes to freshen her palate.

'Shall we adjourn to the lounge for coffee?' Antonia queried when it appeared everyone had had their fill.

They were the sweetest words Michelle had heard in hours, and she subdued her enthusiasm as she stood to her feet and joined her parents.

Chantelle Gerard cast her daughter a thoughtful glance. 'I had no idea you knew Nikos Alessandros.'

Money was important. Breeding, equally so. The Bateson-Burrows possessed both. But the Alessandros' fortune couldn't be ignored.

Michelle could almost see the wheels turning in her mother's brain. 'I intend leaving very soon.'

'You're going on somewhere with Jeremy, darling?'

'No.'

'I see,' Chantelle voiced sagely. 'We'll talk in the morning.'

'Believe me, *Maman,* there is absolutely nothing to tell,' Michelle assured with an edge of mockery, watching as her mother lifted one eyebrow in silent chastisement. 'Nothing,' she added quietly.

Twenty questions at dawn wasn't her favoured way to begin the day. However, Chantelle was well-practised in the art of subtle manipulation, and Michelle was able to interpret every nuance in her mother's voice.

'We can easily give you a lift home if you're prepared to wait awhile.'

She should have brought her own car. Except Jeremy had insisted he collect her. Not a wise move, she decided wryly in retrospect.

The mild headache she'd thought to invent was no longer a figment of her imagination. And Jeremy was fast becoming a nuisance. Her apartment was less than a kilometre away, a distance she'd entertain no qualms in walking during the day. However, the night hours provided a totally different context for a woman alone.

'I'll call a taxi.'

Antonia offered a superb blend of coffee, together with liqueur, cream, milk, exotic bite-sized continental biscuits and a variety of Belgian chocolates.

Michelle added milk and sugar, and sipped it as quickly as etiquette allowed. Placing her cup and saucer down onto a nearby side-table, she turned towards her hosts, and her stomach executed a slow somersault as she discovered Antonia and Emerson deep in conversation with Nikos Alessandros.

Just pin a smile on your face, thank them for a pleasant evening, and then exit the room. Two or three minutes, five at the most.

Almost as if he sensed her hesitation, Nikos lifted his head and watched her approach.

Jeremy appeared at her side and draped an arm over her shoulder. His hand lingered a hair's-breadth from her breast, and she stepped sideways in an effort to avoid the familiarity, only to have Jeremy's hand close firmly over her arm.

'Finished doing the duty thing with your parents?'

She took exception to his tone, and his manner. 'I don't regard talking to my parents as a duty.'

'You obviously don't suffer parental suffocation as a result of being the only child,' he alluded cynically.

'No,' she responded evenly.

'Ready to leave?' Nikos queried smoothly as she joined Jeremy's parents. 'If you'll excuse us,' Nikos announced imperturbably to his hosts. 'Michelle and I have some catching up to do.' He caught hold of her hand and drew her forward, inclined his head towards a startled Jeremy, then led her from the lounge.

'What do you think you're doing?' she hissed as soon as they reached the foyer.

'Providing you with a lift to your apartment.'

'Michelle.' Jeremy drew level with them. '*I'll* take you home.'

She felt like hitting each of them. One for being overly possessive and childishly jealous. The Greek for his arrogance.

'There's no need to leave your parents' guests,' Nikos intoned pleasantly. 'Michelle's apartment building is almost opposite my own.'

How did he know that?

'She's *my* girlfriend,' Jeremy reiterated fiercely as he turned towards her.

This was getting worse by the second.

'Michelle?' Nikos' voice was silk-encased steel.

Jeremy's hand closed over her shoulder, as if staking a claim. 'Damn you, *tell him.*'

'There's nothing to tell,' she assured quietly, and winced as Jeremy's hold tightened.

'I don't think so, my friend,' Nikos drawled with dangerous softness, and Jeremy turned towards him with emboldened belligerence.

'This is none of your business!'

'I disagree.'

'Why would you do that?'

'Because Michelle is with me.'

'Damned if she is!' Jeremy's face contorted with fury.

'You want proof?' Nikos demanded silkily.

Michelle didn't get the chance to say a word in protest as Nikos drew her into his arms and covered her mouth with his own.

Possessive and frankly sensual, he took advantage of her surprise to taste and plunder at will, then before she could protest he gathered her close and turned the kiss into something incredibly erotic.

Her heart jumped, then raced to a quickened beat as one hand slid to hold fast her nape while the other cupped her bottom and brought her into startling contact with hard male arousal.

Each and every one of her senses intensified as he sought her response.

Passion…electric, magnetic, *shameless,* it tore through all the conventional barriers to a primitive base that was wholly sexual.

It was as if an instinctive knowledge existed between them, she registered dimly. Something that sanctioned the way his mouth wreaked havoc with her own.

She was supremely aware of him, everything about him. The faint layers of texture and smell heightened her senses…the subtle tang of his cologne, the texture of his skin, the fine fabric of his clothing.

There was a part of her that wanted to travel with him wherever this sensual path might lead, while the sensible *sane* part registered alarm.

With a groan of disgust she dragged her mouth away. Her breathing was ragged, and for the space of a few seconds she had no knowledge of where she was. There was only the man, and a mesmeric helpless hunger.

'What in hell do you think you're doing?'

Jeremy's voice seemed to come from a distance, and she struggled to focus on the immediate present.

'Right now, taking Michelle home,' Nikos declared

with deceptive mildness. Without missing a beat he lifted one eyebrow in silent query. 'Michelle?'

Dammit, his breathing was even, steady, while hers seemed as wild and ragged as her heartbeat.

'Walk away from me,' Jeremy warned. 'And I won't have you back.'

She registered Jeremy's rage and felt vaguely sickened. 'You never *had* me in the first place.'

The sound of voices and the appearance in the foyer of two other guests had a diffusing effect, and Jeremy's expression underwent an abrupt change from anger to affability.

'Let's get the hell out of here,' Nikos instructed quietly, taking hold of her arm.

He led her down the few steps to the driveway, and she made a futile effort to wrench her arm free from his grasp as they drew abreast of a large BMW.

'Don't,' he warned silkily. 'You'll only hurt yourself.'

It was difficult to determine his expression in the dim half-light as he withdrew a set of keys, unlocked the door, then handed them to her. 'Drive, if it will make you feel safer to be with me.'

The soft crunch of gravel as footsteps approached intruded, and she stood stiffly as they drew close.

'Goodnight, Michelle. Nikos.'

Nikos returned the acknowledgement as the couple slid into the car immediately behind them, and in an unbidden gesture Michelle thrust the keys at him, then she unlatched the door and slid into the passenger seat.

Nikos took his position behind the wheel, fired the engine, then eased the car onto the road. Minutes later the powerful car entered the main northbound highway, traversed it for less than a kilometre, and took the next turnoff that led into suburban Main Beach.

She was supremely conscious of him, the slight flash of gold on his wrist as he handled the wheel.

'We'll stop at a café for coffee,' Nikos informed as they paused at a set of traffic lights. 'There's something I'd like to discuss with you.'

'The subtle "your apartment or mine?" spiel?' Michelle mocked with light sarcasm. 'Forget it. One-night stands aren't my thing.'

'I'm relieved to hear it.'

The lights changed, and within minutes the powerful engine purred down a notch as he decelerated and touched the brakes, then he eased the vehicle to a halt.

Michelle reached for the door-clasp, a word of thanks ready to emerge from her lips.

Then she froze.

The underground car park was similar to a multitude of beneath street-level concrete caverns. Except it wasn't *her* apartment car park.

CHAPTER TWO

'WHERE THE HELL are we?'

'My apartment building,' Nikos drawled. 'It happens to be in a block a short distance from your own.' He opened his door and slid out from behind the wheel.

Michelle copied his actions, and stood glaring at him across the roof of the BMW, then she turned and walked to the sweeping upgrade leading to the main entrance.

'The security gate is activated by a personally coded remote.' He paused a beat, then added with killing softness, 'Likewise, the lift is security coded.'

She swung back to face him, anger etched on every line of her body. 'Kidnapping is a criminal offense. If you don't want me to lay charges, I suggest you allow me free passage out of here. Now,' she added with deadly intent. If she'd been standing close enough, she'd have lashed out and hit him.

Nikos regarded her steadily, assessing her slim frame, the darkness of her eyes. There was no fear apparent, and the thought momentarily intrigued him. Self-defence skills? His own had been acquired and honed to a lethal degree.

'All I want is fifteen, maybe twenty minutes of your time.'

Her heartbeat thudded painfully against her ribs. The car park was well-lit, there were a number of cars lining marked bays, but it was eerily quiet. There was no one to whom she could appeal for help.

Michelle extracted her mobile phone and prepared to punch in the requisite digit that would connect her with Emergency Services and alert the police.

'You have nothing to fear from me.'

His voice was even, and controlled. Too controlled. He emanated an indefinable leashed quality, a watchfulness that only a fool would disregard. And she didn't consider herself a fool.

'I don't find this—' she swept an arm in silent indication of her surroundings '—in the least amusing.'

'You were averse to joining me in more comfortable surroundings,' he posed silkily.

Anger meshed with indignation, colouring her features and lending her eyes a fiery sparkle. 'Forgive me.' Her voice dripped icy sarcasm. 'For declining your invitation.'

Her passion intrigued him. Dammit, *she* intrigued him. Most women of his acquaintance, aware of his social and financial status, would have willingly followed wherever he chose to lead.

Yet for all that Michelle Gerard felt like an angel in his arms and responded with uninhibited fervour, instinct relayed that it wasn't part of an act.

'By your own admission,' Michelle vented with restrained anger. 'You brought me here to talk.'

She needed to shift the balance of control. *Fear* wasn't an option. Although the word in itself was a misnomer. Nikos Alessandros didn't mean her any harm, at least not in the physical sense. Yet when it came to her emotions... Now that was an entirely different ball game, something which irked her unbearably, for how could she be emotionally spellbound by a man who, in a short few hours, had broken every conventional social nicety?

'I suggest you do so, *now,*' she continued forcefully. 'And condense whatever you have to say into two minutes.' She indicated the mobile phone. 'One wrong move and I'll summon the police.'

He leaned one hip against the smooth bonnet of his car, and regarded her thoughtfully.

'I want you to be my social companion for a few weeks,' he stated without preamble.

Michelle drew in a deep breath and released it slowly. Whatever she'd expected, it hadn't been this. He had only to beckon and women would beat a path to his side. 'Surely you jest?'

His attention didn't falter. 'I'm quite serious.'

'Why?'

'For much the same reason it would suit you.'

She didn't pretend to misunderstand. 'What makes you so sure?'

'Body language,' Nikos drawled.

Her eyes flashed golden fire. 'I can handle Jeremy.'

'I don't doubt you can.' One eyebrow lifted. 'The question is, do you want to?'

'I don't need anyone to fight my battles,' she said dryly. 'Any more than you do. So why don't you cut to the chase?'

'I thought I already had.'

Her head tilted to one side. 'You expect me to be-

lieve there's a female you can't handle?' The prospect
was almost laughable.

'The widow of a very close friend of mine,' Nikos
enlightened her slowly. 'Her husband was killed several months ago in a skiing accident.'

'She is emotionally fragile, and genuinely misin-
terprets the friendship?' Michelle posed. 'Or has she
become a calculating vixen intent on snaring another
rich husband?'

His expression imperceptibly hardened, a subtle
shifting of muscle over bone that reassembled his
features into a compelling mask.

'You presume too much.'

So she'd struck a tender nerve. Interesting that he
didn't answer her question.

'You feel honour-bound to spare—' She paused
deliberately.

'Saska.'

'Saska,' she continued. 'Any embarrassment during what is a transitional grieving period?'

'Yes,' he declared succinctly.

'I see.' She regarded him thoughtfully. 'And on
the basis of one meeting, an appraisal of *body language,* you virtually kidnap me and suggest I have
nothing better to do with my time than act out a part
for your benefit.'

'There would be a few advantages.'

Topaz flecks shone in the depths of her green eyes,
a silent evidence of her anger. 'Name one.'

'All of the pleasure and none of the strings.'

'And a bonus, I imagine, if I'm sufficiently convincing?' The flippant query slipped from her lips,

and she glimpsed the faint edge of humour tilt the corner of his mouth.

'I'm sure we can come to an amicable arrangement.'

The entire evening had been a complete farce, including Jeremy's behaviour. As for Nikos Alessandros... *Impossible* didn't come close!

'Just who the hell do you think you are?' she demanded fiercely.

His expression hardened slightly, and his eyes took on the quality of steel. 'A man who recognises an opportunity, and isn't afraid to seize it.'

She could still feel the touch of his mouth on hers, his taste...and the way her senses had flipped into a tailspin.

His indolent stance was deceptive. She had the instinctive feeling that if she turned away from him, he would simply reach out and haul her back.

'Go find some other female,' Michelle directed. 'I'm not willing to participate.'

She caught the dark glitter in his eyes, glimpsed a muscle tense at the edge of his jaw, and experienced momentary satisfaction at besting him.

'There's nothing I can do to change your mind?'

Her gaze didn't waver. 'No, not a thing.'

He examined her features with contemplative scrutiny. 'In that case, we'll take the lift to the ground floor and I'll escort you to your apartment.'

She wanted to argue with him, and almost did.

'Wise,' Nikos drawled.

Michelle felt her stomach twist as they stepped into the small electronic cubicle. She was incredibly aware of the emotional pull, the intangible meshing of the senses.

Seconds later she preceded him into the main lobby, passed reception, then emerged into the fresh evening air.

Less than a hundred metres distant lay several trendy restaurants and cafés, each with outdoor chairs and tables lending the area a cosmopolitan air.

Michelle's apartment building was situated fifty metres distant on the opposite side of the road, and when they reached its entrance she paused, a polite smile widening her lips as she turned towards him.

There was nothing to thank him for, and she didn't make a pretense of doing so. The polite smile was merely a concession.

'You forgot something.'

She caught the purposeful gleam in those dark eyes an instant before hands captured her face.

His head descended and his mouth covered hers in a kiss that plundered deep, savouring the inner sweetness without mercy, his tongue swift and incredibly clever as he took his fill.

This was skilled mastery, she registered dimly, and a silent gasp of outrage remained locked in her throat as he cupped her bottom and brought her close up against him so that she was in no doubt of his arousal.

Potent, shimmering heat sang through her veins and pooled at the centre of her feminine core. She could feel the thrust of her breasts as they swelled in anticipation of his touch, their tender peaks hardening into sensitive buds craving the tantalising succour of his mouth.

This was insane. A divine madness that had no place, no basis in *anything*.

Almost as if he sensed her withdrawal, he gradually lightened the kiss to a gentle brush of his lips against her own. Then he lifted his head, and released her.

'Pleasant dreams, *pedhi mou,*' he bade gently.

His eyes were warm, and deep enough to drown in. The flip response she sought never found voice, and she turned away from him, activated the security code on the external door, then hurried into the lobby without a backward glance.

Damn him. He was the most arrogant infuriating devastating man she'd ever met. Infinitely dangerous, she added as she jabbed the call button to summon one of two lifts.

As soon as the doors slid open she entered the cubicle, stabbed the appropriate panel button, and barely suppressed a shiver as the lift sped swiftly upward.

If she never saw him again, it would be too soon. Which was a total contradiction in terms, she grimaced as the lift came to a halt at her floor.

Seconds later she let herself into her apartment, hit the light switch, checked the locking mechanism was in place, then she moved through to the kitchen.

Caffeine would keep her awake, so she opted for a glass of chilled water, sipped the contents, then crossed to her bedroom.

It was several minutes this side of midnight, and she divested her clothes, took a leisurely warm shower, then slid between cool percale sheets in an effort to cull sleep.

Without success. There were too many images

crowding her mind. A tall dark-haired Greek whose eyes seemed to haunt her. His voice, with its slightly accented timbre that curled like silk round every sensitive nerve-end, invading without license as a vivid reminder of his touch. The feel of his hands on her body, their caressing warmth, and the taste of his mouth on hers as it devoured, savoured, and sought to imprint his brand.

It was almost as if she could still sense the exclusive tones of his cologne, the clean smell of fine tailoring and fresh laundered cotton. And a subtle masculine scent that was *his*...

Dammit. She didn't want to be this *disturbed* by a man. To have her senses invaded by a pervasive sexual alchemy.

She'd met scores of men, been charmed by several, discovered an affection for a few, and loved none. At least, not the *swept off my feet, melting bones* kind of emotion portrayed on the cinema screen and extolled between the pages of many a romance novel.

When it came to attraction, she was still waiting for the earth to move. Warm and fuzzy somehow didn't come close to hungry shattering sensual sexuality.

Yet tonight she'd experienced it in the arms of a stranger.

For the space of...how long? Two, three minutes? She'd lost all sense of time and place. There was only the man, the moment, and raw unbridled passion.

Her body had curved into his, and clung, moulding in a perfect fit as his mouth had taken possession of her own.

And it had been *possession*. Demanding, compelling, and frankly sensual, his kiss was a promise. Primitive, raw, libidinous.

It should have frightened her. Instead, for the space of those few minutes she'd felt exhilarated, *alive,* and aware. Dear God, so aware of every pulse beat, the heat that flared from every erogenous zone as her whole body coalesced into a throbbing entity, almost totally beyond her control.

If he could initiate such an effect with just a kiss, what sort of lover would he be?

Intensely vital, passionate, and incredibly sensual. Hungry, wild...*shameless,* she added with certainty.

What was she thinking?

Nikos Alessandros was the last man on earth she would want to have anything to do with.

She lifted her head and thumped her pillow. Damn the hateful images invading her mind. They clouded her perspective, dulled commonsense, and played havoc with her nervous system.

All she had to do was fall asleep, and in the morning a fresh new day would dispense with the night's emotional turmoil.

CHAPTER THREE

THE INSISTENT RING of the telephone penetrated Michelle's subconscious, and she reached out a hand, searched blindly for the handset, and succeeded in knocking the receiver onto the floor.

Oh hell. What a way to start the day.

She caught hold of the spiral cord and tugged until her fingers connected with the receiver.

'Michelle.'

Inches away from her ear she recognised the feminine voice, and she stifled an unladylike oath.

'Maman,' she acknowledged with resignation. Just what she needed.

'Are you still in bed, *cherie?*' There was a slight pause. 'Do you know what time it is?'

Seven, maybe eight, she hazarded, sparing a quick glance at the bedside clock before drawing a sharp breath. *Nine.*

'You are alone?'

Michelle closed her eyes, then opened them again. 'No, *Maman.* Two lovers have pleasured me all through the night.'

'There is no need to be facetious, darling,' Chantelle reproved, and Michelle sighed.

'I'm sorry. Blame it on lack of sleep.'

'I thought we might do lunch.' Chantelle named a trendy restaurant at Main Beach. 'Shall we say twelve?' And hung up before Michelle had a chance to confirm or refuse.

'Grrr.' The sound was a low-pitched growl that held a mixture of irritation and compliance. She could ring back and decline, except she knew almost word for word what Chantelle would say as a persuasive ploy.

Emotional blackmail of the nicest kind, she added mentally as she replaced the receiver and rolled onto her stomach.

Lunch for her mother inevitably meant a minuscule Caesar salad, followed by fresh fruit, a small glass of white wine and two glasses of water. Afterwards they would browse the trendy boutiques, drive the short distance to Marina Mirage, relax over a leisurely *latte,* then wander at will through the upmarket emporiums.

It was a mother-daughter thing they indulged in together on occasion. Michelle was under no illusion that today's invitation was a thinly-veiled guise to conduct an in-depth discussion about her association with Nikos Alessandros.

In which case she'd best rise, shine and meet the day. Routine chores and the weekly visit to the supermarket would occupy an hour and a half, and she'd need the remaining time to shower and change if she was to meet her mother at noon.

Chantelle ordered her favourite Caesar salad, and mineral water, while Michelle settled for something more substantial.

'Antonia and Emerson have insisted we join them on their boat for lunch tomorrow.'

Sunglasses shielded her mother's eyes, successfully hiding her expression. Although Michelle wasn't fooled in the slightest.

Chantelle had conversation down to a fine art. First there would be the pleasantries, some light humour in the form of an anecdote or two, followed by the main purpose of the meeting.

'That will be nice,' Michelle commented evenly.

'We will, of course, be back in time to attend the Gallery exhibition.'

This month's exhibition featured an up and coming local artist whose work had impressed both Gallery partners. Arrangements for each exhibition were made many months in advance, and it said much for the Gallery's reputation that they had bookings well into next year for future showings.

Emilio possessed an instinctive flair for what would succeed, and their combined talents and expertise had seen a fledging Gallery expand to become one of the most respected establishments on the coastal strip.

Invitations had been sent out to fifty patrons and their partners, the catering instructions had been given. All that remained were the final touches, and placement of the exhibits.

Something which both she and Emilio would attend to this afternoon and complete early tomorrow morning. 'Do you have any plans for tonight, darling?'

Michelle wound a portion of superb fettuccine

marinara onto her fork and held it poised halfway above her plate. 'An early night, *Maman*.'

'Oh, I see.'

Did she? 'You know how much effort Emilio and I put into each exhibition,' Michelle said lightly. 'There are so many things to check, and Emilio is particular with every detail.'

'I know, darling.'

Chantelle considered education as something important for Michelle to acquire. The private school, university, time abroad to study at the Sorbonne. Except she really wasn't expected to *do* anything as a result of such qualification and experience.

The Gallery had been viewed as a frivolous venture. Michelle's partnership with Emilio Bonanno was expected to be in name only, something she quickly dispelled as she steadfastly refused to join her mother on the social circuit, confining herself to the occasional charity dinner or gala, much to Chantelle's expressed disappointment.

You could say, Michelle mused, that for the past three years her mother had graciously accepted that her own social proclivities were not shared by her daughter. However, it didn't stop Chantelle from issuing frequent invitations, or, for the past year, indulging in subtle matchmaking attempts.

'I think you've succeeded in making Jeremy jealous.' Chantelle took a sip of mineral water, then set down the glass. 'He wasn't quite himself after you left last night. Has he telephoned you this morning?'

'No,' Michelle responded evenly. 'I don't particularly want to hear from him.'

'Because of Nikos Alessandros?'

'Nikos Alessandros has nothing whatsoever to do with it.'

'He's quite a catch, darling.'

She chose to be deliberately obtuse. 'Jeremy?'

'Nikos,' Chantelle corrected with a tolerant sigh.

'As I have no intention of indulging in a fishing expedition, whether or not he's a catch is totally irrelevant.'

'Do you have time to do a little window shopping?' Chantelle queried. 'I really think I could add something to my wardrobe.'

To give her mother credit, she knew when to withdraw. 'I promised Emilio I'd be at the Gallery at two-thirty.'

Chantelle savoured the last mouthful of cos lettuce, then replaced her fork. 'In that case, darling, do finish your pasta. We'll share a coffee later, shall we?'

Clothes, shoes, lingerie, perfume. Any one, or all four, could prove a guaranteed distraction, and Michelle accompanied her mother into one boutique after another in her quest to purchase.

An hour and a half later Chantelle held no less than three brightly emblazoned carry bags, and there was no time left to share coffee.

'See you tomorrow, darling. Don't work too hard.'

Michelle placed a light kiss on her mother's cheek, then watched as Chantelle stowed her purchases in the boot before crossing to slide in behind the wheel of her Mercedes.

It was almost two-thirty when Michelle entered the Gallery. A converted house comprising three levels, it had been completely renovated. Polished wooden floors gleamed with a deep honey stain, and the walls were individually painted in several different pale colours providing a diverse background for carefully placed exhibits. Skylights threw angled shafts of sunlight, accenting subtle shadows as the sun moved from east to west throughout the day.

She experienced a degree of pride at the decor, and what she'd been able to achieve in the past three years.

'Emilio?'

She returned her keys to her bag and carefully closed the door behind her.

'Up here, *cara,*' an accented voice called from the mezzanine level. 'Brett is with me.'

A short flight of stairs led to the next level. Above that were Emilio's private rooms.

Michelle moved swiftly towards the upstairs studio where Brett's exhibition was to be held. 'Hi,' she greeted warmly as she joined them. Both men glanced up, gave her a penetrating look, then switched their attention to the stack of paintings propped carefully against one wall.

'*Cara,* stand over there, and tell us what you think,' Emilio commanded.

For the next four hours they worked side by side, then when the artist left they ordered in pizza, effected a few minor changes, satisfied themselves that every exhibit was strategically placed according to their original plan.

'He's nervous,' Michelle noted as she bit into a slice of piping hot pizza. Melted cheese, pepperoni, capsicum...delicious.

'It's his first exhibition,' Emilio granted, following her action.

The light glinted in reflection from the ear-stud

he wore. Designer stubble was at odds with his peroxided crew cut. A lean sinewy frame clothed in designer jeans and T-shirt, he bore the visual persona of an avant garde. His sexual preferences were the subject for conjecture, and he did nothing to dispel a certain image. However, it was part of the tease, the glamour associated with a role he chose to play, and the knowledge very few close friends knew he was straight and not at all what he appeared to be, only amused him.

Behind the image lay a very shrewd business brain, an almost infallible instinct for genuine talent, and an indefinable *nous* for what appealed to the buying public.

It was something Michelle also shared, and their friendship was platonic, based on mutual knowledge, affection and respect.

'You are pensive. Why?'

Forthright, even confrontational, Emilio possessed the ability to divine whenever anything bothered her. She delayed answering him by pulling the tab on a can of soft drink and taking a long swallow of the ice-cold liquid.

'A man, huh?' Emilio pronounced. 'Do I know him?'

She replaced the can onto the table, and took another bite of pizza. 'What makes you so sure it's a man?'

'You have soft shadows beneath those beautiful green eyes.' His smile was gentle, but far too discerning. 'Lack of sleep, sweetheart. And as you rarely party 'til dawn, I doubt a late night among the social elite was the cause.'

'I could merely be concerned about tomorrow's exhibition.'

'No,' he declared with certainty. 'If you don't want to talk about him, that's fine.'

Michelle cast him a level look. 'He was a guest at a dinner I attended.' She paused fractionally. 'And if I never see him again, it'll be too soon.'

'Trouble,' Emilio accorded softly. 'Definitely.'

'No,' she corrected. 'Because I won't allow him to be.'

'*Cara,* I don't think you'll have a choice.' His quiet laughter brought forth a vexed grimace.

'Why do you say that?'

'Because you're a beautiful young woman whose fierce protection of self lends you to eat lesser men for breakfast,' he mocked. 'The fact you haven't been able to succeed with this particular one is intriguing. I shall look forward to meeting him.'

'It won't happen,' Michelle vowed with certainty.

'You don't think so?'

'I know so,' she responded vehemently.

'OK.' Emilio lifted both hands in a conciliatory gesture, although his smile held humour. 'Eat your pizza.'

'I intend to.' She bit into the crisp crust, then reached forward, caught up a paper napkin and wiped her fingers. 'I'll help you clean up, then I'm going home.'

'An empty pizza carton, a few glasses, soft drink cans. What's to clean?'

'In that case,' she inclined, standing to her feet in one fluid movement. 'I'm out of here.' She leaned forward and brushed her cheek to his. *'Cíao.'*

* * *

The Gallery opened at four, and an hour later the full complement of guests had gathered, mingling in small clutches, glass in hand. Taped baroque music flowed softly through strategically placed speakers, a soothing background to the muted buzz of conversation.

Michelle had selected a classic fitted dress in black with a lace overlay. Stiletto heels, sheer black hose, her hair swept high, and understated make-up with emphasis on her eyes completed a picture that portrayed elegance and style.

Hired staff proffered trays containing a selection of hors d'oeuvres, and already a number of Brett's paintings displayed a discreet *sold* sticker.

Success, Michelle reflected with a small sigh of relief. Everything was going splendidly. The finger food couldn't be faulted, the champagne was superb, and the ambience was *perfecto,* as Emilio would say.

She glanced across the room, caught his eye, and smiled.

'Another triumph, darling.'

Her stomach tightened fractionally as she recognised Jeremy's cynical voice, and she summoned a polite smile as she turned to face him. 'I didn't expect you to honour the invitation.'

'I wouldn't have missed it for the world.'

He leaned forward and she moved slightly so that his lips brushed her cheek. An action which resulted in a faint intake of breath, the momentary hardening of his eyes.

'The eminently eligible Nikos has yet to put in an

appearance, I see.' He moved back a pace, and ran light fingers down her arm.

Michelle tilted her head a little and met his dark gaze. 'A little difficult, when he wasn't issued an invitation.'

'Dear sweet Michelle,' Jeremy chided with sarcastic gentleness. 'Nikos was an invited guest on the parents' cruiser today. The enchanting Chantelle issued the invitation to your Gallery soiree.' He paused for effect before delivering the punch line. 'As I recall, Nikos indicated he would grace us with his presence.'

Her heart tripped and raced to a quicker beat. 'Really?'

One eyebrow slanted in mockery. 'Am I mistaken, or is that not pleasurable anticipation I sense?' He primed a barb and aimed for the kill. 'Didn't he come up to scratch last night, darling?' His smile held thinly veiled humour. 'Jet lag can have that effect.'

Calm, just keep calm, she bade silently as she moved back a pace. He didn't release her arm, and she gave him a deliberately pointed look. 'This conversation is going nowhere, Jeremy.' She flexed her arm, felt his grip tighten for an instant before he released her. 'If you'll excuse me, I really must mingle.' Her voice assumed an icy formality. 'I hope you enjoy the exhibition. Emilio and I are confident of Brett's talent and potential.'

'Ah, the inimical Emilio,' Jeremy drawled. 'You do know he's bisexual?'

As well as being untrue, it was unkind. She didn't miss a beat. 'Slander isn't a pretty word. Watch you don't find yourself in court on a legal charge.'

'A mite too protective, darling.'

'And you,' she declared with quiet emphasis. 'Are a first-class—'

'Michelle.'

Her body quivered at the sound of that faintly accented voice, and her pulse went into overdrive. How much of her argument with Jeremy had Nikos Alessandros heard?

Everything came into sharp focus as she slowly turned to face him.

'Nikos,' she acknowledged, and imperceptibly stiffened as he placed a hand at the back of her waist.

His expression gave nothing away, but there was a hint of steel beneath the polite facade as he inclined his head.

'Jeremy.'

Michelle's nerves flared into sensitised life at his close proximity.

'Is there a problem?' Nikos asked smoothly, and she felt like screaming.

Yes. Jeremy for behaving badly, and *you* just for being here!

A determined sparkle darkened her eyes. 'If you'll excuse me? I really should mingle.'

She turned away, only to find that Nikos had joined her.

'Just what the hell do you think you're doing?' she queried with quiet vehemence the instant they were out of Jeremy's earshot. She made a concerted effort to shift out of his grasp without success.

'Rescuing you.'

'I didn't need rescuing!'

His smile held a hint of cynical humour. 'Especially not by me.'

'Look—'

'Save the indignation for a more suitable occasion.'

'Why?' Michelle vented with quiet fury. 'When I have no intention of seeing you again.'

'Considering your parents and the Bateson-Burrows have issued me with a few interesting invitations, that's most unlikely,' Nikos assured silkily.

She wanted to hit him. It was enough she had to deal with Jeremy, whose recalcitrance in the past twenty-four hours could be directly attributed to the man at her side.

Had Nikos not been a guest at the Bateson-Burrows' dinner table, she could have conducted a diplomatic discussion last night with Jeremy, and he wouldn't now be behaving quite inappropriately.

Or would he? Jeremy had displayed a side to his personality she'd never suspected might exist.

'Suppose we embark on a conducted tour of your protegé's work.'

'Why?' she demanded baldly, and found herself looking into a pair of amused dark grey eyes.

'I could be a potential buyer, and you do, Chantelle assures me, have an excellent eye for new talent.'

Did she realise just how beautiful she looked when she was angry?

'Mother has excelled herself in lauding my supposed talents,' she stated dryly.

'Cynicism doesn't suit you.'

In any other circumstance, she would have laughed. However, tonight she wasn't in the mood to see the humorous side of Chantelle's machinations.

They drew close to one exhibit, and she went into a professional spiel about light and colour and style,

Brett's unusual technique, and indicated the painting's possible worth on the market in another five years.

Nikos dropped his arm from her waist, and she wondered why she suddenly felt cold, even vaguely bereft.

Crazy, she dismissed. Every instinct she possessed warned that Nikos Alessandros was a man she should have nothing to do with if she wanted to retain her emotional sanity.

CHAPTER FOUR

'WHICH OF THE collection is your personal favourite?' Nikos queried as they moved from one exhibit to another.

There were interruptions as she was greeted by a few guests, and on each occasion good manners demanded she introduce the man at her side.

She could sense their masked speculation, sense their curiosity, and she wasn't sure whether to feel angry or resigned.

Michelle's lips parted to make a flippant response, only to change her mind at the last second. 'The little boy standing on a sandhill looking out over the ocean.'

He lifted a hand and tucked a stray lock of hair back behind her ear. He watched her eyes dilate, and felt the slight shiver his touch evoked. 'Why that particular painting?'

'Because it seems as if the ocean represents his world, and he's curious to know where it ends and what's beyond the horizon. If you look at his features, there's wonderment, excitement.' Her voice softened. 'He's trying not to be afraid, but he is. You can see it in the faint thrust of his lower lip, the way his chin tucks in a little.' She raised her hand, then let it fall again to her side.

It was more than just a painting, it represented life. The promise of what might be. Even though the logical mind relegated the image to the skilled use of paint on canvas and artistic flair.

'Consider it sold.'

Michelle glanced up and examined the chiselled perfection of his features. 'You haven't asked the price.'

'It's listed on the programme.' His smile was wholly sensual. 'What discount are you prepared to offer me?'

She badly wanted to say *none,* except 'business' was a separate category to 'personal,' and anyone with sufficient *nous* ensured the two were kept apart. 'It depends on your method of payment.'

'I'll present you with a bank cheque at midday tomorrow, and organise delivery.'

Michelle didn't hesitate. 'Five per cent.'

It shouldn't concern her where he intended to hang it, in fact she told herself she didn't care.

'Something is bothering you?'

His light tone didn't fool her in the slightest. He was too intuitive, and she loathed his ability to tune into her thoughts. It made her feel vulnerable, and too acutely sensitive.

'Why should anything bother me? I've just sold the most expensive painting featured in this exhibition.'

'By your own admission, it's the one you admire most,' Nikos pursued softly. 'I imagine you can offer a suggestion how it should be displayed to its best advantage?'

She could tell him to do what he liked with it, but professional etiquette got the better of her.

'It should occupy centre stage on a wide wall,' she opined slowly. 'Preferably painted a very pale shade of blue, so the colours mesh and there's a sense of continuity.'

Interesting, he perceived, that her love of art overcame her instinctive wariness of him.

'Now, if you'll excuse me,' Michelle said purposefully. 'There's something I need to check with my business partner.' She offered him a polite smile, then turned and went in search of Emilio.

'So he's the one,' Emilio said in a quiet aside several minutes later.

'I don't know what you're talking about.'

'Yes, you do.'

'I'd prefer not to discuss it.'

'As you wish.'

'Dammit, I don't even like him!'

'So… What's liking got to do with anything?' Emilio queried mildly.

'Grrr,' she vented softly, and incurred his soft laughter.

'Stephanie.' He was suddenly the businessman, the art entrepreneur, assuming the faintly affected manner he'd honed to perfection. 'How are you, darling?'

Michelle followed suit, according the wealthy widow due deference. The money Stephanie Whitcomb had spent in their Gallery over the past few years went close to six figures.

'Such a success, *cherie,*' Chantelle complimented as Michelle crossed to her parents' side. 'We are very proud of you.'

'Indeed. A stunning exhibition.'

'Thank you, *Papa.* Naturally you're prejudiced.'

Etienne smiled as he leaned forward to bestow a light kiss to her cheek. 'Of course.'

'Tomorrow we're hosting a small cocktail evening. Just very close friends. Six o'clock. You'll join us, won't you?'

Her mother's idea of a small gathering could number anything from twenty to thirty people. Drinks on the terrace, a seemingly casual but carefully prepared finger-food buffet.

'*Maman,* no,' Michelle voiced with regret. 'I have plans.'

'What a shame. We included Saska in Nikos' invitation. I thought you might like to bring Emilio.'

There was a silent message evident which Michelle chose to ignore. 'Another time, perhaps?'

'If you reconsider...' Chantelle trailed delicately.

'Thank you, *Maman.*'

Guests were beginning to drift towards the door, and as always, it took a while for the Gallery to empty.

Michelle organised the hired staff as they packed glassware into containers. Much of the cleaning up had already been done, and Emilio handed over a cheque, then saw them off the premises.

'Go home,' he ordered without preamble. 'You're tired, it shows, and I'll deal with everything in the morning.'

'I had no idea I looked such a wreck,' Michelle said dryly.

'Darling, I am an old friend, and I can tell it like it is,' he said gently.

'It was a successful evening.'

All of Brett's paintings had sold, and they'd succeeded in confirming a tentative date in April to host another exhibition of his work.

'Very,' Emilio agreed, as she reached up and brushed his cheek with her lips. 'For what it's worth, I approve of the Greek.' He lifted a hand and smoothed back a stray tendril of hair that had escaped from the chignon at her nape. 'I enjoyed watching him watch you.'

Something inside Michelle's stomach curled into a tight ball. 'Since when did you become my protector?'

'Since I fell in love with you many years ago…as a sister,' he teased gently.

She smiled with genuine affection. 'In that case, *brother*, I'm going home and leaving you with all that remains of the clean-up chores.'

'Tomorrow morning, ten,' Emilio reminded. 'Take care.'

Her car was parked about twenty metres distant, the street was well-lit, and as the Gallery was situated off the main street housing numerous cafés and restaurants, there were several parked cars in the immediate vicinity.

Michelle gained the pavement and stepped in the direction of her car, only to pause at the sight of a male figure leaning against its bonnet.

The figure straightened and moved towards her. 'I thought you were never going to leave,' Jeremy complained.

She stepped forward to cross the grass verge, and felt his hand grasp her arm.

'It's been a long day, and I'm tired,' she said firmly. Her patience was getting thin, but she recognised a

certain quality about him that made her very wary.
'Goodnight.'

'Dammit, Michelle, you can't just walk away from
me.'

'Please let go of my arm. I want to get into my car.'

She was unprepared for his sudden movement
as he twisted her close with vicious strength, then
ground his mouth against her own.

Instinct and training combined to allow her to un-
balance him, and one swiftly hooked foot sent him
falling to the ground.

Michelle moved quickly round to the driver's side,
unlocked the door, and was about to slide into the seat
when Jeremy caught hold of her arm and dragged
her out.

'I believe the lady said no,' a slightly accented male
voice drawled hardily.

Jeremy's fingers tightened with painful intensity,
and she could feel his palpable anger.

'Bitch!'

'Let her go,' Nikos commanded with dangerous
softness. 'Or else I promise you won't walk easily
for days.'

Michelle caught her breath as Jeremy's fingers bit
to the bone, then he flung her arm free, turned and
crossed the road to his car, fired the engine with an
ear-splitting roar, and sent the tyres spinning as he
sped down the road.

Nikos said something vicious beneath his breath as
she stiffened beneath his touch, and he swore briefly,
pithily, in his own language.

Michelle edged the tip of her tongue over her lips

and discovered several abrasions where her teeth had split the delicate tissues.

'I'll drive you home.'

'No.' She told herself she didn't need his concern. 'I'm fine.' To prove it, she slid in behind the wheel, only to have him lean into the car and bodily shift her into the passenger seat.

Seconds later he took her place and engaged the ignition.

'There's no need for you to do this,' Michelle asserted as he set the car in motion.

Three blocks and two minutes later he swept through the entrance to her apartment building and paused adjacent the security gate leading to the underground car park.

'Do you have your card?'

She handed it to him wordlessly, and when the gate was fully open she directed him to her allotted space.

'What about your own car?'

He directed her a dark glance as he led her towards the lift. 'I walked.' He jabbed the call button, and when the lift arrived, he accompanied her into it. 'Which floor?'

'There's no—'

'Which floor?' Nikos repeated with dangerous quietness.

He was icily calm. Too calm, she perceived, aware there was something apparent in his stance, the set of his features, that revealed anger held in tight control.

'I appreciate your driving me home. But I'm fine.'

She glimpsed the darkness in his eyes, the hard purpose evident, and was momentarily bereft of speech. 'Really,' she added seconds later.

One eyebrow rose slightly, and she met his silent scrutiny with unblinking equanimity.

'Look in the mirror,' Nikos bade quietly, and watched as she spared the decorative mirrored panel a glance.

Her hair was no longer confined in a neat chignon, her eyes were dark, dilated and seemed far too large in features that were pale, and her mouth was swollen.

'Now, which floor?' he queried with velvet softness, and she hesitated momentarily before capitulating.

'Fifteenth.'

They reached it in seconds, and she silently indicated the door leading to her apartment.

Once inside she had the compelling urge to remove Jeremy's touch from her skin, and she wanted to scrub her teeth, cleanse her mouth.

'I'm going to take a shower and change.' She no longer cared whether Nikos Alessandros was there or not, or whether he'd have gone when she returned. Uppermost was the need to be alone, shed and dispense with her clothes.

Hell, she'd probably burn them, she determined as she reached the bedroom and began peeling each item from her body.

Michelle activated the shower dial and set it as hot as she could bear, then she lathered every inch of skin, rinsed, and repeated the process three times. Satisfied, she turned the dial to cold and let the needle spray revive and revitalise her before she reached for a towel.

Minutes later she donned clean underwear, then reached for jeans and a loose cotton top. She discounted make-up, and applied the hair dryer for as long as it took to remove most of the dampness, then she simply wound it into a knot and pinned it on top of her head.

Michelle walked into the kitchen and saw Nikos in the process of brewing coffee. He'd removed his jacket and his tie. He'd also loosened a few top buttons and folded back the cuffs of his shirt.

His appraisal was swift, yet all-encompassing. 'I've brewed some coffee.'

There were two cups and saucers on the countertop, sugar and milk, and she watched as he filled her cup.

He looked comfortably at ease, yet instinct warned that anger lurked just beneath the surface of his control.

'You don't have to do this.' She hugged her arms together across her midriff, and temporarily ignored the cup and saucer he pushed towards her.

'No,' Nikos responded evenly. 'I don't.' He added sugar to his cup, stirred, then lifted it to his mouth.

She should suggest the more formal surroundings of the lounge, but the last thing she wanted to do was indulge in meaningless conversation.

'Do you intend laying charges?'

Her eyes widened slightly. Oh God, that meant involving the police, filing a complaint. The facts becoming public knowledge. Jeremy's parents, her parents, their friends...

'I don't think so,' she said at last.

His piercing regard unsettled her, and after what seemed an age she averted her gaze to a point somewhere beyond his right shoulder.

'What about the next time he lays in wait for you?' Nikos queried relentlessly.

Michelle's eyes snapped back into focus. 'There won't *be* a next time.'

'You're so sure about that?'

'If there is, I can handle it,' she reiterated firmly.

'Such confidence.'

'I handled you.'

His smile lacked any pretense at humour. 'At no time did my motives stem from a desire to frighten or harm you.'

'I didn't know that.' Any more than she knew it now.

'No,' he qualified, and glimpsed the way her body jerked imperceptibly, and the defensive tightening of her arms as she sought to control it. He wasn't done, and he derived no satisfaction or pleasure in what he intended to say. 'Don't presume to judge the son by his parents.'

'Hidden messages, Nikos?' Her eyes were clear as they met his.

The unexpected peal of the telephone startled her.

'Aren't you going to answer that?'

She moved to the handset and picked up the receiver.

'Michelle.'

Jeremy. Her fingers tightened. 'I have nothing to say to you.' She hung up without giving him the opportunity to utter a further word.

A minute later it rang again, and she ignored it for several seconds before snatching the receiver.

'I'm sorry.' His voice was ragged, and came in quick bursts. 'I was jealous. I didn't mean to hurt you.'

She didn't bother answering, and simply replaced the receiver.

Within seconds the telephone rang again, and she caught up the receiver, only to have it taken out of her hand.

'Call once more, and I'll ensure Michelle notifies the police,' Nikos directed brusquely. The tirade of abuse that followed was ugly. 'What you're suggesting is anatomically impossible. However I'm quite prepared to get a legal opinion on it. Would you care for me to do that?'

It was obvious Jeremy didn't want anything of the kind, and she watched as Nikos replaced the receiver.

'Does he have a key to your apartment?'

'No.' Indignation rose to the fore, and erupted in angry speech. 'No, he doesn't. No one does.'

'I'm relieved to hear it.'

Michelle fixed him with a fulminating glare. 'What I do with my life and who I do it with is none of your business.'

He admired her spirit, and there was a part of him that wanted to pull her into his arms and hold her close. Except he knew if he so much as touched her, she'd scratch and claw like a cornered cat.

'Tonight I made it my business.'

'I didn't leave the Gallery until half an hour after everyone else,' Michelle flung at him. 'How come you happened to still be hanging around?'

'I was on foot, remember? I noticed Jeremy sitting in a car he made no attempt to start.'

Nikos didn't need to paint a word picture. She got it without any help at all, in technicolour.

'I should thank you.'

His mouth tilted fractionally. 'So—thank me.'

Her eyes met his. 'I thought I just did.'

'And now you want me to leave.'

'Please.'

She watched as he extracted his wallet, withdrew a card, scrawled a series of digits and placed it onto the countertop.

'My mobile number. You can reach me on it anytime.'

She followed him from the kitchen, paused as he caught up his jacket, then crossed the lounge to the front door.

Nikos lifted a hand and brushed his fingers down her cheek. 'Goodnight, *kyria*.'

He didn't linger, and she told herself she was glad. She closed the door, set the locking mechanism in place, and threw the bolt.

Then she crossed to a comfortable chair and activated the remote.

Cable television provided endless choices, and she stared resolutely at the screen in an effort to block out what had transpired in the past hour.

She focused on the Gallery, its success, Emilio, until it became increasingly difficult to keep her eyes open, then she simply closed them, uncaring where she slept.

CHAPTER FIVE

MICHELLE WOKE AT dawn to the sound of male voices and lifted her head in alarm, only to subside as realisation affirmed the television was on and the voice belonged to actor Don Johnson as Sonny in a rerun of 'Miami Vice.'

Her limbs felt stiff, and she stretched in an effort to ease them, then she checked her watch.

There was time for a swim in the indoor pool, then she'd shower and change, grab some breakfast, and drive to the Gallery.

It was almost nine when she swung the Porsche into a parking bay, and she used her key to unlock the outer Gallery door.

'Buon giorno.'

'Hi,' she greeted, and cast Emilio an appreciative smile as she saw the fruits of his labour in highly polished floors and everything restored to immaculate order. 'You're an angel.'

'Ah, from you that is indeed a compliment.'

'I mean it.'

The corners of his eyes crinkled with humour, and his smile was warm and generous. 'I know you do.'

'As you've cleaned up, I'll do the book work, enter the accounts, make the phone calls.'

'But first, the coffee.' He moved towards her and caught hold of her shoulders, then frowned as he saw her wince. His eyes narrowed as he glimpsed the shadows beneath her eyes. 'Headache, no sleep, what?'

'A bit of all three.'

She bore his scrutiny with equanimity. 'Elaborate on the *what*, Michelle.'

Emilio called her *darling, honey, cara,* but rarely *Michelle.*

'It was such a successful evening,' she prevaricated.

'Uh-huh,' he disclaimed. 'We've achieved other successful evenings, none of which have seen you pale, wan, and hollow-eyed the next morning.'

She opted to go for the truth. Or as much of it as he needed to know. 'I watched a film on cable, then fell asleep in the lounge.' She arched her neck, and rolled her head a little. 'I'm a little stiff, that's all.'

He didn't say anything for several long seconds. 'Nice try, *cara.*'

'You mentioned coffee?'

Michelle took hers into the office, and set to work entering details from yesterday's sales into the computer. She double-checked the receipts and entries before printing out the accounts, then stacked them in alphabetical order. A few of their regular clientele had paid by personal cheque, and she organised the banking deposit sheet.

She made telephone calls and arranged packing

and delivery, then checked with the clientele to ascertain if the times quoted were convenient.

When the intercom beeped, she activated it. 'Yes, Emilio?'

'Jeremy Bateson-Burrows is here. Shall I send him in?'

'No.' Her refusal was swift, and she breathed in deeply before qualifying, 'I don't want to see him.'

A minute later the intercom beeped again. 'He says it's of vital importance.'

Michelle cursed beneath her breath. 'Tell him I'll be down in a minute.'

Her stiletto heels made a clicking noise on the polished floor, and she saw Jeremy turn towards her as she drew close.

Emilio was within sight some distance away arranging a display of decorative ceramic urns.

'Jeremy,' she greeted with cool formality.

'I wanted to apologise in person.'

Careful, an inner voice cautioned. 'It's a little too late for that,' she said evenly. 'If you'll excuse me, I have a considerable amount of work to get through.'

'I need to talk to you, to explain. Have lunch with me. Please?' He was very convincing. Too convincing. 'I don't know what came over me last night,' he said desperately.

'I'd like you to leave. Now,' Michelle said quietly.

He reached out a hand as if to touch her arm, and she stepped back a few paces.

'Michelle.'

Emilio's intrusion was heaven-sent, and she turned towards him in silent query.

'I'm in the middle of an international call,' Emilio

announced smoothly. 'Nikos Alessandros has arrived to arrange delivery and payment. Can you attend to him?'

He held the mobile phone, and she almost believed him until she glimpsed the dark stillness apparent in his expression.

'Yes, of course.'

Nikos watched as she walked towards him, and controlled the brief surge of anger as she drew close. She looked as fragile as the finest glass.

'Good morning.' Or was it afternoon? Hell, she'd lost track of whether it was one or the other.

His eyes met hers, dark, analytical, unwavering, and her eyes widened slightly as he leaned forward and cupped her face with both hands.

His mouth covered hers with a gentleness that made the breath catch in her throat, and she was unable to suppress the shivery sensation scudding down her spine as his tongue softly explored the delicate tissues, slowly traced each abrasion, then tangled briefly with her tongue before withdrawing.

He let both hands drop to his side, then he circled her waist and drew her close.

'What's going on? Michelle?' Jeremy's voice was hard and filled with querulous anger.

Nikos' arm tightened fractionally in silent warning, and the look he cast down at her was warm and incredibly intimate. 'I don't see the need to keep it a secret, do you?' He shifted his attention to Emilio. 'Michelle and I have decided to resume our relationship.'

She heard the words, assimilated them, and didn't

have a chance to draw breath as Nikos soundly kissed her.

Why did she have the feeling she was one of three players on a stage, with an audience of only one? Because that was the precise scenario, and it came as no surprise when Jeremy brushed past them and exited the Gallery.

Emilio locked the door after him and turned the "open" sign round to read "closed."

'You can't do that,' Michelle protested.

'I just did. So what are you going to do about it?' Emilio queried lightly, adding in jest—'Sue me?'

She looked from one to the other, then fixed her gaze on Nikos. 'You've really put the fat in the fire now.' Reaction began to rear its head. 'Do you realise the news will probably reach my parents? What will they think?' She closed her eyes, then opened them again in the knowledge that her darling *maman* would undoubtedly be delighted. Another thought rose to the fore, and her expression became fierce. 'This situation plays right into your hands with Saska, doesn't it?'

'Who is Saska?' Emilio asked with interest, and Nikos informed him urbanely.

'The recently widowed wife of a very close friend.'

'Whom Nikos suggested I collaborate with him to deceive,' Michelle added.

'Ah,' Emilio commented with a shrug in comprehension. 'But you wouldn't play, huh?'

'No, she wouldn't,' Nikos said smoothly.

A wide smile showed white teeth and lent dark eyes a lively sparkle. 'I think you should, *cara*. Play,' Emilio added quizzically. 'It would do you good.'

'Emilio,' Michelle warned. 'I don't find this in the least amusing.'

'No, darling, I don't expect you do.' His expression sobered slightly. Jeremy was the catalyst, and Nikos, unless he was mistaken, was a man with a hidden agenda. 'You'll forgive me if I say I shall enjoy the show?' He didn't give her the opportunity to respond.

'I don't need to tell you that your secret is safe with me. Now, why don't you go have lunch together, and fine tune your strategy?'

'Yes,' Nikos agreed. 'Why don't we do that?'

She cast him a discerning look, opened her mouth to argue, then closed it again. 'I'll get my bag.' She crossed to the office, retrieved it, then swung back to the entrance.

Emilio was talking into the mobile phone, and she fluttered her fingers at him, checked her watch, and silently indicated she'd be back at two.

'I suggest somewhere close by in air-conditioned comfort,' Nikos indicated silkily as they walked into the midsummer sunshine.

Michelle slid down her sunglasses, and was aware he mirrored her actions. 'Fine. You choose.'

Ten minutes later they were seated in seclusion at a table overlooking an outdoor courtyard filled with potted flowers and greenery plants of numerous description.

'Your parents have invited Saska to their home this evening.'

Michelle looked at him over the rim of her glass. He looked relaxed and at ease, and far too compelling for his own good. '*Maman* is the consummate hostess,' she said evenly. 'I'm sure you'll both enjoy yourselves.'

She replaced the glass as the waiter delivered their order.

'I'll collect you at five to six.'

'I have other plans.'

'Change them.'

'Those plans involve other people. I don't want to let them down at such short notice.'

His eyes speared hers. 'I'm sure they'll understand if you explain.'

Yes they would, but that wasn't the point.

Michelle picked up her fork and stabbed a crouton, some cos lettuce, and regarded the poised fork with apparent interest. She was bargaining for time, and it irked that he knew. 'Surely the charade can wait a few days?'

'Antonia and Emerson Bateson-Burrows are fellow guests,' Nikos intimated. 'Won't they think it a little strange if you're not there?' He waited a beat. 'And Saska is seen to be my partner?'

She had to concede he had a point. 'I guess you're right.'

Why did she feel like she'd just made a life-changing decision? How long would this pretense need to last? A few weeks? A month? It wasn't as if they had to attend every party and dinner in town. It was likely she'd only have to see him a couple of nights a week.

Just keep your emotions intact, a tiny voice taunted.

Michelle took a sip of mineral water, then speared another morsel of food. The salad was delicious, but her appetite diminished with every mouthful.

What about the chemistry? The way she felt when he touched her? Each time he kissed her, whether in sensual exploration or passion, she'd just wanted to die.

Dear heaven, she'd experienced more emotional upheaval in the past two days than she had in…a long time, she admitted.

Nikos observed each fleeting expression, and wondered if she realised how expressive her features were? Or how easily he was able to define them?

'I guess we should set down some ground rules.' That sounded fair, she determined. How had Emilio put it? *Fine tune your strategy.*

'What did you have in mind?'

Michelle looked at him carefully, and was unable to see beyond the sophisticated mask he presented. Oh God, was she *mad*? She wasn't even in the same league, let alone the same game. So why was she choosing to play?

'You don't make decisions for me, and vice versa,' she began. 'We consult on anything that involves the both of us.'

'That's reasonable.'

So far, so good. 'No unnecessary—' She was going to say *intimacy,* but that sounded too personal. 'Touching,' she amended, and missed the faint gleam in those dark eyes.

'I'll try to restrain myself, if you will.'

He was amused, damn him! 'This isn't funny,' she reproved, and he proffered a crooked smile.

'My sense of humour got the better of me.'

'Do you want to put a time limit on this?'

One eyebrow slanted. 'Lunch?'

'Our supposed relationship!'

'Ah—that.' He expertly wound the last of his fettuccine onto his fork and savoured it. 'How about… as long as it takes?'

Of course. That was the entire object of the exercise. She'd had enough salad, and she pushed the bowl forward, then sank back in her chair.

'I'm intrigued,' she ventured. 'To discover how you knew I'd studied at the Sorbonne?'

He looked at her carefully. 'I endeavour to discover background details of the people who claim to want to do business with me. It's a precautionary measure.'

Michelle's eyes narrowed slightly. That meant being able to access confidential data on file. Although with the right contacts and connections, it wouldn't be difficult.

'Emerson Bateson-Burrows has been vigilant in baiting the figurative hook,' Nikos revealed with wry cynicism.

As her parents mixed socially with Jeremy's parents, they, too, had come beneath Nikos' scrutiny. It didn't leave her with a comfortable feeling.

'We didn't meet in Paris.'

'Yes, we did,' he corrected.

'Where?' she demanded. 'I would have remembered.'

'At a party.'

It was possible. She'd attended several parties during her Paris sojourn. Although she was positive she'd never seen Nikos Alessandros at any one of them. 'We weren't introduced,' she said with certainty.

'No,' Nikos agreed. 'It was a case of too many people, and I was with someone else.'

Now why did that suddenly make her feel jealous? It didn't make sense.

'You'd better let me have your phone number in case I need to contact you,' he said smoothly, and she lifted one eyebrow in mocking query.

'You mean you don't already have it?'

His gaze was steady. 'I'd prefer you to give it to me willingly.'

She looked at him for a second, then she reached into her bag, extracted a card and handed it to him.

'Would you like something else to eat?' When she shook her head, he indicated, 'Dessert? Coffee?'

How long had they been here? Half an hour? Longer? 'No. Thanks,' she added. 'I have a few things to do before I go back to the Gallery.' She didn't, but Nikos wasn't to know that. 'Would you excuse me?'

He lifted one hand, gained the attention of the waiter, and rose to his feet. 'I'll walk back with you.'

She opened her mouth to say 'there's no need,' saw his expression, and decided to refrain from saying anything at all.

Nikos signed the proffered credit slip, pocketed the duplicate, then accompanied her onto the street.

Finding 'things to do' didn't stretch her imagination, and she made the bakery first on her list, where she selected bread rolls, a couple of Danish pastries. For Emilio, she justified. To lend credence, she entered the small local post office and stood in line to buy stamps.

Did Nikos suspect her mission was a sham? Possibly. But she didn't care.

'Are you done?'

The sound of that soft slightly accented drawl

merely added encouragement, and she stepped into the pharmacy, picked up some antiseptic liquid, paid for it, then emerged onto the pavement.

The fruit shop was next, and she selected some grapes, an apple, a banana, and two tomatoes, justifying her purchases, 'I won't have time to get anything after work.'

It took only minutes to reach the Gallery, but they were long minutes during which she was acutely conscious of his height and breadth as he walked at her side.

Twice she thought of something to say by way of conversation only to dismiss the words as being inane.

At the Gallery entrance she paused and thanked him for lunch, then looked askance as he followed her inside.

'If you remember there was a distraction,' Nikos reminded indolently. 'I need to give you a cheque, and have you arrange delivery.'

Michelle tended to it with professional efficiency, then accompanied him to the door.

'What have we here?' Emilio queried, indicating her purchases shortly after Nikos' departure.

'Things.' She selected the bakery bag and handed it to him. 'For you.'

His soft laughter was almost her undoing. 'You initiated a small diversion?'

'Minor,' she agreed, and he shook his head in silent chastisement.

'Tonight could prove interesting.'

Michelle merely smiled and headed towards the office.

* * *

It was after five when she parked her car in its allotted space and rode the lift to her apartment.

The message light was blinking on the answering machine, and she activated the 'message' button, listened to Jeremy's voice as he issued an impassioned plea to call him, deliberated all of five seconds, then hit 'erase.'

His increasingly obsessive behaviour disturbed her, and she stood in reflective silence, aware that at no time had she given him reason to believe they could share anything more than friendship.

A quick glance at her watch revealed she had half an hour in which to shower and dress before she was due to meet Nikos downstairs.

Michelle entered the lobby as Nikos' BMW swept into the bricked apron immediately adjacent the main entrance, and she reached the car just as he emerged from behind the wheel.

Nikos noted the slight thrust of her chin, the cool expressive features, and suppressed a faint smile at the sleek upswept hairstyle. The make-up was perfection with clever emphasis on her eyes, the generous curve of her mouth.

The classic "little black dress" had a scooped neckline, very short sleeves and a hemline that stopped mid-thigh, with high stiletto-heeled black pumps accenting the length of her legs.

Everything about her enhanced the sophisticated image of a young woman in total control.

Michelle slid into the passenger seat and offered him a faint smile in greeting.

He looked relaxed, and she wished she could feel comfortable about deceiving her parents.

The car gained clear passage onto the road, and Nikos headed towards the main arterial road leading into Surfers Paradise.

'Ten minutes to countdown.'

'Less,' Nikos declared. 'It begins when we collect Saska from her hotel.'

Within minutes he drew the car to a halt adjacent the Marriott. 'I won't be long.'

She watched as he disappeared through the automatic glass doors, crossed to one of several armchairs in the large lobby, and greeted a tall elegantly dressed woman.

Beautiful wasn't an adequate description, Michelle decided as Nikos escorted the brunette to the car.

The mental image Michelle had drawn of a depressed and desperately unhappy widow didn't fit the vital young woman who conversed with ease during the ten-minute drive to Sovereign Islands, a group of seven manmade residential islands situated three kilometres north, and reached by an overbridge from the mainland.

Chantelle and Etienne Gerard's home was a modern architectural tri-level home, with two levels given over entirely to entertaining.

There were several cars lining the driveway, and Michelle experienced a vague sense of uneasiness as she entered the house at Nikos' side. She was all too aware of the role she'd committed herself to play and the deceit involved.

Almost on cue, Nikos caught hold of her hand and

linked his fingers through her own, and the smile he cast her was intimately warm.

It stirred her senses and made her acutely aware of each breath she took. The blood seemed to race through her veins, quickening her pulse.

Oh God. What had she let herself in for?

CHAPTER SIX

'NIKOS, SASKA, how nice to see you.' Chantelle, ever the gracious hostess, greeted them with pleasant enthusiasm, then she leaned forward and touched her daughter's cheek with her own. 'Darling, I'm so pleased you could come.'

Her mother's 'just a few friends' extended to more than thirty, Michelle estimated as Chantelle led them through the house and out onto the large terrace overlooking a wide canal.

Hired staff were in evidence to ensure trays of finger food and drinks were constantly on offer.

Introductions and greetings were exchanged with the ease of long practice as they mingled with fellow guests.

Every now and then she felt the pressure of Nikos' fingers on her own, and several times she made a furtive attempt to free them without success.

Antonia and Emerson Bateson-Burrows were among the guests, and Michelle's stomach twisted a little at the thought that Jeremy might put in an appearance.

'Have you known Nikos for long?'

Was this a trick question? Surely Nikos had already provided Saska with *some* basic information?

'We met while Michelle was studying in Paris,' Nikos answered for her, and Michelle wrinkled her nose at him.

'Really, darling,' she chastised teasingly. 'I'm quite capable of answering for myself.' She turned towards Saska and rolled her eyes. 'At a party.' Surely it would do no harm to elaborate a little? 'Five years ago.' That fit in well. 'I was a student with a very new Arts degree, which my parents agreed should be followed by a year at the Sorbonne.' She lifted her shoulders in a typically Gaelic shrug. 'Intense study, you know how it is. I was dragged off to a party with friends. Nikos was there.'

Saska's eyes assumed a faintly quizzical gleam. 'Alone?'

'Of course not.' This could almost be fun, meshing fact with fiction. 'His companion for the evening was a stunning blonde.'

'He was obviously attracted to you.'

'Very much so,' Nikos admitted as he carried Michelle's hand to his lips, and she felt the graze of teeth against her knuckles in silent warning.

Which she took delight in ignoring. 'He played the gentleman, and was very circumspect in his interest.' She met his gaze and openly dared him to refute her words. 'Weren't you, darling?'

'Until the next time.'

The *knowledge* was there, apparent, and acted as a subtle reminder that when it came to game-playing, he was more than her equal.

'Michelle. Nikos.'

It was a relief to have Emilio join them, and she cast him a generous smile as Nikos introduced Saska.

'Pleasant evening,' Emilio commented, switching his attention to the widowed brunette. 'You're here on holiday?'

'Yes. Nikos suggested I take a break for a few weeks.'

'Perhaps we could have dinner together one night soon? Tuesday?'

My, Emilio was moving quickly, Michelle acknowledged silently, watching as Saska effected a slight lift of her shoulders.

'If that is acceptable to Nikos and Michelle?'

Whoa. A foursome? *Tomorrow?*

'We'll be delighted, won't we, *pedhi mou?*'

The endearment was deliberate, and she was tempted to say *no,* but knew it would sound churlish. 'Delighted,' she agreed. At the first opportunity, she decided, she would have words with Nikos about the frequency of such 'dates.'

Michelle took another sip of excellent champagne and removed a seafood savoury from a proffered tray. It seemed hours since she'd picked at a salad over lunch.

'What a magnificent view,' Saska enthused as she gazed out over the water. 'Nikos, you must tell me the history behind the design of these islands.'

'Take Saska down onto the jetty,' Michelle directed, and felt a tingle of pleasure at thwarting him. 'It's possible to obtain a more effective view from there.'

This was not part of the plan. It was evident from the faint warning flare in the depths of those eyes.

'Michelle is more knowledgeable,' he responded smoothly.

It was a very neat manoeuvre, and one she couldn't really extricate herself from without appearing impolite.

The ground was landscaped on three terraced levels from the outdoor pool down to the water's edge. Lavish landscaping included concrete steps, a decorative rockery, a large fountain, flower-edged paths, and expanses of lush green lawn.

Michelle led the way, and when they reached the jetty she stepped out to its furthest point as she directed Saska's attention towards the Broadwater.

'The stretch of land immediately in front of us is known as south Stradbroke Island. Beyond it lays the Pacific Ocean.'

Saska leaned forward. 'And these islands?'

'Manmade. Each small island is connected to the other by a series of bridges. It's very effective, don't you think?'

Saska didn't speak for several minutes. 'Nikos is a special friend,' she relayed conversationally. 'We've known each other a long time.'

Michelle didn't pretend not to understand. 'I imagine there's a purpose to you telling me this?'

'I find it unusual he has never mentioned you.'

Why did she suddenly feel as if she'd just stepped into a minefield? 'As you know, Nikos has diverse business interests in many European cities.' She was plucking reasons out of nowhere. 'We met not long before I was due to return to Australia to discover my niche in the art world.' A small elaboration, but much of it had its base in truth.

'And now?' Saska persisted. 'I understand you've only recently rediscovered each other?'

'Yes.'

'Do you love him?'

Think, she directed mentally. You can hardly say *no.* 'I care,' she said simply, and added for good measure, 'Very much.' May the heavens not descend on her head for such a transgression!

'So do I,' the brunette declared.

'What are you advocating? Swords drawn at dawn, and a fight to the death?'

Saska smiled, then began to laugh, and the effect transformed her features into something of rare beauty. 'I like you.'

'Well now,' Michelle drawled. 'That's a bonus.'

'In fact,' Saska deliberated. 'I think you'd be very good for Nikos.' The smile widened. 'But then, so would I. We share the same heritage, the same interests, the same friends. As much as I grieve for my dead husband, I have discovered I do not like being alone. Do we understand one another?'

'Yes. But haven't you neglected the most important factor?'

Saska lifted a finely arched eyebrow. 'I don't think so.'

'Nikos. The choice is his to make, don't you think?'

'Of course.'

Confidence was a fine thing. 'Now we've had this little chat,' Michelle said evenly, 'shall we rejoin the other guests?'

'By all means.'

The evening air was still, and although light, there was a hint of impending dusk as shadows began to lengthen. The water lost its deep blue and began to acquire a shade of grey as the colours lost their sharp intensity.

Numerous garden lights sprang on, together with lit columns around the pool, illuminating the terrace and surrounding area.

Nikos moved forward to meet them, and although his smile encompassed both women, his hand settled in the small of Michelle's back for an instant before his fingers began a soothing movement up and down the indentations of her spine.

It felt warm, electric, and did crazy things to her composure. A sensation that was heightened when he leaned towards her and brushed his lips close to her ear before proffering her a plate of food.

It was then she caught sight of Jeremy, and her appetite became non-existent.

'I thought you might be hungry.'

'Not really.'

He picked up a savoury and held it temptingly close to her mouth. 'Try this.' When she shook her head, he took a small bite and offered her the rest.

What was he doing, for heaven's sake? She took the savoury from his fingers and ate it, then looked at him in exasperation when he followed it with another. 'Isn't this overkill?'

'You could at least look as if you're enjoying it.' His voice was pure silk, and she retaliated by biting more deeply than necessary, caught his finger with her teeth as she intended, then managed to look incredibly contrite. 'Oh darling, did I bite you? I'm so sorry.'

'I think I'll live.'

'Perhaps you could get me a drink?'

'Champagne?'

She deliberated for all of five seconds. 'Of course.' Not a wise choice, but she'd sip it slowly for a while, then discard it in favour of mineral water.

'Saska?'

All he had to do was catch the waiter's attention, and seconds later their drinks were delivered. Nikos possessed a certain air of command that drew notice. Add a compelling degree of power with sophisticated élan, and the combination was lethal.

Her eyes were drawn to those strong sculpted features, the broad facial bone structure, the well-defined jaw, and the firm lines of his mouth.

What would he be like if ever he lost control? A faint shiver slithered its way over the surface of her skin. Devastating, a tiny voice prompted. Unbridled, flagrant, *primitive*.

At that moment his eyes met hers, and held. Her own dilated, and she felt as if her breath became suspended. Then his lips curved to form a lazy smile that held knowledge and a sense of pleasurable anticipation.

He couldn't *see* what she was thinking...could he? And it wasn't as if she *wanted* to go to bed with him. Heaven forbid! That would be akin to selling her soul. Besides, you might never recover, a secret inner voice taunted.

She'd seen women who never experienced their sexual equal prowl the party circuit in search of an adequate replacement. They tended to possess few scruples, dressed to kill, and drank a little too much.

She needed to get away for a few minutes, and

the powder room provided an excellent reason. 'If you'll excuse me?' She handed her champagne flute to Nikos. 'I won't be long.'

Michelle paused several times en route to extend a greeting to a number of her parents' friends. Indoors there were two guests lingering adjacent the powder room, and she by-passed them and headed for the curved flight of stairs leading to the upper floor which housed her parents' suite and no less than five guest rooms with en suite facilities.

She chose one, then lingered to tidy her hair and retouch her lipstick.

Michelle emerged into the bedroom, and came to a shocked standstill at the sight of Jeremy leaning against the doorjamb.

'These are my parents' private quarters,' she managed evenly.

She kept walking, hoping he would move aside and allow her to pass. He didn't, and she paused a few feet in front of him. 'Jeremy, you're blocking my way.'

Her instincts were on alert. However, the upper floor was well insulated from the people and noise on the terrace out back of the house. Even if she screamed, it was doubtful anyone would hear a thing.

She took a step forward only to have him catch hold of her arm.

'Wasn't I good enough?' Jeremy demanded softly.

'Your father and mine are business associates,' she said carefully. 'Our parents share a similar social circle. We were friends,' she added.

'You're saying that's all it was?'

'For me, yes.' She looked at him, glimpsed the darkness apparent in his eyes, and knew she'd need to tread carefully. 'I'm sorry if you thought it was more than friendship.'

'If Nikos hadn't put in an appearance that night...' He trailed to a halt.

She was silent for several long seconds. 'It wouldn't have made any difference.'

'That's not true,' he said fiercely. 'You have to give me another chance.'

Not in this lifetime. She chose not to say a word.

'Michelle!' The plea was impassioned, and desperate. Too desperate.

'What do you hope to achieve by holding me here?' She had to keep talking. And pray someone, *Nikos,* would think it curious she'd been away so long and investigate.

His face contorted. 'Have you slept with him yet?'

'You don't have the right to ask that.'

'Damn you. I'm making it my right.' He yanked her close up against him, twisted her arm behind her back and thrust a hand between her thighs. His fingers were a vicious instrument for all of ten seconds before she went for the bridge of his nose, but he ducked and the side of her palm connected with his cheekbone.

'I doubt Nikos will want you when he knows I've had you first.'

All of a sudden she was free, and Jeremy lay groaning on the carpet.

'You won't have the opportunity.' Nikos' voice held the chill of an arctic floe. 'A restraining order will be put into effect immediately. If you violate it, you'll be arrested and charged.'

Nikos swept her a swift encompassing glance, and

his eyes darkened as he took in her waxen features, the way her fingers shook as they smoothed over her hair.

'You can't have me arrested,' Jeremy flung wildly as he scrambled to his feet, and Michelle almost quaked at the controlled savagery evident in Nikos' response.

'Watch me.'

'My father—'

'Doesn't have enough money to get you out of this one. Attempted rape is a serious charge.'

Jeremy's face reddened, and he blustered—'I didn't touch her.'

Nikos reached out a hand and sought purchase on Jeremy's jacket.

'What are you doing?'

'Detaining you while Michelle fetches your parents.'

'Everything comes with a price. My father will pay yours.'

'As he has in the past?' Nikos queried silkily. 'Not this time,' he stated with a finality that moved Jeremy close to hysteria as Michelle stepped through the doorway.

'Don't bring my mother. She'd never understand.'

'Then perhaps it's time she did,' Nikos said pitilessly.

'Michelle, don't,' Jeremy begged. 'I'll do anything you want. I promise.'

'We can do this one of two ways. Michelle fetches your parents and you're removed from these premises without fuss. Or I force you downstairs and onto the terrace for a very public denouncement. Choose,' he commanded hardily.

Michelle smoothed a shaky hand over her hair in a purely reflex action as she descended the stairs. Reaction was beginning to set in, and she drew a deep breath in an effort to regain a measure of composure.

What followed wasn't something she would choose to experience again in a long time. Parental love was one thing. Blind maternal devotion was something else.

Nikos dismissed Emerson's bribe, and suggested the Bateson-Burrows remove their son as quickly as possible.

At which point Chantelle arrived on the scene, took everything in with a glance, and demanded an explanation.

'Jeremy has had a little too much to drink,' Emerson indicated smoothly. 'We're taking him home.'

As soon as they were alone Chantelle looked from Michelle to Nikos. 'Would one of you care to tell me what really happened here?'

Michelle didn't say a word.

'Nikos?'

'Jeremy failed to accept Michelle and I have a relationship.' His eyes were hard, his expression equally so. 'He hassled her last night when she left the Gallery, and tonight he went one step further.'

Chantelle looked suitably horrified. '*Cherie,* this is terrible. Are you all right?'

'I'm fine, *Maman,*' Michelle reassured her quietly.

'I'll see to it that Michelle initiates a restraining order. Jeremy has a history of violence,' Nikos informed grimly. 'One recorded offense in Sydney three years ago.'

'The Bateson-Burrows moved to the Coast almost three years ago,' Chantelle reflected slowly.

'He was expelled from two private schools, and kicked out of University,' Nikos continued. 'In Perth, Adelaide, and Melbourne.'

Chantelle straightened her shoulders. She didn't ask how he acquired the information. It was enough that he had. 'It's to be hoped they soon leave the Coast.'

'It appears to be a familiar pattern.'

'Meanwhile, Michelle—'

'Will stay with me.'

'Now just a minute,' Michelle intervened, and met his dark gaze.

'It's not negotiable, *pedhi mou.*'

'The hell it's not!'

'*Cherie,* for my sake, as well as your own, do as Nikos suggests. Please.'

'I'll tell Saska we're leaving early,' Nikos declared. 'If she wants to stay, she can get a taxi back to the hotel.'

'Can I get you something, darling?' Chantelle queried as soon as Nikos disappeared down the hallway. 'A drink? Some coffee? A brandy?'

'I'm OK. Really,' she assured in a bid to lessen her mother's anxiety. 'Just a bit shaken, that's all.'

'Antonia and Emerson—Jeremy. I had no idea,' she said wretchedly. 'Thank heavens Nikos was here.'

All this has happened *because* of Nikos, she felt like saying. Yet that wasn't entirely true. Nikos' presence had only accelerated Jeremy's irrational jealousy.

'*Maman.*' She paused, then changed her mind against confiding that her purported relationship with the powerful Greek was just a sham.

'Yes, darling?'

'I'll just go tidy up.' She felt the need to remove Jeremy's touch, preferably with a long very thorough soaping in the shower. But for now, she'd settle for pressing a cold flannel to her face and redoing her hair.

Nikos had returned by the time she emerged, and she met his swift gaze, held it, then she crossed to brush her lips to her mother's cheek.

'I'll ring you in the morning.'

Chantelle hugged her close, then reluctantly released her. 'Please. Take care.'

Minutes later Nikos eased the powerful BMW onto the road, and she didn't offer a word as he drove to Main Beach.

'I'll be fine on my own,' Michelle stated as he parked the car outside her apartment building and slid out from behind the wheel.

'Nice try.'

She faced him across the car roof, glimpsed the dark glittery look he cast her, and felt like stamping her foot in frustrated anger. 'Look—'

'Do you want to walk, or have me carry you?' Nikos' voice was hard, his intention inflexible.

'Go to hell!'

'I've been there. Twice in the past twenty-four hours. It's not something I plan to repeat.' He moved round the car to her side. 'Now, which way is it going to be?'

'If you dare—' Whatever else she planned to say was lost in a muffled sound as he simply hoisted her over one shoulder, walked to the entrance, activated the door with her security card, then strode towards the bank of lifts at the far end of the lobby.

'Put me down, dammit!' She beat fists against his back, aimed for his kidneys, and groaned in frustration when he shifted her out of range. A mean-intentioned kick failed to connect, and she growled as fiercely as a feline under attack as he gained the lift, punched the appropriate panel button, then when the lift stopped, he walked calmly to her apartment, unlocked the door, and only when they were inside did he let her slide down to her feet.

'You want to fight?' he challenged silkily. 'Go ahead.'

She wanted to, badly, and right at this precise moment she didn't care that she couldn't win.

'You,' she vented with ill-concealed fury. 'Are the most arrogant, egotistical man I've ever met. I want you to leave, now.'

'It's here,' Nikos stated ruthlessly. 'Or my apartment. Choose.'

Something about his stance, the stillness of his features slowly leeched most of the anger from her system.

'Don't you think you're taking the *hero* role too far?'

'No.'

Succinct, and clearly unmoveable. Maybe she should just concede defeat now and save her emotional and physical energy. It would be a whole lot easier than continuing to rage against him.

'I could ring the police and have them evict you.' It was a last-ditch effort, and she knew it.

'Go ahead.'

She badly wanted to call his bluff. Except she had no trouble visualising how such a scene would evolve, and how it would inevitably prove to be an exercise in futility.

Occasionally there could be success in conceding defeat. 'You can sleep in the spare room.'

She turned away from him and crossed the lounge to her bedroom and carefully closed the door.

If he insisted on staying—*fine*. She was going to have a long hot bath with bath oil and bubbles...the whole bit. Then when she was done, she'd dry off and climb into bed, hopefully to sleep until the alarm went off in the morning.

Michelle stayed in the scented water for a long time. It was bliss, absolute bliss to lay there and let the perfumed heat seep into her bones and soothe her mind.

It had a soporific effect, and she closed her eyes. For only a minute, she was prepared to swear, when a rapid knock on the door caused her to jackknife into a sitting position.

Seconds later the door opened and Nikos walked calmly into the bathroom.

'What the hell are you doing in here?'

She looked like a child, was his first thought, with her hair piled on top of her head, and all but buried beneath a layer of frothy foam.

'Checking you hadn't fallen asleep and drowned.'

Her eyes were huge, the pupils dilated with anger.

Most women would have sank back displaying most if not all of their breasts, and behaved like a sultry temptress by inviting him to join them.

'You could have waited for me to answer!'

'You didn't,' he relayed coolly. 'That's why I came in.'

'Well, you can just turn around and go out again!' Indignation brought pink colour to her cheeks, and she looked at him through stormy eyes. Then, in a totally unprecedented action, she did the unforgivable. She scooped up water and foam and threw it at him in a spontaneous action that surprised her almost as much as it did him.

Her aim was good, it drenched the front part of his shirt, and she watched in fascination as a patch of foam began to dissipate. Then she lifted her gaze to lock with his. And wished fervently that she hadn't, for what she glimpsed there made her feel terribly afraid.

There was strength of purpose, a knowledge that was entirely primitive. For a moment she thought he was going to reach forward and drag her out of the bath and into his arms.

It was uncanny, but she could almost feel his mouth on hers, savour the taste of him as he invaded the soft inner tissues and explored them with his tongue. Staking a possession that could only have one ending.

The breath caught in her throat, and for seemingly long seconds she wasn't capable of saying a word.

'You provoked me,' she managed at last.

'Is that an apology?' Nikos demanded silkily.

'An explanation.'

His eyes speared hers. 'Pull the plug, and get out of the bath.'

She looked at him incredulously. 'While you're still here? Not on your life!'

He reached out, collected a large bath towel, unfolded it and held it out.

Nikos saw the anger drain out of her. Her eyes slowly welled, leaving them looking like drenched pools. It twisted his gut, and undid him more than anything she could have said. Without a word he replaced the towel, then he turned and walked from the en suite.

Michelle released the bath water, towelled herself dry, then she pulled on a huge cotton T-shirt and slid into bed to sit hugging her knees as she stared sightlessly at a print positioned on the opposite wall.

The events of the past few hours played and replayed through her mind until she made a concerted effort to dismiss them.

Where was Nikos? Ensconced in the spare bedroom, or had he left the apartment?

She had no way of knowing, and told herself she didn't care. Except she had a vivid memory of the way her body reacted to his; the protective splay of his hand at her back; the intense warmth in his eyes when he looked at her. The feel of his mouth on hers, the way he invaded her senses and stirred them as no man had ever done before.

Michelle shifted position, picked up a book from the pedestal and read for a while. Three nights ago she'd been so engrossed in the plot she hadn't been able to put the book down. Now, she skimmed sentences and turned pages, only to discard it with disgust at her inability to focus on the plot.

All she needed, she determined as she switched off the light, was a good night's sleep.

CHAPTER SEVEN

MICHELLE WOKE WITH a start, the images so vivid for the space of a few seconds that she was prepared to swear they were real.

Jeremy, maniacal. Nikos, dark and threatening.

It was as if she was a disembodied spectator, watching the clash of steel as they fought, the thrust and parry as they each meshed their skill with physical prowess.

Then there was darkness, and she heard a cry of pain, followed by silence. She tried to ascertain who was the victor, but his features eluded her.

'Dear heaven,' Michelle whispered as she shifted into a sitting position and switched on the bedlamp. Light flooded the room, and she relished the reality of familiar surroundings. Then she lifted her hands to her cheeks and discovered they were wet.

She scrubbed them dry, then she slid out of bed, pulled on a wrap, and walked quietly out to the kitchen. The digital display on the microwave relayed the time as one-o-five.

A cold drink would quench her thirst, and she selected a can, popped the top, and carried it into the lounge.

The night was warm, and she had an urge to slide open the wide glass doors and let the fresh sea air blow away the cares of the past few days.

Michelle stepped out onto the terrace and felt the coolness wash over her face. There was the tang of salt, a clean sweetness that drifted in from the ocean, and she breathed deeply as she took in the sweeping coastal view.

Street lamps, bright splashes of neon, pinpricks of light that diminished with distance from enumerable high-rise apartment buildings lining the coastal strip.

It resembled a fairyland of light against the velvet backdrop of an indigo night sky and ocean.

She lifted the can and took a long swallow of cool liquid. The breeze teased loose a few stray tendrils of hair and pulled at the hem of her wrap.

It could have been ten minutes or twenty before she returned indoors, and the sight of a tall male figure framed in the lounge brought her to a shocked standstill.

Her rational mind assured it was Nikos, but just for a split second with the reflected hall light behind him, her imagination went into overdrive.

'How long have you been standing there?' Was that her voice, sounding slightly high and vaguely breathless?

'Only a few minutes,' Nikos ventured quietly.

A towel was draped low on his hips, his chest and legs bare. It occurred that she hadn't even bothered to consider he wouldn't have anything to change into.

'I noticed the hall light go on half an hour ago.'

'So you decided to investigate.' She didn't mean to sound defensive. Except he could have no idea how vulnerable she was feeling right now, or be aware of the image he presented.

For one crazy moment she wanted to walk up to him and take comfort from the warmth of his embrace. Yet that was a madness she couldn't afford.

'I didn't mean to frighten you.'

Hadn't he been able to sleep? Or did he simply wake at the slightest sound? His features were dark, and in this half-light it was difficult to read his expression.

Her senses leapt at the electric energy apparent. It was almost as if all her fine body hairs rose up in anticipation of his touch, and she felt her heart quicken to a faster beat.

Get out of here, *now,* a tiny voice urged. Except her legs wouldn't obey the dictates of her brain.

The slow ache of desire flared deep inside, and she was aware of her shallow breathing, the pulse throbbing at the base of her throat.

Nikos didn't say a word as he took the few steps necessary to reach her, and his eyes held hers, compelling, dramatic, unwavering. Dark onyx fused with emerald, and she was unable to look away.

A hand closed over her shoulder, while the other slid beneath the heavy knot of her hair, loosened it, then when it fell to her shoulders he threaded his fingers through its length and smoothed a few stray tendrils behind her ear.

She felt him move imperceptibly, then sensed his lips brush over her hair and settle at the edge of one temple.

Unbidden she linked her arms round his waist and sank into him. She didn't want to think, she just wanted to feel. To become lost in sensation, transported to a place where there was only the moment, the man, and the passion.

She lifted her face to his, and felt the soft trail of kisses feather across her cheek, then descend to the generous curve of her mouth, tantalising, teasing, nibbling as he explored the soft fullness of her lower lip, tracing it with the tip of his tongue before delving in to make slow sweeping forays of the sweetness within.

It wasn't enough, not nearly enough, and she opened her mouth to him, angling her head in surrender as passion swept her to new heights.

Michelle dragged his mouth down to hers as his hand slid to her thigh and slowly crept up to her bottom, shaped it, then pressed her in close so she could be in no doubt of his arousal.

'Put your arms round my neck,' Nikos instructed, and she obeyed, only to catch her breath as he lifted her up against him and curved each thigh round his waist so that she straddled him.

Then he walked towards the bedroom, every step providing an erotic movement that heightened the ache deep inside.

She wanted, needed the physical joining, the hard thrusting primal rhythm as he took her with him to a place where there was only acute primitive sensation. Michelle was dimly aware they reached the bed. She felt him pause as he tossed back the bedcovers and drew her down onto the percale sheet, stilling as his eyes locked with hers.

He saw slumberous passion, desire, and something else that gave him pause. It would be so easy to take her, to sink into those moist depths and slake a mutual need until they reached satiation.

Instead he took the slow route, the long sensual tease that began with a sensory exploration of all her pleasure pulses, the sensitive crevices, as he used his lips, the soft pads of his fingers to touch and tantalise.

Michelle was unaware of the slight sounds she made deep in her throat as he took the tender peak of her breast into his mouth and began to shamelessly suckle until she cried out for him to desist. Then he merely shifted to its twin and brought her to the edge of pain.

Not content he caressed a path to her navel, explored it, then travelled low over her belly, teased the dark blonde curls with his tongue, then indulged in an intimacy that took her to the brink, then tipped her over the edge in a free fall that had her threshing against him, imploring him to stop…to never stop.

For one wild moment, she didn't think she could handle the intensity, then mercifully it began to ease, and she met his kiss hungrily, her hands eager, searching, wanting to bestow some of the pleasure he had gifted her.

She cried out as he caught her hands together and pressed them to his lips. There were a few emotive seconds as he paused to use prophylactic protection, then he positioned his length and eased into her, exulting in the gradual feeling of total enclosure as he slid deep. And stayed there for several long seconds before repeating the action. Longer and deeper, then harder and faster until she cried out and fell off the edge of the world.

What followed became a feast of the senses as

he soothed her fevered flesh with a gentleness that brought her close to tears. He explored each sensitive pulse, felt her quivering response and savoured it in a long after-play that stirred her senses to a point where it no longer became possible to lay supine, a willing supplicant to everything he chose to bestow.

She wanted to stir him to passion, to render him mindless beneath her touch until he begged her to stop.

With one easy movement she dragged herself free, then she captured his head between her hands and kissed him, thoroughly, slaking a sensual thirst as she employed sufficient pressure to roll him onto his back.

His eyes were dark, slumberous, and intent as she straddled his waist, then she trailed an exploratory path along one collarbone with her lips, dipped into the faint hollows, using her teeth to tease the hair on his chest, nibbling, savouring, tasting, until she reached one hard brown male nipple.

With extreme delicacy she laved it with her tongue and slowly suckled until the peak began to swell, then she took it between her teeth and employed the lightest pressure.

She felt, rather that heard his slight intake of breath, and she rolled the slightly distended peak with her teeth, then suckled with greedy sensitivity, all too aware of his fingers lightly brushing the soft fullness of her breasts.

Not content, she trailed a path of lingering kisses across his chest to bestow a similar treatment to its twin, and was unprepared for the sharp arrow that was part pleasure part pain as he took her nipple between two fingers and rolled it.

She gently swatted his hand and slid slowly down his torso, caressing the line of dark hair until she reached his stomach, hovered there for long tantalising seconds, then descended with such painstaking slowness.

Nikos held his breath as she began to explore with such devastating gentleness, it took all his willpower not to haul her into his arms and take control.

Yet he'd tested the measure of her endurance with an equally lingering sensual torture.

Nevertheless when she touched him lightly with the tip of her tongue, the breath hissed between his teeth, and her tentative examination brought a surge of powerful emotion. Not for the degree of her expertise. It was her touch, the desire to please him as he had pleasured her that brought him to the brink of climax.

Did she know she had this effect on a man? On *him?* Somehow he doubted it.

When he was almost ready to take independent action, she rose up in one graceful movement, carefully positioned herself, then slid slowly down until he was buried deep inside her.

It felt good, so very good. As if every nerve fibre, every sensory cell heightened as she sheathed and held him tightly.

There was a part of her that didn't want to move, simply to be. Yet there was a primal need for sensory stimulation, and she placed a hand on either side of his shoulders, then began to withdraw. Just a little, increasing the action until it became something primitive, and she cried out as his hands curved into her waist, held her still, then assumed the position of supremacy, lifting her high as his hips rose and fell endlessly until it was she who cried out, she who clutched hold of him.

Afterwards he held her, his fingers drifting a lazy pattern back and forth along her spine until her breathing quietened.

Michelle felt his lips graze her ear, then slip to the sensitive curve of her neck, linger there, before moving to the edge of her mouth.

His kiss was incredibly soft, the lightest touch as he savoured a path over the fullness of her lower lip.

'We're still—'

'Connected.'

She felt his mouth part in a humorous smile. 'Uncomfortable?'

'No.' The sound sighed from her lips. She felt as if she could lay here forever, absorbing the man, his texture and taste.

There were words she wanted to say. Words that would adequately express what she'd just experienced. How special it had been. Emotionally, spiritually, physically. For the first time she knew what it was like to be a part of someone on every level. To share, possess, and be possessed.

Frightening. For inevitably there would follow a sense of loss. *Don't think about it,* she bade silently. Just enjoy the night, and forget about what the new day might bring.

It wasn't love. Love was a slow process, a gradual learning, appreciation, understanding. An attunement of the senses.

Yet what they'd just shared was more than lust. That much she knew. Lust didn't leave you caught up with introspective thought, wishing for something beyond reach, or cause you to wonder if what had just happened could irreparably change your life. Or if, she decided a trifle wildly, there would be any choice.

There was no magic wand she could wave to remove the past few hours. Tomorrow would be dealt with when it arrived. Now all she wanted to do, all she had the energy for, was sleep.

She was unaware of Nikos carefully shifting her to lay at his side, or that she instinctively curled into the curve of his body as he settled the bed-covering over her sleeping form.

Michelle felt something soft drift across her arm, and she burrowed her head more deeply into the pillow. It was early, her alarm hadn't sounded, and she was tired.

Minutes later there it was again, whispering along the curve of her waist. It had to be an early morning breeze teasing the sheet, and she kicked the tangle of soft percale, freeing it from her body.

This time there was no mistaking the brush of skin on skin, and her eyes swept open to see Nikos propped up on one elbow, watching her. His expression was slumberous and deceptively indolent, and he looked as sexy as hell with stubble darkening his jaw.

She'd experienced the entire gamut of emotions in his arms. Physical, emotional, spiritual had combined to make their coupling as good as she imagined it could possibly get.

Even thinking about what they'd shared brought

a surge of heat flooding her body, and her eyes widened as he stroked gentle fingers over her breast. The sensitive peak hardened beneath his touch, and she drew in her breath as he rolled it gently between thumb and forefinger. Answering sensation flowered deep within, instantly so she ached with need, and her breathing hitched as he leaned forward and began teasing her breast with his lips.

His hand trailed low, conducting a seeking path with unerring accuracy, and within seconds she scaled the heights, begging as he held her there, then she tipped over the brink in a sensual free fall that left her breathing ragged, her voice an indistinguishable groan as she whispered his name.

He slid into her in one deep movement, nestled momentarily, then slowly withdrew, only to repeat the controlled thrust again and again. There was little of the hard passion of the night, just long and sweet and slow as she became consumed by a deep pulsing flame, intensely exquisite as it swirled and shimmered through her body like a treacherous heat haze.

She decided dreamily that it was a wonderful way to start the day.

'You have the most beautiful smile.'

'Mmm?'

His husky laughter curled round her nerve-ends and tugged just a little too much for comfort, activating a renewed spiral of sensation infinitely dangerous to an equilibrium already off balance.

Assertiveness was the key, she determined as she reached out and ran an idle forefinger down the slope of his nose. And humour.

'Time to begin all those mundane things like

shower, breakfast, and don the business suit.' She traced the groove creasing his upper lip, then pressed down on the fullness beneath it, only to have him take her fingertip between his teeth. 'Ouch, that hurt.'

'It was meant to,' Nikos chided solemnly, although his eyes were darkly alight with amusement. 'We have an hour.'

Her heart lurched. 'I dislike being rushed.'

'I don't think you'll object.'

'Personal grooming,' Michelle said helplessly as he slid out of bed. 'A leisurely breakfast,' she intimated as he scooped her into his arms. 'And two cups of coffee. Where are you taking me?'

'The shower.' He reached the en suite bathroom in a few long strides. 'You can have that second coffee at the Gallery.'

With economy of movement he turned on the water dial, adjusted it, then stepped into the large glassed cubicle.

Nikos picked up the huge sponge, poured perfumed liquid soap onto it, then became intent on smoothing the sponge over every inch of her body.

It was an erotic experience, as he meant it to be, and she balled her hand into a fist and playfully struck his shoulder.

'Is that a complaint?'

The thought of sharing this kind of morning experience on a regular basis made her mouth go dry.

'Yes. I think I'm going to miss breakfast.'

His eyes were impossibly dark with lambent emotion as he lowered his head down to hers. 'Then I guess tomorrow we'll just have to make an earlier start, hmm?'

She didn't answer. She couldn't. The words were locked in her throat as his mouth took possession of her own.

She became oblivious to the warm spray of water, for there was only the hard strength of his body. Strong muscle and sinew that bound her close, so impossibly close that all she had to do was wind her arms up around his neck and hang on as he parted her thighs.

His arousal was a potent force he withheld in a bid to heighten her desire, and she was almost crazy with need when he finally surged into her. She cried out as sensation washed through her body, taking her higher than she'd thought it was possible to climb.

His mouth ravaged hers as he reached the physical peak with her, and she exulted in the primitive shudder that shook his large frame as they clung to each other in mutual climactic rapture and its aftermath.

Michelle missed breakfast entirely. There wasn't even time to do more than take a few hurried sips of the coffee Nikos brewed while she put the finishing touches to her make-up.

'I'll book the restaurant,' Nikos intimated as she collected her shoulder bag and turned towards the door. 'We're dining with Emilio and Saska, remember?' he prompted as she swivelled to face him, 'By the way,' he gently teased, 'Cute butterfly tattoo.'

It was small, and positioned low on the soft curve of her right buttock.

His smile was slow, musing. 'A moment of madness, flouting of parental authority, or what?'

'A dare. Paris.' A mischievous gleam lit her eyes. 'It was the tattoo or a navel ring.'

The phone rang, and for a moment the humour drained away. If it was Jeremy— She crossed the room and picked up the receiver.

'Michelle? Everything OK?'

Relief poured through her. 'Emilio. Yes. I'm just leaving now.' She cut the connection, and looked at Nikos. 'Just—lock up when you leave.'

'I'll contact my lawyer and set the paperwork in motion for a restraining order, then ring you.'

She was already crossing the lounge. 'Thanks.'

A chill slithered down her spine as she rode the lift down to the underground car park. The thought of Jeremy and just how close she'd come to assault was the reason why Nikos had stayed overnight in her apartment.

Not part of the agenda had been their shared intimacy. Who had initiated it?

Dear heaven, did it matter?

Michelle discovered that it did, very much, for it made a farce of their charade, and provided an unexpected twist in that they no longer needed to pretend.

A paradox really, for the lines determining their supposed relationship had shifted. For the better, if one believed in a transitory affair. Sadly, she didn't. What had begun as a mutual arrangement, now took on a different context. Jeremy was an unknown quantity. And there was Saska.

How long would it take to effect a resolution? A week? Two? Then what? Would Nikos extricate himself, move base to wherever in the world he chose, and never seek to contact her again?

That surely was part of the master plan. It had to be.

Wasn't that what she'd wanted?

The Gallery was just up front, and she parked the car, locked it, then ran up the short flight of steps to the main door.

Work, she decided, was a panacea for many things. All she had to do was keep herself busy, her mind occupied, and deal with each day as it occurred.

A hollow bubble of laughter rose and died in her throat. In theory, the analogy was fine. The problem was reality.

CHAPTER EIGHT

THE MOBILE PHONE rang as Michelle eased the car onto the road, and she assured her mother she was fine, she'd slept well; and no, she hadn't forgotten the charity function at a city hotel scheduled for Thursday evening.

'Nikos can partner you, darling. You'll sit at our table, of course.'

Michelle parked outside the Gallery, and cut the connection as she reached the main entrance.

It proved to be a hectic morning. A shipment due to be unloaded from a dockside container in Sydney was caught up in a strike, and numerous phone calls were necessary to reschedule and put a contingency plan in place.

There was paperwork requiring attention, data to enter into the computer, and several phone calls to make confirming collection and delivery of items ordered on consignment.

The phone pealed, and she automatically reached for the receiver and intoned a professional greeting.

'Michelle. Nikos.'

His voice was deeper and slightly more accented

over the phone, and the sound of it evoked a pulsing warmth flooding her veins.

'I've arranged an appointment with my lawyer at twelve-thirty.'

The restraining order. 'I'll reorganise my lunch hour.'

'I'll meet you at the Gallery and take you to Paul's office,' Nikos intimated, and she sank back in her chair, swivelled it to take in the view across the Nerang river.

'I don't think that's necessary.'

'Twelve-fifteen, Michelle.'

He hung up before she had the opportunity to argue.

'Problems?'

Michelle swung back to face Emilio, who had walked into the office during the conversation. 'Nothing I can't handle.' It was said more to convince herself than Emilio. Somehow she didn't think any woman could manipulate Nikos. Unless he permitted it.

'You left early last night.'

It was better she went with the fictional excuse. 'I had a headache.'

He placed both hands on the desk and leaned forward. 'This is Emilio, remember?'

She kept her gaze steady as he raked her pale features, then settled on the pulse at the base of her throat.

'So, do we play guessing games, or are you going to tell me?'

'OK.' She used facetiousness and shock value as a

form of defence. 'Nikos took me home, and we made wild passionate love all night.'

His eyes lit with amusement, and something else she was unable to define. *'Brava,'* he said gently. 'I approve. Of the loving, and the Greek.' He straightened away from the desk. 'Jeremy was the catalyst, am I right? For someone who knew what to look for last night, it wasn't difficult to put two and two together. Your absence, Jeremy, then Nikos.' His expression hardened fractionally. 'I'll wring his neck.'

'Jeremy, or the Greek?'

'Don't jest, *cara.* If there's a problem, I want to know about it.' He waited a beat. 'We're more than just business partners, we're friends.'

She spent a major part of her waking hours at the Gallery. Emilio deserved to be on the alert if Jeremy continued to prove a nuisance.

'Nikos insists I file a restraining order.'

Emilio's eyes sharpened. 'Give,' he uttered in succinct command.

'Last night was the third—' *Assault?* She settled for '—attack, in seventy-two hours.'

'Son of a bitch!' The words were uttered with such silky softness, it sent a shiver down her back. 'He won't get a foot inside the Gallery. Your apartment is secure.' His expression became ruthlessly hard. 'Don't go anywhere alone. *Comprende?'*

'I just love it when you lapse into Italian,' Michelle teased at his protective stance.

'I'm serious.'

She tilted her head to one side, her eyes solemn. 'I'm a big girl. And capable of defending myself, remember?'

She was good, he visited the same *dojo* and had witnessed a few of her training sessions. However, expertise in formal surroundings was a different kettle of fish to the reality of an unexpected attack with brutal intent in a dark deserted street.

'Stand up,' he instructed quietly. 'Turn with your back to me.'

'Emilio—'

'Do it, *cara*.'

'This really is unnecessary,' she protested, and caught his faint smile.

'Indulge me.'

The electronic buzzer attached to the main door sounded, heralding entrance of a customer, and Emilio spared a quick glance in the overhead monitor.

'Nikos.'

It was twelve-fifteen already? She should go powder her nose and ensure her hair was OK.

'We'll continue this later.'

'What will you continue later?' Nikos drawled from the open doorway.

His tall frame almost filled the aperture, and Michelle was positive the room seemed to shrink in size. He looked the epitome of an urbane sophisticate attired in impeccably cut trousers, a dark blue shirt unbuttoned at the neck and a jacket hooked casually over one shoulder.

'A test against a real attack attempt, as opposed to an orchestrated practised manoeuvre,' Emilio enlightened, meeting Nikos' steady gaze with one of his own.

'Michelle has filled you in.' It was a statement, not a question.

'Yes.'

'I take it you have no objection if she has an extended lunch hour?'

'As long as it takes.'

'I'm moving her into my apartment.'

Michelle thrust the swivel chair forward, and glared from one man to the other. 'Now, just wait a damn minute.' She settled on Nikos. *Excuse me. You're doing what?*

'Moving you temporarily into my apartment,' he reiterated calmly.

Her eyes flashed emerald fire. 'The hell you are.'

'Then I'll move into yours. Either way, it makes little difference.'

'It makes plenty of difference!'

'Then choose.'

'Just who has granted you the God-given right to take over my life and order me around?' She was so furious, her body was almost rigid with anger.

'I did,' Nikos relayed with deceptive ease. 'Your apartment, or mine, *pedhaki mou?*'

'I am *not* "your little one"!'

Nikos' eyes flared. 'Yes, you are.'

Emilio watched the by-play with interest. Intriguing the sparks that flew between these two. He smiled, despite the gravity of the situation at hand. Unless he was very wrong, Michelle had met her match in the forceful Greek.

'I'd rather move home.'

Nikos shook his head. 'Due to your parents' social commitments, they're rarely in residence except for a few requisite hours each night, and they don't have live-in help.'

'While you,' she vented with deliberate emphasis, 'intend to stand guard over me every minute of the day?'

'And night,' he added equably, although his tone was deceptive. The eyes had it. Inflexible, compelling. Invincible.

'No.' She refused to be ordered about like a child.

'No?' His voice was pure silk.

'I'll book into a hotel.'

'Where, without independent security, Jeremy could access your room in a minute?'

'Don't you think,' she inclined carefully, 'you're getting just a bit carried with all this?'

'I have your parents' approval.'

'That's a low trick.'

'They're just as concerned about your safety as I am.'

She was angry, so angry at the way he was taking control. 'I don't doubt that. But I can take care of myself. I don't need a minder, or a baby-sitter!'

He wanted to take hold of her shoulders and shake her. Instead, he used words to create a similar effect.

'Jeremy has a history of previous violence. In this instance, it's been activated by his jealousy of me and what he sees as my involvement with you. Which makes me responsible to a degree.'

He looked at her carefully. 'What if I hadn't been there when he accosted you outside the Gallery Sunday night?' It gave him little pleasure to see her eyes dilate at his implication. 'Or last night?' he pursued relentlessly. 'Was anyone else aware Jeremy might use any opportunity to get you alone? Was there anyone who became alarmed when you didn't return within a reasonable time?'

He paused, then slid home the final barb. 'Have you considered what would have happened had I not come in search of you when I did?'

She opened her mouth to refute what he'd said, then closed it again.

'Jeremy has attacked you three times,' Emilio stated inexorably. 'You want to try for four?'

Nikos' eyes pierced hers, their depths dark and inflexible. 'Don't you think you're protesting too much...after last night?'

He was too skilled a tactician not to choose his weapons well, she perceived, and silently cursed him for his temerity.

'Aren't we late for an appointment?' she posed stiffly, and heard his drawled response.

'I'll ring Paul and let him know we've been delayed.'

'If it's all right with you,' Michelle declared with deliberate mockery, 'I'll just go powder my nose.'

Nikos Alessandros, she decided, had a lot to answer for. At this very moment her feelings were definitely ambivalent.

Damn, damn, *damn*. Why was she objecting? The man was a lover to die for. Why not just go with the flow, enjoy the perks, and live for the day?

Last night had been *heaven*. Was it such a sin to enjoy responsible sex?

Without commitment? And what happens when it ends, as it inevitably will? a small imp taunted. What then? Do you think you'll be able to walk away, heart-whole, smile, and thank him for the memory?

'Give me a break,' she pleaded with the inimical imp, snapped on the lid of her lipstick, then she reentered the office and shot Nikos a dark glance.

Which merely resulted in a raised eyebrow. 'Ready?'

'Take your time,' Emilio bade as Michelle preceded Nikos out onto the mezzanine balcony.

They traversed the short flight of stairs down to the main Gallery.

'Do what you need to do, and if you don't make it back by five, I'll see you at the restaurant at six.'

'I'll be back midafternoon,' she declared firmly, as she leant forward and brushed Emilio's cheek.

Nikos unlocked the BMW and she slid into the passenger seat, watched as he crossed round to slip in behind the wheel, then she sat in silence as he eased the large car into the flow of traffic heading towards the main highway.

'You're very quiet.'

'I'm saving it all for later,' she assured, and heard his husky laughter. 'If you weren't driving, I'd *hit* you,' she said fiercely.

Southport was merely a few kilometres distant, and within five minutes Nikos drove into a client car park adjacent a modern glassed building.

Nikos' lawyer led her through a series of questions as he compiled a detailed draft statement, informed what a restraining order entailed, perused a sheaf of faxed reports Nikos provided him with, then he advised her as to her personal safety, and requested she call into the office at four that afternoon to sign the statement.

It was one-thirty when they emerged from the

building, and within minutes Nikos headed the car towards Main Beach.

'Where are you going?' Michelle queried sharply when he turned towards the Sheraton hotel and its adjacent marina shopping complex.

'Taking you to lunch.'

'I'm not hungry.'

'The seafood buffet should tempt your appetite.'

'Nikos—'

'I've never known a woman who argues the way you do,' he drawled with amusement.

'You,' she stated heatedly. 'Are the most domineering man I've ever met!'

He eased the BMW into an empty parking space and killed the engine. Then he released his seat belt and leaned towards her.

His mouth settled on hers, hard, as he shaped her jaw to his, and he employed a sensual ravishment that tore her anger to shreds and left her breathless and trembling.

She was incapable of uttering a word, and he brushed a gentle finger over her lower lip.

'You talk too much.' He reached for the clip of her seat belt, released it, then he slid out from behind the wheel and led her towards the restaurant.

It was peaceful to sit overlooking the huge pool with its lagoon bar, and the buffet offered a superb selection which proved too tempting for Michelle to resist.

'Feel better?' Nikos queried when she declined dessert and settled for coffee.

'Yes,' she answered simply.

'We need to discuss whose apartment we share.'

'I don't think—'

'Yours or mine?'

'Are you always this dictatorial?'

'It's an integral part of my personality.' The waiter presented the bill, and Nikos signed the credit slip, added a tip, then he drained the last of his coffee. 'Shall we leave?'

Within minutes Nikos turned the car into the street housing both their apartment buildings, and she opened her mouth to protest when he swept down into the car park beneath his building.

'Come up with me while I collect some clothes.'

She turned towards him. 'I don't like people making decisions for me.'

His expression assumed an inflexibility, accenting the vertical grooves down each cheek, and his mouth settled into a firm line. 'Get used to it, *pedhi mou*.'

Michelle rode the lift with him to the uppermost floor. 'We're going to have to draw a few ground rules,' she insisted as she entered his penthouse apartment.

It was beautiful, marble tiled floors, Oriental rugs, imported furniture and exquisite furnishings. Interior decorating at its finest.

'Make yourself comfortable,' Nikos bade. 'I won't be long.'

There were a few framed photographs positioned on a long mahogany table, and she crossed to examine them. Family, she perceived, noting an elderly couple pictured in one, while the others were presumably siblings with a number of young children.

She knew so little about him, his background.

Why, when his family obviously resided in Europe, he chose to spend part of his time in Australia.

Which inevitably led to how long he intended to stay on this particular occasion. Weeks, or a month or two? With business interests on several different continents, he wouldn't remain in one place for very long at a time.

Nikos returned to the lounge with a garment bag hooked over one shoulder, and a hold-all in his hand.

'Two sisters,' he revealed, anticipating her question. 'Both married. One lives in Athens, the other in London. My parents reside on Santorini.'

'While you wander the world.' She could imagine the high-powered existence he led. International flights, board meetings, wheeling and dealing.

'I have houses in several countries.'

'And a woman in each city?'

'I have many women friends,' he said with dry mockery.

Now why did that suddenly make her feel bereft? Did she really think *she* was different? Special? Get real, an inner voice mercilessly taunted. You're simply a momentary diversion.

With determined effort she spared her watch a glance and turned towards the door. 'Shall we leave?' She needed some space and time away from him. 'You can drop me off at the Gallery. I'll give you a key to my apartment.'

Minutes later he drew the car to a halt outside the Gallery. 'I'll pick you up at five.'

She was about to argue, but one look at his implacable expression was sufficient to change her mind, and she refrained from saying a word as she handed him her keys, then she slid out, closed the door, and trod the bricked path to the Gallery's main entrance without so much as a backward glance.

If Emilio was surprised to see her, he didn't say so, and she went straight through to the office and booted up the computer.

With determined resolve she set her mind on work, and refused to give Nikos Alessandros a second thought.

Until he appeared with Emilio in the doorway a few minutes after five.

'Time to close down for the day, *cara*.'

Michelle saved the data, closed the programme and shut down the machine. Without a word she collected her bag and preceded Nikos out to the car.

It was a bright summer's evening, the sun was still warm, and she could easily have walked. She wasn't sure whether it bothered her more that her freedom of choice had been endangered, or that Nikos had nominated himself as her protector.

Or perhaps she was more shaken at the thought of sharing her apartment with him. Last night… Hell, she didn't even want to think about last night!

Nikos parked in the bay next to hers, and they rode the lift to the fifteenth floor in silence.

Nikos unlocked her apartment, and she swept in ahead of him.

'Fix yourself a drink if you want one,' Michelle suggested politely as she tossed her bag down onto the coffee table. 'I'm going to shower and change.'

She entered her bedroom and went straight to the walk-in wardrobe. If he'd *dared* invade her space by hanging his clothes here…

He hadn't, and she told herself she was glad as she entered the shower.

Half an hour later she caught up an evening purse and paused in front of the cheval mirror to briefly examine her appearance.

The emerald-coloured evening pantsuit complemented her slim frame and highlighted her eyes. Minimum jewellery and an upswept hairstyle presented an essential sophisticated image, given that Saska would undoubtedly appear at her stunning best.

Michelle took a deep breath, released it, then joined Nikos in the lounge.

His appraisal was swift, encompassing, and caused a shivery sensation to scud across the surface of her skin.

She offered him a brilliant smile. 'Do you think Saska will be impressed?'

He didn't offer a word as he crossed the short distance to her side, and her eyes widened as he cradled her face, then settled his mouth on hers in passionate possession.

When he lifted his head she wasn't capable of saying so much as a word.

'Better,' he drawled. He touched the pad of one finger to her lips. 'Lipstick repair.' The edge of his mouth curved. 'Although personally, I prefer the natural look.'

'Don't overdo the play-acting,' she managed evenly. 'I doubt Saska will be fooled.'

It was just after six when they reached the nominated restaurant, and within minutes Emilio and Saska joined them in the lounge bar.

As Michelle predicted, Saska could have stepped

from one of the fashion pages of *Vogue*. In classic black, the style was deceptively demure…a total contradiction when Saska removed the fitted bolero top to reveal the dress was virtually strapless, with a thin shoestring strap over each shoulder.

'It's a little warm in here, don't you think?'

Oh my. Were those generous curves for real? They just begged to be shaped and caressed by a man's hand.

She caught Emilio's eye, saw the faint glimmer of amusement apparent, and prepared to shift gears into 'compete' mode.

This was, Michelle accorded silently, going to be quite an evening!

'Michelle,' Saska almost purred. 'One hopes you no longer suffer from your headache?'

The faint emphasis gave the malady quite a different interpretation. 'Nikos took good care of me.'

How was that for an understatement? If Saska were to guess the manner in which he'd cared for her, the sparks would surely fly!

It was fortuitous the maître d' chose that moment to indicate their table was ready, and within minutes the wine steward appeared to take their order.

CHAPTER NINE

'CHAMPAGNE?' SASKA SUGGESTED. 'We should drink to our continuing friendship.'

'Yes,' Michelle agreed with a winsome smile. 'Why don't we do that?'

'Nikos and I go back a long way.'

'So he told me.'

Saska's eyebrow arched. 'I imagine you know I was married to his best friend?'

'You must miss him very much,' she said gently. Saska deserved some compassion. It would be devastating to be widowed at any age, but for someone so young, the loss must be terrible.

Eyes dark and faintly cloudy regarded Michelle with contrived steadiness. 'Dreadfully. But life moves on, and so must I.'

With Nikos, Michelle deduced. She could hardly blame Saska for pursuing the possibility. Nikos was a man among men, irrespective of his wealth, status and social position. As a lover... Just the thought of what she'd shared with him was enough to melt her bones.

Nikos ordered a bottle of Dom Pérignon, and together they perused the menu, their choices varied as they deliberated over a starter, main and dessert.

The waiter presented the champagne with a flourish, eased off the cork, then part-filled each flute before setting the bottle in the ice bucket and retreating.

'To old friends,' Saska said gently, touching the rim of her flute to that of Nikos'.

His answering smile was equally gentle, then he silently saluted Emilio and turned to Michelle.

'To us.'

His eyes were dark, and so incredibly sensual, she had to consciously prevent her eyes dilating with shock.

Her mouth shook slightly as he caught her hand and linked her fingers with his.

He'd missed his vocation as an actor. If she hadn't known better, she could almost believe he meant the light touch on her arm, the slight brush of his fingers against her cheek. The warmth of his smile, the way his eyes gleamed with latent emotion.

Together, they decided on a selection from each course, gave their order, then discussed a range of topics from art to travel as they sipped champagne.

Emilio added authenticity to Nikos and Michelle's 'romance' with anecdotes from his years as an art student in France.

'Remember, *cara?* That little café on the Left Bank, where the waiter plied you with coffee and pledged his undying love?'

Saska looked from one to the other, her fork poised as she posed a question. 'You studied together and shared accommodation?'

Michelle wrinkled her nose, then laughed, a faint

husky sound that was unintentionally sexy. 'Yes, with four other students. Communal kitchen, bathroom. Tiny rooms. It was little more than a garret.'

'But you adored it,' Emilio endorsed. 'Too much coffee, too little food, and too much discussion on how to change the world.'

'You lived in a garret?' Saska queried in disbelief. 'With little money? Didn't your parents help you?'

'Of course. Except I didn't want a nice apartment in the right quarter, with smoked salmon and caviar in the fridge.'

'She gave all that up for the baguettes, sardines, and cheese.'

'And wine,' Michelle added with an impish smile. 'It was fun.'

'Pretending to be poor?'

'Dispensing with the trappings of the rich,' she corrected with quiet sincerity. 'Had I not done that, my time in Paris would have been very different.'

'Yet you managed to meet Nikos.' Saska gave a faint disbelieving laugh. 'I cannot imagine him slumming it.'

'We met at the home of mutual friends,' Nikos drawled, embellishing the original fabrication.

'It was one of those rare occasions when we ventured into the sophisticated arena of the rich Parisians,' Emilio revealed with droll cynicism.

'So you were at the party, too?'

'As Michelle's bodyguard,' he declared solemnly. 'She rarely left home without me. And no,' he added quietly at Saska's deliberately raised eyebrows. 'We were never more than just very good friends.'

'And now you're business partners.'

Emilio inclined his head in mocking acquiescence. 'Our friendship is based on trust. What better foundation to establish a business?'

'How—quaint,' Saska acknowledged. 'Pretending to be impoverished students, then returning home to open a Gallery.'

You don't get it, do you? Michelle queried silently. We needed the struggle, the very essence that combines naked ambition with the perspicacity to survive and succeed. A nebulous element that shows in the art as something more than talent. We wanted to be able to recognise that flair through personal experience, not as judgmental eclectics.

It was perhaps as well the waiter delivered the starter. Although she wasn't so sure as Nikos played the part of attentive lover by tempting her with a morsel of food from his plate.

It was relatively easy to take up his challenge by spearing a succulent prawn from its bed of lettuce and offering it to him from the edge of her fork. She even managed to adopt the role of temptress with a melting smile, which brought an answering gleam and a flash of white teeth as he took a bite of the fleshy seafood.

Michelle daren't glance in Emilio's direction, for if he acknowledged her performance with a surreptitious wink she would be in danger of subsiding into laughter, and that would totally destroy the illusion.

Saska was not about to be outdone. Although her attempts to gain Nikos' attention were infinitely more subtle with the light touch of her hand on his arm, the few 'remember' anecdotes that served to endorse a long friendship.

Michelle had to concede it was a fun evening, for

she enjoyed the nuances, the interplay, and the elusive rivalry, albeit that on her part it was contrived.

Or was it? There was nothing false about her reaction to Nikos' touch. Or the warmth that radiated through her body when he smiled. The brush of his lips caused a spiral of sensation encompassing every nerve cell.

It provided a vivid reminder of the exquisite orgasmic experience they'd shared, and the need to recapture it again.

Which would be the height of foolishness. Sexual gratification was no substitute for lovemaking. It was something she'd vowed to uphold. Selective sex with someone she cared for, and who she believed cared for her. It didn't sit well that last night she'd broken her own rule.

They chose to decline dessert in favour of the cheeseboard, and lingered over excellent coffee.

Michelle was surprised to see it was after eleven when they parted outside the restaurant, and she offered her cheek for Emilio's kiss.

'*Brava,* darling,' he murmured close to her ear, then offered, 'Your performance was incredible. See you in the morning.'

Saska followed suit by pressing her lips to Nikos' cheek, then lightly, briefly on his mouth. 'We must do this again soon.'

Nikos' smile held warmth. 'We'll look forward to it.' He caught Michelle's hand and threaded her fingers through his own, then brought it to his lips. 'Won't, we?'

Oh my, he was good. She offered him a melting smile. 'Of course. Thursday evening there's a charity ball being held at the Marriott. *Maman* is on the committee. I can arrange a ticket if Saska would like to join us.'

Saska didn't hesitate. 'I'd love to.'

Nikos waited until they were seated in the car before venturing with silky amusement, 'Do you delight in setting the cat among the pigeons?'

Michelle turned towards him and offered a stunning smile. 'Why, *darling, Maman* will be gratified at the sale of another ticket, and Saska will enjoy the evening.'

'And you, *pedhaki mou,*' he drawled. 'What will you enjoy?'

'Watching you,' she responded sweetly.

'Playing the part? Isn't that what we all do on occasion? In business, socially?'

'You do it exceptionally well.'

'Let me return the compliment.'

'In the interest of establishing our pseudo relationship, the evening was a success.'

He didn't answer as he negotiated an intersection, and she lapsed into a silence that stretched the several minutes it took to reach her apartment building.

'There's no need for you to stay,' Michelle declared firmly as he rode the lift with her to the fifteenth floor.

'We've already settled this issue.'

'Last night was different.' The lift came to a halt and she retrieved her key in readiness.

'No.'

She crossed the carpeted lobby to her apartment and unlocked the door.

'What do you mean—*no?*'

'Your apartment or mine,' Nikos reiterated hardily. 'It's irrelevant. But we share.'

'I doubt Jeremy will attempt to enter the building, and even if he did, he'd never get past my front door.'

He thrust a hand into each trouser pocket, and looked at her with open cynicism. 'You don't think he's sufficiently devious to disguise himself as a delivery messenger?' He continued before she had a chance to answer. 'Or utilise some plausible ploy to get past reception?'

A week ago none of these possibilities would have entered her head. Now, she had good reason to pause for thought. And she didn't like any of the answers.

'You're not prepared to give in, are you?' she queried wearily.

'No.'

She didn't say a further word, and simply turned and walked through to the kitchen. She needed a drink. Hot sweet tea to take the edge off the champagne and an excellent meal.

Michelle filled the electric kettle and switched it on, then she extracted a cup, teabag, sugar and milk, and stood waiting for the water to boil.

She was conscious of Nikos' presence, and all too aware of him silently watching her actions as she poured hot water into the cup, sweetened it and added milk.

If he stayed there much longer, she'd be tempted to throw something at him.

She discarded the spoon into the sink, and looked at him. Then wished she hadn't.

Eyes that were dark and frighteningly still held

her own captive, and she felt like an animal caught in a trap.

Everything faded into the background, and there was only a mesmeric quality apparent as he closed the distance between them.

'Fight me, argue with me,' Nikos berated silkily. 'But don't turn your back and walk away.' He lifted a hand and caught hold of her chin between thumb and forefinger, then tilted it. 'Ever.'

It was impossible to escape that deep assessing gaze, and her own anger lent an edge of defiance.

'Don't say a word,' he warned with deceptive mildness, as she opened her mouth to give vent to his actions.

'Why?'

His mouth angled over hers, then took possession in a kiss which tore the breath from her throat as he plundered at will.

Then the pressure eased, and she almost cried out as he began an evocative tasting with such sensual mastery it was almost all she could do not to respond.

A flame deep within ignited and flared into vibrant life, until her whole body was consumed with it, and she wound her arms up around his neck, leaned into him, and simply went with whatever he dictated.

It was a long time before he gradually broke contact, and she could only look at him in stunned silence as he lightly traced the swollen contours of her mouth.

'There's no one here to observe the pretense,' Michelle said shakily, and his smile held musing warmth.

'Who says it's a pretense?'

His hand brushed across her collarbone, back and

forth in a hypnotic movement, and she bit back a gasp as he settled his lips at the base of her throat.

'Let's not do this,' she pleaded fruitlessly, and felt his mouth part in a soundless smile.

'Frightened?'

'Scared witless,' she admitted.

He savoured the sweet valley between her breasts, then slowly nibbled his way back to her lips. 'Don't be.'

She had to stop him now, or she'd never find the willpower to break away.

'Last night was a mistake,' she said desperately, and almost died at the force of his arousal.

'Something which felt so good could never be a mistake.'

Michelle made a last-ditch effort. 'Foolish, then,' she amended.

'What makes you say that?'

Self-preservation and remorse reared its head. 'I don't do this sort of thing,' she assured, then attempted to clarify. 'We haven't even known each other a week.'

His eyes held hers, and there was wry humour, sensuality, and something else she couldn't define. 'A lifetime,' he mocked lightly.

'It has to mean something,' she protested.

'And this doesn't?'

'No—yes. Oh hell. I don't know.' She was supremely conscious of the sensual warmth stealing through her veins, heating her body until her bones seemed to liquify and dissolve beneath the flood of sensation.

She felt bare, exposed, and frighteningly vulnerable, and she needed to explain why. 'I like to plan things, have a reason for everything. Not dive off the deep end with—'

'Someone you've known less than a week?'

'Yes!' She was out of her depth, and flailing. 'Where can this—this farce, possibly lead? In a few weeks it'll all be over. Then what?'

Nikos brushed gentle fingers down her cheek and let them rest at the edge of her mouth.

'Why not wait and see?'

Because I don't want to be hurt, she cried silently. Too late, a tiny gremlin taunted. You're already in this up to your neck, and in a one-sided love, pain is part of the deal.

Love? She didn't love him. Lust, maybe. Definitely lust, she amended as he hoisted her high up against him and walked towards the bedroom.

Michelle wound her legs around his waist and held on, exulting in the feel of him, the broad expanse of his chest, the tight waist, the strength of his arms.

In the bedroom he switched on the lamp, then let her slide down to her feet.

For a moment she just looked at him, then he lowered his head and took her mouth, gently this time, employing such acute sensitivity she felt she might cry.

Together, they slowly divested their clothes, pausing every now and again to brush a tantalising path over bare flesh in a teasing discovery.

She adored the texture of his skin, the hard ridges of muscle and sinew, the clean faint musky aroma. There was the faint tightening of muscle, the soft intake of breath as she caressed him, and she groaned out loud when he wreaked havoc with one sensitive peak, then the other as he suckled at each breast.

There were no questions asked, no answers given, as they embarked on a sensual feast that was alternately gentle and slow, then so hard and fast sweat beaded their skin and their breath became tortured and ragged.

It was a long night, with little sleep, only the mutual sharing of something infinitely special. Wholly sexual, blissfully sensual, and to Michelle, incredibly unique.

On the edge of exhaustion she wondered if it all wasn't a figment of her fervent imagination. Except there was a hard male body to which she clung, and something terribly *real* to the scent and feel of him.

'Orange juice, shower, breakfast, work,' a husky male voice tormented. 'Rise and shine, *pedhi mou*. You have forty minutes.'

Michelle lifted a hand, then let it fall back onto the bed. 'It's the middle of the night.'

'Eight-fifteen on a bright and warm Wednesday morning,' Nikos assured, and pulled the sheet from her supine form.

He could, he thought regretfully, get very interested in the slender lines of her back. The twin slopes of her bottom were firm mounds his hands itched to shape. And as for that daring little butterfly tattoo... It just begged to be kissed, tasted, and savoured. Like the cute dimple on each side of her lower spine.

'Five seconds,' he warned musingly. 'Or I'll join you, and you won't surface until midday.'

That had the desired effect, for she rolled onto her back and opened her eyes. 'Five?'

'Three, and counting,' Nikos assured, laughing softly as she swung her feet to the floor.

'Orange juice.' He handed her the glass and watched her drain half the contents before handing it back to him.

'Shower,' Michelle said obediently, and searched for her wrap.

'Nice view,' he complimented gently, and glimpsed the tinge of pink colour her cheeks.

'You're dressed,' she observed as she pushed a tumbled swathe of hair behind one ear.

'Showered, shaved, and I've just cooked breakfast.'

'A gem among men.' She found the wrap and shrugged her arms into it. 'I hope you've made coffee?'

'It's percolating.'

'Are you usually so energetic at this hour of the morning?' She caught his gleaming smile, and her mouth formed a wry grimace. 'Don't answer that.'

Michelle crossed to the en suite, and adjusted the water dial in the shower to hot. Afterwards she'd turn it to cold in the hope it would encourage her blood to circulate more quickly and force her into bright-eyed wakefulness.

A fifty per cent improvement was better than none, she perceived half an hour later as she sipped ruinously strong coffee and sliced banana onto cereal.

By the time she finished both, she felt almost human.

Five minutes remained to take the lift down, slip

into her car and drive the short distance to the Gallery.

'I have meetings scheduled for most of the day,' Nikos informed as they took the lift together. 'I should be back about six. If there's any delay, I'll phone you.'

'Oh hell,' Michelle said inelegantly as they crossed to where their cars were parked.

'Problems?'

'A flat tyre.' Disbelief coloured her voice, and Nikos swore softly beneath his breath.

'I'll drop you off at the Gallery. Give me your car keys, and I'll arrange to have someone fix it.'

Closer examination revealed the tyre had been very neatly slashed.

'You don't think—'

'This is Jeremy's handiwork?' He was certain of it. 'Possibly.' Just as he was sure there would be no evidence.

He unlocked the BMW and Michelle slid into the passenger seat. Within seconds he fired the engine and eased the large car up the ramp and out onto the road.

Two blocks down he pulled into the kerb, let the engine idle, and reached across to unlatch her door. 'I'll ring you through the day.' He kissed her, hard, briefly, then straightened as she released the seat belt and stepped out from the car.

It was a hectic morning as Michelle caught up on a batch of invoices, liaised with the framing firm, and made countless phone calls.

Lunch was something she ate at her desk, and it

came as something of a shock when Nikos rang at three-thirty.

'I've had your car delivered to the Gallery. Don't forget your four o'clock appointment with the lawyer. I'll collect you in fifteen minutes.'

Oh hell, she hadn't forgotten, she simply hadn't expected the time to come around so fast. 'Thanks.'

There was a sense of satisfaction in attaching her signature to the legal statement, and a degree of relief the matter was now in official hands.

It was almost five when Nikos drew the BMW to a halt outside the Gallery, and it was a simple matter to slip behind the wheel of her Porsche and followed him the few blocks to her apartment.

The message light was blinking on her answering machine, and she activated the button and listened to the recorded message.

"Eloise, Michelle. You haven't called. So this is a reminder. Don't forget Philippe's party tonight. Six-thirty."

'Philippe?' Nikos queried.

'My godson,' she explained. 'He's three years old, and tonight is his day-care Christmas party.' She lifted a hand and pushed a stray lock of hair behind one ear. 'I can't believe I didn't remember.' She checked her watch. 'I'll have to shower, change and leave.'

'I'll come with you.'

Michelle cast him a wry glance. 'To a children's party?'

'To a children's party,' he repeated mockingly.

It was fun. Parents, family, gathered in front of a large open-air stage at the day-care centre, young

children dressed in costume as the teachers led them
through their practised paces. Taped music, and childish voices singing out of tune and synch. Smiles and
laughter when some of the children forgot they were
supposed to act and waved to their parents.

Michelle stood among the crowd, with Nikos positioned behind her, secure within the light circle of
his arms.

Afterwards she searched for and found Eloise and
her husband, and spent time with Philippe, who displayed his delight at her being there, as well as curiosity for the man at her side. She whispered in his
ear in French, and made him giggle.

'I am a bon tot,' Philippe repeated in English to
his parents. 'Tante Michelle says so.'

It was almost nine when the pageant concluded,
and after bidding Philippe an affectionate goodnight
she walked with Nikos to the car.

Minutes later she leaned back against the headrest
and closed her eyes. It had been an eventful day, following on from a very eventful night.

When they stepped inside her apartment Nikos
took one look at her pale features, the dark shadows
beneath her eyes, and gently pushed her in the direction of her bedroom.

'Go to bed, *pedhaki mou*.'

She needed no second bidding, and within minutes
she'd divested her clothes, cleansed her face of make-
up and was laying supine beneath the bedcovers.

Sleep came almost instantly, and she woke in the
morning, alone. Except the pillow beside hers held
an indentation, and there was the soft musky aroma

of male cologne as a vivid reminder that Nikos had shared her bed.

Michelle took a hurried shower, then she dressed ready for work and emerged into the kitchen to discover Nikos dressed and speaking into his mobile phone in a language she could only surmise as being his own.

One glance at the countertop was sufficient to determine he'd already eaten, and she finished a small plate of cereal with fruit before he'd completed his conversation.

'Good morning.' He crossed to her side, brushed her lips with his own, then he picked up a cup and drained his coffee. 'Almost ready? I'll drop you at the Gallery.'

CHAPTER TEN

IT HADN'T BEEN the best of days, Michelle reflected as she entered her apartment just after five. Whatever could have gone wrong, had.

Nikos had called to say he'd be late, and while she told herself she was pleased to have the apartment to herself for more than an hour, that wasn't strictly true.

She craved the warmth of his arms, the feel of his mouth on hers, the heat that pulsed through her veins at the mere thought of him.

The light on her answering machine blinked, and she ran the message tape, only to hear three hang-ups, which she considered mildly disturbing, given that her mobile number was recorded for contact.

Jeremy? Would he revert to nuisance hang-up calls?

A shower would do much to ease the tension, and ten minutes later she donned denim cut-offs, a fitted rib-knit top, left her hair loose, and applied minimum make-up. It was way too early to begin dressing for the charity ball, and she didn't fancy floating around the apartment for more than an hour in a wrap.

The intercom buzzed, and she crossed to activate it.

There was silence for a few seconds. 'Having fun with your live-in lover, Michelle?'

A sickening feeling twisted her stomach at the sound of Jeremy's voice, and she released the intercom, only to hear it buzz again almost immediately. She hugged her arms together, hesitated, then picked up the receiver.

Her fingers clenched, and her voice assumed an unaccustomed hardness. 'Don't be a fool, Jeremy.'

'Wisdom isn't my forte.'

'What do you hope to achieve by harassing me?'

'Haven't you worked it out yet? I find it a challenge to skate close to the law and remain unscathed.'

She hung up on him, and almost didn't answer the phone when it rang twenty minutes later.

'Michelle? We have a delivery of flowers for you at reception.'

Michelle's lips curved into a smile. 'I'll be right down.' She caught up her key and went out to summon the lift.

A beautiful bouquet of carnations in delicate pastels encased in clear cellophane greeted her, and she reached for the attached envelope.

A single word was slashed in black, and showed starkly against the white embossed card. *Bitch*.

She didn't need to question who'd sent them.

'Will you dump these for me?'

'Excuse me?'

'Dump them,' Michelle repeated firmly.

'But they're beautiful,' the receptionist declared with shocked surprise.

'Unfortunately the intention behind them isn't.'

A fleeting movement on the bricked apron beyond the automatic glass entrance doors caught her eye, and she recognised Jeremy execute an elaborate bow before he moved quickly out of sight.

It was a deliberate taunt. A reminder that he was choosing to play a dangerous game by his own rules.

'It seems a shame to waste them.'

Michelle merely shrugged her shoulders and headed towards the double bank of lifts.

She had an hour in which to change, apply make-up and do something with her hair.

The thought of attending a pre-Christmas ball to aid a prominent charity held little appeal. Women spent days preparing for this particular annual event. Chantelle, she knew, would have gone from the masseuse to the beautician, had her nails lacquered, then spent hours with the hairdresser.

Ten minutes later she'd stripped down to briefs, added a silky wrap, then she crossed to the vanity to begin applying make-up.

It was there that Nikos found her, and he wondered at the faint shadows beneath her eyes, the slightly too bright smile.

'Bad day?' He felt his loins tighten as she leaned close to the mirror.

'So-so,' Michelle answered cautiously.

'Are you wearing anything beneath that wrap?' he queried conversationally.

She glimpsed the purposeful gleam apparent in those dark eyes, and shook her head in silent mockery. 'There's not enough time.'

His smile tugged at her heart and did strange things to the nerves in her stomach. 'We could always arrive late.'

'No,' she declared. 'We couldn't.'

He moved to stand behind her, and her eyes dilated at their mirrored image. One so tall and dark-haired, while the top of her blond head barely reached his shoulder.

His hands slid round her waist, released the belted tie, then moved to cup each breast.

Liquid warmth spilled through her veins, heating her body as desire, raw and primitive, activated each nerve cell.

Michelle watched with almost detached fascination as her skin quivered beneath the sweet sorcery of his touch, and she felt her breath catch as one hand splayed low over her abdomen, seeking, teasing the soft curling hair at the apex of her thighs.

The lacy bikini briefs were soon dispensed with, and when she would have turned into his arms he held her still, then he lowered his mouth to the curve of her neck and gently savoured the delicate pulse beating there.

Her bones melted, and she sank back against him, wanting more, much more.

'You're not playing fair.' The words emerged as a sibilant groan as he pressed her close in against him.

His arousal was a potent force, and the need to have him deep inside her was almost unbearable.

Michelle caught a glimpse of herself in the mirror, and almost gasped at the reflected image. She looked like a shameless wanton experiencing a witching ravishment.

Her eyes were large, the pupils dilated, and her lips had parted to emit a soundless sigh. Pink coloured her cheeks, and her body arched against his in silent invitation.

'Nikos, please.'

Without a word he grasped hold of her waist and lifted her to sit on the wide marbled vanity top, then he lowered his head to her breast and caressed one pale globe.

It was an erotic tasting that held her spellbound as she became consumed with treacherous sensation, and when she could bear it no longer she caught hold of his head and forced it up, then angled her mouth to his in a kiss that was urgent, hungry, and passionately intense.

How long before they slowly drew apart? Five minutes, ten? She had no idea. All she knew was that the slightest touch, the faintest sound, would tip them both past the point of no return.

It was Nikos who rested his forehead against her own as he effected a soothing circular movement over her shoulders.

'I guess we should take a raincheck, hmm?'

She wasn't capable of saying a word, and she looked faintly stricken as she inclined her head in silent acquiescence.

He cupped her face and kissed her gently, then he drew her down onto her feet. 'I'll go shower, shave and change.'

When he left she leaned both hands on the vanity and closed her eyes. She felt as if all her nerves had stretched to breaking point, and then shredded into a thousand pieces.

No man had ever had this effect on her before. Not once had she felt so *consumed,* so helpless. Or so deeply *involved.* It was frightening. For what happened when it ended, as it inevitably would? Could she walk away, and say, Thanks, it was great while it lasted?

The thought of a life without him in it seemed horribly empty.

You're bound to him, a tiny voice taunted. Until Saska relinquishes her widow's hold, and Jeremy has been removed, voluntarily or forcibly, from the picture.

So what do you suggest? she demanded silently. Love and live each day as if it's the last? That's the fiction. Reality will be a broken heart and empty dreams.

The sound of water running in the adjacent en suite acted as an incentive to gather herself together. She was a mess. Hair, make-up… She'd have to begin from scratch.

Michelle forced herself to work quickly, and after a shaky start she used expert touches to heighten her delicate bone structure, highlight her eyes, and outline her mouth.

Her hair was thick, and it wasn't difficult to add extra thickness with the skilful use of a brush and hair dryer.

The gown she'd chosen to wear was an ankle-length slinky black silk sheath with a softly draped bodice and slim shoestring shoulder straps. Black stiletto-heeled shoes completed the outfit, and she caught up a matching black stole, a small beaded evening bag, then walked out to the lounge.

Nikos was waiting for her, looking resplendent in a dark evening suit, white cotton pin-pleated shirt and black bow tie.

Michelle felt her heart stop, then quicken to a rapid

beat. His broad facial bone structure lent him a primitive air, the chiselled cheekbones, dark eyes, the perfectly moulded nose, and a well-shaped mouth that could wreak such sensual havoc.

He was an impressive man, in a way that had little to do with the physical. There was a ruthlessness apparent that boded ill for anyone who dared to cross his path. There was also a gentleness that was totally in variance with his projected persona.

If he were to gift his heart to a woman, it would be a gift beyond price. A wise woman would treasure and treat it with care.

Such wayward thoughts were dangerous. She couldn't afford them, daren't even pause to give them a second of her time.

'Shall we leave?' She couldn't believe her voice sounded so steady, so cool.

The lift descended nonstop to the ground floor, the doors slid open to admit the receptionist before resuming its descent to the car park.

'Michelle. I put the flowers in a vase on the lobby side-table. It seemed such a pity to waste them. I hope you don't mind?' The lift slid to a halt and they emerged into the concrete cavern. 'Have a great evening.'

'What flowers?' Nikos queried as he led Michelle in the opposite direction towards his car.

'A bouquet of carnations.'

One eyebrow rose slightly. 'I'll rephrase that. Who sent you flowers?' He caught hold of her elbow and drew her to a halt when she didn't answer. 'Michelle?'

There didn't seem any advantage in prevaricating. 'Jeremy.'

Nikos' eyes hardened measurably. 'He delivered them personally?'

'Yes.'

'He spoke to you?' he demanded sharply.

'No. He merely stood outside and choreographed an elaborate bow.'

Nikos bit off a pithy oath. 'That young man seems to choose to dance with danger.'

She could almost feel the palpable anger emanate from his powerful frame as he unlocked the BMW, saw her seated, then he crossed round the car and slid in behind the wheel.

'Has he rung you at any time today?' He fired the engine, then eased the car towards the ramp.

'This evening, shortly after I arrived home.'

There was something primitive in his expression as he turned briefly towards her. 'Tomorrow morning we transfer to my apartment. And don't,' he warned bleakly. 'Argue. The penthouse can only be accessed by using a specially coded security key to operate the lift. Even the emergency stairwell is inaccessible from the floor below.' His eyes became hard and implacable. 'At least I know you'll be safe there.'

This was all getting a bit too much! 'Look—'

'It's not negotiable,' Nikos decreed with pitiless disregard.

'The hell it isn't!'

'We're almost there.'

He was right, she saw with amazement. It was less than two kilometres to the Marriott hotel, and they'd traversed the distance in record time.

'We'll discuss this later,' Michelle indicated as he cruised the car park for an empty space.

'You can count on it,' Nikos agreed with chilling bleakness.

Anger at his highhandedness tinged her mood, and her back was stiff as she walked at his side to the lift. There was a group of fellow guests already waiting to be transported to the ballroom, and she forced her facial muscles to relax as they rode the necessary two flights.

From that moment on it was strictly smile-time as they mixed and mingled in the adjoining foyer. Uniformed waiters circulated with trays loaded with champagne-filled flutes, and she accepted one, sipped the sparkling liquid, and endeavoured to visually locate her parents.

'There you are.'

Michelle heard Saska's slightly accented voice, summoned a smile, then she turned to face the tall brunette.

'Saska,' she acknowledged politely. 'It's nice to see you.' How many mistruths did people utter beneath the guise of exchanging social pleasantries? Too many, she perceived cynically as she tilted her cheek to accept Emilio's kiss.

The guests began to dissipate as staff opened up the ballroom, and Michelle was supremely conscious of Nikos' arm along the back of her waist, the close proximity of his body as they moved slowly into the large room.

Circular tables seating ten were beautifully assembled with white linen, gleaming cutlery and glassware, beautiful floral centrepieces. Each table bore a number, and they gravitated as a foursome towards their designated seats.

Saska deliberately positioned herself next to Nikos, and Michelle was intensely irritated by the widow's deliberate action.

There was, unfortunately, very little she could do about it without causing a scene. A fact Saska had already calculated, and her smile was akin to that of a cat who'd just lapped a saucer of cream.

The evening's entertainment was to be broken into segments during the elaborate four-course meal, with a fashion parade as the conclusion.

Chantelle and Etienne Gerard joined them, together with two young couples. There was time for a brief round of introductions before the obligatory speech by the charity's fundraising chairman, which was followed by a delicious French onion soup.

A magician dressed in elegant black, grey and white fatigues, white-painted face and black-painted lips demonstrated a brief repertoire with a multitude of different coloured scarves, silver rings, and a small bejewelled box.

A seafood starter was served, and Michelle nibbled at a succulent prawn, forked a few mouthfuls of dressed lettuce, then reached for the iced water.

Saska held Nikos' attention in what appeared to be a deep and meaningful conversation. Michelle caught Emilio's eye, saw his almost imperceptible wink, and felt her lips twitch.

He held no fewer illusions that she did. Emilio enjoyed the social scene, deriving cynical amusement from the many games of pretense the various guests played for the benefit of others. He was rarely mistaken in his assessment.

The starter dishes were collected by staff as the

lights dimmed and a gifted soprano gave an exquisite solo performance from a popular opera.

Michelle sipped champagne and endeavoured to ignore the spread of Saska's beautifully lacquered nails on Nikos' thigh. The slight movement of those nails didn't escape her attention, and she felt the slow build of anger. And jealousy. Although she refused to acknowledge it as that emotion.

'Oh well done,' Saska accorded as the guests burst into applause.

Michelle watched her turn towards Nikos, say something in Greek, laugh, and touch the sleeve of his jacket.

Perhaps, she decided, it was time to play. The young man seated next to her was about her own age, and had partnered his sister to the function.

Michelle leaned towards him. 'I would say it's going to be a very successful evening.'

Two spots of colour hit his cheekbones. 'Yes. Yes, it is.' He indicated the soprano accepting a second round of applause. 'She's really quite something, isn't she?'

'Quite something,' Michelle agreed solemnly.

'The food is good, don't you think?' he rushed on earnestly. 'Can I help you to some wine? More champagne?'

She gave him a slow sweet smile. 'You could fill my water glass, if you don't mind.'

He didn't mind. In fact, he couldn't seem to believe his luck, given that the beautiful blonde who seemed to want to talk to him was in the company of a man whose power, looks and degree of sophistication were something he doubted he'd ever aspire to.

'Do you attend many of these charity functions?'

He was nice, pleasant and easy to talk to. 'My parents are very supportive of a few major charities,' she revealed. 'So yes, I attend a few each year.'

'Is—' he began awkwardly. 'Are you— Would you dance with me later?'

'I'd like that,' she said gently.

They were interrupted as the waitress deftly served the main course, and Michelle offered him a faint smile as she transferred her attention to the food.

She felt the light brush of fingers against her cheek, and she turned towards Nikos in silent query.

'He's just a boy,' he chided softly, and glimpsed the brilliant flare of gold in the depths of those beautiful green eyes.

'Are you saying,' she said with extreme care, 'that I shouldn't talk to him?'

'I doubt he's equipped to cope with your flirting.'

She met his gaze with composed tolerance. 'While you, of course, are well able to cope with Saska.'

'You noticed.' It was a statement, not a query, and she wanted to say she noticed everything about him. Except to acknowledge it would be tantamount to an admission of sorts, and she didn't want to betray her emotions.

He took hold of her hand and lifted it to his lips, then kissed each finger in turn. 'Eat, *pedhaki mou*.'

Dynamic masculinity at its most lethal, she accorded silently. All she had to do was look at him, and she became lost. It was if every cell in her body wanted to fuse with his, generating a sensual chemistry so vibrant and volatile, it was a wonder it didn't burst into flame.

'In that case, you'd better let me have my hand back,' she managed calmly, and glimpsed the musing gleam evident in those dark eyes so close to her own.

'Don't be too sassy,' Nikos drawled softly. 'Remember, we eventually get to go home together.'

'I'm trembling.'

'It will be my pleasure to ensure that you do.'

'Then I suggest you eat,' Michelle said demurely. 'You'll need the energy.'

One eyebrow slanted in visible amusement, and his eyes gleamed darkly.

'Darling,' she added, sotto voce, and pulled her hand free. She glanced up, caught Emilio's wicked expression, and widened her eyes in a deliberately facetious gesture.

Chicken and fish were served alternately, and she picked at the fish, speared the exotically presented vegetables, then pushed her plate forward. Dessert would follow, accompanied by a cheeseboard, and all she felt like was some fruit and cheese.

She picked up her glass and sipped the iced water, watching with detached fascination the precise movements as Nikos dealt with his food. He looked as if he took pleasure in the taste, the texture of each mouthful.

As he took pleasure in pleasing a woman. Just to see his mouth was to imagine it gliding slowly over her body, caressing soft skin, savouring each pulse beat. The sensual intimacy, the liberties he took, and her craven response.

Dear heaven, she could feel the blood course through her veins, heating her skin, just at the thought of what he could do to her.

Almost as if he sensed a subtle shift in the rhythm of her heart, he paused and slowly turned towards her.

For one millisecond, she was unable to mask the stark need, then it was gone, buried beneath the control of self-preservation, and his eyes darkened in recognition.

It felt as if there was no one else in the room, only them, and she could have sworn she swayed slightly, drawn towards him as if by some magnetic power.

Then he smiled. A soft widening of his mouth that held the hidden promise of what they would share.

She bit into the soft tissue of her lower lip, felt the slight stab of pain, and tasted blood. Her eyes flared, and the spell was broken. The room and its occupants reappeared, the sound of muted chatter, background music.

The waiters moved unobtrusively, removing dishes, plates, while a noted comedian took the microphone and wove jokes into stories with such flair and wit, it was impossible not to laugh.

Dessert comprised glazed strawberries in a chocolate basket decorated with fresh thickened cream. Sinful, Michelle accorded silently as she bit into the luscious fruit. She abandoned the chocolate and cream, and reached for the crackers and cheese as the compere announced the fashion parade.

Models took the stage in pairs, displaying an elegant selection of day wear, after five, and evening wear.

Coffee was served as the last pair of models disappeared from the stage, and it acted as a signal for the deejay to set up the music. It was also a moment when several guests chose to leave their respective tables to freshen up.

'Do you think—' a male voice inclined tentatively. 'Would you care to dance with me?'

Michelle turned towards him with a smile. 'Yes.' She placed her napkin on the table and rose to her feet.

He was good, very good, and she laughed as he led her into a set of steps she could only hope to follow. This was fun, *he* was fun, and for the next few minutes she went with the music.

'You do this very well,' she complimented as the music slowed to a more sedate beat.

'My sister and I are ballroom dancing competitors.'

'It shows,' she assured.

'I don't suppose—' He shook his head. 'No, of course not. Why would you?'

She looked at him and saw the enthusiasm of youth. 'Why would I *what?*' she queried gently.

'Agree to go out with me. The movies, a coffee. Anything.'

'If I wasn't with someone, I'd have loved to.'

'Really?' He could hardly believe it. 'You would?'

'Really,' she assured.

The track finished, and Michelle took the opportunity to thank him and indicate a return to their table.

CHAPTER ELEVEN

NIKOS MET HER eyes as she took the seat beside him, and he refilled her glass and handed it to her as the young man led his sister onto the floor.

'Did you let him down gently?'

'He asked me out.'

'Naturally you refused.'

She decided to tease him a little. Heaven knew he deserved it. 'I gave it considerable thought,' she said demurely. 'And I decided I would—' She paused deliberately, then offered an impish smile. 'Dance with him again.'

Nikos pressed a forefinger to the centre of her lips. 'Just so long as the last one is mine.'

'I'll try to remember,' she responded solemnly.

'Minx,' he accorded. 'Do you want some coffee?'

'I think so,' Michelle said solemnly. 'Any more champagne, and I might not be held responsible.'

His smile almost undid her. 'Responsible for what?'

'Doing Saska an unforgivable harm.'

'She's a friend.'

'I know, I know. It's just that the boundaries of her friendship with you seem to be expanding.'

'At the moment. Soon they'll shift back to their former position.'

'I admire your faith in human nature, but don't you think you're a little misguided?'

'No.'

A waitress appeared with a carafe of coffee and she poured them each a cup. Michelle reached for the sugar and stirred in two sachets.

'Nikos? Perhaps we could dance? Michelle, you don't mind, do you?'

She gave Saska a brilliant smile. 'Of course not. I intend to finish my coffee.'

'You and Nikos appear to be getting along together exceptionally well,' Chantelle inclined when Nikos and Saska had moved out of earshot.

She wanted to tell her mother the truth, but what was the truth? She wasn't sure any more. 'Yes,' she responded carefully. How would her mother react if she relayed they fought like hell on occasion and their lovemaking resembled heaven on earth?

Be amused, probably, offer a good argument cleared the air, and add the making up was always the best part.

'We're leaving soon, darling,' Chantelle relayed. 'It's quite late, and your father has an early flight to catch tomorrow. Maybe we could have lunch together? I'll call you, shall I?'

Nikos and Saska resumed their seats, and Michelle tried to ignore the arm he draped across the back of her chair. It brought him close and implied a deliberate intimacy.

'Please, *Maman*. I'll look forward to it.'

'Saturday, perhaps?'

'Not the weekend,' Nikos disputed. 'We'll be in Sydney.'

She cast him a challenging look. 'We will?'

'I have business there,' he enlightened with a mocking drawl that didn't fool her in the slightest.

'The break will do you good, *cherie,*' Chantelle enthused.

Since when had Nikos gained the God-given right to organise her life? Since he first walked into it, she acknowledged cynically.

Which didn't mean she'd simply give in without a struggle, and she said as much as he drew her on to the dance floor.

'I don't like being told what to do.'

'Especially by me, hmm?'

'Look—'

'No, *pedhi mou,*' Nikos stated with deceptive mildness. 'This is the way it is.' His eyes were at variance with his voice. 'Tomorrow I have a two o'clock meeting in Sydney, which will conclude with a social dinner. I plan to fly back to the Coast on Sunday. You get to go with me.'

'And just how do you propose to indicate my presence?'

His appraisal was swift, calculating, and brought a tinge of soft colour to her cheeks. 'I am answerable to no one.'

Michelle closed her eyes, then slowly opened them again. 'Well, now there's the thing. Neither am I.'

'Yes,' he refuted with silky tolerance. 'You are. To me. Until the situation with Jeremy is resolved.'

Anger and resentment surged to the surface, lending her eyes a brilliant sparkle. 'Let's not forget Saska in this scheme of things.'

An indolent smile curved the generous lines of his mouth. 'No,' he drawled with an edge of mockery. 'We can't dismiss Saska.'

Her back stiffened in silent anger. 'I don't think I want to dance with you.'

His lips brushed her temple, and his hands trailed a path up and down her lower spine in a soothing gesture.

'Yes, you do.'

Caught close in his arms wasn't conducive to conducting an argument, for she was far too conscious of the feel of that large body, the subtle nuances of sensation as her system went into overdrive.

'Always so sure of what I want, Nikos?'

His eyes held knowledge as he held her gaze. A knowledge that was infinitely sensual and alive with lambent passion. 'Yes.'

She was melting, subsiding into a thousand pieces, and there wasn't a sensible word she could frame in response.

His cologne combined with the scent of freshly laundered clothes and a barely detectable male muskiness. It proved a potent mix that attacked her senses, and she felt the need to be free of him, if only for the five or so minutes it would take to freshen up.

'I need to visit the powder room.'

It was late, and already the evening was beginning to wind down. In another hour the venue would close, and those inclined to do so would go on to a nightclub.

Michelle left the ballroom and entered the elegantly appointed powder room. After using the facilities, she crossed to the mirror to repair her make-up, and barely glanced up as the door swung in to admit another guest.

Saska. Coincidence, or design? Michelle opted for the latter.

'I have to hand it to you,' Saska complimented as she crossed to the mirror. 'You move quickly.'

No preamble, no niceties. Just straight to the heart of the matter.

'It's taken you less than a week to have Nikos delight in playing your knight in shining armour.'

Michelle capped her lipstick and placed it in her bag. 'I'm very grateful for his help.'

'Very convenient, these little episodes which have occurred with Jeremy.' She spared a glance at Michelle via the mirror, and one eyebrow arched in disbelief. 'You must agree it raises a few questions?'

'Are you accusing me of contriving a situation simply to manipulate Nikos' attention?'

'Darling, women are prepared to do anything to get Nikos' attention,' Saska declared with marked cynicism.

'Does that include you?'

'I would be lying if I said no,' Saska admitted.

Michelle drew in her breath and released it slowly. 'And the purpose of this little chat is?'

'Why, to let you know I'm in the race.'

'There is no race. Nikos isn't the prize.'

'You're neither naive nor stupid. So what game are you playing?'

'None,' Michelle said simply. 'Blame Nikos. He's the one intent on being the masterful hero, without any encouragement from me.' Without a further word she turned and left the room.

Nikos and Emilio were deep in conversation when she slid into her seat, and she met Nikos' swift glance with equanimity.

'More coffee?'

'Please.'

He signalled the waitress, and instructed her to refill both cups.

It was almost midnight when they left, and Michelle looked at the towering apartment buildings standing like sentinels against a dark sky. Lit windows provided a sprinkling of regimented light, and she wondered idly at the people residing there. A mix of residents and holiday-makers intent on enjoying the sun, surf and shopping available on this picturesque tourist strip.

Nikos paused at the lights, then turned into suburban Main Beach. Within minutes the car swept beneath her apartment building.

'I'm going to bed,' Michelle announced the instant Nikos closed the front door behind them.

'If you want to fight, then let's get it over and done with,' Nikos drawled with amusement.

She swung round to face him, and her chin tilted fractionally as she lifted one hand and began ticking off one finger after another. 'I'm not moving into your penthouse, and I'm not—' she paused and gave the word repetitive emphasis ' —*not* spending the weekend in Sydney with you.'

'Yes, you are.'

She was on a roll, and unable to stop. 'Will you please do me a favour and inform Saska that I did not contrive to gain your attention by playing a *pretend assault* game with Jeremy!'

His eyes narrowed. 'She's—'

'Delusional,' Michelle accused fiercely.

'Temporarily obsessive,' Nikos amended.

'That, too!'

He crossed to where she stood and placed his hands on her shoulders, kneading them with a blissfully firm touch that eased the kinks.

Dear Lord, that felt good. Too good, she perceived. Any minute now she'd close her eyes, lean back, and give in to the magic of his touch.

His lips brushed against the sensitive hollow at the edge of her neck, and she stifled a faint groan in pleasure.

She felt his fingers slide the shoestring straps over her shoulders, and the trail of kisses that followed them.

'This isn't going to resolve a thing,' Michelle inclined huskily as she acknowledged the slow curl of passion that began building deep inside. Any second now she wouldn't possess the will to resist him.

'Nikos, please—don't,' she almost begged as he kissed a particularly vulnerable spot at her nape.

'You want me to stop?'

No, but I daren't allow you to continue. Not if I want to retain any vestige of sanity.

'Yes,' she answered bravely. The loss of his touch made her feel cold, bereft, as she slowly turned to face him. Self-preservation caused her to move back a pace.

'I don't see the necessity for me to move into your penthouse. Removing myself to Sydney for the weekend is tantamount to running away. You're not responsible for me. What has happened with Jeremy would have happened anyway.' It came out sounding wrong, and Nikos used it to his advantage.

'You're saying you want to stay here alone,' he began with chilling softness. 'And risk having Jeremy utilise devious means and front up to your door? Or maybe lay in wait in the underground car park for the time you return home alone?'

His words evoked stark images from which she mentally withdrew. 'Suffer probable trauma as well as possible injuries? For what reason? Simply to prove you can protect yourself from an emotionally unbalanced young man with a history of previous attacks?'

Put like that, it sounded crazy. But what about *her* emotions? With each passing day she became more tightly bound to him on every level. What had begun as an amusing conspiracy was now way out of hand.

'You expect me to go to Sydney for the weekend, and spend every waking moment worrying if you're all right? Forget it.'

'Dammit. Why should it matter to you?'

His eyes hardened to a bleak grey. 'It matters.'

It was too much. *He* was too much. Without a word she crossed the lounge and entered her bedroom.

She closed the door, and wished fervently it held a lock and key. Although it would hardly prove an impenetrable barrier, for he possessed the brute strength to break the door down if he was so inclined.

With hands that shook she released the zip fastening at the back of her dress and slipped out of it. Next came her shoes, and she gathered up a cotton nightshirt and slipped it over her head.

It took only minutes to remove her make-up and brush her teeth, then she slid in between the sheets, snapped off the light to lay staring into the darkness.

Michelle had little knowledge of the passage of time as thoughts meshed with dreamlike images, and it was only when she stirred into wakefulness that she realised she must have fallen asleep.

She moved restlessly, and her hand encountered warm male flesh, hard bone and muscle. Her body went rigid with shock.

'Nikos?'

'Who else were you expecting, *melle mou?*' He brought her close and lowered his mouth to nuzzle the sweet hollows at the base of her throat, then trailed up to capture her mouth in a slow evocative kiss that stole her breath away.

It would be so easy to lose herself in his embrace, and she told herself she needed the warmth of his touch, the feel of him deep inside, and the mutual joy of lovemaking. At this precise moment she refused to label what they shared as *sex*.

Tomorrow she'd deal with when it dawned. But for now there was only the man and the wild sweet heat of his loving.

And the passion. Mesmeric, provocative, ravaging, until she went up in flames and took him with her.

Michelle rose early the next morning, then showered and dressed, she gathered together a selection of clothing suitable for a weekend in Sydney, added personal items and make-up, and packed them into a bag.

She'd considering making a final protest about the need to move into Nikos' penthouse, then dismissed it before she uttered a word. One look at his compelling features was sufficient to convince her that he intended to win any verbal battle she might choose to initiate.

'Leave your car here,' Nikos instructed as he stowed her bags in the boot of the BMW. The larger bag was destined to be deposited in the penthouse. 'I'll pick you up from the Gallery at ten.'

'OK.'

He shot her a musing glance. 'Such docility.'

'It's your forceful personality,' she assured sweetly. 'It has a cowering effect.'

His laughter was soft, husky, and sent renewed sensation spiralling through her body as she slid into the car beside him.

'No,' he mocked. 'It doesn't.' He fired the engine and sent the car up the ramp and onto the road.

It was at her insistence she spend an hour at the Gallery to dispense with some of the paperwork, rather than linger in her own or Nikos' apartment.

It was after midday when their flight touched down in Sydney, and almost one when they registered at an inner city Darling Harbour hotel.

'What do you plan to do this afternoon?' Nikos queried as he unfastened his garment bag and slotted it into the wardrobe.

'Shop,' Michelle declared succinctly as she followed his actions.

'I should be back by six. I'll make dinner reservations for seven.'

'Fine,' she acknowledged blithely, then gasped as

he cradled her face and kissed her. Hard, and all too briefly.

He trailed gentle fingers along the lower edge of her jaw. 'I'll have my mobile if you need to contact me.' He caught up his suit jacket and pulled it on. 'Take care.'

Five minutes later Michelle took the lift down to reception, had the concierge summon a taxi, and she gave instructions to be driven to Double Bay.

The exclusive suburb was known for its numerous expensive boutiques housed in a delightful mix of modern glass-fronted shops and converted terrace cottages.

The sun shone, and the gentlest breeze stirred the leaves of magnificent old trees lining the streets.

Boutique coffee shops and trendy cafés with outdoor seating beneath sun umbrellas created a cosmopolitan influence.

Michelle pulled down her sunglasses from atop her head and prepared to do some serious shopping.

Two hours later she took a brief respite and ordered a cappuccino, then fortified, she caught up a selection of brightly emblazoned carry-bags and wandered through the Ritz-Carlton shopping arcade, paused to admire a display of imported shoes, fell in love with a pair of stilettos and after declaring them a perfect fit, she added them to her purchases.

It was after five-thirty when a taxi deposited her at the door of the hotel, and on entering their suite she took pleasure in examining the contents of numerous bags before storing them in the wardrobe.

With quick movements she gathered fresh underwear and a wrap, then escaped into the adjoining bathroom.

Nikos found her there, in a cloud of steam, her body slick with water, so completely caught up with her ablutions that she didn't even hear him enter.

The first Michelle knew of his presence was the buzz of his electric shaver, followed minutes later by the rap of his knuckles against the glass door as he slid the door open and stepped in beside her.

'Communal bathing, hmm?' she teased, loving the feel of his hands on her waist. 'Sorry to disappoint you, but I've nearly finished.'

'No, you haven't.' He slid his hands up over her ribcage and cupped each breast.

His fingers conducted an erotic teasing of each sensitive peak, and she felt desire arrow through her body.

'No?'

He didn't answer. He merely reached forward and closed the water dial, and she was incapable of saying another word as his mouth touched her own, teased, tasted, nibbled, then hardened with possessive masterfulness.

His tongue laved hers, and encouraged participation in an erotic dance that eventually became an imitation of the sexual act itself.

She wasn't conscious of leaning into him, or lifting her hands to hold fast his head. There was only the need to meet and match his passion until the heat began to dissipate.

Her skin was acutely sensitive to his slightest touch as he trailed gentle fingers back and forth across each collarbone, then slowly traversed to the slopes of her breasts.

His lips found the sweet hollow at the edge of her neck, and nuzzled. One hand splayed low over her abdomen, and caressed her hip, her buttock, then teased the soft curling hair at the apex between her thighs.

Michelle felt as if she was dying. A very slow erotic and incredibly evocative death as he brought her close to orgasm with tactile skill. Unbidden, her neck arched and a soft almost tortured moan escaped her throat as her feminine core radiated heat and ignited into sensual flame.

It was almost more than she could bear, and she cried out as he lifted her up against him. With one easy movement she linked her arms around his neck and wound her legs over his hips, glorying in the feel of him, the surging power, his strength.

Pagan, electrifying, primeval.

Michelle sensed the moment he let go, the slight shudder that shook his body, then the stillness, and she kissed him with such exquisite gentleness her eyes ached from unshed tears.

With infinite care they indulged in a long afterplay, the light brush of fingers over sensitised skin, kisses as soft as the touch of a butterfly's wing.

She touched his face with the pads of her fingers, and slowly traced the strong bone structure with the care of someone who needed to commit his features to memory.

The firm eyebrows, broad forehead, the slightly prominent cheekbones and the wide firm jaw-line. She explored his lips, the clean curves, the firm flesh that could wreak such havoc at will.

Then she gave a soft yelp as he drew the tip of her finger into his mouth and gently nipped it.

Without a word he reached forward and turned on the water dial, set it at warm, then palmed the soap and began to smooth it over her body.

When he finished, she took it from his extended hand and returned the favour.

'Food,' Michelle inclined in a voice that shook slightly as he closed the water dial.

Nikos' eyes gleamed dark and his lips parted to form a musing smile. 'Hungry?' He leant forward and extracted a towel, draped it over her shoulders, then collected another and wound it round his hips.

'Ravenous.'

'Now wouldn't be a good time to tell you I've put our reservation back to eight.' He lifted a hand and smoothed a damp tendril of hair behind her ear. 'Or that we're joining three of my associates and their partners for dinner.'

She reached up and kissed his chin. 'I forgive you.'

'Do you, indeed?'

'Uh-huh.' Her eyes sparkled with devilish humour. 'I bought a new dress to wear tonight. And shoes.' She began to laugh. 'You get to see what I'm not wearing beneath it.' She wrinkled her nose at him. 'And suffer,' she added in an impish drawl.

'We can always leave early.'

He watched beneath hooded eyes as she went through the deodorant and powder routine, then she stepped into lacy thong bikini briefs, and his loins stirred into damnably new life.

She activated the hair dryer and brushed the damp

curling length until it bounced thick and dry about her shoulders, then she began applying make-up.

If he stayed any longer, they wouldn't make it out of the suite, he perceived wryly. And for all that the evening was social, the prime criterion was business.

With that in mind he walked into the bedroom and began to dress.

When Michelle emerged from the bathroom all he had to do was fasten his tie and don his jacket.

She crossed to the wardrobe, extracted the dress, then stepped into it and turned her back to him.

'Would you mind?'

He moved forward and slid the long fastener closed over her bare skin. Minuscule briefs, no bra. Throughout the course of the evening he was going to go crazy every time he looked at her.

Michelle swung round to face him. 'What do you think?'

The cream silky sheath with an overlay of lace fell to just above her knees. Its scooped neckline was saved from indecency by a swathe of lace, and a single shoestring strap extended over each shoulder. Very high stiletto-heeled shoes in matching cream completed the outfit.

'You were right,' he drawled with an edge of mockery, and she laughed, a soft throaty sound that was deliciously sexy.

'It works both ways,' she assured with sparkling humour, and spared him an encompassing look.

Dark tailored trousers, blue shirt, navy silk tie, hand-stitched shoes. Expensive, exclusive labels that showed in the cloth and the cut. But it was more than that, she perceived a trifle wryly. The man wore them well, but it was the man himself who attracted attention. His height, breadth of shoulder, tapered waist, slim hips and long muscular legs would intrigue most women to wonder or discover if the physique matched up to the promised reality. Michelle could assure that it did.

He pulled on his suit jacket and extended a hand. 'Let's go.'

They took a taxi, got held up in traffic, arrived late, and opted to go straight to the table rather than linger at the bar.

In retrospect it proved to be a pleasant evening. Beneath the social niceties, it was clear that a deal had been struck and cemented during the afternoon. In Nikos' favour, Michelle perceived.

She found it intriguing to witness him in the executive role. He was a skilled tactician. His strategy was hard-edged, and she was reminded of the iron fist in a velvet glove analogy.

Tenacity, integrity. He possessed them both. His associates admired those qualities and lauded him for them. They also coveted his success.

It was after eleven when the bill was settled and they converged briefly outside the entrance.

Nikos went to hail a taxi, only to pause when Michelle caught hold of his hand.

'Our hotel is just across the causeway,' she indicated, pointing it out. There were people enjoying the warm summer evening. 'It's a beautiful night. Why don't we walk?'

Nikos cast her a wry glance. 'In those heels?'

'They're comfortable,' she assured. 'Besides, after that sumptuous meal we need the exercise.'

'I think I prefer a ten-minute taxi ride to a ten-minute walk.'

Her laughter was infectious. 'Conserving energy, huh?'

'Something like that.' His drawl held musing mockery.

'And I thought you were at the peak of physical fitness,' she teased unmercifully, and laughed at his answering growl. 'We walk?'

It took fifteen minutes because they paused midway to admire the city-scape. Myriad lights reflected in the dappled surface of the water, gunmetal in colour beneath the night sky. The air was fresh, tinged with the tang of the sea, and she felt the warmth of his arm as it curved along the back of her waist.

There was a part of her that wished this was real. That the sexual chemistry they shared was more, much more than libidinous passion.

How could you care deeply for someone in the space of a week? More than care, a tiny voice prompted. With each passing day she found it more difficult to separate the fantasy and the reality.

How much was pretense? Could a man kiss a woman so deeply, and not care? Make love with her so beautifully, and feel nothing more than sexual gratification?

And even if there is affection, is that all it would be?

Worse, when this is all over, what then?

What do you want? A convenient relationship for as long as it lasts? Then heartache? Don't kid yourself, she silently derided. Nikos doesn't want the *forever* kind, with a marriage certificate and children. Nor do you. Or at least, you didn't think you did until now.

Her life had been good until Nikos Alessandros walked into it. She'd been satisfied with the status quo. Content to run the Gallery jointly with Emilio. Happy in her own apartment, and with her social life.

Now, it didn't seem to mean as much.

Apprehension seeded and took root. How could she bear to live without him?

'Shall we continue?'

Michelle brought her attention back to the present and she tucked her hand into the crook of his elbow. 'Yes, let's go back.'

There was a sadness in the depths of her heart as they undressed each other and made love in the late hours of the night.

CHAPTER TWELVE

'DO YOU WANT to go down to breakfast, or shall we order in?'

'The restaurant,' Michelle said at once. 'Staying in could prove dangerous.'

'For whom, *melle mou?*'

'I might ravish you,' she teased mercilessly, and heard his soft mocking laughter.

'I tremble at the mere thought.'

'Well you might,' she threatened as she slipped from the bed, aware that he followed her actions.

'Today you have plans, hmm?'

Nikos sounded amused, and she picked up a pillow and threw it at him, then watched in fascination as he neatly fielded it. 'If you don't want to play, *pedhaki mou,*' he drawled, 'I suggest you go shower and dress.'

She escaped, only because he let her, and re-emerged into the bedroom to quickly don elegantly tailored trousers and a deep emerald singlet top.

Nikos followed her actions, and after a superb breakfast they spent almost two hours in the Aquarium viewing the many varieties of fish displayed in numerous tanks before walking across the causeway to Darling Harbour to explore the many shops.

It was a beautiful summer's day, the sun shone, there was just the barest drift of cloud, and a gentle breeze to temper the heat.

They had lunch at a delightful restaurant overlooking the water, then they boarded a large superbly appointed catamaran for a cruise of Sydney harbour.

Mansions built on the many sloping cliff-faces commanded splendid city views, and the cruise director pointed out a few of the exceptionally notable residences nestling between trees and foliage.

Coves and inlets provided picturesque scenery, and there were craft of every size and description moored close to shore.

Sydney was famous for its Opera House, a brilliant architectural masterpiece instantly recognisable throughout the world, and its Harbour Bridge.

Of all the cities she'd visited, this one represented *home* in a vast continent with so many varying facets in its terrain. It tugged a special chord in the heart that had everything to do with the country of one's birth, patriotism and pride.

Nikos rarely moved from her side, and he appeared relaxed and at ease. The suit had been replaced by tailored trousers and a casual polo shirt which emphasised his breadth of shoulder, the strong muscle structure of his chest.

Michelle was supremely conscious of him, the light brush of his hand when they touched, the warmth of his smile.

Here, they were a thousand miles away from the

Gold Coast, and Jeremy. Let's not forget Saska, she added wryly.

There was no need to maintain any pretense. So why hadn't Nikos abandoned the facade the moment they touched down in Sydney?

Because the sex is good? an inner voice taunted.

She should, she reflected, have insisted on separate suites. They could have each gone their separate ways for the entire weekend, then simply travelled to the airport together and caught the same flight to the Gold Coast.

So why didn't you? a silent voice demanded.

The answer was simple…she wanted to be with him.

Oh great, she mentally derided. Not only was she conducting a silent conversation, she was answering herself, as well.

It was almost five when the cruise boat returned to the pier, and afterwards they wandered at leisure along the broadwalk at Darling Harbour, and sat in one of many sidewalk cafés with a cool drink.

'Let's eat here,' Michelle suggested. The area projected a lively almost carnival ambience, and she loved the feel of a sea breeze on her face, the faint tang of salt in the air.

'You don't want to go back to the hotel, change, and dine *a deux* in some terribly sophisticated restaurant?' Nikos queried.

He looked relaxed, although only a fool would fail to detect the harnessed energy exigent beneath the surface.

'No,' she declared solemnly.

They ate seafood, sharing a huge platter containing a mixture of king-size prawns, mussels, oysters, lobster and Queensland crustaceans cooked in a variety of different ways, accompanied by several sauces and a large bowl of salad greens.

Dusk began to fall, and the city buildings took on a subtle change, providing a delightful night tapestry of light, shadow and increasing darkness.

'We could take in a movie, a show, visit the casino,' Nikos suggested as they emerged from the restaurant.

Michelle offered him a sparkling glance. 'You mean, I get to choose?'

'Last night was business,' he drawled, and she bit back a laugh.

'Not all of it.'

He took hold of her hand and linked his fingers between her own. 'Behave.'

'I shall,' she said demurely. 'Impeccably, for the next few hours. At the casino. Then,' she added with wicked humour, 'I plan to ravish you.'

'Two hours?'

'Uh-huh. It's called *anticipation*.'

It was worth the wait, Nikos accorded a long time later as he gathered her close on the edge of sleep. She'd made love with generosity and a sense of delight in his pleasure. And fun, before the intensity of passion had swept them both to a place that was theirs alone.

His arm tightened over her slender back, and she made a protesting murmur as she burrowed her cheek more deeply against his chest.

He soothed her with a gentle drift of his fingers,

and brushed his lips against her hair, listening, feeling, as her breathing steadied into a deep even pattern.

'The Rocks,' Michelle chose without question when Nikos queried over breakfast what she would like to do with the day. Their flight to the Gold Coast was scheduled for midafternoon.

'Trendy cafés, shops, and—'

'Ambience,' she intercepted with a wicked smile.

They took a taxi, and spent a few pleasant hours wandering the promenade, examining the various market stalls, chose a café where they enjoyed a leisurely meal, then it was time to return to the hotel, collect their bags and head for the airport.

With each passing hour she felt an increasing degree of tension. And sadness the weekend was fast approaching a close.

'Thank you,' she said quietly as they waited for their bags to arrive on the carousel from the flight. 'It was a lovely break away.'

Nikos glimpsed the subtle edge of apprehension apparent, and divined its cause. A muscle hardened along the edge of his jaw. Jeremy's behaviour pattern was predictably unpredictable. His parents' method of dealing with their son's recurring problem, however, was not.

For the past week he'd deliberately scaled down his business commitments to an essential few, and chosen to work via the computer link-up in his apartment, instead of his company office overlooking the Southport Broadwater.

Nikos sighted their bags and lifted them off the carousel. Five minutes later he was easing the large BMW out from the security car park.

'Do you mind if I make a phone call?' Michelle queried soon after they entered the penthouse.

'Go ahead. I'll be in the study for an hour.'

She rang her mother, put a call through to Emilio, then she retreated to the bedroom to unpack.

Michelle left early the next morning for the Gallery, and by midday she'd managed to catch up with most of the paperwork. Lunch was a sandwich washed down with mineral water and eaten at her desk.

Preliminary festive season parties were already under way, and tonight they were to join her parents and several of her father's associates for dinner at the Sheraton.

It was after five when she entered Nikos' penthouse, and after a quick shower she tended to her make-up, swept her hair into a smooth French pleat, then she donned a cobalt blue fitted dress with a sheer printed overlay, slid her feet into stiletto-heeled shoes, and collected her evening purse.

'OK, let's go.'

'There's something you should know before we leave.'

Her smile faltered slightly. 'Bad news?'

'Jeremy and his parents left the country early this morning. Their home is up for sale, and Emerson's office is closed.'

'Thank God,' she breathed shakily, as surprise mingled with relief.

'Rumour has it they intend settling in Majorca.'

It was over! She could hardly believe it. No longer would she have to look over her shoulder, suspect every shadow, or be apprehensive each time the phone rang. She could resume a relatively carefree life, move back into her apartment...

Nikos caught each fleeting expression and successfully divined every one of them.

A weight sank low in her stomach as comprehension dawned. Nikos' protection was no longer necessary. Which meant—*what?* Did she thank him, then walk out of his life? *Would he let her?*

'The news has already leaked and speculation is rife,' Nikos said quietly. 'I wanted you to hear it from me, rather than an exaggerated version from someone else.'

'Thank you.'

He could sense her tentative withdrawal, see the hidden uncertainty, and he wanted to shake her.

'We'd better leave,' Michelle said brightly. '*Maman* said six-thirty.' It was almost that now.

It was a beautiful evening. Except she didn't really *see* the azure blue of the sky as Nikos drove the short distance to the Sheraton hotel.

Michelle drew in a deep breath, then slowly released it as he slid from the car and consigned it to the concierge's care for valet parking.

She'd have to go inside and act her socks off in an attempt to portray an air of conviviality.

It didn't help to discover Saska was present in the company of one of her father's business associates. Although it was hardly surprising given the associate had been a guest on the same night as Saska at her parents' home the previous week.

Champagne on an empty stomach was not a wise move, and her appetite diminished despite the superb seafood buffet. While everyone else filled their plates and returned for more, all she could manage to eat was a few mouthfuls of salad and two prawns.

Michelle conversed with apparent attentiveness to the subject, but within minutes she retained only a hazy recollection of what had been said.

Her mind was consumed with Nikos as she reflected on every detail, each sequence of events that had brought and kept them together.

She reached out and absently fingered the stem of her champagne flute.

'Michelle?'

Oh Lord, she really would have to concentrate! She looked across the table and saw Saska's bemused expression. 'I'm sorry,' she apologised. 'What did you say?'

'I'm leaving for Sydney tomorrow to spend a few weeks with friends before flying home to Athens.'

Sydney, *Athens?* Saska was leaving the Gold Coast *tomorrow?* Her brain whirled. Did that mean Saska had given up any hope of turning Nikos' affection into something stronger, more permanent?

'I'm sure you'll enjoy Sydney,' she managed politely. 'There are so many things to see and do there.'

'I'm looking forward to it.'

Michelle wasn't sure how she managed to get through the rest of the evening. She even managed to pretend to eat, and followed mineral water with two cups of very strong coffee.

It was after eleven when Etienne settled the bill and brought the evening to a close. Some of the guests had taken advantage of valet parking, others had chosen to park in the underground car park. Consequently farewells and festive wishes were exchanged in the main lobby.

Within minutes of emerging from the main entrance the concierge had organised Nikos' car, and Michelle sat in silence during the short drive.

The penthouse had been a haven, now it seemed as if she was viewing it for the last time. Dammit, she daren't submit to the ache of silent tears.

She was breaking up, fragmenting into countless pieces. Tomorrow... Dear heaven, she didn't want to think about tomorrow.

Nikos lifted a hand and tilted her chin, then held fast her nape as he angled his mouth over hers in a kiss that tore at the very depths of her soul.

It became a bewitching seduction of all her senses, magical, mesmeric, and infinitely flagrant as he led her deeper and deeper into a well of passion.

There was something almost wild about their love-making, a pagan coupling filled with raw desire and primitive heat.

Afterwards Michelle lay quietly in Nikos' arms, listening to his heart as it beat in unison with her own.

Then when she was sure he slept, she carefully eased herself free and slid from the bed.

She moved quietly into the kitchen, found a glass,

filled it with water, then drank it down in the hope it would lessen the caffeine content of the coffee.

For the life of her she couldn't return to that large bed and pretend to sleep. Without thought she crossed to the lounge and moved the drape a little so she could see the night sky and the ocean.

CHAPTER THIRTEEN

'PENNY FOR THEM?'

Michelle turned her head at the sound of that drawling voice, and her stomach did a backward flip as he linked his arms around her waist and pulled her back against him.

'It's all worked out well,' she managed evenly. 'The Bateson-Burrows have relocated, and—'

'Saska has reevaluated her options, and accepted I'm not one of them,' Nikos drawled as he rested his chin on top of her head.

So where does that leave us?

Fool, she accorded silently. Where do you think it leaves you? You'll go back to your own apartment. Nikos will remain in his—until he returns to Athens, or settles in France, or any other European city where he has a base.

Sure, he might promise to call, and maybe he will, once or twice. He'll simply take up with any one of several beautiful females, and continue with his life. While you fall into a thousand pieces.

The mere thought of him with another woman made her feel physically ill.

'I should thank you,' Michelle said quietly. 'For everything you've done to help protect me from Jeremy.'

The night sky held a sprinkle of stars, pinpricks of light against dark velvet, and less than a kilometre distant the marina stood highlighted beneath a series of neon arcs.

If I tried really hard, she thought dully, I could count some of the stars. Perhaps I should wish on one of them. Although wishes rarely came true, and belonged to the fable of fairy tales.

'I consider myself thanked.'

Did she detect a slight edge of mockery in his voice? Dear God, of course she had thanked him. With her body, from the depths of her soul, every time they'd made love.

She was almost willing to swear that their lovemaking had meant something more to him than just a frequent series of wonderfully orgasmic sexual experiences.

Women faked it. But were men capable of faking that ultimate shuddering release?

Nikos possessed control…but he'd lost it on more than one occasion in her arms, just as she'd threshed helplessly in his against an erotic tide so tumultuous she was swept way out of her depth. Only to be brought back to the safety of his embrace.

'I'll pack and move into my apartment in the morning.'

Was that her voice? It sounded so low, so impossibly husky, it could have belonged to someone else.

'No.'

Michelle's heart stopped, then accelerated to a rapid beat. 'What do you mean—*no?*'

His hands moved up to her shoulders. 'Do you want to leave?'

Dear heaven, how could he ask such a question?

She was incapable of movement, and he slowly turned her to face him.

'Michelle?'

'I—how—' Oh hell, she was incapable of putting two coherent words together. 'What are you suggesting?' she managed at last.

'I want you to come with me when I fly out to New York.'

Want, not *need,* she noted dully.

Did she have any idea how transparent she was? Eyes so clear he glimpsed his reflected image in their depths. A pulse hammered at her temple, and was joined by another at the base of her throat.

Go, an inner voice urged. Enjoy the *now,* and don't worry what will happen next month, next year. Just... hop on the merry-go-round and enjoy the ride for as long as it lasts.

But what happens when the music winds down and the merry-go-round slows to a stop? Would the break be any easier then, than it is now? Worse, she knew. Much, much worse.

Yet life itself came with no guarantees. If she walked away now, she'd never know what the future might hold.

It was no contest. There could be only one answer.

'Yes,' Michelle said simply.

Nikos covered her mouth with his own in a kiss so incredibly gentle, she wanted to cry.

'There's one more thing.'

He pressed his thumb over her lower lip. 'Marry me, *agape mou.*'

Her eyes widened measurably, and for an instant her whole body stilled, then she became conscious of the loud hammering of her heart and the need to breathe.

'Yes.'

His smile almost undid her. 'No qualifications?'

Michelle shook her head, not trusting herself to speak.

'How do you feel about a Celebrant marrying us in the gardens of your parents' home two weeks from this Saturday?'

She did swift mental calculations. 'Two days before Christmas?' Dear heaven. 'My mother will freak.'

He stroked the rapidly beating pulse at the base of her throat. 'No, she won't.'

Two weeks. 'Nikos—'

'I love you,' he said gently. 'Everything about you. The way you smile, your laughter, the sound of your voice. The contented sigh you breathe when you reach for me in the night.' His mouth settled briefly on hers. 'I need you to share my life, all the days, the nights. Forever.'

Michelle closed her eyes in an attempt to still the sudden rush of tears. 'I knew you were trouble the first moment I set eyes on you,' she stated shakily.

'An arrogant Greek who took control and turned your life upside down, hmm?'

Stifled laughter choked in her throat. 'Something like that.' Her eyes gleamed with remembered amusement. 'You were always there, in my face.' Her expression sobered momentarily. 'Thank God.'

'Fate, *pedhaki mou*.' He cupped her face and smoothed away the soft trickle of tears with each thumb. 'It put us both in the same place at the same time.'

Yes, but it had been more than that, she acknowledged silently.

Much more.

'You never did intend this arrangement to be temporary, did you?'

He dropped a soft kiss onto the tip of her nose.

'No.'

'When did you decide?'

'I walked into the Bateson-Burrows' home that first evening, took one look at you, and knew I wanted to be in your life.'

'Why?'

He smiled, a self-deprecatory gesture that was endearing in a man of his calibre. 'Instinct. Then Fate dealt me a wild card.'

'Which you didn't hesitate to use,' she acknowledged musingly.

'Do you blame me?'

Michelle lifted her arms and linked her hands at his nape, then she drew his head down to hers. 'I love you,' she said with quiet sincerely. 'I always will. For as long as I live.'

'Come back to bed.'

She couldn't resist teasing him a little. 'To sleep?'

'Eventually.' He kissed her with hungry possession. 'After which we'll rise and face the first of several hectic days.'

* * *

Nikos had been right, Michelle mused as she kissed her mother, then hugged Etienne.

Each day had proven to be more hectic than the last. Yet superb organisation had achieved the impossible by bringing everything together to make their wedding day perfect.

There had been tears and laughter as the Celebrant pronounced them man and wife, and Nikos kissed the bride.

Photographs, the cutting of the cake, and an informal reception had completed the afternoon.

Now it was time to leave in the elegant stretch Cadillac hired to transport them to a Brisbane hotel where they'd stay prior to catching an international flight early the next morning.

'We made it,' Michelle said jubilantly as the driver eased the long vehicle away from Sovereign Islands towards the arterial road leading to the Pacific Highway. From there, it was a forty-five-minute drive to Brisbane city.

Nikos took hold of her hand and raised it to his lips. 'Did you think we wouldn't, *agape mou?*'

Her smile melted his heart. 'Not for a moment. You and my mother make a formidable team.'

He kissed the finger which held his rings, and praised his God for the good fortune in finding this woman, his wife.

When he reflected on the circumstance, the chance meeting, and how close he had come to delegating his trip to Australia... It made his blood run cold to think he might never have met her, never experienced the joy of her love or had the opportunity to share her life.

He had never seen her look as beautiful as she did today. The dress, the veil, they merely enhanced the true beauty of heart and soul that shone from within.

A man could drown in the depths of those brilliant deep green eyes, and be forgiven for thinking he'd died and gone to heaven when those soft lips met his own.

'Champagne?'

Michelle looked at the man seated close beside her, and gloried in the look of him. There was inherent strength apparent, an indomitability possessed by few men. She wanted to reach out and trace the groove that slashed each cheek, trail the outline of his firm mouth, then have those muscular arms hold her close.

'No.' She leaned against him and laid her head into the curve of his shoulder.

'Tired?'

'A little.'

'We'll order in room service, and catch an early night.'

She smiled at the delightful vision that encouraged. 'Sounds good to me.'

Nikos lifted a hand and threaded his fingers through the length of her hair, creating a soothing massage that had a soporific effect.

'Did I tell you we're spending two weeks in Paris after I've concluded meetings in New York?'

'Paris?' The Arc de Triomphe, the Eiffel Tower, the ambience that was the soul of France.

'Paris,' he reiterated. 'A delayed honeymoon.'

'Now I know why I fell in love with you.'

'My undoubted charm?' he mocked lightly, and felt her fingers curl within his.

'The essence that is Nikos Alessandros, regard-less of wealth and possessions. *You,*' she emphasised.

'There is an analogy that states "'tis woman who maketh the man."'

'I think it's reciprocal,' she accorded with wicked amusement.

Michelle lapsed into reflective silence.

Everything had been neatly taken care of. She'd arranged to lease out her apartment; together, she and Emilio had interviewed several people to act as her replacement at the Gallery, and had finally settled on a competent knowledgeable young woman who would, unless Michelle was mistaken, give Emilio a run for his money.

She intended to liaise with Emilio from wherever she happened to be in the world. New York, Paris, Athens, Rome. In this modern technological age, dis-tance was no longer an important factor.

It was almost dark when the Cadillac slid to a halt outside the main entrance to their hotel. Check-in took only minutes, then they rode the lift to their designated suite.

Flowers, champagne on ice, fresh fruit and an as-sortment of Belgian chocolates were displayed for their enjoyment, and Michelle performed a sedate pirouette and went straight into Nikos' waiting arms.

His kiss was both gentle and possessive, a gift and a statement which she returned twofold.

'Mmm,' she teased. 'I could get used to this.'

'The hotel suite?'

'You—me. Sharing and working at making a life together. Happiness, *love.*'

'Always,' Nikos vowed. His mouth fastened over

hers, and he deepened the kiss, exulting in her response until their clothes were an unbearable restriction.

'I guess we don't get to eat for a while,' Michelle murmured as she nibbled his ear.

'Hungry?'

'Only for you.' Always, only you, she silently reiterated.

Love. The most precious gift of all, and it was theirs for a lifetime.

* * * * *